every secret thing

every secret thing

a novel

LILA SHAARA

BALLANTINE BOOKS NEW YORK

Published in the United States by Ballantine Books,
an imprint of The Random House Publishing Group,
a division of Random House, Inc., New York.

BALLANTINE and colophon are registered trademarks
of Random House, Inc.

ISBN-13: 978-0-345-48565-6
ISBN-10: 0-345-48565-3

Printed in the United States of America

Book design by Lisa Sloane

To Rob, obviously.

acknowledgments

IT SEEMS TO ME that when writing a book like this, you could legitimately thank everyone you've ever known, since fiction can require that you call upon experiences and relationships from anywhere, anytime. But there are a few people whose contributions to this particular work are specific and so deserving of mention. Four (!) psychologists were extremely helpful to me in various ways: Patricia Marterer and Laura Hickok, in addition to cheerleading me in general, each gave me help on issues of child psychology. (They also happen to be two of my dearest friends.) In addition, Jodi Peppel and Judy Grumet were immensely helpful in ways both professional and personal.

I have quoted my friend Sara Sturdevant at various points, with her gracious permission, since she has a great way with a phrase. I "borrowed" some stories from two priceless buddies, the extraordinary artist and drummer Sue Sneddon and the brilliant scientist Karen Martin, both fabulous raconteuses. Ellen Madono contends that the book itself was in part a product of my taking a chronic homeopathic remedy that unblocked my creative pathways; assuming she's right, I thank her, especially since she's my homeopath as well as my friend. Lipika Mazumdar, Martha Terry, Juanita Menchaca, and Barb Madaus also gave me great all-around, "you can do it" sorts of support, as did the "anthro spices," Ed Boytim, Philip Bittenbender, and David Arndt.

My brother Jeff generously gave me the name of his editor, considerably reducing my anxiety. I also should thank my travel buddy from long ago, Margaret Moore, who shared an experience or two that made it into this book.

A lot of the more charming aspects of the twins' behavior in the story were taken more or less directly from that of my two sons. I hope that when they're old enough to read the book, they won't hold this against me. Much.

I also have one of the greatest husbands, without whom I could have produced nothing so time- and energy-consuming as this book. May you all be so fortunate as to be blessed with such a partner. Amen.

"For God shall bring every work into judgment, with every secret thing, whether it be good, or whether it be evil."

ECCLESIASTES 12:12–14

part one

part one

chapter one

―――――――――

[Y]ou were kicked off the edge of a precipice when you were born, and it's no help to cling to the rocks falling with you. If you are afraid of death, be afraid. The point is to get with it, to let it take over—fear, ghosts, pains, transience, dissolution, and all. And then comes the hitherto unbelievable surprise: you don't die because you were never born. You had just forgotten who you are.

ALAN WATTS, *The Book*

I HAD A DREAM on the clammy November day I turned thirty-three. I was standing on the edge of a cliff, talking to my deceased grandmother. I was saying something to her to the effect that I was undecided about taking the plunge off the cliff. She looked at me with some disgust, grabbed my wrist fiercely, and flung me off the edge, saying, "It's too late, honey, you're already falling." I woke up then with a small yelp, wrist aching. At the time, I couldn't figure out what big venture I had started but wasn't admitting that I had started. I think now that I knew, on however unconscious a level, that I was about to undergo one of those unpredictable, lurching life changes that I was prone to. I am always planning, strategizing, saving, investing, but the architecture of my life seems to be constructed for me, often without any participation on my part till the last minute. I'm in the midst of making my peace with this; on my thirty-third birthday I was still in denial that I had so little control over my life. Numerology isn't highly thought of in the academic circles I inhabit now, but I have always found it interesting. Thirty-three is significant; it was the final age of Christ and is the number of resurrection, of enlightenment.

I only got one present, and as it turned out, it was a gift of such importance, opening it should have sent psychic shivers through me, sent my heart pounding so much that I should have been swaying visibly with the force of it. But I merely thought it a curiosity, vaguely creepy but nothing threatening. Not a portent.

There was no return address on the package, which was about the size of a sandwich, small enough to fit inside the mailbox. It was wrapped in brown paper and held together with ribbed tape that had been applied meticulously. It had been sent to "Gina P." at my address, written in black marker. I didn't think it likely that I was a target of a terrorist threat or anything else that sinister. I thought maybe it could have been a mistake of some kind, but it was difficult to see how that was very likely, either. So I opened it.

Inside what turned out to be plain corrugated cardboard was a smaller, purple gift box, only about an inch deep and foiled with embossed irises. I thought briefly that if I had had a daughter, she might have loved to have such a box for little girly things. Having boys who fit the cultural mold in most ways, I knew they would have found the mere suggestion of using such a thing supremely offensive.

I removed the lid. Lying on a bed of soft white cotton was a pendant on a fine gold chain: a pale jade heart the size of a half dollar and the color of pistachio ice cream. It looked real and expensive. I thought again, this must be some mistake, but I couldn't imagine how such a thing might happen. There was no note, no card. In hindsight, the truth, or at least part of it, should have been as obvious as the daylight. But at the time I was dim and relatively worry-free about the pendant. I didn't like it much; it seemed sentimental and gaudy. I didn't wear much jewelry then, anyway, and this was not something I ever would have worn, even in the past when my life dictated that I be more decorated. I put it in the bottom compartment of my largest jewelry box, where it lay while curiosity about it bothered me for a few days, and then I forgot its existence completely. I'm grateful now that I didn't worry over it like a kitten with a dead mouse. It wouldn't have been out of character. But birthdays tended to depress me a little; this wasn't the only time when the distractedness of depression brought me a little peace.

Anyone who seeks out the single mother experience by choice, I think, must be insane. Or stupid. I am not talking about the millions of single moms in the world who are what they are by chance or misfortune, like me. I'm talking about the working women who choose to get pregnant on their own to be fulfilled or whatever. I had no plans to become a mom of any kind, but a combination of chance circumstances, stupidity, and some dubious choices (on my part), as well as deception on the part of another, conspired to bring me here, not only a single mother but the mother of *twin boys*. I have known people, as I'm sure you have, who are the product of large and busy families. They have many siblings or lots of cousins; holidays are noisy and crowded with lots of things and smells and singing. And the world is filled with children. It's a regular thing that kids are everywhere, their needs are dealt with routinely by whatever adults are available, and discipline is easy and communal. In other words, having kids around is, well, normal.

That was not my personal experience. My parents chose to live well away from human congress for reasons that are still not entirely clear to me. They didn't even seem to like each other very much but adhered in that unfortunate alchemy that keeps miserable couples incomplete without each other. They bought a large, drafty, and not very sound farmhouse parked in the middle of a fallow sugarcane field five miles outside of sparsely populated Stoweville, Florida, when I was about five. After a few years the visits from the few friends my parents still possessed and from the few relatives my father had ever tolerated dwindled to nothing. And so, dealing with other children became a total mystery to me. On the long bus rides through the canopy roads to my underfunded public school, I sat alone. I saw other children at school but had no idea what to do with them. After I finished playing with dolls at about age nine, I never again fantasized about having babies, or being a mom, or being a wife, or any of that. I can't really remember what I did fantasize about, which is odd, because I lived almost completely in my head. One sister was six years older and had no use for me whatsoever. My younger sister had the mysterious (to me) power of attracting friends no matter how remote we were physically from them, and so was at other people's houses a lot of the time. When she wasn't, we played ceaselessly, so that when she was gone, I ached with loss and jealousy. I never understood her secret for—seemingly without effort—getting people to transport her wherever she wanted to go. Her friends seldom came to our unwelcoming house. So when she was away I missed her and envied her, and I reveled in her when she was home, until she got sick. Then she was home all the time, and I have lived with the guilt ever since, of having enjoyed the last six months of her life more than I enjoyed any others of my childhood. The aftermath was, of course, one of the blackest times of my life, but until then, being a child, I didn't for a moment really believe that she was going to die. I didn't know that children could die. But, of course, as we all must, I learned.

So now, I thought, the portion of the universe that pays attention to me, if any, must be laughing. I, through a series of stupid accidents, became a spectacularly unprepared single mom. I am also an extremely paranoid one, because I know that children can die.

CINDY, THE ADMINISTRATIVE ASSISTANT in our department, said, "You want to hear about David Renouart or not?"

"It's okay. I can take it," I said.

"He just broke up with his girlfriend."

Kay Reynolds, the chairperson, said, "The psych department secretary? I can never remember her name. Probably can't stand to think of the poor girl's sex life." Kay was a deeply decent person, but her husband had left her with three youngish children years before while he engaged in an orgy of adultery. He ended up living on an organic dairy farm in Vermont with one of his conquests. Kay had raised their children, now all postcollege, by herself.

"No, no, *they* broke up at least two months ago. This is a new one. I don't know this one's name—Frieda, Frances, something. She's a new part-time instructor in the criminology department. But she dumped him." Cindy dropped her voice, already at a discreet volume, even lower. "After finding him having sex with Nedra Kelly."

I squeaked, "Fine arts Nedra Kelly?"

"Yep. They were doing it in his office. Can you believe some people? He and this Frieda or whatever would sometimes just go into his office together, close the door, stay in there for a half an hour, and then come out all rumpled. I mean, no discretion whatsoever. So it turns out he was doing exactly the same thing with the chair of the fine arts department, and his trashy girlfriend walks in on him. Jo Kinsey"—the secretary in the economics department, Renouart's campus home—"told me that she, the girlfriend, made a huge scene, screaming and crying. But the worst thing was that she left the door to his office open while they were still trying to, you know, get themselves together. Students and faculty are all running into the hall to see what's going on, and there are David and Nedra, half undressed, falling off the top of his desk."

I was beaming and Kay was trying not to blow crumbs of coffee cake through her nose with laughter, when the remaining two faculty members walked in together: Vincent Capinelli, in his thirties, handsome, tall, and enthusiastically gay, and Ida Weiss, the great lady of the College of Arts and Sciences at Tenway University. Ida was fabulous, sweet, smarter than any of us, tiny, dedicated to the principles of a liberal arts education, and prone to short haircuts, tweed suits, and comfortable shoes. I liked her a lot, although I often almost displayed my southern upbringing by wanting to call her Ida May. For all her wonderful qualities, she didn't have much of a sense of humor. When I first met Ida, Kay had told me that everyone thought of her like a grandmother. I couldn't help but flash to Grammy Paletta. She had been very tall, a beauty in her day, and tended to wear makeup an inch deep for all occasions and skirts with slits up the sides until her death at eighty-six. No, Ida Weiss didn't remind me in the slightest of Grammy.

The two newcomers were now understandably interested in why Kay was laughing so hard. The three of us looked at one another. We could have explained honestly to Vince what was so funny, but we all knew Ida would be disappointed by our mean-spiritedness. Also, Ida wasn't someone you felt comfortable discussing anyone's sex life with.

"Oh, dumb stories about my cat," I said nonsensically, and went off to grade papers.

After school that day my boys had gone to their friend Josh Hepple-white's house, three doors down from ours. It was getting near dinner-time, and I was about to go reclaim them. I liked going outside on our modest little dead-end street even in this premature bone-snapping cold. There hadn't yet been much snow, so the lawns and trees were gray and dead, as was the sloped wood that dropped away across the street from my house. But I loved stripped trees and brown crunchy grass; I loved winter. It was still a novelty to me, this almost super-natural changing of the world's condition from month to month. Where I'd been raised, we'd had seasons, but the actual weather asso-ciated with them wasn't of much concern to anyone but farmers; the calendar told us when to go to school, when to celebrate certain holi-days, when to plant gardens if you were so inclined. Other than that, winter mostly meant relief from the crushing watery heat that sat on Florida's interior for half the year.

And I liked long nights and short days and fireplaces, all alien to me till adulthood. And the preholiday light shows that my neighbors indulged in delighted, fascinated, and repulsed me all at the same time. I couldn't imagine investing so much in that, but I could appre-ciate the results of other people's efforts. The Hepplewhites' home was so laden with strings of lights, motorized deer, and giant inflated Santas that it buzzed and hummed loudly enough to hear from the street. Tenway was a nice middle-class suburban sort of place, woods and playgrounds mixed with a small but bustling business district and actual neighborhoods of a limited socioeconomic but wide ethnic range; the presence of a small, semibackwater university combined with just a touch of blue-collar sensibility kept it from being snooty or too beige or fascist in terms of taste. At Christmastime most households let their collective hair down enough to enjoy garish displays of Yuletide spirit without too much yuppie competitiveness. And the sprinklings of menorahs and Kwanzaa decorations seemed unself-conscious, nonthreatening, and nonthreatened. It soothed me somehow, this simple joy in electric rococo.

My house, however, had only a simple wreath on the front door. I had no outside electrical outlets, and so despite the boys' pleading, there wasn't much we could do to add to the local splendor. The house of my elderly next-door neighbor, Jessie, was similarly dark. Her only acknowledgment of the upcoming holiday season was a small doll dressed in lacy angel robes, once white, now sepia, tacked diagonally to her front door.

As I walked out of my house, I saw that Jessie was in her front yard. No one ever referred to her as Mrs. Foxhall; everyone called her Jessie, even the teenagers on the block. She looked comical, stock still on her front walk, facing her door. Given the weather, my first thought was that she appeared frozen solid.

"Jessie? Are you all right?"

"Well, I can't seem to get back to my front porch." Her voice had a tremor in it that I didn't remember.

I walked through her front gate, took her by the arm, and got her up the steps to her front door, almost carrying her. It wasn't particularly hard. I noticed that the sad, discolored little angel doll was chronically smashed by her storm door, so that its wings were bent and crippled-looking. I felt an irrational pity for it.

Jessie had been my neighbor for two years. I knew her name and knew that she was old but little else. I'd brought her a tin of cookies when I first moved in. She'd told me abruptly that she was diabetic and couldn't eat sweets. That had been pretty much my entire experience with her, other than her telling my boys to get out of her yard the previous summer. There hadn't been anything frail about her then. Now she looked about ten years older, her hair sparser and shorter;

even her height was diminished. It had been a hard winter so far; I was suddenly worried about her.

Together we made it into her house, which was approximately the temperature of the surface of Mercury.

"Well, you think you'll be all right now?"

"I think so. I'm going to make some tea. Would you have some?"

She still looked a little wobbly. I thought I'd better hang out for a bit. "That would be great. Can I help?"

She let me, although she didn't seem happy about it. She led me through a house with tiny rooms full of boxes and dolls and many objects made of yarn. There was dark, thick furniture underneath those things and small paths through which you could walk from room to room. There was no light from the outside at all. It was so hot, you could almost see the air shimmer above the yellowy lamps. We wound up in a narrow kitchen. The walls were covered with shelves displaying miscellaneous pieces from a variety of sets of cheap china. Many of the teacups were cracked. Lots of them were pink.

It's been my experience with the elderly that the best tack to take is simply to take the blame for everything.

"I'm so sorry I haven't been a better neighbor," I said. "I have two seven-year-olds, as I guess you know. It keeps me pretty busy."

"Twins, right?"

"Yes."

"They don't look much alike."

"Fraternal twins."

"No daddy, huh?"

"I'm a widow." She had to know this. I might not have been the most interesting thing on the street, but a tidbit like that had to have circulated. She asked a number of impertinent questions about my dead husband, my marriage, where I'd lived, and so on.

"I bought this house to be near my cousin Mo. Do you know Maureen Hannigan? She and her . . . partner live a few blocks away. You know the big Victorian on the corner of Circuit and Truro? They're fixing it up," I said.

"That's two women?"

"Yes."

"Hmmm. I've heard about them. She's a Hannigan? Frank and Rosa's daughter?"

"Yes. Their oldest. Do you know them?" I asked, only mildly surprised. Tenway is not very big.

"I grew up next door to the Lodovicos. That's still where Rosa lives now, right?"

"Yes."

"So you're Rosa's niece, then? You're not Francesca's daughter, are you? You'd be about the right age, I think."

I said, "I don't really know Aunt Franny, but you knew she was a nun from forever, right? She wouldn't have had a daughter. My mother is Maria."

"That's right; the Lodovicos had lots of girls. Maria was the snooty one. Although Rosa was pretty snooty herself. Lottie and Francesca, they were the sweet ones. Francesca had a daughter, all right. I remember. I was still living next door when that happened."

"You lived next to the big house on Acton?"

"Yes. I only moved here when my husband and I wanted something smaller, so we sold the Acton Street house and bought this one. Turned out to be a good decision. People are a lot nicer here on Circuit Lane than on snooty Acton. It's funny that you live next door to me now, being related to the Lodovicos. But Tenway's a small town; there's no getting around it."

"So I didn't know anything about Franny having a daughter. Was this before she entered the convent?"

"Oh, no! That was the big scandal at the time. She'd been a nun already for a few years. She was pretty young when she went in, eighteen or nineteen or something like that. She was the baby, so she always seemed young to me. It was just a few years later when she came home in shame, you know. I was still living next door to them then. I can remember Leo Lodovico was very loud about the whole thing. I'd never seen a man cry like that before. He actually sobbed, cried out loud like a woman. It was a terrible thing." She didn't look like she thought it all that terrible; she looked pretty happy, actually. "I never heard a peep from Angela, your grandmother. Just him. The baby was born at home, though. Then someone, a lawyer or social worker or something, came and got it. I don't know what happened after that." Jessie squinted at me. "Now, tell me, whose daughter are you?"

"Maria's," I repeated.

"She married that southern fella, right? Angela hated him. Said he was the worst of all the no-goods her daughters married."

I wasn't surprised that Nonna would have been unhappy with one of her daughters marrying someone like my father: charming, excessive, and completely untrustworthy.

"Maria had girls, too, am I right?"

"Yes, three of us."

"One of them died."

"Yes."

"It's terrible when children die young. I had a twin sister, Ann. God took her when I was ten years old. It's funny that you have twins, too. We were identical; people couldn't tell us apart. My mother always called me Jessie Ann after she died. I'd just been plain old Jessie before that."

I wanted to get back to this baby of Franny's but felt awkward about dragging the conversation back to my concerns after this sad story. My mind skittered away from the thought of having one of a pair of twins die at ten.

"That's my sister, Ann." Jessie pointed to one of an identical pair of dolls, huge, three feet high at least. I'd been raising boys; I'd forgotten about the various permutations of doll lust to which little girls were prone. The pair were standing observing us from a corner of her small living room. They were dressed in long frilly dresses of red satin and white lace, Christmas finery. "That's me," she went on, pointing to the farthest doll. I had no idea how she knew which was which. Placement, I supposed. "We got those for Christmas the year Ann died, the year we were ten." I considered for a moment telling her my story but found the idea extremely uncomfortable. I had a feeling she didn't want to hear anyone's stories but her own, anyway.

Jessie went on. "We looked so much alike, no one could tell us apart, not even my mother. We used to fool people a lot. It was easy, since she put us in the same clothes most of the time." I've always found this practice creepy, but apparently Jessie's mother thought differently. "After she died, my mother still kept confusing us, calling me Ann half the time. I think that's why Mother didn't seem to miss her too much: She had me around, and to her it was almost the same as before." Then Jessie was crying, hot tears slowed in their progress by deep wrinkles. "I wonder what my life would've been like, shared with someone." You were married, I wanted to say, but knew all too well that it wasn't the same and that all marriages aren't created equal.

I made a move to put my arm around her bony shoulders. She jerked away from me as from an unexpected flame. "I'm all right," she said, irritable now. Embarrassed, too. "I'm feeling all right now. You don't need to stay."

During finals week in December I did lots of baking and gave out baked goods promiscuously, especially in my department at the university. My colleagues tried to reciprocate with offers of socializing, Christmas dinners, and celebrations honoring Hanukkah and Kwanzaa. I went to none of them, making various excuses. Having children is handy for this; you can always find some reason you can't leave them or bring them. I debated taking Jessie some sugar-free cookies but didn't feel up to the probable rejection.

The Christmas that followed my thirty-third birthday, beginning my year of waking up, wasn't too bad. I got myself a toaster oven and was genuinely happy with that. My old one had crapped out on me right after Thanksgiving. My sons, Toby and Stevie, got pretty much everything they had asked Santa for. Sidney, my cat, got a cloth mouse stuffed with catnip. My sons each gave me some pieces of chocolate with pink sticky wrappers and some drawings of Christmas trees and bells, along with two handmade calendars for the new year. Those projects had been inspired and supervised by their second-grade teacher, Mrs. Bernson.

I did exchange gifts with two adults, though it only netted me one present, since they are a couple. My cousin Mo (Maureen) and her partner, Ivy, gave me a leather-bound blank book. "You need to write," Mo said. But I thought even as she said it, no, I don't, because finally, after all this time, my life is working out. You write when things abrade you, and writing is the best way to put the rasp somewhere else for a time, to bring some relief. My sons are healthy, my roof doesn't leak, I have a job that makes sense for me. Things are okay. I don't need anything.

chapter two

---

*Nothing in the universe can stand by itself—no thing, no fact,
no being, no event—and for this reason it is absurd to single
anything out as the ideal to be grasped. For what is singled out
exists only in relation to its own opposite, since what is is defined by what is not, pleasure is defined by pain, life is defined
by death, and motion is defined by stillness.*

ALAN WATTS, *The Way of Zen*

TOBY SAID, "So Grandma's coming?"

"Yes," I said.

"Why?"

"Because her sister died, and they're having the funeral here. On
Friday. This is her hometown, where she grew up. Her other sisters
are here, too: Aunt Lottie and Aunt Rosa."

"Did I know the lady who died?"

"No, honey. She lived in Africa. I never met her, and neither did
you." I caught myself before telling him that the reason the funeral
was so late was that her body had had to be shipped back to the States

from Kenya. Unnecessary information about dead bodies was probably best avoided for sensitive seven-year-olds, I thought.

"Will Grandma bring us presents?"

"I doubt it, honey."

"She hasn't been here in a really long time."

"You're right."

Toby was sitting at the small kitchen table, eating a bowl of cereal. Stevie came into the room and circled the table while pressing a small plastic truck against the side of his head and simultaneously singing in an atonal sort of drone, "I have a truck on my *head,* I have a truck on my *head.*" He was naked from the waist down.

I said, "Stevie, go get some pants on." No response. "Stevie." Nothing. "Stevie." The weird singing and marching continued. *"Stevie,"* I said, putting a firm hand on his shoulder and turning him to face me.

"What?" he said, genuinely puzzled at my tone.

"You don't have any pants on," Toby commented, bored.

Stevie looked down, saw it was true, looked back at me, and laughed. I sighed, then joined him.

The term started without fanfare; only a blizzard. I lived close to the university and had all-wheel drive, so I didn't have to cancel any classes, much to my students' chagrin, I'm sure. My colleague Vincent missed a class or two; whether he really couldn't make it in was something of a question.

The first day of school was a Tuesday, and I had three classes. Two of these were introductory courses filled with lots of freshmen, but the third was an upper-level class in religion and gender. A lot of the students were majors in the department; a majority of them were male. This is highly unusual in any class with "gender" in the title. Clearly, something was up. A cluster of boys who sat in the back of the room seemed to be having a really good time, although they weren't too disruptive. I wasn't terribly concerned with this; it was a curiosity, nothing more. Now I can't believe that I couldn't sense the undercurrents, the speculation, the reassessing in the eyes of many of my students. All I thought was that as the term went on, I might develop a good enough rapport with some of the students in the class to ask them what it was that I didn't know.

An academic schedule can be very child-friendly. I did a lot of my work at home. It is easier to do that in an electronic era when students can communicate easily with professors via e-mail; I rarely took lunch, so I was almost always able to pick up my boys from the bus stop around three-thirty. On a Monday afternoon in early January, the second Monday of the new semester, Jessie Foxhall flagged me down as soon as I got back to my house with the boys. She was on her porch with a coat draped over her shoulders and washed-out lavender mules on her feet. The wind was blowing the flurries back up to the sky, and the temperature was well below freezing. I hollered to her that I would be over as soon as I got the boys settled.

A half hour or so later I knocked on her door. She took a few minutes to answer, then let me in with enthusiasm. "I'm cleaning out," she said.

"Oh?" I said, wishing she'd just let me get on with my business.

"Yeah. You need clothes. Come in, I'm going to give you some."

I considered telling her that I had been a model in New York City for many years and that I had more clothes stored in my attic than I could ever wear in the life I had now. I decided against it.

The interior of her house was no more comfortable than it had been before. She had a photo album out on the cramped coffee table. It was one of the old kind; Grammy had had one like it, dark brown paper sheets bound with yarn, covered with sepia and black-and-white rectangles, attached with bits of tape long disintegrated. The edges of the pages looked like silverfish had been at them. She said, "Look, look, this is the house I could have had." She pointed to a shiny black-and-white photo with pinked edges of a plain white farmhouse surrounded, as far as you could tell, by tall grass. The house looked to be quite small, smaller perhaps than the one we were in. She said, "That was Charles Willis's house, upstate in Warsaw. The man who wanted to marry me. I was twenty years old. Things would've been different if I'd married him."

"Why didn't you?" I asked, a little afraid the question was rude. I knew she was a widow, so this was confusing. But I was in a hurry and wanted to get home more than I wanted to hear the story.

"My mother wouldn't let me. She needed me to clean her house, to take care of all the kids, to take care of her. She wasn't well. She got spells, you know the sort of thing."

No, I didn't. "I didn't know you had a large family."

"We didn't. She took in poor kids, and she got money for it. It was good money, but she was too sick to do any of the work, so I had to do it. Of course, we had a bigger house, the one on Acton. We had as many as eight kids at a time."

I thought it sounded like a nice racket for her mother, but who knew the circumstances, really? "Did your father help?"

"Hah! He was long gone by then. He left when Ann died. I only saw him once after that, at my mother's funeral, twenty-seven years later."

"So what happened to Charles?"

"He got married to somebody else, had a son, then got killed in a fire." I was afraid she might start crying again, but she stayed bone-dry. This was old, old news. "His wife's gone now, too." She pulled a thready tissue from the pocket of her housecoat and blotted her face. "The bags are upstairs, in the hall. Would you get them for me?"

I was simultaneously curious and fearful about the rest of her house. The upstairs was mostly narrow and poorly lit, filled with heavy dark furniture, much like the first floor. At the top of the stairs I found two grocery bags filled with mildewy polyester clothing. "I'm sure some of your friends can use those. Maybe some of your students." I thanked her, said sure, and made my way home, mentally adding them to the next load for Goodwill.

The next morning I was pulling out of my driveway to go to an early before-class appointment, having already gotten the boys to school. I saw a pleasant-looking middle-aged black man standing on the porch of the house next door. Jessie opened the front door and with a quick, nervous look at me pulled him in. I tried to wave a neighborly greeting, but she had already closed the door. I still felt bad that I hadn't tried harder to give her some Christmas cookies. I knew she wouldn't have taken them, but I should have made the gesture, I thought.

———

I DIDN'T SEE JERI, my therapist, much anymore. I had to quit seeing her weekly when I started teaching at the university full-time. But I still felt depression licking me around the edges, a tiny unraveling, so I thought a New Year's check-in with her was warranted.

She had a hippie office, which I liked, with lots of incense, candles, muslin, and Indian brass. (I wanted to be more of a hippie myself but was constitutionally too tense.) She dressed in beautiful dripping earth tones and didn't worry at all about the effect of the sun on her aging process. She wasn't old enough to be my mother, but I wished she were.

In these occasional sessions she had a checklist she went through to get up to speed on my most egregious past issues.

"Okay," she said. "How is your house? Can you walk from one room to another without stepping over anything? Is it possible?"

"Oh, yes," I said.

"What does it smell like?"

"Uh, I don't know."

"Dirty cat litter?"

"No!"

"Rotten food?"

"No! It smells fine, Jeri."

"Can you eat off the floor?"

"God, no," I said.

"Good!" she said. I was known to inhabit extremes in the past.

"How are the boys?"

"Healthy. Reasonably happy. Doing well in school. Stevie's still a little withdrawn. Toby's still a little too eager to please. But we're working on it."

"Are they still seeing Dr. Silverman?"

"Not regularly. I check in with him periodically, but he says he thinks they're doing okay. I keep an eye on things pretty closely."

"I know you do. Do they go to other kids' houses at all?"

"They're starting to more. I think they're still a little young for sleepovers. Toby gets nightmares sometimes. I kind of want him home." I curbed my defensiveness. "They do have a best friend now in the neighborhood, Josh Hepplewhite, who's a year older but very sweet. I like his mother, too. I'm pretty sure she's still married, but I've never met the husband. Every time she's invited me in for coffee, he's been at work. She's home during the day. She's willing to help me out in a pinch by getting them at the bus stop or whatever. It's a real relief."

"And you let them spend a good amount of time there?"

"Yes, I think so."

"Do you have them in any sports, any outside activities besides school?"

"I signed them up for baseball this coming spring. They are only moderately interested, and I don't know anything about this, really. But I'm trying, Jeri, I'm trying. I want them to be normal boys; I really do."

"I know you do, Gina. I know you do. That's great. You know, sometimes kids get hit by balls, sometimes they get a little hurt, even in Little League."

"Yes, I know that."

"Anybody been sick?"

"Only colds. Nothing big."

"Any episodes of premourning lately?"

"A few. Not so many. That's getting better."

"Give me an example of a recent one."

"Hmmm. My cousin Mo just got this CD for Christmas. It was a gift from her partner, Ivy. The CD is by a woman named Eva Cassidy. Have you heard of her?"

"No."

"Well, Mo brought it over one day over the holidays because she really likes it. And there's a really sad story to it. This woman was really talented: a beautiful voice, a good musician, an artist. She was also really shy and sweet and beloved by a lot of the other musicians around DC, where she lived. Then she gets some sort of cancer, and she's dead in a few months. Boom, gone. She was around my age."

"So, that's a possible scenario for you, dying like that, suddenly?"

"Well, of course, but that's not the thing. It's her parents. I mean, they're the ones putting out all her music now. As a tribute to her life and all, which is great, of course. But all I can think as Mo's reading me the liner notes—like it's a fucking TV movie, isn't it tragic, and so on—is, you mean you can raise your kids, you can get them through childhood, get them self-sufficient, get them out on their fucking own, and they can still up and die on you? I have no idea if I like the CD or not; I can't even have it in the house."

"Maybe that would be a good exercise, to borrow it for a day or two, make yourself listen to it."

"I'm not interested in exercises in masochism. I don't care if it would be therapeutic or not."

"Well, maybe now is not the time. Any other episodes of pre-mourning that we need to talk about?"

"That was the big one. Although now you've got me thinking about it happening to *me,* and then the boys would be without me, and they'd be fucked. Thanks a lot."

"Sorry. You've got Mo, right? And Ivy? The boys wouldn't be entirely alone."

Deep breath. "No, I guess you're right."

"Okay. Let's talk about your love life. Have you been out on any dates?"

"No."

"None at all since the Awful Bragging Man?"

"Not a one."

"How is that for you?"

"It's okay. I'm not pining about it. I think those systems have largely shut down."

"Hmmm. Well, be careful. If you try to put your libido totally to sleep, most likely it'll rear up and take a chomp out of you, probably when it's really inconvenient. How are things with your cousins, all that part of your family?"

"The same. Some of them are nice enough. Others are terrifying. It's hard to hang out only with the ones I like, though. They make themselves a package deal so much of the time."

"Families will do that. You in contact with any of your friends from before? School or the city?"

"No."

"Why not?"

"Well, it's been hard to have conversations with a lot of them that don't focus on my sons one way or another. I mean, most of those people are seriously career-focused. It's hard to share with any of them the necessary obsessions of parenting. You know: Is their school okay, do you like your pediatrician, are they happy, do you have a good source for hand-me-downs, how much computer or TV time do you allow, do they wet the bed, have bad dreams, autism, ADD, ADHD, do they hurt pets, do you give them an allowance, how much, at what age, are they happy?"

"You said that last one twice."

"Which?"

"Are they happy."

"I guess I should also ask, when do you stop taking them to the shrink? Haha."

Jeri didn't laugh.

"Anyway, that part of my life's all done with. I think I fill most of my old friends with contempt now."

"How do you know that?"

"I just do. But my mother's coming up. My aunt Franny, her sister, just died."

"I'm sorry. Was this an aunt you were close to?"

"No. I'm not even sure I ever met her. She was a nun, did missionary work in Kenya. She hasn't been here since I've lived in Tenway."

"But your mother's coming for the funeral?"

"You bet. As you can imagine, I can't wait."

chapter three

Yet the more surely and vividly you know the future, the more it makes sense to say that you've already had it. When the outcome of a game is certain, we call it quits and begin another. This is why many people object to having their fortunes told: not that fortunetelling is mere superstition or that the predictions would be horrible, but simply that the more surely the future is known, the less surprise and the less fun in living it.

ALAN WATTS, *The Book*

ON THURSDAY I had finished teaching my early-morning class and had a break of several hours before my afternoon class, the lopsided one on religion and gender. I rarely went out for lunch during that time, preferring to remain in my office and get as much work done as possible. As I settled in behind my desk, I was feeling enthusiastic about my job, as my morning lecture had gone particularly well. I had been funny and articulate, and my students had seemed bright-eyed and interested. My imagination does such piercing damage to me at times, you'd think it would be attuned to the least tremor in the psychic energy around my life. But that day I was simply congratulating myself on how organized and efficient I was being and how inspired a lecturer I had been. When my phone rang, my desk lamp flickered, yet I still expected nothing more earth-shattering than a student pleading to be allowed to turn in an assignment late. When I answered, an unfamiliar male voice asked if I was who I am and, when I said yes, identified himself as Tucker McCandless, the constable of Tenway. He then demanded that I come see him as soon as possible. When I asked why, he simply said it was an important police matter and there wasn't any time to waste. He was very polite, but scared the bejesus out of me.

There were plenty of spaces, so I parked my car in the closest non-handicapped one, locked up, wondering if that was really necessary in the police station parking lot, and went in through the glass doors. Behind a counter on the left was a short, moist, balding man whose uniform no longer fit him; he looked pink and balloonish, as if his uniform would pop if you poked him with a sharp object. At first he didn't look my way; he was distracted by the sudden flickering of the overhead fluorescent lights. I got his attention and asked him where I could find the constable. (I was appalled to realize I couldn't remember his name.) His face lit up when he heard mine, like I was an old friend, a rescuer from boredom, a celebrity. I had managed to keep anything like panic from working its way into my belly; for some reason, this joy at my appearance made my stomach tighten in a way the phone call hadn't. He pointed me in the right direction, smiling and obsequious.

I was grateful that the office door had "Constable T. McCandless" painted on it. The Tucker part came back to me, but I knew I never would have remembered his last name. I wondered how long the constable had held the office and if I would still be in Tenway during the next election, whenever that was. I hadn't been for the last one. I was somewhere between uneasy and terrified. I knocked, and after hearing "Come in," I opened the door. Three men sat in a pleasant cream-colored room. There was a large picture window facing the door that expanded the feel of the room considerably. You could see the river, and the light was from the east. There were potted ferns and cacti and succulents on the long windowsill, and the place had a warm humidity that felt comfortable after the dry cold outside.

All three stood at my entrance. Behind the giant oak desk was a middle-aged man in a khaki uniform who I assumed was Constable McCandless. On the other side of the desk, backlit by the huge window, were two men in blue suits. My first impression was that one was big and one was little, but that wasn't strictly true. One was extremely tall, broad-shouldered, with short, curling dark hair over a serious brow and deep-set eyes. The other was of medium height, slender but fit, with light brown hair, intense blue eyes, and an absolutely beautiful set of teeth. He was displaying pretty much all of them for me in a huge and charming grin. The other two men were not smiling; in fact, the big man seemed angry about something. The constable simply looked confused.

I consider it important to learn my students' names as soon as possible, but unfortunately I am not a quick study. I've developed a system of giving people nicknames based on their appearance and then associating their real names with them later, after the faces have become familiar. It's involuntary and frequently internally embarrassing; they're rarely names people would enjoy being called. I automatically gave these two the names Big Bear and Cutie Pie. I knew they would never know this, but I had a horror of those names somehow slipping out in conversation. The constable was easier; he was simply "the constable." He had a comb-over on an egg-shaped head that teetered on top of his body like a lonely cone atop a slender new pine. He seemed to waver in the breeze created by my entrance, but he gave the impression of being a comfortable, avuncular, homely sort of man, unlike the other two. Not one thing about either of them seemed even remotely comfortable.

They greeted me in what seemed to me a blur, taking my coat, and offering me a seat and coffee. We stared at one another for a moment. If you had told me right then that my life would forever be different, had already become different even without my knowing it, then, finally, I would have believed you. I was not a total stranger to law enforcement, but I had never approached it from this angle before, from what seemed to me to be the wrong end of it, the really dangerous end.

No one said anything for an odd few moments. The copier in the next room buzzed as someone used it for some form or other. You could hear the *click click* of a woman's thick heels on the linoleum in the hall. They all seemed awkward, as though something had thrown them, but as I didn't know why I was there in the first place, I couldn't for the life of me imagine what was holding them back, restraining them from telling me why I had been summoned.

The constable leaned in first, looking me in the eye. He said in a gentle, quavery voice, "Dr. Paletta, there are three students at the university whom we are very interested in. We want to know if you know them."

The constable introduced the other two men. They were NYPD detectives, who came from the city at the request of frantic parents. Cutie Pie was Detective Barnes and Big Bear was Detective Galloway, but their names didn't stick, as usual, and their first names were lost the moment they were spoken. One was grim and one seemed almost happy, but I couldn't have told you then who was who. They showed me pictures, told me names. It turned out that I did know two of the three boys: Tim Solomon and Jason Dettwiler were roommates who had taken a course of mine together last term, and were in one now. But the third, Bradley Franco, was familiar only to the extent that he looked like many other white college boys with even, smooth, and unmemorable faces. Age had written little on it as yet; and the three men led me to believe that it never would. Bradley had disappeared.

"We think Tim, maybe with Jason's help, killed him," said Cutie Pie.

"That's horrible," I said. This was such a foreign concept, so much the province of fiction, that I couldn't register an emotion about it, at least not yet. I tried to picture the two students, which I could do only vaguely. I didn't know them well, didn't have a sense of them as people. That, however, made the idea of their possibly being murderers no less horrific.

"I can't tell you anything helpful, I don't think," I said weakly. I wondered why they hadn't contacted Tim and Jason's advisers, classmates, fraternity brothers. Of course, maybe they had. They must be talking to all their professors, I thought. But I couldn't imagine anything useful coming out of a conversation with me, and I couldn't understand why they made me come to the station, as opposed to them visiting the campus. Certainly that would have been more efficient. I said something to that effect. They all looked at one another in a series of shifty glances that started the fear reflex in my middle again. "What aren't you telling me? I don't have anything to do with this. I don't even know the poor missing boy."

Cutie Pie spoke first, finally. "You don't know about Tim's website?" He was trying not to smile.

"No. What website?"

"The one about you. And some other women, too, but you're definitely the star."

My shock was deep and left me with nothing to say. Then I said, "I don't understand." I was getting a nasty presentiment, at last. You think website, you think frat boys, you think women, the most likely thing it adds up to is pornography. My heart was starting to flutter. There were old photographs that I thought were not bad, not explicit, not too terrible. But out of context, Jesus, out of context, oh my God. "Can I see it?"

The constable moved aside from his chair behind the big desk, waved me over, and pushed a suspiciously small number of keys. I realized that this meant that they, of course, had been looking at the site before my arrival. I saw it, saw familiar pictures, mostly thumbnails: me at twenty, at twenty-two, in Venice, on the French and Italian rivieras, in the Bahamas, lots of beaches, lots of chaise longues, lots of boudoiry-looking sets. Then some other pictures, a blurry brunette, the back of her head all that was visible, performing fellatio on some obviously willing male. Not me. Oh my God. Not me. There was also text, a story: "Gina, my lush and luscious Gina," horrible treacly filthy stuff about love and sex in some phantasmagoric academic setting. Ridiculous sex. Stupid sex. Adolescent male notions of sex.

"This is on the Internet? Anyone with a computer can see this?" Three heads nodded.

They let this set in for a few moments, and then I got up and asked where the bathroom was. The constable led me out of his office with a light hand on my shoulder and pointed me to a door down the hall that said "Ladies." Safe inside, I spent ten minutes or so sobbing.

After some period of time, I don't know how long, I cleaned myself up and left the restroom. I found a water fountain and drank a lot from it. I then thought to look at my watch. I had to be back by one o'clock, but I was shocked to see it read eleven-seventeen. At least it was close to that; my watch appeared to have stopped. I felt fifteen years older than when I'd gone to work that morning.

There were several other people in the hallway where I found myself, some in uniforms and some in civvies. It opened into the lobby where I had entered, and I could hear soft murmuring from the desk where Balloon Man was stationed. I wondered if any of these people were concerned in this matter, if they, too, had been looking at the offending website. If they thought it was funny. I was no longer used to being looked at. I grew calmer but couldn't stop shivering. Be brazen, I told myself. But my brazen days were past. My children had sucked every bit of brazen out of me.

I limped back into McCandless's office. The three of them were all still there. Cutie Pie was all helpful and solicitous, delighted to get me a cup of hot coffee. I again imagined the three of them combing through that website before I showed up.

I said, "So are you going to arrest him or what?"

"We can't," said Cutie Pie. "We know that the three of them are linked in some pretty bad ways. We know that Brad and Tim and Jason are involved in drug trafficking at the university here. That's one of the reasons we've been having a conversation with our new friend, Constable McCandless." He nodded toward the older man. "The Francos, Bradley's parents, haven't heard from him in two weeks, and all they've been told at his frat house is that he left, with luggage, a while ago. They're scared; they know that Tim Solomon is bad news and that Bradley is, or was, tight with him. Given what we suspect about Tim, we're pretty confident that there's been foul play, which is what the Francos are most afraid of, obviously. But we don't have enough evidence, including a body, to do anything about it yet. Bradley isn't a minor. He can leave town if he wants to. There's nothing concrete that says he hasn't."

This was so surreal as to make my mind close off to it, to the possibility of actual violence on this scale among a category of person I saw every day. But I said, "You can arrest Tim for that shit," pointing to the constable's computer. "It's all made up. That's got to be illegal, putting crap like that out on the Internet. I'll press charges or whatever if you need me to." Although I wasn't sure that was such a good idea, pushing it, getting the site more notoriety.

Big Bear spoke up for the first time, in a soft sibilant voice. "Nothing he said is actually illegal. You could try to sue him, but it would give him more publicity, which would defeat some of the purpose of the suit. And he can claim that the content is fiction. He doesn't use your last name in the text."

"But it has pictures of me."

"Yes, but nothing actually saying that he's talking about you or that the graphic photos are of you. It's all implied, and that's really tricky stuff legally. You might want to talk to a lawyer, but you want to be very careful before you take any of this into a courtroom."

I could feel a little whisper of panic. I breathed at it, then said, "So why am I here?"

The constable answered this time. "These big-city boys think that you can help them get this rich little son of a bitch, excuse my language."

"Why can't you just arrest him?"

"His dad is a well-known attorney in Manhattan," said Cutie Pie. "They have more money than God, and Tim knows all about skirting the law. We can't tie him to the drugs or his other illegal business ventures. He was actually already tried for rape as a juvenile."

"Why isn't he in jail?"

"The case was dismissed." This from Big Bear. "Tim had the best legal defense team in the city, and the case was only the girl's word against his."

"So you can't arrest him, and you think he's murdered someone, and he's busy murdering my reputation. How sure are you of all this?"

Detective Big Bear said, "We're very sure. But that's different from being able to prove anything in court. Tim is definitely a psychopath. We think he's becoming extremely dangerous."

"And how can I possibly help you?"

The constable said, "I'd like to know that as well." For the first time he looked a little less gentlemanly, more overtly put out.

The short, handsome detective went back to Cutie Pie mode for a moment. He dimpled, showing another lovely grin. "Listen." He looked quickly at his partner. "We've both been on the job since seven, and I'm starving. Dr. Paletta, why don't we take you out to lunch, and we can talk over the ideas we've been knocking around."

The constable stood up. "I have other work to do around here, Detectives." He seemed even more put out. "I can't go with you." Sigh. "You three go on, and you boys fill Dr. Paletta in on the rest of our conversation here this morning. Dr. Paletta, here's my card." He wrote something on it and handed it to me across the desk. "I added my direct number so you can call me later if you have any questions or problems. You boys let me know afterward what course of action you decide to pursue. I mean it; keep me in the loop. My town may be small, but I'm not a dumbass." He looked again at me. "Pardon my language," he said.

chapter four

There are, then, two ways of understanding an experience. The first is to compare it with the memories of other experiences, and so to name and define it. This is to interpret it in accordance with the dead and the past. The second is to be aware of it as it is, as when, in the intensity of joy, we forget past and future, let the present be all, and thus do not even stop to think, "I am happy."

Both ways of understanding have their uses. But they correspond to the difference between knowing a thing by words and knowing it immediately. A menu is very useful, but it is no substitute for the dinner. A guidebook is an admirable tool, but it is hardly to be compared with the country it describes.

ALAN WATTS, *The Wisdom of Insecurity*

GENERALLY, I DON'T have a high opinion of policemen. At this point in my life I had already seen a few representatives of the famous NYPD in action. Models and the people who work or socialize with them do a lot of coke, a lot of Ecstasy, a lot of heroin, a lot of other stuff. Not so much pot; it makes you hungry. I'd see cops let beautiful, rich, skinny people get away with all kinds of stuff if the girls would simper enough, would show the proper respect or give favors of the right kind. Sometimes money, sometimes sex, sometimes access. You learned early, don't belittle them, don't blow them off, don't treat them like they don't matter, because then they'll hunt you down or get their friends to hunt you down, find whatever you have, bust you for anything at all. Alex Grady, a six-foot Texan who had a record number of *Vogue* covers on her résumé, had consumed four Long Island iced teas on an empty stomach and insisted on driving her convertible BMW down Fifth Avenue at ten o'clock on a Friday night. Erin Steele, Katie Cameron, and I were in the car with her. Four grams of coke were sitting stupidly in a baggie on the console between the two front seats. Her driving was outrageously drunken; we were pulled over within five minutes. Alex made no effort to hide the goodies, I think because she was simply too drunk to think of it. She flirted ridiculously with the young policeman, as did the rest of us, energetically and shamelessly, and he let us go. I later heard that that same young, sweet-faced officer had beaten a drunken homeless man almost to death less than a week after our encounter. He obviously wasn't always soft on crime.

But most of my ideas about officers of the law came from my experience with my father the sheriff and his deputies; the latter hung out in the Stowe & Go Truck-O-Tel, where I waitressed at fifteen, a tall, virginal fish out of water. These were mountainous good old boys named Otis and Mel and Buddy, bellies audibly creeping over crisp black belts, shirt buttons so strained they had to be sewn on again and again by trusting wives. The three of them would come in every morning for breakfast, which was always on the house. Sometimes one of them would disappear for about ten minutes or so, as would Tammy Kaye, my senior by four years. I thought for a mortifyingly long time that the nickname "Twenty-Dollar Tammy" had been given to her by all our regular truckers because she was such a good waitress and received really good tips. An older waitress, Canasta Frechette, either felt sorry for me or simply got tired of the running jokes about my innocence and told me what the name really meant. I was so horrified, I couldn't look Tammy in the face or speak to her for several shifts. Tammy was matter-of-fact about the whole thing. She already had two small children for whom she was the sole support, and waiting tables was only so lucrative. By the time I left a year later, she had a third. I occasionally wondered what had happened to Tammy Kaye and her three kids, who would be in high school or beyond by now.

In any case, I never forgot the drooly, vaguely mean-spirited way the three deputies would flirt with Tammy and then with me. It always made me feel under threat, those three beefy men with guns and nightsticks and radios and lots and lots of local power, making kissing faces at me, occasionally rubbing against me, brushing an "accidental" hand over my ass. They knew they could never push it further since my father was their boss. That was a relief but not enough of one to ever make me comfortable around them. When I thought "cop," I thought about many unpleasant things, three of which were Otis and Mel and Buddy taking turns with Twenty-Dollar Tammy while their radios crackled.

The New York detectives asked my advice about where to go for lunch, preferably somewhere not near the campus. Detective Big Bear offered to move my car to one of the spaces in the back of the municipal building so that no one would recognize it parked there. I accepted and suggested a diner out toward the North Hudson Mall that no one I knew frequented. They agreed, and I rode with them in a generic dark blue American car that smelled thickly of many cigarettes. I was gradually becoming numb to the idea that there was porn out in the ether with my name on it. I was doing quiet yoga breaths, telling myself that people survive much worse, thinking of my kids and my mother. Then I thought about how much my cousin Lizzie would enjoy this. My mind avoided the thought of Uncle Frank altogether.

We found a window booth in the smoking section. Detective Cutie Pie sat next to me, preventing escape, and Detective Big Bear faced us. They both whipped out packs of cigarettes and lit up before saying anything. I remembered the compulsion with a vague nostalgia, relieved that I'd overcome that particular addiction during my pregnancy. Belatedly, Big Bear asked if I minded; Cutie Pie looked appalled, as though the thought that I might be prissy enough to insist on a smoke-free environment hadn't occurred to him. I said I didn't care.

Under the window there was one of those old tabletop jukeboxes, loaded with songs by country singers I hadn't heard since my waitressing stint. I hadn't thought anyone this far north would have even heard of most of them: Merle Haggard and Tex Ritter, Kitty Wells and Faron Young, Dottie West and Tennessee Ernie Ford. The voices, in my memory, of Stoweville. I idly flipped the pages, but the light on the top had burned out; I was reasonably certain the thing wouldn't work if we fed it quarters.

We ordered from a waitress with "Cola" etched on her name tag. In other circumstances I would have made a joke about this. Cutie Pie ordered a cheeseburger with a root beer. Big Bear had an egg salad sandwich with coffee. I ordered a chef salad, no dressing, and an iced tea. After Cola left, clearly already smitten with the cute one, I asked them to tell me exactly what they had in mind for me. Cutie Pie got chummy with me first, stalling. He worked his dimples hard and said, "First, why don't we get to first names here. We may be seeing a lot of each other. Is it all right if we both call you Gina? I'm Russell, and this is Tommy." He pointed at his partner with fingers that held his unfiltered Camel.

"Okay," I said, already irritated by his overly friendly manner. "Please tell me what else you want from me."

After some surprisingly coy dithering on Cutie Pie's part, something finally became clear. They'd thought that I'd been sleeping with Tim, that these fantasies had some truth to them. They thought they could use me to get to him. This made something in my throat swell; I felt like I'd swallowed a box of chalk. My mouth opened, but I literally couldn't say anything. Even Cutie Pie's high spirits seemed to dim a little as my rage became evident. "Look," he said, soothingly now, handling me. "We obviously had the wrong impression. But we need your help. We've got alternate plans. Please don't dismiss us without hearing us out." Hands open, big blue eyes pleading, no trace of the offensive smirk.

I looked at Big Bear. Detective Galloway was still not saying much. He looked even angrier than he'd looked before, and the smoke coming out of his nostrils just underlined that; I would have laughed in another life. It wasn't clear to me at whom this anger was directed. Cutie Pie looked at Galloway, then said, "Tommy doesn't like the idea of us approaching you. To be honest, our captain isn't too happy with it, either, but Bradley's disappearance has made the matter a whole lot more urgent."

It figured, I thought. A rich white boy's propensity for date rape and drug dealing didn't merit anywhere near as much concern as the disappearance of another similarly privileged kid. But, of course, murder, I thought, murder. The worst thing.

"We think you're under threat now," Cutie Pie Barnes continued, looking less cute to me every minute. "And maybe the other women in the site."

"Have you contacted them?"

"Not yet," said the detective. "You seem to be its major focus, so we thought we'd approach you first. We're afraid of what Tim Solomon might be capable of and of some escalation. Even Tommy agrees that these two are getting more dangerous. You gals need some protection. But maybe we can use the situation to our advantage."

I figured Detective Galloway wasn't articulate enough to express what his doubts were, but I was. "I'm a lousy actress if you want to do some sort of sting or whatever. And I have two kids. I can't possibly put them at risk."

"They already are," said Russell Barnes.

I looked at my salad, wondering if it was worth getting a to-go container for it. Detective Barnes was still talking. "Is there somewhere you could send them? To their dad's, maybe? Just for a week or two?"

"Their father's dead."

That shut him up for a beat. Then, "Anyone else?"

I thought of Mo and Ivy. "Maybe, for a night or two. You really think they'd try to hurt me or my kids?"

Barnes looked at Galloway and raised his eyebrows. Detective Galloway finally spoke, reluctantly. "Possibly. But the constable has people watching both Solomon and Dettwiler, so we know where they are at all times. That should keep you safe for the moment."

I thought about trusting my sons' safety to Otis and Buddy and Mel.

"You're single, right?" Barnes asked.

"Yes," I said.

"Not anymore, sweetheart," he said, teeth blazing.

The plan, briefly, was this: Russell Barnes would sit in on the class Tim and Jason were in and stay at my house, at least sometimes. They had reason to think Tim Solomon was watching me at home. That creeped me out as nothing else had so far. Tommy Galloway and some of the members of the local constabulary would keep an eye on us as well as the two alleged criminals. I had some grave, grave, grave doubts about all this.

I said to Detective Galloway, "You think this is a boneheaded idea, too, don't you?"

He looked broodily at me, breathed out a long slow breath, and said, "I don't have a better idea. And Russell's right. You may already be at some risk here."

I sat with this, blood cooling and stomach coiling. I couldn't think, had no idea what to ask, what the smart thing was to do, what my rights were in these peculiar circumstances. Something did occur to me suddenly, though, popping up from my unconscious like a submerged cork.

"And my last name was not on the website anywhere?"

Both men were at once expressionless.

"No," said Russell.

"Then how did you find out who I was?"

Tommy Galloway looked angry again, and Russell actually blushed. He and Tommy looked at each other again. I'd seen lots of cop shows. According to them, partners were like twins; they developed linguistic shorthands and quasi-telepathic methods of communication. This was how I interpreted what was going on, but they seemed antagonistic, as well, in ways I couldn't fathom.

"Tell her," Tommy Galloway rumbled.

Russell hesitated just an instant, then said, "I recognized you."

I hadn't worked in that business for a long time, and I hadn't been particularly famous or notorious, as far as I knew. Plus, I had used another name.

"How?"

"I'm kind of, um, a connoisseur." There was a pause. He said, defensive, "Only classy ones. I have good taste." A watered-down smile.

"Oh." A connoisseur of lingerie catalogs. Oh Jesus.

"I knew your professional name. We just called the catalog, identified ourselves, found out your agent's name, and so on."

"We were pretty sure from the text on the website that you had something to do with Tim's school," Tommy said softly. "But we were surprised that you were on the faculty."

I let the insult hang there along with the silver smoke. "So how many other people have you let in on this?" I said, feeling sick again.

"No one," Tommy said. "We didn't tell them why we needed the information. We understand that this is a potentially humiliating situation for you. We're really not trying to make it worse."

I didn't believe for a second that they gave a hairy rat's ass about my humiliation or discomfort. "So what now?" I finally said, trying not to start crying.

"Well," Russell said, stretching and lighting his third cigarette. "I start pretending to be another, you know, professor type, start hanging out, trying to get Tim to get upset and jealous and act out. We'll keep a close eye on him and catch him when he does." He paused and brushed his finger across my cheek. "Don't worry, Gina, we'll protect you. And your kids, too."

His condescension made me want to grind the saltshaker into his blue, blue eyes. "You both totally look like cops in those blue suits, and you, Russell, wouldn't pass for a professor of dirt, visiting or otherwise, for one minute. You're pompous enough, but that's about it. If this is the best you've got, forget it." I had never before in my life been that rude to anyone, with the exception of my late husband's mistress at his funeral. I knew I was going to feel really bad about this later but was too angry to settle down.

Russell actually looked hurt, which made things worse. They

were both silent and then shared another one of those hostile ESP looks. Russell finally said to Tommy, lips jutting, "All right, genius. *You* do it."

Tommy didn't look particularly happy to be the one to "do it." I wasn't all that happy, either; I was even less comfortable with Big Bear than I was with Cutie Pie.

I left them to talk it over, going to the bathroom for a while. I looked at myself in the mirror through the black streaks on the glass, where the silver had worn away. I said aloud, "So glad I never did nude pictures. So worried it would bite me in the ass one day. Good for me." I jumped as the door swung open and a woman with long, dry hair the color of margarine walked in. I wasn't sure if she'd heard me chattering at myself. I immediately became busy at the sink, washing my hands.

I sat down, pinning Detective Barnes in the booth this time. "So what now? Tell me who you're supposed to be." I looked at Tommy.

"I'm going to be Dr. Galloway from Columbia."

"You know, in this day of information access, Tim will be able to find out you're not on the faculty with a few mouse clicks."

"Good point. I'll talk to some people in the philosophy department there and get them to add me to the website. If they can't do that rapidly, I'll just make sure that there's a story in place that because I'm on sabbatical, I'm not listed or something. I doubt Tim understands academic protocol all that well. I can come up with something plausible."

"You know people at Columbia?"

"Yeah. I actually did go there, and I do know people in that department. I guess I'm pretty well prepared to pass as an academic."

"Philosophy?"

"I got my master's in philosophy a few hundred years ago."

I tried not to appear as insultingly surprised as I was.

Russell was sulking. "I have a BA in criminology. I'm not an illiterate idiot." I said the appropriate soothing platitudes about how smart and skilled you must be to be a detective, still feeling guilty about my earlier outburst, glad for a chance to be nice to him. In reality, I had no idea what kinds of skills you needed.

"So," Tommy said, after Russell was placated sufficiently, "when's your next class where you see these boys?"

"Next Wednesday night," I said.

As they drove me back to my car at the police station, I remembered unhappily that my mother was arriving that evening, that I had a funeral to go to the next day, that I didn't need this drama in my life at all right now. I discussed it with them; they said they'd leave me alone for the weekend and we'd start the whole mess in earnest the following Wednesday. However, today they wanted to come to my house to suss out arcane things having to do with surveillance and access and security. At the station Tommy said he would go in and brief Constable McCandless and make some calls to New York. Russell suggested that I drive the two of us back to campus and let him look around. Tommy would pick him up in their car while I was teaching, and we'd rendezvous at my house later. I didn't know how to say no to any of that.

I parked in the faculty lot and took Russell on a very abbreviated campus tour, since I had little time to get everything done I needed to do before my class. We were walking by a row of student housing, including Tim and Jason's fraternity, when I saw two men walking toward us. One I recognized vaguely but didn't know. The other was David Renouart, professor of economics, two-timer of Frances or Freida with Nedra Kelly. He was a slender, fair man with wire-rim glasses on a long thin nose, medium height, in jeans, a sport shirt, and a tweed jacket. Dressed for the part. He was very good-looking, very urbane, very clever. Thin-faced, sharp, well published, ambitious. His classes were full of happy coeds. I didn't hate him exactly, but I would have loved never to have to see him again. He was the only man I had slept with since Scott died.

Scott had been gone for four years, and David pestered me for almost six months till I finally relented. He was good at making me feel special, chosen. I writhe to think about this now. I kept the relationship quiet. I didn't expect it to last too long. He actually told me he was in love with me, which I found both startling and suspicious even at the time. I confided in Mo and Ivy about seeing him; this was inevitable, anyway, since they were my primary babysitters. Then Ivy sat me down and filled me in on the world according to David Renouart. She's the assistant to the dean of the faculty of arts and sciences and knows everything that happens at the university. She was kind about it but said that David had been doing a lot of talking. Some of it may have been to his current companion in the stupid gray running suit. A *lot* of talking. About how he was having all kinds of wild and athletic sex with a certain former lingerie model and former cover girl for *Cosmo* and *Vogue*. Everyone knew, she said. He was pretty proud of himself, she said. Also fairly explicit. Lots of people at the university, primarily males, appeared to be interested: professors, security guards, maintenance men, gardeners, you name it.

I confronted David. He denied it, then admitted it. But, he said, that was before he actually *knew* me. That was before he understood the *magnificence* that was Gina. I ended it precipitously. Fortunately, I had kept him away from my boys, not that he had any interest in them. I realized through the humiliation and hurt that I hadn't been all that interested in him even as a boyfriend, much less as a replacement daddy.

So here was my scummy braggart smiling and extending his hand. I never knew what to do when I saw him on campus. Usually I opted for chilly but civil, so that was what I did now.

"Gina, how are you? You remember Rege Bellisario, don't you? From the business school?"

No, of course not. Why would I, asshole? "Hello," I said pleasantly.

"Are you heading for class?"

"Yes."

"Gina, I don't know if you've heard, but Deepak Chopra is coming to campus to give a talk, pretty informal. I sort of got him to come here. He's kind of a friend, actually. You *have* to be there. I knew with your interest in religion and philosophy, you'd want to know."

It's not an *interest,* fuckwit. I have a Ph *fucking* D. "Most religion scholars don't take him all that seriously, David. He's kind of religion-light, if you know what I mean. Self-help, pop psych, you know. But thanks, anyway."

He looked predictably taken aback, and I felt a little ashamed, but I mean, please. I was trying not to simply see him as an idiot, but it was hard.

David decided wisely to change the subject. "And you are . . . ?" David looked at Russell.

"Russell Barnes. I'm a visiting professor here in criminology." Fortunately, my face stayed blank.

"Oh? And how do you know our Dr. Paletta?" Hearty, collegial smile.

Our Dr. Paletta? What a craphead poseur. My dislike for him put a bad taste in my mouth.

Russell was a detective, for all I hadn't given him much respect earlier. He had picked up on something and obviously didn't like David much, either.

"I sat in on one of Gina's classes last term and decided that I needed to come to Tenway." It turned out he was a pretty good mimic; he'd captured that faux British academic-speak accent beautifully. He looked at me with a besotted smile and put a gentle arm around my shoulders. "I think she's the most brilliant, talented, and beautiful woman I've ever met. I might even stay."

I just goggled at him, but David and Rege looked gobsmacked, as the British say. I managed a fake smile, gave a weak "We've got to go. Nice to see you. Bye," and took us both quickly away.

"What?" was all I could manage when we were out of earshot.

"You have a history with him? It was dripping off the two of you."

"Sort of" was the best I could respond. Then I said, "What about Tommy?"

"Rumors saying that you're dating two guys aren't going to hurt our operation at all. It won't hurt to have that asswipe hear it, either, will it?"

"No, I guess you're right. My reputation is probably for shit, any-way, if the website is already common knowledge." Oh Christ, did that asshole David know about it? I needed to talk to Ivy about all this as soon as possible.

"You have a foul mouth for a southern belle."

"Blow it out your ass."

I led us back to my department's building and quickly got my notes in order while Russell charmed Cindy at the front desk. I gave her a story about him being a friend visiting from out of town but said nothing about him being an academic or from Columbia for fear that some of the other faculty members would overhear and come out of their offices to jolly around with an unfamiliar colleague. In this instance, being part of a nice, friendly department made me queasy with anxiety. I bundled my notes and books together so that I wouldn't have to stop in my office again before class and then pulled Russell away from an enamored Cindy. I made a point of asking her to say hi to her husband before dragging him out the door.

I gibbered quick directions to my house at him and left him talking to Tommy on his cell phone. Then I went off to class, about to give one of the most disjointed lectures of my life.

At three-thirty I waited at the boys' bus stop, chatting with a few of the other moms I had a speaking acquaintance with, along with one dad and one grandmother. A few minutes later I hugged two skinny little boys who came flopping off the bus. Stevie wanted to be carried; I said to this what I always said: "You've *got* to be kidding!" Then Toby wanted to be carried as well. I had to call them lazy bums repeatedly to get them to stumble back to our house after shouting good-byes to the other adults and kids at the corner. Stevie in particular engaged in his favorite drama, "I'm soooooo tired," dragging feet, lolling head, tongue out, panting. They then of course had to burst into the house, almost sending the storm door flying off its hinges as one of them threw it open and let it slam shut. *Bang!* "Every day," I muttered, by this time exhausted. This one had already been excruciatingly long.

They were, of course, startled by the appearance of Tommy and Russell at our front door a few minutes after our arrival. I told them that the men were new teachers at the university and I was showing them around. That didn't explain why the two of them were so interested in the locks on the windows and doors, but the boys were blessedly oblivious to those details. Tommy took me aside for a moment and told me that he had talked to his connections at Columbia and that some sort of cover story was already in place. They poked around for a while, and then I did my best to get rid of them, since they didn't seem in a hurry to leave. Finally, they departed in a flurry of handing me cards with numbers on them: their cell numbers, the station house, even the direct number to their lieutenant in the city. They warned me, sotto voce, to drill the boys on basic safety: Don't let in strangers, don't tell people on the phone too much, and so on. I tucked their cards in my address book, hoping never to see either of them again.

chapter five

The contrast between the insecure, neurotic, educated "modern" and the quiet dignity and inner peace of the old-fashioned believer, makes the latter a man to be envied. But it is a serious misapplication of psychology to make the presence or absence of neurosis the touchstone of truth, and to argue that if a man's philosophy makes him neurotic, it must be wrong.

The common error of ordinary religious practice is to mistake the symbol for the reality, to look at the finger pointing the way and then to suck it for comfort rather than follow it.

ALAN WATTS, *The Wisdom of Insecurity*

MY MOTHER HAD SURPRISED ME by announcing that she was going to stay with me, when she had called about Francesca's death. "The Big House will be full of people," she said. She didn't mention the possibility of staying at her sister Lottie's house, which she had dubbed, more than once, a dump. "You still have that cranky old cat? What's his name, Barney?"

"Sidney. Yes."

"Oh. Well."

"The boys haven't seen you in, what, two years?"

"Three."

She lived in an upscale retirement community in the Buckhead area of Atlanta, fairly near my well-off banker sister. Their relationship remained mysterious to me, although they seemed close, or at least closer than my mother and I were. My sister wasn't married and had no children. I had no idea how my mother felt about that.

She came that Thursday evening. The funeral was scheduled for the next day. The boys were terribly excited about her arrival; I was careful not to say anything too deflating. My mother had taken a cab to our house; she swayed a bit under the weight of the boys' jubilance but bore it better than I had expected. She walked into my house, which she had never seen, and after a while said, "At least it seems pretty clean."

She came into the kitchen to watch me cook, sitting at the table with a glass of wine. She was telling me something about a trip to Cancún recently taken by her friend Nell Johnson, when Toby popped into the kitchen, saying, "Mom! Mom! Mom! I need a glass of water. Can you get it for me, please?" He does not have a soft voice, and my mother was still talking, so I had to ask her to repeat herself while I got him what he wanted.

After he left the room with the water, she said, "Doesn't that boy know that you don't yell in the house? And that you don't interrupt an adult?" This was said softly, but it still made my stomach clench.

I thought that his saying "please" was pretty good, actually. I made the mistake of saying so, adding, "He's seven, Mom. He doesn't know anything."

"Well, he won't know anything if you don't teach him." She'd been raised in New York, yet some forty years of southern living now shaped her speech. "I don't know why you don't teach those boys some manners. If you had talked to me the way they talk to you, I'd've whacked you upside the head so fast, you'd've been hit before I swung my arm. You need to show them that actions have consequences, Gina."

I knew that phrase well. Without humor, I wondered what her take on Tim Solomon's website would be and felt a little sick.

Later, after both my mother and my sons were asleep, I felt drained and wired at the same time, a condition that didn't bode well for easy sleep. I decided to talk to my sister Ellie instead, someone I could actually be honest with about the disturbing events of the day.

"*Murder?* Jesus. And a website devoted to your *lusciousness?* What the hell do you wear when you teach those classes?"

"The baggiest, most shapeless things possible. Half the time I don't even comb my hair, and I almost never wear makeup. I swear I'm not doing anything to provoke this."

"When you don't comb your hair, maybe you look all bedroomy. But the murder thing is pretty awful. You never saw any of this coming? Never had a sense that these kids were nuts?"

"Nope. Lots of students seem on the edge to me. I obviously can't distinguish between tense and psychotic, at least with the superficial contact I have with most of them. This doesn't speak well for my ability as an adviser."

"What I want to know about are these detectives. Like on TV! Are they single, young/old, hot/ugly, or what?"

"I have no idea about the marital status of either of them; they're both in their thirties, I'd guess. Neither is repulsive. In fact, one is quite the matinee-idol type, blow-dried do and all. The other is kind of a hit-man, hulky type. But don't cops get divorced all the time— they're never home, too much job stress, and so on? Don't they have a really high incidence of spousal abuse?"

"Okay, so you don't need to marry one. You've just been celibate for way too long, and here's your chance, someone who's in your life and out, back to the city when this is all done. You can bat your eyes at them and make them feel all protective and get them all hot for you."

"Them?"

"Well, one of them. Whichever floats your boat."

"My boat is dry-docked. Forget it, Ellie. And they're cops."

"Oh, forget the Three Bubbas of Stoweville. Not all of them can be that bad. These are detectives from the big city, anyway. They have to take tests and stuff. They can't be the idiots those three were."

"That's an assumption, Ellie, based on watching TV shows. You don't know any more about this than I do. They had on bad suits and leered at my old pictures and thought I was a cradle-robbing slut before they met me."

"Okay, okay. What names did you give them?"

I sighed, then told her.

She was delighted. "So it looks like you're bound to sleep with Cutie Pie. It's been how long? A year since that pathetic French-named goober? Russell sounds just your type."

"What, shallow?"

"No, hunky. I'm paying you a compliment. Although usually you like 'em more eggheady."

"He seems about fifteen to me. I don't think I ever found fifteen-year-old boys sexy, at least not since I was about eleven."

"Well, maybe you should go for the older one."

"I don't know that he's older, E. He's just not as icky-cute."

"Icky-cute. I like that. Well, I think you should give 'em both a chance. Throw 'em both against a wall, see which one sticks."

"That's a gross metaphor."

"Well, you know what I mean. In any case, the funeral should be fun. That's sarcasm, G., by the way.

"I gathered that."

The weather for my aunt Francesca's funeral the following morning was appropriately frigid, with sleet coming down from the sky like a rain of icy razor blades. I decided not to take the boys out of school for it. The last funeral they had attended had been their father's. They had been only three years old at the time, but I didn't think that another one at this point, even for a relative they had never met, was a good idea. My neighbor Patsy Hepplewhite, mother of Josh, agreed to get them at the bus stop and said she'd keep them for dinner as well. I thanked her and vowed silently to come home as early as I could.

. . .

"Well, Maria," her brother-in-law said to my mother as we came in the door of the church. "Where's your other daughter?"

"She has a living to earn, Frank. She never met Francesca. I told her it wasn't necessary to come to this and disrupt her schedule."

"She should be honoring a holy woman in the family."

"None of the Palettas are serious Catholics, Frank. Leave us be."

Frank huffed off. My mother wasn't usually this assertive with blustery males. I admired her for standing up to him and told her so.

"Oh, Frank's not so bad," she said, "but just because Rosa obeys his every whim and whisper doesn't mean I have to."

The service itself wasn't grand, nor was it well attended. I recognized most of the people there: Franny's three sisters and their families made up most of the crowd. There was one crying priest, very thin, past middle age, sitting in the last pew. Aunt Lottie spoke to him quietly and briefly. Everyone else left him alone.

The reception was held at Uncle Frank's restaurant, unimaginatively named Hannigan's. It wasn't a very good place to eat, in my opinion, but that wasn't the main reason I seldom went there. You never knew when Frank was going to be on the premises; I made a policy of not being where he was without lots of other Hannigans around as a buffer.

Half the restaurant was reserved for the funeral party. His chef had set up a large buffet with lots of chicken wings, salads, and sandwich fixings. I couldn't touch any of it; I was unaccountably melancholy, given my emotional distance from the subject of all this. I know wakes are for many people a healthy way to deal with death, but they don't do much for me. And the stress of wondering if any of them knew, or what they would think if they did, was draining everything I had. I might not have known Franny, but that didn't excuse being completely self-absorbed at her funeral. I resolved to leave as early as possible.

The first person I spoke to was the older of Aunt Lottie's two girls, Donna. She was about my age, though it was hard to tell for sure; I didn't know her or her sister, Bobbie, well. Donna was a little on the heavy side but quite pretty, I thought. Well-hidden beauty was the hallmark of the Eberle girls. Both plump, but pleasantly so, with glasses and no real concern about dressing to look like anyone's idea of the It girl, if you know what I mean. Good teeth, good skin, good hair, but nothing done with any of it. I always had to resist the urge to give beauty or fashion advice to both of them. It was an occupational hazard, or a former one. But Grammy had given me a talking to a long time ago, when I was only seventeen and flush with my new success in New York. I was giving well-meaning suggestions to my dowdy sister about "slimming" clothing.

Grammy took me aside. "Genie"—she was the only one who called me that—"if someone asks for your advice, it's help. If not, then it's an insult." I suddenly saw the resistance of my sister to my "tips" not as pure stubborn envy, although that may have been in the mix as well, but as hurt. I never did it again, figuring I would wait until she asked my advice on something. She never did.

Donna and I started talking about a recent film we'd both seen, and then her younger sister Bobbie came up and grabbed my arm. She was fresh and happy with a new boyfriend, a roundish, freckly young man with thick, swirly auburn hair. She introduced him to me as Clark Dewars.

"Like the good stuff," he said with a bounce.

"Oh, the Scotch," I said, catching on. I shook his hand and rambled off as quickly as possible. No sooner had I successfully avoided conversation with Clark and Bobbie when Maggie swooped down on me. Maggie's my age and the only other cousin who has bred. Other than that, we had absolutely nothing in common. She was moderately pregnant for the seventh time. She'd miscarried once, but the other five had taken. The only one of her children I could see now was her youngest, two-year-old Ewan, who was engaging in his favorite habit, standing next to Maggie with a handful of her skirt in his mouth. I don't know if this was to her credit, but she let him, so she always had large damp spots near her hem. I couldn't decide if I found this repulsive or funny or endearing or all three. No one else among the Hannigans ever seemed to acknowledge it as unusual.

Maggie proceeded to tell me of a hapless and worthy divorcé new to her parish who, it was implied, would make a wonderful father for my children. She told me John Fagin was a reporter for the *Tenway Express,* a weekly, and by no means good, newspaper. This was not the first time Maggie had tried to set me up. Each time I hoped it was the last. I often wondered if her own marriage was happy. She was determined to make me as happy or as miserable as she was.

"No, thanks," I said.

"You always say no," said Maggie.

"Yes," I said.

She pursed her lips and waved someone over before I could get away from her. He turned out to be a man of medium height, weight, coloring—medium everything—about forty years old. "John," said Maggie, "meet my cousin Gina."

His smile was broad, revealing medium teeth, and looked sincere as he took my hand in his hot, damp one and shook it. I pulled away; Maggie then left, Ewan weirdly trailing behind, and John Fagin (whom I immediately dubbed Doughboy, feeling low and mean-spirited) and I began an exhausting conversation about our jobs, our kids (he had a daughter who lived with his ex-wife), and our living quarters. He had an apartment south of town that he wasn't too happy with. He talked about his impending annulment (always confusing to me about Catholic annulments; doesn't that make the children bastards, and isn't that bad?). His job at least had the potential to sound interesting for a few minutes. As we talked, I could feel everything left of my energy oozing out of me through my feet and into the floor. I gave him all the cues I could: glancing at my watch, gazing over his shoulder at other people, moving slightly away. Nothing worked.

I couldn't get a grip on how he looked and knew, sadly, that ten minutes after he was gone from view, I wouldn't be able to pick him out of a lineup. That made me feel sorry for him, which is the worst way to feel about a new acquaintance, especially if he wants romance to be on the table. Long after I felt like an empty social vessel, he finally came to the point, asking if I'd like to go to dinner sometime. He didn't know about my tenuous relationship to the deceased; even if he had, this was a terribly inappropriate time and place to troll for dates. But I'd been brought up to, at all costs, be nice. I said, "Thanks, but I don't really date."

"How can someone like you not date?"

I couldn't think of an answer to that, so I just looked at him with my mouth open.

"Look," he said, "it would just be for dinner. You've got to eat!"

"I eat with my kids," I said.

His smile was gone now. He said, "Maggie said you'd been widowed for a while."

"Yes."

"You've got to move on, you know. It's time to get out there."

Anger started to fill up the space left by all the energy that had fled a short while before.

"Why?" I said.

"What? Well, life's too short and is for the living and all that."

"What does that have to do with dating? I don't date." I was trying not to raise my voice.

"You think maybe I can't afford you or something?"

I was almost relieved. This was actually insulting; I could legitimately walk away. As I did, he grabbed my arm, saying, "I'm sorry. That came out wrong."

I looked at him. The nice reflex kicked back in. "That's okay. But I don't date. I have to go talk to my cousins." I pulled away, not looking back.

The easiest cousin to find turned out to be Bobbie Eberle, the bubbly Clark at her side, as she seemed to be looking for me. "We're leaving," she said, "with Donna and Mom. We'll see you in a week, right? You're still having the party for Mo's birthday?"

"Yes. Be there by four if you can."

Mo's actual birthday was the upcoming Thursday, but she'd committed to spending it at the Big House with her parents, and that meant that she and Ivy couldn't be together for the celebration. So Ivy and I had schemed to give her a small surprise dinner party two days later. The Eberles were in; I hoped nothing, like two psychotic students, for example, would intervene to keep the dinner from happening.

The Eberles and Clark departed, and I was left mostly with Hannigans. I found Mo lingering by a vat of Swedish meatballs. I didn't tell her about my encounter with Maggie's latest project. Mo could get defensive about her siblings' awkward behavior, and she was stressed enough as it was. She was, as usual at family affairs, partnerless. I linked arms with her, and she said, "I really wish Ivy were here. In just a few days I'm going to be thirty-five. Do you think advancing age will help me be less of a weenie where my father is concerned?"

I couldn't think of a diplomatic answer to that. She went on, "Or do you think the time will ever come when my dad likes me without straightness?"

"Not everyone can dig the nonlinear, baby. Ivy understands. Family sucks."

"You shouldn't say that. You have kids. You can't teach them that. Family's most important when you have kids."

"To do that, I need some help from the aforementioned family. Ivy has the same problem. Her parents don't deal with you, either, right?"

"Yeah, I guess. Still," Mo said unhelpfully, gazing with pained, besotted eyes at her father, my uncle Frank, sitting at the head of a long table.

After a bit more commiserating, I decided that I needed to put in some time with the rest of my family. Farther down the buffet table I spotted Mo's younger sister Lizzie, who was ladling some sort of meaty-looking, mayonnaisey salad onto her plate. I was always trying to get Lizzie to like me, without success. I never knew why it was so important to me. Lizzie was fair, lean, and very tightly wrapped. That was ironic, given that she was a massage therapist. She was pretty, though not so drop-dead gorgeous as the baby of the family, Molly, and much fairer as well. Completely natural, too, no makeup, no hair color, though narrow streaks of gray were finding their way into her ash-blond curls. If you liked a girl who looked like she ate a lot of granola, you'd love Lizzie, so I was surprised to see her about to eat what looked like greasy ham salad.

I'd once told her admiringly that she was lucky to be naturally curly, which she dismissed with a sharp hand gesture. Lizzie also shaved nothing. She held me in great contempt for giving in to the patriarchy by shaving my legs. In response to this, I admitted my envy of the beautiful blond down that covered hers. I was descended from nothing but Italians; the hair on my legs was both formidable and unattractive. If untended, it could make wearing tights excruciating. When I said this, her expression didn't alter, and she continued talking as though I had said nothing. This interchange had occurred about a year before, and little had changed in our relationship since.

Lizzie didn't look too thrilled to see me now. She simply said, "Are we still on for next Saturday?" referring, presumably, to Mo's surprise party. I told her that we were and she asked if she could help in any way. I said no, the servers had everything under control, and she slid away.

Adrift, I put some damp salady-looking greenery on a plate and was looking for a napkin when Maggie's husband, Stu, came up to me.

"Hey, Gina. Nice to see you here."

"Hey, Stu."

"I was wondering how happy you were with your house."

"What?" Stu was in real estate.

"I've noticed that your neighborhood seems to be in transition."

"What does that mean?"

"It means it's changing."

"I know what the word 'transition' means, Stu. I just don't know what kind of transition you're talking about. Geological? Architectural? Meteorological? What?"

"Well, I don't know what you call it exactly. Ethnic, maybe?"

"Are you referring to the fact that a black family moved in a few months ago?"

"Well, partly. You have to think of your property value."

"No, actually, I don't. I don't have any plans to move anytime soon. Besides, I've met them. The Corbins. They have a daughter who's prime babysitting age, so I have my eye on her. Not, probably, for the same reason that you would. Anyway, I can't see how they would be likely to do anything to lower anybody's property values." I sighed. Looking at his vaguely irritable and smug face, I realized this was hopeless. Maybe he had even been trying to be genuinely helpful. Who knew? "Never mind, Stu. Thanks for your input. But I'm fine. I'm not planning on selling or buying any time soon." He was still a little put out, I think, that two years before I hadn't consulted him. I also hadn't taken him up on a few offers to help me do repairs around the house.

I decided I'd had enough of the limp salad and of Stu, so I left him, pleading a genuine need to find the bar. It was a popular spot and so was easy to find. Mo was talking to her youngest sister, Molly, by far the prettiest of the Hannigan girls. They were engaged in a conversation that looked both drunken and intense, so I left them alone after getting a martini in a plastic cup, looking around to see where else duty might lead me. My eyes found Aunt Rosa, who was talking to Maggie, who still had Ewan glued to her dress like a sucker-fish. Rosa saw me and waved me over, looking glad to see me. Maggie seemed less so. I wondered if she'd already gotten a report from John Fagin. She didn't bring it up, though. Instead, she said, "I was glad to see Donna. She never comes to anything. She's supposedly always working, but I don't believe that."

"She's an obstetrical nurse. She does work night shifts a lot and on weekends, too," Aunt Rosa said, putting up a mild defense of her most elusive niece.

"It's not like she's a doctor," Maggie said. "They wouldn't miss her if she took off once in a while for family."

Trying to change the subject, I asked Aunt Rosa about her garden. She was known for her green thumb; Uncle Frank had built her an attractive little greenhouse in their backyard with a small walled-in rose garden behind it. It was her favorite topic of conversation. She had won a number of awards for her roses; she was at least as proud of them as she was of any of her children.

Aunt Rosa said, "I have a new rose that's coming along beautifully. It's a special one that Frank got me from Italy, called La Dolorosa della Vecchia. The line is very, very old. I'm planning on entering it in the Tendale County rose show in the spring. I'm very optimistic about its chances." She was as animated as she ever got, soft brown and gray hair wisping out from her loose French twist, eyes crinkled in a small smile.

"Good for you," I said. "You've got a real gift. I'm trying to get some stuff growing. Maybe in the spring you could give me some tips."

"I'd be glad to. It all comes down to good compost."

"Doesn't everything?" I said.

Maggie's gaze was drifting away; I followed it to where it came to rest, on two of her children who were playing behind the main food table. I watched as little Kelsey whacked the back of six-year-old Conor's head with her doll with a great deal of force for a four-year-old. Conor turned around and yelled at her, but her face stayed blank. She waited till he got distracted, and then she did it again with complete and almost clinical premeditation. I expected Maggie to show some concern, to run over and intervene. Instead, she smiled and shook her head. She even chuckled a little. Stu was nowhere to be seen.

I'd had enough; I'd met all the familial obligations I could stomach. I looked at my watch and said it was time for me to leave, to collect my kids. A rambling discussion of why I hadn't brought them ensued in which I had to strain hard for tact; I left Maggie plainly convinced that I wasn't properly exposing my kids to death, God, and family. I relentlessly said my good-byes, hugging Aunt Rosa and giving her a quick peck on the cheek.

I didn't say that one of the main reasons they hadn't come was that neither I nor my boys enjoyed being around Maggie's horrible children. Seeing Kelsey's blank violence reminded me of the previous Easter, the last time I'd dared to take the twins to the Big House. I had been drawn upstairs, heart pounding, to where all seven of the kids had been playing. I found Toby sobbing on the floor. Next to him was a large Styrofoam cross, the kind they use for some funeral arrangements. Stevie was watching with big blue eyes from a few feet away, and ten-year-old Caitlin had what looked like a belt in her hand. She was screaming, "Get up, Jesus! You have to get up." Adam and Conor were standing with their backs against the wall. Kelsey, three years old then, was crying, too.

Toby had a welt the size and shape of an oyster on his cheek. You could see a small cut at the bottom of it. It matched the shape of the buckle on the belt.

"You were hitting him with this?" I looked at her, unbelieving. She started crying, too, in grating hiccups. "Mom says that's what made Jesus's life so good. He got beat by the Jews, but then he rose from the dead."

Maggie's only response had been "Oh, Gina, lighten up. They're kids. That's what kids do. Sometimes they get hurt. You're so over-protective."

Over dessert everyone seemed to be getting progressively drunker. Even my mother appeared to be having a good time, laughing glee-fully at some anecdote Stu was telling her. I saw Uncle Frank, seated kinglike as before, and knew that even rudimentary courtesy de-manded that I at least minimally thank him before I left. It was his restaurant; presumably he'd paid for everything. I swigged the last of the bitter martini and made my way over.

Frank had a glass of dark red wine in his hand. He was of the school that believed that if it was wine, it didn't really count as alcohol. He saw me approaching, raised bushy brows, and gave a one-sided smile. "Hey, here's the doll of the family," he said to his audience, several men seated around him, about his age; I knew none of them. I smiled limply at them and, staying out of his reach, said quickly, "Thanks so much for doing this. I've got to go, but it's been good to see every-one."

"Hey, not so fast." He reached out and grabbed my hand. "She's the one I was talking about," he said to the bald, bobbing heads around him. "The New York model. But I guess you can tell, huh?" Low, gurgly drunken chuckles. His hand felt like prison; I really wanted him to let go but didn't want to do anything unseemly, God help me. It horrified me how unassertive I was being.

"Hey, Gina," he went on amid the rumbling, "an idea I had: Why don't you give some beauty tips to those Eberle girls? You know, Donna and Bobbie," as if I wouldn't know who he meant. He looked sincere, as if he really had their welfare in mind. "They could use it.

Hell, even my girls could stand a few pointers, especially from some-one like you. Whaddya say?" He looked like this was a suggestion both reasonable and brilliant.

I gave him an unsuccessful smile. "I think they're all just fine the way they are."

"Oh, come on!" he chortled. More nodding from the collected Evil Geezers. I finally got up the energy to pull my hand away, re-iterated my need to go, thanked him again, and scooted away, look-ing desperately for my mother.

I found her, still grinning drunkenly with Stu. "We're leaving," I said. I finally got her to leave but, she made it clear, not willingly.

In the car I said to her, "Don't you wonder what they say about you, or me, when we're not there?"

"Not really," she said.

After I got home with the boys, my mother wanted to discuss the fu-neral in some detail. It seemed to bother her that they had dressed Franny in her formal habit. I tried to get her to stop, to change the subject, but she wouldn't. I wound up having to explain more of what had gone on that day than I wanted to Toby, who was deter-mined to understand all the nuances of a Catholic funeral. Later that night I heard wailing across the hall. I got out of bed and got the sob-bing Toby out of the lower bunk. I carried him, crying more softly now, back to my room. It woke my mother; I saw her look out her door, but she didn't say anything.

chapter six

THE NEXT DAY I decided to assuage my curiosity. "Hey, Mom, Jessie next door said that Franny had a baby. Is that true?"

My mother looked at me as though I had started spewing poisonous snakes from my mouth. "Of course not. That's ridiculous."

"Really? Why did she say that, then?"

"Is that Jessie Hays?"

"Jessie Foxhall."

"Oh, she used to be Jessie Hays. I remember her. She was trouble. She was crazy, too. Don't believe anything she says. It's a pretty strange coincidence, her living next door to you here."

"She lived next door to you folks, growing up?"

"Yes. But Mama didn't think much of her. She was nosy. And kind of trash, if you know what I mean."

"No, I don't. What does that mean?"

"Just trash. You know it when you see it."

I couldn't get her to tell me any more about this supposed baby of Franny's. But she said, "I'm going to be gone this afternoon for a while. I have some business to take care of."

"What business?" I said, showing what I thought was polite curiosity.

"Franny's estate. Rosa and Lottie and I have to see a lawyer about some things. We haven't finished going through her effects yet, either." I knew Franny couldn't have much of an estate. She was a nun, for Christ's sake, no pun intended. My mother looked cagey but clearly wasn't going to tell me any more about it.

I went to my room to meditate. After trying long enough to know it wasn't going to work, I found that I was cold, so I changed my clothes. My mother knocked once on my bedroom door, then pushed it open and walked in. I looked at her over the turquoise sweater I was planning to put on, which I was holding up to my chest. She looked me up and down, frowned, and said, "Are you wearing that?"

The answer seemed obvious, but I said, "Yes."

"It's a little dressy, isn't it? Are you going somewhere?"

"No. But it's warm and comfortable, and I wanted to wear it. I'm wearing jeans, Mom. I don't think that's particularly dressy."

Mom said, "I suppose I'm being a busybody." She waited for me to correct her. I didn't. "Well," she snapped, "I hear Rosa's car. I guess it's a good thing that she's driving me. I wouldn't want to put you out any more. We'll be having dinner out, so don't save anything for me."

I rolled my eyes behind her back, feeling like a sulky teenager. After she went downstairs, I finished dressing.

Aunt Rosa brought her back that evening but didn't come in. Toby was drawing at the dining-room table. Stevie was playing a game on the computer in the same room. I kept the desktop on a small corner table there because when I'd put it in the third bedroom, Stevie would disappear upstairs for hours. This way I could see him and know what he was up to. I worked hard to make sure he didn't spend all his time this way, but it was often serious labor to get him off a video game, sometimes even to go to the bathroom or eat. My cousin Lizzie had asked me if he was just a little bit autistic, his powers of concentration were so worryingly strong. It was difficult for me not to overreact. I asked Jeri about the possibility; she explained that there was no such thing as "a little bit autistic" and that Stevie certainly wasn't. She then added, alarmingly, that attention deficit disorder was a possibility, but if he wasn't having trouble in school, I didn't need to do anything about it at the moment. Structure, she said, lots of structure. I had lost only a few nights' sleep over that.

Both boys pretty much ignored my mother's return even though she rumbled loudly through the living room, many crackling and long papers in important brown folders under her arms. She headed for the stairs. To be polite, I said, "Everything go okay?"

She looked at me with her eyebrows raised. "It went fine," she said, then went up, plodding heavily. She looked back when she was halfway up the stairs and said, "I'm going to call Gerald and tell him when to pick me up at the airport." Gerald was my mother's latest boyfriend. I knew next to nothing about him other than that he was younger than she was. "I'll be leaving tomorrow."

Later I put the boys to bed and then, while my mother was downstairs watching TV, did about an hour of yoga. After Mom went to bed, I talked to my sister Ellie for a while. I filled her in about the funeral and then told her about how squirrelly Mom was being about Franny's estate.

"So what the hell is our scary mama up to?" she said.

"I have no idea. She'll tell me or she won't. Maybe Aunt Lottie will tell me sometime."

"You know, if you have anything coming out of Franny's estate, Mama is going to try to keep it from you. You might want to check it out just in case she's trying to screw you out of something."

"I can't imagine I'll inherit anything. It's not like I knew her at all. And if Mom wants more money, she can have it. I'm doing all right, and I don't want to fight about stuff like that."

"Don't give me that Zen crap about accepting what you can't change."

"That's the serenity prayer from Alcoholics Anonymous. It was originally written by Reinhold Niebuhr in 1943."

"Whatever. Don't be a wimp."

"I am a wimp. Besides, I really don't care." I imagined that Ellie was rolling her eyes at me. Then I remembered about Franny's baby. I told Ellie.

"A baby? Adopted out? In this family? I don't think so. Someone from the family would have taken it."

I thought about it for a minute. Oddly, that possibility hadn't occurred to me. "There are a lot of girls among all the cousins. Do you really think one of them is Franny's kid?"

"Maybe. Who could it be? I mean, when did this happen? Were any of the sisters married?"

"I don't know. Franny was the youngest, so they might all have been married by then. I don't know dates. I don't even know anything about when Franny went into the convent."

"Hmmm. Maybe it's not one of them. Maybe it's one of us."

The idea hit me like a bullet. "Ellie, I'll bet it's me!"

"Why you?"

"Because Mom hates me."

Ellie made a few of the noises you have to make when people say something like that, but she knew it was true.

"Ellie, that would explain it."

"You may be right. But you've got to find out some facts before you decide this is the truth, you know."

We hashed it out some more, then decided that Bobbie would be a good person to enlist. She, along with all the female cousins, had a stake in this, too, she had access to Lottie, and she was a librarian. She was good at research.

"Speaking of cousins and Catholics, so Maggie's still trying to get you to date some good old former altar boy?"

"Yes. Sigh."

"If you told her about the website, she might leave you alone."

"Yeah, I can't wait till all the Hannigans hear about it."

Early the next afternoon the toilet backed up. I was manning the plunger when the phone rang. My mother was taking a nap and wouldn't have woken up if the *Titanic* had crashed through the guest-room window. My boys were playing a computer game in the dining room. As I said, Stevie's powers of concentration were legendary; he never heard anything when he was playing a computer game unless you screamed directly into his little ear. Toby was somewhat better, but when the phone rang, he simply went into another room; the loud ringing hurt his sensitive ears.

As I attempted to put the plunger down delicately, without spreading toilet water all over the bathroom floor, it slipped out of my hand and rolled, handle first, under the claw-foot tub. With a muttered "shit" I ran out of the bathroom, nearly tripping over my ancient cat, Sidney. Since I inadvertently touched his backside gently with my foot, he gave me a mean swipe with his right paw, taking a small chunk out of my left ankle. Even if I believed in kicking cats, which I don't, Sidney had a hinky hip, and so it would have been karmically disastrous to kick him even if he'd earned it.

With a loud "Ow!" I hobbled into my bedroom and finally picked up the phone. "What?" I snapped, and instantly regretted it. "I'm sorry," I continued before the other party could speak, "I mean, hello."

"Gina?"

"Yes?" I couldn't place the voice at all.

"It's Erin."

My stomach tightened. "Whoa, it's been a while. How the hell are you?"

"I'm doing okay. But I've been thinking about you a lot lately. I'm sorry I'm so lousy at keeping in touch. I was wondering if we could get together. Like for dinner or something."

"I'd like that." I mostly meant it. "What's going on in your life? I've seen the ads. You look fabulous. 'Lahk an anchell.' " I was making fun of a photographer we both had known.

Erin's laugh was a genuine giggle. "Raphael is still working, you know. He has his own agency, and he's doing very well."

"Good for him. You seem to be a household word. You can still do *Sports Illustrated*. Go, girl, go."

"Well, that's probably the last time. Unfortunately, I've got to go in a minute, but I had a quick break, and I really want to see you. When can we set it up? Do you ever come into the city?"

"Rarely," I said. I then blurted before I had time to think it through, "How hard would it be for you to come here?"

"Pretty easy. I can get a car. When?"

"Well, my mother's in town, but she's leaving this evening. So really, any night." I remembered that I had a date with the cops, innards sinking. "Actually, tomorrow night would be the best time for me if you can make it that soon. And if you don't mind having the kids around. It's not that easy arranging for a sitter." I'd renounced going to lengths to shield people from my children.

"Your *mother*? I thought she hated you."

"She does. She was here for my aunt's funeral."

"God, I'm sorry. Were you close to your aunt?"

"Never met her, actually. But thanks."

"Are things any better between the two of you?"

"Not really."

"That sucks. Tomorrow night would be fine for me. I'll be excited to see your boys." I doubted that, but it was nice of her to say so. "Say around six?"

"Fine. I'll make dinner. It'll be great to see you, Erin."

"It will. Here's my cell in case you need to get in touch." She gave me the number. "I'll see you then."

We rang off, and then I remembered that I should have asked her about what she could/would or couldn't/wouldn't eat. You have to assume dietary restrictions with someone in her line of work. But I didn't want to call her back.

I then returned to the special lure of the toilet.

I was washing my hands from my (successful) toilet labors when my mom peeked out from behind the guest-room door. She looked put out.

"Who was on the phone?"

"An old friend from the city. Erin Steele."

"Would I have seen her?"

"She's the face on the *Jamais* cosmetics ads. I don't know if you've seen those."

"Of course I've seen them. I shop, don't I?"

"I suppose you do." I was trying not to snap back, but it was getting harder and harder. "Anyway, she wants to get together sometime."

"What do you think she wants?"

"I don't know, Mom. Just to talk, to reminisce, I don't know. She's an old friend. I'll be glad to see her."

"Just don't be getting any ideas about returning to that nasty business. You're too old, and you have responsibilities. And you have young boys. I mean, I think it would be totally inappropriate for you to be getting your picture taken with no clothes on when you have children."

"I never took my clothes off, Mom." Not all of them, anyway.

Mom got Lottie to take her to the airport late that afternoon. I think she didn't want to spend that much time in the car with the boys, so she didn't ask me. I was taking out the trash shortly after she left, when Jessie waved to me from her front porch. I leaned back in the front door, calling to the boys that I was going next door for a minute, and wandered over, hugging myself in the sharp air. It occurred to me as I walked the five steps to her porch that I should be asking her if she needed things at the store. But then I thought about the man and the boy who had come to see her. Maybe they ran errands for her.

"Was that Maria?" she asked, voice quavery as she waved me inside her house. Walking in was like having to pierce a membrane between the almost violent cold outside and the weighty bubble of heat inside. "Has she gone?"

"Yes," I said. "She left to go back to Atlanta. Are you okay?"

"I'm fine," she said. "But I don't like Maria. Never did. She's awfully mean." I didn't know what to say to that. "You don't seem to take after her much."

I still couldn't find any appropriate response. "Thank you" seemed like a weird thing to say, so I just stood there.

"Don't you think my hair looks good?" she went on. I hadn't noticed, but it did look thicker, more in unison, than before. I guess that meant it looked good. I was on firmer conversational ground here. I said it looked great, leaving the question of what she'd done to so beautify herself dangling. She said, "It's Eva Gabor."

I thought stupidly for a moment that she knew the deceased Hungarian celebrity personally and had gotten beauty tips of some sort from her. Jessie put her hand to her hair again in a disconcertingly vain gesture. Then the answer struck me. Eva Gabor had had a line of wigs. I was immensely grateful that I remembered that in time to avoid offending her in some way (Jessie, not Eva Gabor). I said, "It's a really good cut for the shape of your face." This was one of those semimeaningless things fashion people say to nonfashion people when they want to be complimentary in a vague way. I figured I was at least doing no harm. "Any special occasion?"

She sobered up quickly. "No," she said. "Well, I'm going out. I wanted some help, though. I need to get my green dress out. It's up high, and I can't get it, and I'm a little shaky with the step stool these days."

I told her I would be glad to help, and she showed me where her little rusty metal step stool lived behind the kitchen door. I took it and followed her as she made her slow way upstairs to a bleak hallway lit by a bulb on a furry cloth-covered wire. She waved at the paneled door to a small room with green foil wallpaper, grand and faded, with silvery roses embossed in crooked vertical jade stripes.

"Wow," I said. "That's great wallpaper."

"I put it up myself," she said.

The room was mostly filled by a high twin bed with a heavy cherry headboard and an enormous cherry dresser with a rose marble top. It was oddly depressing, cheery and dreary at the same time, like a fake grin. She pointed to the narrow closet door, and I helped get an old cardboard box that was soft with age and dust down from the top shelf. There was no light in the closet, and the room was lit only by a tiny bedside lamp that was dripping with yellowed plastic in the shape of teardrops. Reaching up into the dark, teetering on the dented little step, required a leap of faith and a reining in of the darker side of my imagination.

After I deposited the box on the bed, she opened the crisscrossed top and pulled out a folded square wrapped in yellowed tissue paper. Carefully pulling off the wrapping and then unfurling the item itself, she revealed a confection in satiny crème de menthe. Lace and bugle beads competed for attention on the collar and cuffs, and the fifty or so buttons were covered with gold lamé. Jessie's face glowed, some of the intense green reflecting off her cheeks.

I said, "It's something, Jessie. Are you wearing this tonight?"

"Yes," she said, remembering me and clamming up. "Thanks for getting it down for me. You need to go now, to get back to your boys."

"You're right. I shouldn't leave them for long. Can I do anything else for you while I'm here?"

"No, no, get home, get home now." She almost shoved me down her stairs and out of her house, no more thanks coming. I wished then that she had an unheated mudroom or something else that could function as a sort of air lock to prepare you for the heart-clutching temperature changes involved in going through her front door. Outside the temperature was easily in the single digits. I always suspected that inside her house the digits were tripled but never thought to check her thermostat.

chapter seven

I LIKE HAVING a sound track to my life. I can remember events best if I can place them in the context of the music I was listening to at the time. The good thing about this is that I can revisit any time I want simply by playing certain songs or études or whatever. Of course, the bad thing about it is that a certain song, heard unexpectedly in a store or even from a passing car, can just as easily land me in the middle of a memory of trauma or misery.

In the year after I turned thirty-three (the age of resurrection) I was branching out, reawakening from a recent phase of musical conservatism. I found new CDs by Patti Smith, whom I'd always idolized, and played lots of Moby, Lucinda Williams, Missy Elliott, and the Mekons. James Brown and They Might Be Giants remained favorites of the boys, along with Sly and the Family Stone.

The Erin Steele time of my life, however, had a bassier, clubbier sort of sound to it. I couldn't decide if I needed to revisit it before she showed up, then decided that her presence would be reminder enough; I didn't need to inhabit the past any more than that. I missed some things about that time and was relieved to see the ass end of others.

I'm basically a pragmatist and not too prone to nostalgia. On the day of Erin's visit, it hit me as I quickly and sloppily cleaned up the first floor of the house, with grudging and energy-sapping "help" from my sons, that my main worry about seeing her again was that I would simply bore her.

I had a tendency, as have many parents, to talk a lot about my sons. They're pretty interesting as kids go. But that only goes so far with anyone; people who are single and childless generally find even the most remarkable accomplishments or sidesplitting hijinks of someone's kid pretty ho-hum. For seven years, though, they'd been pretty much it for me; it was difficult to disconnect enough to get genuinely engaged in something else. Sometimes I could watch myself being tedious and was still helpless, unable to make myself into someone more interesting.

The hard fact was, I used to be more interesting than Erin. Now I wasn't. I hoped I was big enough to enjoy her life vicariously without being ashamed of mine, but wasn't sure I could pull it off.

After the house was at least passable, I then cleaned myself up as best I could. I even debated whether I should bother putting on makeup. It's not like it's a date, I said to myself. But though I didn't want to admit it, I wanted to look somewhat like the person she knew. A lot of vanity had been beaten out of me, but not all. So I put on a reasonable pair of jeans and enough makeup to look like I was alive and healthy. I made spaghetti because it was easy and could pass for real food and the boys would eat it. I made sure the pasta was whole wheat and the sauce was sugar-free. I had no idea what kind of dietary universe she inhabited these days.

At a little after six Erin appeared at the door. I got her in, got her (incredibly expensive fake) fur coat off. She clearly was not trying to make me feel like a schlub in comparison to her, for which I was grateful. She had on jeans as well, although hers were probably not from Target, and a pale blue silk blouse that fluttered engagingly around her belly, then stopped, exposing a wide band of golden flesh just above her waistband. Leather half boots, a few rings, and that was it. Her hair was shorter than it had been the last time I had seen her.

Then it had been long and yellow; now it was cut in a perfect shag with some darker tones mixed into the blond. She looked fabulous. Glowing. Rich. Young.

I hugged her, surprised at my own delight. "Come in. I'm so impressed you found it so easily. You didn't need to call me once for directions!"

"Well, it's easy when you make a professional driver do all the work, including the navigating. He's got one of those computer locator thingies in the car."

I introduced her to the boys. Toby eyed her with some interest; Stevie paid only the slightest attention to her arrival, as he was busy with the computer. I asked her, "What does your driver do while you're here?"

She raised her eyebrows. "I have no idea," she said. "I've never thought about it." She looked around. "Your house is so cute. It's great," she said unconvincingly.

I got her a glass of wine, yelled at the boys that dinner would be on the table in half an hour, and took her into the kitchen, where we could sit and talk.

"Okay, so first of all, you have to tell me about Dion and DeVonne Van Doren."

Erin answered, "Their spring line killed in both Paris and L.A. I saw them just last month. Of course, before the Paris show they had an epic fight. A lot of folks were wondering if they were going to dissolve the partnership for real this time."

"They always fought before big shows. Is Dion still with Carlton?"

"Yes. It's quite sweet. They're the only truly monogamous couple I know. But DeVonne has a new boy toy. He's only twenty-two and just as cute as can be. Not terribly bright, but you know that never mattered much to DeVonne."

"The last one I knew about was Cain, the blond one everyone called Bam-Bam, like the kid from *The Flintstones*. He was as dumb as a bottle of glue, if I remember correctly. But that was, what, eight years ago?" I sighed, trying not to feel a wave of sadness over the road not taken. Leave it alone. "She dumped him as soon as she found out he was from Flatbush."

"What's wrong with Flatbush?"

"D and D are from Flatbush."

"Really?" said Erin. "You always knew all this stuff about people. How did you know everything like that?"

"People talked to me. I don't know why."

"Well, probably because you never blabbed."

"Till now, anyway. If I tell you their real names, will you keep it a secret?"

"Absolutely! This is gold."

"Brace yourself. Donny and Doreen Komarchek."

"From Flatbush?"

"Yep. Local siblings done made good. With the help of elocution lessons. Their dad still owns a little drugstore there."

Erin laughed, then said, "Well, Bam-Bam's long gone. There's a brand-new one now, but I don't know his name. She doesn't talk about her boyfriends much anymore. Has them but doesn't talk about them. By the way, Raphael said to say hi. I told him I was coming to see you. He's told me a few dozen times that he misses shooting us together. Nobody does the pouty thing the way you used to."

"Well, no one has your fabulous smile. I never did figure out what was up with my teeth."

"I don't know, either, because they look normal in real life."

For any photographer besides Raphael Priazzi, I'd smile, and it would look okay. I even had a few covers where I was grinning like a maniac and still looked like you're supposed to. But every time he put us together and tried to get me to smile, they just looked huge. I once heard him say "Gina has-a teet"—and I'm pretty sure he meant teeth, but of course you couldn't be sure—"like-a piano keys." All I could do was hope he meant the white ones. It was pretty humiliating at the time.

"Oh, and Philippe says hello, too," Erin added. I had forgotten all about Philippe Congère, another photographer who did lots of work for *Lavish*. He was famous for bilingual non sequiturs. "Can't you feel the dangére, *chérie*? Can't you love it like a rose? Like a petal? Can't you spread your lips and glow, my love? You are so raaadiant, so glowy. I love you; fuck me with your happiness, my Chinese love sweetness." None of us ever knew exactly what the hell he was talking about, but it didn't seem to matter. We all looked great in his shots. Even if we were saggy-faced from hangovers or menstrual cramps or breakup-induced crying jags, we still looked willowy, pouty, ethereal, raaadiant. Philippe was a genius, if a bit of a jerk. He played the role of the gay fashionisto, but he wasn't; he had been married at least twice and had three children, although I was never clear on how many kids went with which (ex) wife. That, of course, never stopped him from sleeping with the occasional new girl. He favored bulimics; I don't know why.

I finished getting the spaghetti ready and got the boys to join us. Fortunately, Erin understood that the topic had to change a bit until the boys were done eating. They both took to her, especially Toby, who liked girls of all ages. He did his best material for her, including his famous imitation of Foghorn Leghorn and his limited but effective repertoire of French and Spanish words. Erin tried not to be too uncomfortable.

She didn't eat much, which didn't surprise me, nor did it hurt my feelings. After dinner, the boys went to watch a movie in the living room while Erin and I talked some more. I asked her if she'd hang out while I got them to bed. Later, I came downstairs for our first completely uncensored chat of the evening.

I said, "I had a realization when I hit my thirties. Women like me are supposed to like wine better than liquor. But I finally had to admit that wine makes me feel kind of crummy and gives me a terrible hangover. But good gin, ahhh, that's a different story. In moderation, of course. Or occasionally vodka. But it's got to be Tanqueray or Stoli. Everything else just feels like it's rotting my insides. So what do you say? Want a martini? It's not like you have to drive."

"Sounds absolutely fabulous. It really will be like old times."

She reminded me about a time I had forgotten, when we were in Venice. All the models were booked into this *pensione* off Canal Street, where the members of an Italian soccer team were also staying. I don't think they were a very good team. In any case, they were the tiniest male athletes I'd ever seen. They were on the floor above ours; they kept craning over the railings of their balconies, trying to work up the nerve to swing themselves down. They kept whispering nonsensical English words, as if they could get to us if only no one spoke out loud. Finally, some of them found the courage and dangled above the windows of our three adjoining rooms, hissing and frantic. The distance was pretty far, and to drop onto our balcony was likely to be painful, if not fatal.

She started laughing again. "Oh my God, remember how Signore Fiorio went after them after Katie Cameron complained?"

We said in unison, "Fucking boy!" Signore Fiorio was the proprietor of the place, and he saw himself as a sort of protector or chaperone of this female swarm, as many of us were quite young and, presumably, delicate. His English was only marginally better than that of the little soccer players. After Katie had fetched him to our room and he saw the simian athletes hanging outside the windows like an uneven row of icicle lights, he ran after them, waving a heavy cherry cane, scaring them back up, to scramble back into their own rooms. The whole time he was yelling "Fucking boy! Fucking boy!" He then looked at Erin, in whom he had shown a particular paternal interest. "Is this right, 'fucking boy'?" Erin had no choice but to nod. It's not like it was exactly wrong.

"He was so sweet," I said. "Thank God we managed to wait until he left to start laughing. I think I ruptured something. Then we drank way too much, and I couldn't sleep very well, and we had to get up early, and I was totally bloated the next day. Those pictures of me always made me look like I'd just had dental work."

"Babe, when people looked at those pictures, they weren't looking at your face."

We both snorted. Actually, a picture from that shoot had become the most widely published one of my career. I was in a string bikini, posing in Saint Mark's Square among the pigeons. It was utterly preposterous, but that wasn't really a concern of the editors of *Lavish*. I understand that the scantily clad nature of the photo was the selling point, but I'd looked better in other pictures. In that one my face was puffy. I'd always referred to it as the bloat picture.

Then I asked Erin about her love life, of course. She said there wasn't anyone in particular right now, although she'd been engaged the year before to Rodney Bailey, a big name in arena rock. I loathed his music and everything he stood for, but Erin still seemed to have a soft spot in her heart for him, so it seemed rude to say anything. She asked me about mine.

"I had a brief affair with another professor about a year ago. It was a disaster. A few other academic types seemed promising, then turned out to be married, which I found out in time, but still. Other than that I've been staying out of it. I can't just bring a guy home for sex with the boys here. Too weird, too trailer trash, too oedipally awful. I mean, it can't be a good idea to rub their noses in their mother's sexuality."

"You still like 'em little and nerdy?"

"I guess. I don't like 'em much at all right now. I miss sex, but it doesn't seem worth it at the moment."

She looked at me for a moment. "Do it at his house. Or in a car if you have to. Life's too short."

"Hmmm."

"You didn't *used* to be so . . . careful."

"I didn't used to have children." I didn't know how she felt about that, didn't want to come off as smug. "I'm not sure I'm someone who should have them, but I do. So I'm screwed. Or not." I laughed. I was having a great time. I was remembering why I had liked her so much, why we'd been so close.

———

"JESUS, ERIN."

"Yeah, well, they think I'll be all right. But I'm going to have to have a mastectomy and then chemo and radiation and all that shit."

I felt like I was on a falling elevator. "When do you go in?"

"Soon. They want to do it as soon as possible. So"—she started crying—"the *Sports Illustrated* shoot is probably the last one I'll do. I sure can't do *Lavish* anymore."

"Honey, I'm so sorry." I hugged her as she cried for a while. I asked how she was fixed for practical needs, money, people to take care of her, and so on. But Erin had fame, family, beauty, and money, so none of those were real concerns.

"But Jesus, Gina, my whole career is fucked, you know, and I'm not like you; I'm not cut out for much else. And I can't act, I can't sing. What the hell am I going to do? I mean, I can probably live on what I've made for a good while, but I don't know any man I want to marry who'd take care of me, and even if I did, what am I going to *do*? I've got to do *something*!" Her tears were coming out fast now.

I held her and said, "Erin, you could work again if you want to. It's not all swimsuits and underwear. What do the *Jamais* people say? Do they know yet?" I was wondering if all her contracts would bail on her. I entertained a momentary fantasy: Erin Steele, cover girl and breast cancer survivor. The poster girl for breast cancer chic. Beauty survives cancer. A new age in advertising, the age of the real woman. If her agent pushed it right, maybe a whole new career, a new kind of career.

Never in a million, billion years, I thought. She said her agent was working on postoperative gigs for her. I didn't believe it, and neither did she.

"Oh, Erin, honey, I'm so sorry," I repeated, and continued to hug her while she cried. We talked for a bit longer, drank a bit more. Then Erin called her driver. She was tired and a little drunk, and the surgery was set to happen in a few days. I thanked her for coming out to my house and for trusting me enough to tell me all this.

"My publicist is releasing the information to the press in a couple of days. I just didn't want you reading about it in *Entertainment Weekly*." I thought, quickly and sadly, that I doubted they'd care. But who knew? "We'll see how the surgery goes," she went on, "and take it from there."

I told her that I really wanted to stay in close touch, especially now, and we hugged again. I watched her get into the limousine and then went back inside, hugging myself from the cold. I wondered how bad the cancer really was. I thought about the cold hand of the Universe. An icy finger touched here, wealth, there, cancer, here, both, there, neither.

That night I had a really bad dream. I didn't remember it when I woke up, except that it had to do with knives and cutting and blood. It made me feel off and punky all day long.

chapter eight

DETECTIVES BIG BEAR and Cutie Pie showed up on Wednesday afternoon shortly after I got the boys from the bus stop. Seeing them at my door flattened me completely; I had hoped that somehow this would all resolve itself, evaporate like some criminal condensation. When Toby and Stevie asked about them, I said that Russell would be helping Molly look after them tonight and Tommy was going to help me teach. Toby was promising to be a good chaperone; he was a friendly fellow, and he immediately grabbed Tommy's hand, taking him to see an elaborate Hot Wheels track he had gotten for Christmas. We had not yet managed to get the whole thing assembled, and he wanted help with it. I intervened, saying that there were other matters to attend to first. With only a little yelling I got them to do homework, fetched them both a snack, and cleaned out their lunch boxes and backpacks, readying them for the next day. Ten minutes later, homework done, snack eaten, Stevie went to the computer. Toby approached Tommy and Russell again about the Hot Wheels track; to my relief, neither man seemed to mind.

While the males were thus occupied, I cleaned up the kitchen, threw the laundry I'd started that morning in the dryer, fed the cat, petted him, and scooped his litter. Then I got out some money for pizza. At a little after four o'clock my cousin Molly appeared at my door, looking cold and red-nosed but very, very pretty and very, very young. She was a graduate student in physical therapy at the university. She was only half-Italian but looked more like it than I did. Where my hair was light brown, hers was chestnut, quite straight, quite long. She had a symmetrical oval face. She was a lot smaller than I was in general. I always felt a bit gawky and large around her, which is unusual for me. I was never really sure if Molly even liked me. She treated me with a coolness that I found difficult. She had taken to chiding me, a habit she seemed to have picked up from her older sister Lizzie. But Molly and the boys got along well, and she needed the money I paid her for babysitting every Wednesday night, when I taught the class Tim and Jason were in. And she was extremely convenient; she lived with Mo and Ivy, two blocks away.

I had a hard time figuring out how to explain the detectives to her. But as it turned out, Russell was very good at telling women things. I took her into the dining room, which was fast becoming Hot Wheels Heaven, and introduced her to the men. Russell practically lit up at her arrival and interjected that he and his friend were visiting the criminology department at the university and I was helping them out on a confidential matter. That seemed to be enough. He and Molly seemed to take to each other right away, which didn't surprise me. They were pretty similar from what I could tell, charmingly predatory toward the opposite sex. She barely glanced at Tommy, whose expression hadn't strayed from grim since the previous week. It seemed permanent, like a tattoo. She seemed satisfied that I could vouch for Russell and so had no problem hanging out with him for a while. She was also willing to help with the Hot Wheels track. I would put up with a lot for that.

Stevie surprised me by suddenly leaving the computer. He walked directly up to Tommy, looked him in the eye, and said, "You will really like the tower that I'm building in this game. Come see it."

It was not a request. Stevie was the graver, more reserved of the two boys, and he rarely took to newcomers. But he grasped Tommy's hand and pulled him over to the computer. They sat down on the bench there side by side, the huge man and the little boy, and together continued constructing the ornate virtual Lego tower that Stevie was very proud of. This was more touching than I wanted to admit. I realized that the detectives needed my kids to at least tolerate them for the next few days, so maybe I could relax about how nice they were likely to be.

I took a moment to go upstairs, do a few deep-breathing exercises, and fix my face. I put on some makeup and paid more attention to my hair than I usually do for my classes. I was feeling vulnerable and needed all the camouflage I could get. I was careful, however, not to put on too much. I wasn't in the habit of wearing makeup much anymore, as I wasn't too interested in people looking at me that way, like a makeup-wearing person. And tonight I was sorely aware of the possibility of sending mistaken messages to any number of people in class. Better to look dowdy than like a slut. I was wearing jeans and a big sweater. I figured that was shapeless enough.

Before I left my bedroom, I thought quickly about Ellie, wishing desperately that I had time to talk to her.

As I was getting ready to leave, the phone rang. I made the mistake of picking it up. It was John Fagin. It took me a moment to put the name to what little I remembered of Doughboy's face. I tried to tell him I was on my way out. He didn't endear himself to me by acknowledging that fact, then completely ignoring it. He wanted to chat for a bit before getting down to the business of asking me out. I gathered that he thought the chummy approach would help his case.

He gabbed on and on about the funeral, which I found surreal. I was trying to break in, to remind him that I needed to leave, when he told me that he regretted not meeting my mother there. I couldn't help asking why.

"Well, you know, women all turn into their mothers when they get older. I wanted to see what you'd be like in a few years."

"Look, John," I said, reeling a little, "I have to go to work. Right now. I'll talk to you some other time." That, as it turned out, was a big mistake.

Tommy and I didn't speak much in the car during the ten-minute drive to campus. If he was at all curious about the phone call, he gave no sign of it. In nicer weather I tended to walk to the campus and back, but given the intense cold this time of the year, I generally drove my trusty old all-wheel-drive wagon. Tommy had reminded me in the car that neither of us had had dinner and the class wouldn't get out till nine. It was still early enough that we could pop into the student union cafeteria and grab something. I tended not to eat much before class, but I realized that a man Tommy's size needed to eat a lot more, and more often, than I did. So we went in, chose some food from various coolers, salad bars, and kiosks, paid, and sat down. I said, feeling genuinely sorry for him, that there wasn't any indoor smoking area near us on campus. He shrugged and said he'd be willing to risk pneumonia by stepping outside to smoke. He was used to it.

I was getting more and more nervous, so I decided the best thing to do was to talk about it. He wasn't going to beat me up. I should be able to relax more around him. He asked me how the intervening time had gone. Did I notice anything weird, did Tim and Jason contact me, and so on. I told him that I basically just denied it all in my head, which is what I had been doing all week.

"But I'm scared shitless about tonight." That didn't come out the way I'd intended. "I'm sorry. My language deteriorates when I'm nervous and I'm out of the hearing range of children. I generally don't talk like this around them. But when I'm tense and with only adults, it's like I get some temporary form of Tourette's syndrome. I guess you guys all talk like the cops on TV or in movies and swear all the time, so it won't bother you. But then again, I don't really know that, do I?" After that idiotic ramble I managed to put the verbal brakes on. Tommy just looked at me, eyebrows raised.

Finally, he took in a slow, deep breath and said, "I would have thought this was something that you'd have a lot of experience with."

"What? Swearing?"

"No, I mean, your whole profession was about creating an unreal image, right?"

"My former profession. I haven't done that for a lot of years now. And other people created the images. I was just a prop."

"You didn't do any acting?"

I absurdly thought at first that he was referring to pornography again and was accusing me of making blue movies. "No," I said quickly. I reconsidered. "Well, yes, but I was terrible at it. A few commercials and one appearance on a sitcom. *My Pal Bernie.* I doubt you'd remember it. Bernie was an orangutan. My character was listed as 'Clueless Cheerleader' in the script. I still can remember the lines: 'He seems really strong. Who's his trainer?' and 'I think he's hot. Look at that six-pack!' This was all, of course, referring to Bernie."

The grim look almost changed then, although to what, I had no idea.

"Look, I just babble when I'm nervous. I'm really nervous now. Lucky you, you get to spend the evening with a profane babbler. I have a lecture planned tonight. I sure as hell hope I can stick to it and don't just yammer nonstop obscenities at them." What the hell was I doing? I felt like the biggest idiot on campus, which was saying something.

He shrugged. "You don't have to be charming, you know. You don't have to work so hard. Just do your job, and I'll do mine."

That was pretty deflating, even though it was said almost gently. I got a grip and said, "Look, we've got to go. Is there something special I should do or say about you? I was wondering if I should introduce you or just say nothing and wait to see if anyone asks who you are at the break."

"Why don't you just say at the beginning of class, 'This is Dr. Galloway. He's visiting us from Columbia University,' and leave it at that? Then we can see what happens. I'll try to ogle you adoringly"—he made it sound like he'd rather be eating bad pork—"and maybe Tim will go ahead and try to beat me up, and we can arrest him on assault charges. Then we can search his room, his house, and so on. That would make all this easy."

. . .

I made it more or less on time to class. Tommy stayed outside for a few minutes to smoke. I scanned the room quickly for the two young felons. I was a little surprised to see that they weren't there. As soon as he came in, Tommy took a seat in the back row. I did a quick head count, getting a total of thirty-five. I made an announcement.

"Look, there are more students here than are registered. The class is full, and drop/add ends this weekend. It isn't likely that I'll let in any more students. So if you're not registered, you need to leave. Let's see. How many of you here are not actually registered for the class?" Ten hands went up. I understood why the class was so unusually popular all of a sudden, and I could feel a blush coming. Every single one of the extra bodies was male. I told them again that they had to leave, and one by one the nonregistered students filed out. I tried to act nonchalant, as if I had no clue why they were all there. I have no idea if it was convincing.

I was starting to hope that Tim and Jason wouldn't come; maybe they'd been hit by a bus and wouldn't be bothering anyone anymore. Although I then thought about the poor bus driver, having to live with that for the rest of his life. I needn't have worried about him; five minutes into class time there was a muffled commotion in the hall. Then Tim Solomon strutted into the class (there is just no other word for it), and Jason followed him in, looking cowed, gangly, and vacant. Tim was sort of handsome in a bullet-headed, Aryan frat boy sort of way. He was stubby, meaty, with oversized, gnarly bodybuilder arms. He also had short blondish hair with jeans and an Argyle sweater on; I swear he could have just emerged from a time portal to the fifties. Jason was stringy, pale, and pimply and wouldn't be considered attractive by most of the cultural standards I'm aware of, anytime, anywhere. Even his clothes dangled awkwardly from him.

Tim turned to me and was deferential, respectful, and apologetic in equal measure. His grin showed big, strong milk-fed teeth. I would have found it amusing if it hadn't been so creepy. I suddenly remembered the names I had given them at the start of the last semester, before I knew who they were: Hitler Youth and Klan Boy.

"I apologize, Dr. P. We were praising the class to some pledges at the house and lost track of time. We'd be deeply grateful if you'd forgive us both." He then bowed extravagantly from the waist.

I forced a smile and said merely, "Sit down, Tim. You, too, Jason." I was hoping my tension looked like irritation and nothing more as I tried to reorganize my thoughts.

That class (Religion and the Modern World) was one of the most nausea-inducing, creepy experiences of my life. I introduced Tommy as "Dr. Galloway" without too much fanfare and then began the lecture for the evening. I was talking about the theories of Ian Lewis concerning the relationship between ecstatic (trance-related) religion and social class, applying them to the so-called New Religious Movements of Japan. I had intended the lecture to be political in content, hoping that the students would be motivated to talk, argue, whatever. Now I just wanted to be able to get through it without screaming and running out of the room. However, the topic was interesting enough and incendiary enough that many of the students did ask questions and started challenging one another. I called the break early; I was afraid I would sweat through my clothes and needed a rest and some water.

I dashed out to the restroom and cooled myself off with some strategically placed wet paper towels. I then got a bottle of water from a vending machine in the hall. I hated spending money on it, but in all the confusion I'd forgotten to bring my bottle from home.

Tommy appeared next to me and said, "I'm going to get one, too, then a quick smoke outside. It's really dry in that room."

"Especially if you're nervous as hell," I said, looking up. I thought, I'm almost five-nine, and I still have to stare up at him from way, way below.

"How tall are you?"

He looked understandably surprised. "Six five."

"Oy," I said. "No wonder I have to look up so far."

He said, "What's up next?"

"A film. A great one, by the way. *Holy Ghost People*. Have you ever heard of it?"

"Yes, I've seen it. My . . . I have a friend who is a filmmaker." I was surprised that he admitted anything of a personal or even human nature.

"A girlfriend, you mean."

He looked squirmy all of a sudden, which I found slightly irritating. "I guess. It's not a serious thing or anything."

What are we, twelve? I thought unkindly. I wonder if she thinks it's serious. Probably. Poor wench.

He lowered his voice. "Listen, sit next to me during the film so we can start looking cozy. Tim has already gotten a little chafed at my presence, and I think we should amp it up as much as we can. Hopefully, we can drive him to want me dead soon."

"Okay," I said, "but be careful what you wish for."

Sure enough, when I brought the lights up at the end of the film, Tim was looking a lot less smug and fun-loving than he had when he first had come in that evening. Tommy and I had hardly canoodled when the lights were down, but we did sit next to each other. I asked the class some questions about the film, and we talked about Lewis some more. I reminded them about assignments. Then I dismissed them, a little early, it's true, but no one complained.

Most of the students fled as soon as they could, but Tim meandered up to the podium, where I was gathering my notes. Jason lingered in the background, waiting. Tommy came up, almost next to Tim, then deliberately edged a tiny bit ahead of him. He said, softly but loud enough so that Tim could hear, "You want to go get some coffee before you have to go home?" I looked at him and said, impressed by my own sangfroid, "Sure."

I then looked over his shoulder at Tim like a normally concerned instructor, I hoped. "What's up, Tim? What can I do for you?" Aside from smacking you in the head with a two-by-four, I thought.

"Dr. Paletta, it was an unusually good lecture tonight."

The hell you say. "Thank you. Can I help you with something?" Eyebrows raised in polite inquiry.

"Well, I'm having some trouble deciding what to do after graduation, actually. I was hoping there might be a time when I could come talk to you about graduate schools and postgraduate work." Tim was one of those people who continuously look at a woman's chest while addressing her. This is a terribly disconcerting habit, and with students I never knew how blatantly I could call them on it. I was wearing a loose turtleneck sweater over a rock-solid bra; there wasn't much more I could do to keep attention away from my breasts. I chickened out and decided to pretend he was talking to me normally.

"You'd be better off talking to your adviser. You're not a religious studies major, so I couldn't really help you much, I'm afraid."

"But I'm thinking about changing my major." Eyes down, up, down. "It would only require a few extra classes, and my parents are all right with it. You see, I'm thinking about graduate school in religion. I've gotten some material from Yale, and I'm really interested in their program." I'll just bet you are, you little shit, I thought. "I know that's your alma mater."

"Uhmmm. Well, I'd be glad to tell you what I can," I said. "I have office hours next Monday. If you want to come see me then, that would be fine."

A small pout, eyes meeting mine now. "Isn't there any way I could see you sooner?"

"I'm done teaching tomorrow by about two-thirty. But I can't stay that long afterward." I didn't want to say anything about having to go get my kids.

Tommy nudged up a bit, smiled chummily at Tim, and then casually put his arm around my shoulders. I thought, this is the second time in a week someone I barely know has done that to piss off someone on this campus. This is really weird.

And Tim was pissed off. It wasn't obvious, but you could see a small tic under his right eye, and Jason was looking a little less vacant. But Tommy appeared oblivious. He said, "Dr. Paletta and I have to discuss the possibility of me being a visiting professor here. I need her help sorting out some of the administrative details. Can this wait until her office hours?" I almost expected this sentence to be ended with "young man?" He was giving a really convincing performance as the asshole blowhard eager to get me alone.

Tim agreed to wait until Monday, although he was quite irritable about it, looking darkly at Tommy between terse acquiescences. "Good night, Dr. Paletta," he finally said, working his way toward the door. "Let me know if I can help you in any way," he added, looking at Tommy, then back at me.

After he and Jason were gone, I heaved a huge sigh. Tommy said, still quiet in case there were ears lurking in the hall, "That went incredibly well, I thought. You're a better actor than you give yourself credit for. Let's go out and get some coffee. We can talk over strategy and look legit if they are watching us." I just wanted to go home but said yes, anyway.

After calling Molly on my cell phone and being assured that being out a little later was all right, we wound up at the Tin Whistle, a bar and coffee shop not far from the college that was open late, allowed smoking, and had decent snack-type food. He was interested in that. I was interested only in some tea and lots of water. I debated getting a posttraumatic stress martini but thought I was going to have enough trouble getting up the next morning. I told Tommy this, deciding that I no longer cared if I was charming or not. He asked what I had to do tomorrow; I explained that I had to teach three classes. Only two preparations, since two of the classes were the same, but it was still an exhausting day. Tommy said that three classes seemed like a lot.

"If you're used to Columbia's faculty's teaching load, yes, it is, where you're there primarily to do research and to produce graduate students. But in a dinky department in a dinky liberal arts college, my main value is to teach. I don't have to do much else other than be on some committees and advise students. That's enough."

"Not much prestige."

"Almost none. But that's okay with me. I don't need the stress. I like to hang out with my kids and grow tomatoes." I was tired of talking, tired of being so embarrassingly self-disclosing. "So what about you? Are you climbing to the top in your profession? Are you being groomed for police commissioner or something?"

He blushed, which I wasn't expecting. "Not really," he said. "I'm very good at what I do. I'm not very good at the politics, though."

No shit, I thought. You look like a mafia hit man.

"Yeah, right," I said. "Well, since my kids' safety and mine are in your hands, I hope you're the best in the universe at what you do."

He actually smiled. It was oddly upsetting, like it was in the wrong place. I always felt that way when I saw Mr. Spock smile in old *Star Trek* episodes. I imagine that when hit men smile, no one else around them does. "So where did you go to undergraduate school? At Columbia as well? I'm an academic, so I can only relate to people in terms of their education."

He looked at me. The smile was gone. "Princeton. A double major in psychology and literature."

"Aren't you a little, er, well-schooled for a cop?"

"I get some shit for it."

He shifted in his seat. He looked angry with me, though not frighteningly so, as he had before. He looked at me again. He said, "Did you always look like this, or did you, um, bloom?"

My hostility returned. "I bloomed. How about you? Were you always big, or did you, um, grow?" I glared at him.

He looked a little hurt. I instantly felt terrible, wished I could retract it. All he said, though, was, "I'm sorry. That wasn't very, um, polite, I guess."

I was now deflated. "Well," I said lamely, "that's okay. Really, you're fine."

The Tin Whistle is known for the owner's terrible taste in incidental music. As we sat there, asking prickly questions of each other, some horrible flannelly song from the late seventies trickled from above, making everything we said even more banal. The conversation was pretty much halted after that last interchange, so we quickly got up. Tommy wanted to pay for my tea, which surprised me. I told him not to be ridiculous.

We got back by about ten-thirty. Sidney came in the front door with us; I avoided stepping on a mole he'd sweetly left for me on the welcome mat. When I looked out later to dispose of it, it was gone. I didn't know who had thrown it out for me but doubted it was Molly.

The boys were sound asleep. Molly had told me this, but I still double-checked. She and Russell seemed awfully smug about something. I feared that they had hit it off more thoroughly than I had expected. I just prayed that if they'd done it, the boys had in fact been asleep. The whole idea made me tense.

I took Molly aside and paid her. Russell offered to see her home; she accepted, which I thought was smart. Tommy said that he and Russell were prepared to stay the night at my house if I could stand it. I had a guest room with a double bed, and a daybed in the dining room, so I told him it was fine with me. I found an ashtray in the back of a cupboard and gave it to him, wishing I'd thought to give it to Russell before I'd left; I imagined a pile of butts in the front yard. At that point I was so exhausted, I didn't care who slept where as long as neither of them tried to sleep with me, mess with my boys, or kick my cat. Tommy insisted on helping tidy up a little before we both retired, as we were waiting for Russell, anyway.

He came back about twenty minutes later. The two detectives wouldn't let me go immediately to bed. We had to talk about the next few days, since I was leaving early in the morning. They made sure that I had all their numbers again; they told me that Tim and Jason were being watched, although I couldn't imagine there were the resources to do it around the clock. But supposedly, if they came near my house, there would be alerts sounded somewhere. I was too tired to take it all in. I just hoped that my sense that I was being protected was accurate.

Tommy said, "I thought I'd come back this weekend. This all depends on what Tim and Jason are doing, of course. We'll come back sooner if they do more than watch you." Horror brought me out of my lethargy for a moment. Then I remembered the significance of Saturday. I'd had so little social interaction that wasn't centered on my kids for so long, and now my universe was practically exploding with adult contact.

"Saturday I'm giving a surprise birthday party. A dinner, actually. For my cousin Mo."

Russell smiled suddenly, broadly. "Can we come?"

Oh God, I thought. I mentally flung my hands in the air. I said, "If you can figure out how to explain yourselves to my guests, fine." I gave them some of the details, then said I'd had enough and was going to bed. Tommy followed me upstairs so that I could show him where to find sheets, towels, and whatever else they might need. As we walked past my open bedroom door, he noticed the poster of Alan Watts that I had tacked to my wall. He said, "That's a great poster. Where'd you get it?" I shushed him, since we were right outside Toby and Stevie's room.

"I got it in San Francisco a long time ago," I whispered.

"I've read most of his stuff. I have at least five or six of his books."

"Good for you." I led him back down to where Russell was eating some of my ice cream in the kitchen. I left them to decide who was going to sleep where and went to bed.

Thursday morning I saw a glimpse of a bleary-eyed Russell headed for the bathroom as the boys and I were preparing to leave the house. He looked awfully good even with a puffy morning face and rumpled hair. Of Tommy we saw nothing. I wrote them a note on how to lock up and left.

chapter nine

ON THURSDAY my classes went adequately, but I certainly didn't set the students' minds on fire with the love of learning. I hadn't had enough sleep or food for two days. By the time I got home with the boys, I was afraid I was going to pass out from exhaustion. I had a whole lot less patience with Toby and Stevie than usual, and I reduced Toby to tears when he resisted doing his homework. At one point he was so angry with me, he told me he wished that Molly was his mother. Stevie tuned me out as much as he could. All in all, it was a crappy day.

There was a message on the machine from John Fagin. I was dismayed and wasn't sure what to do. I opted to ignore it.

I remembered that I needed to talk to Ivy about our additional guests on Saturday. I called her instead of Doughboy, knowing that Mo was at the Big House with her parents and so would be safely out. Ivy was a little put out and understandably confused about who they were and why I had invited them. I was vague, telling her that all would be explained later, but that it was pretty important that they be there. It turned out that Molly had already mentioned Russell, so Ivy was a bit curious about him. Sister (in-law) love won out, and she said she didn't mind. I said they were nice and seemed willing to work for food. And after all, it was my house, although I said nothing about that. After I rang off, the boys and I made up while they ate ice cream. I got everyone, including myself, to bed early.

After taking the boys to school Friday morning, I went to see Jeri again. I couldn't afford the time to see her every week, and I usually felt I'd spent enough money on my mental health already. But things were getting out of hand, and I could feel myself spiraling down into something not identical to depression but more like a dark panic.

Since she had just seen me, she didn't go down the checklist again. We talked about the Hannigans first and the strange subject of Franny's child.

"There's a family you could probably write an entire book about if you wanted to," I said. "Going to dinner there is like sitting in a big pot of dysfunction soup. It makes it pretty hard to breathe." I went on to tell her about my young stalker, although I left out the degree of police involvement in my daily life. I wasn't sure why.

"Wow, your life has been seriously upended of late. How are you dealing with all this?"

"I've been trying to meditate more regularly."

"Trying?"

"It doesn't work usually."

"How so?"

"The kids interrupt me, I start making grocery lists in my head, I notice the enormous diameter and density of the cobwebs hanging from my ceiling, or I fall asleep."

"Hmmm. That's all okay, you know."

"No, it isn't. You're supposed to empty your mind of thought. I can't do that."

"No, you're supposed to *attempt* to do that. The attempt is the point."

"Spoken like someone who is a good meditator," I said.

"Keep trying." She looked at me for a moment. "For some reason the note that seems to be ringing loudest to me at the moment is the issue of the adopted child. Let's shelve the other stuff, however big, just for now. Do you know anything about where this cousin of yours is?"

"No," I said. I hesitated. "I think it's me. I think my parents adopted me. I'm Franny's kid."

"What? Why?"

"Because the dates are about right," I said, although I didn't really know them, "and it would explain why my mother hates me so much."

"Are you sure it's hate?"

"Pretty sure."

"Hate's a complicated emotion sometimes. The thin line and all that."

"She hates me. I think the line here is pretty thick."

"And you think it's because you're adopted."

"It would explain a lot."

"Like what, other than that she hates you?"

"Like why I don't look like her."

"You look like your father, though. You've said so before."

"Yes, but . . ." It explained everything. "Maybe my father *was* my father but my mother wasn't my mother. Of course she'd hate me. And that would also explain why she *did* love both of my sisters."

"You think your father had an affair with your mother's sister? The nun?"

"Well, my father had affairs with lots of women. My mother was certainly not chummy with Franny later. Maybe there was a rift because of an affair. Maybe my mom was jealous. And it's not like my father was so religious that having sex with a nun would have bothered him. Maybe even the reverse, although I don't really want to think about that too much."

"I don't blame you. And so then they adopted you? That would have been a lot for your mother to accept."

"She did accept a lot from him. And he was narcissistic enough to want to keep his own kid by whomever and not care how much it hurt other people."

"Are you sure your father even knew your aunt Franny?"

"I'm not sure of anything like that. But it's possible. I mainly like the idea because it explains why I'm not like anyone else in my family and why they don't like me."

Jeri said, "It would be one explanation."

I spent the rest of the day Friday grocery shopping and cleaning the house. At the grocery store I was lingering over the iceberg lettuce. Stevie is partial to lettuce sandwiches. Since lettuce is the only thing in them besides the bread, I try to make sure it isn't wilted. There were small speckles of rust on all the heads in the bin, so I was trying to find the produce manager to see if there were any others in the back. I also had a tiny flirtation going on with him, to the point where I could call him Arnie. That, according to the plastic tag on his shirt, was his name. He was a charming hippie, probably a few years younger than I was, but we shared an interest in vegetable gardening, compost, and organic produce. I'd long had a weakness for slender, sloppy intellectuals, a predilection that has never once paid off. I knew little else about Arnie and had no real romantic interest in him, but it had made shopping slightly less tedious. Now, reminding myself of my current problems, I thought I might want to put sweet little conversations with younger men, however innocent, on hold. I didn't even want to think about how weird it might seem to him if he ever got wind of the fact that "Mrs. Paletta," as he naïvely called me, was some sort of inadvertent porn queen. Instead of ringing the bell for the manager, I just rooted through the bin for the least rusty head and moved on.

I had just finished putting away the final can of soup in my kitchen when I heard an inexplicable banging noise outside. It sounded as though someone were hitting a sheet of metal with a mallet, right on my front porch. I grabbed my coat from its hook by the door and went outside. No one was there; then I heard a hoarse voice say "Gina" creepily and urgently. I looked to the right and saw Jessie on her front porch, holding the business end of a broom.

"Hi," I said, confused.

Jessie said, "I beat on your downspout. Can you come over? I have some more clothes I want to give you." Oh great, I thought. "Sure," I said.

Her house was so jam-packed with stuff—toys, pictures, doilies, figurines, dishes, not to mention furniture—that I could actually see only a minute portion of it every time I was there. This time I noticed that the walls in the hallway were covered with mediocre still-life paintings, all by the same person, "J. Foxhall."

"Jessie," I said, "are you an artist?"

She looked a little peevish and said, "No, those were my aunt's. Her name was Jean. My aunt and uncle came to live with me after my mother died. They were saving me from being an orphan."

I couldn't tell if this was said with sarcasm. I asked bluntly, "How old were you?"

"Thirty-seven. I waited on them hand and foot."

I kept waiting for the punch line, for the part where she talked about taking some sort of stand, sticking up for herself, not being a doormat. Of course, who knew what the older people in her life would have said? They loved her, they were trying in some way to care for her—who knew? I said finally, "Why?"

"Why what?"

"Why did you wait on them so much?"

"My aunt was sickly."

"Like your mother?"

"Kind of, only she had, you know, woman problems. I had to take care of her. My uncle certainly couldn't. He was an undertaker. When she died, he laid her out himself. He was real proud of how she looked." She stopped, seeming to stare at the tiny dust particles dancing in the lamplight. Then she turned to me. "The bags are in the same place. You get them."

I did and thanked her as though I would be wearing only toilet paper without her castoffs. I thought for the briefest moment about inviting Jessie over to Mo's party on Saturday. But Ivy was already peeved enough at me for all the liberties I'd taken with the guest list. I went home.

By three-thirty the house was clean enough. I picked up the boys at the bus stop and took them to the video store before schlepping them home and making them do their homework ("Think about how *free* you'll be *all weekend* if you do it now!"). I had to do some cooking to prepare for the big dinner the next day. I was making one apple pie and two pumpkin pies. I also thought I'd make the cranberry sauce the night before. I had some grading and class prep to do, as well, but I was hoping that there would be enough time on Sunday to take care of that.

I hadn't made a big dinner like this since I'd shared an apartment in Manhattan with Erin; we entertained a lot in those days, and I'd been able to show off the culinary chops I'd gotten from Grammy Paletta. I'd cooked a fair amount for people in graduate school as well, although on a smaller scale than in New York, because I'd had a bigger apartment and more resources than a lot of my classmates. Even Scott and I had entertained some for a while, especially in that brief period between our no-frills wedding and the birth of the twins. It was the best way I knew to be social: to do it myself, to feed people, to give them something. It was scary to be doing it again, but I was looking forward to it.

Lizzie called right after I ordered pizza for the second time that week. We are only two years apart in age, but we weren't close. However, Lizzie treated me as though we were deeply intimate, making frequent incomplete references to people and events about which I knew nothing. I would not always point this out, as I usually didn't care that much. I never knew if it was narcissism on her part or just a bad memory. Now, however, she was put out with me. She didn't like my additions to Mo's party.

"So Bobbie's going to be there?"

"Yes, with Aunt Lottie and Clark."

"My God, Gina, why not invite the whole freaking parish?"

"There are going to be two other friends of mine coming, too."

"Aren't they supposed to be friends of Mo's? It's her birthday."

"It's my house, Lizzie. My turkey. My plates. They are nice people. Just deal with it. It's only two extra people. Molly knows them already, too."

"Who are they?"

"Just some friends of mine. From school." I figured explaining it all once when everyone was there would be easier.

Weekends were slacker times in our house, so I let the boys eat in the living room while watching one of the movies we'd gotten. I ate one piece of pizza, then my salad. I started doing some exercises with weights while we watched the rest of the movie. The boys had once been interested in weights; they no longer were, although they liked sliding up and down on my weight machine in the basement. They liked the treadmill, too, although as much as a ramp for toy cars as for running on.

Halfway through the movie I finished my exercise routine and sat on the couch with both boys. I had one skinny little butt on each knee. Life wasn't all bad. By the time it was over I had to harass the boys to get them to get ready for bed. An hour and a half later they were asleep, the cat draped across Stevie's feet, and I was putting the pumpkin pies in the oven.

The house was silent. It was often silent at night; I tend not to play music in the kitchen after the boys are in bed, as it's right under their bedroom. I like to cook with the music loud, but I really didn't want them awake again. But the quiet was weirding me out a bit, which it never normally did. That damn website, that damn student. I wanted to call Tim's useless parents and scream at them. I was having trouble feeling compassion for people who would raise a son like that. You hear in parent circles that occasionally the nightmare happens and good people have rotten kids. Bad seeds. Sociopaths. Children born with no inborn capacity for empathy. But if you had a kid like that, wouldn't you try to do something about it? And if your kid was a genuine psycho, the way Tim Solomon might be, wouldn't you have some sense of it? Of course, even if you did, what could you do about it? Shrinks? Maybe, although I don't think psychiatry has much to offer true sociopaths. Should you commit him? You'd have to be damn sure that he (or she) was seriously dangerous, seriously screwed up, to do that to your own child. Maybe compassion for the Solomons wasn't impossible, after all.

I prayed to the universe that this website died a quick death. You could never tell, though. This was a small town, with a smaller campus. I thought again about David Renouart. I had a sudden image of the porn girl in the fellatio pictures on the website. She had a mole on her left shoulder. (You could see her shoulders a lot better than you could see her face.) I was appalled to think that David was the one person in Tenway who would know that I don't have such a mole. Christ. All I could do was hope that he never had to consider it one way or the other.

I felt watched. I peeked out my front window, wondering if there were any cars on the street that I didn't know. I wondered if there was a Tenway deputy in an unmarked car watching my house. Where were Tim Solomon and Jason Dettwiler right now? I decided I needed some reassurance, although it was late. I found the card in my purse that McCandless had given me and picked up my kitchen phone. I dialed the direct number to the constable's office he had written on his card. To my surprise and relief, I got a live human voice. It turned out to be the constable himself. I asked him if he ever slept, and he said simply, "No." I could tell that he thought this very witty. His humor was so dry that I was beginning to fear I was missing half of it. I apologized for calling, which he pooh-poohed; I then asked what the status was with the surveillance.

There was a brief silence, and then he asked, "What phone are you using?"

"What? My home phone. It's not my cell, if that's what you mean."

"No, I mean is it a landline or a cordless?"

"What? A cordless one. Why?"

"Do you have a regular phone with a cord?"

"Of course, for when the power goes out." That happened a lot in Tenway.

"Use it whenever you're calling me or any of the personnel in this matter, Dr. Paletta. In fact, call me back on it now, please." He then hung up.

I was startled but hung up and immediately went upstairs to use the phone by my bed. I called him back.

"Okay," he said. "We know where Tim and Jason are right now. I have them tailed pretty good, and we don't think they've cottoned on to anything yet, but we've got to be careful now that they don't learn about all this. There was a case just a few months ago in Miami where there was some sort of sting going on, but someone was talking about it on a cordless phone. The subject was suspicious, so they just listened with a baby monitor outside the house where the first person was gabbing. Gave the whole thing away. We can broadcast on radio frequencies that are secure, but cordless phones are just too easy to intercept. There are other ways to hear what people are saying. We don't think Tim and Jason have much spy gear, but if they read the papers or if Daddy's said anything about it, they might get the idea to listen to your phone calls just for kicks. Be aware of that. Don't say anything on a cordless that they shouldn't hear, just to be safe."

I was convinced. "You betcha," I said. I decided that as soon as I had the opportunity, I would buy two more old-fashioned phones to place strategically in my house. The cordless ones were too convenient and therefore too tempting. I remembered with a fluttery stomach my earlier conversation with Lizzie. I was pretty sure I hadn't said anything about Tommy and Russell, thank God. I then asked if anyone was watching my house, either good guys or bad guys. He said no, he only had two officers on Tim and Jason. They felt pretty secure that everything was under control, although he'd tell a patrol car to make a pass around my neighborhood from time to time if that would make me feel better. I said it would and thanked him, and he reassured me some more. I insisted that in the future he call me Gina. We then rang off.

What little exposure I'd had to the local constabulary up till then hadn't filled me with much confidence. I'd been stopped a few times in my car for no apparent reason by deputies who just gawped at me and apologized. They all looked about sixteen. But the constable himself seemed to know what he was doing. The jury was still out on the two detectives.

I was just taking the pies out of the oven about a half hour later, when the phone rang. I couldn't bring myself to pick up the cordless, so I ran upstairs and answered the phone by my bed again.

"Hello?"

"Gina?"

"Tommy?"

"I just got a call from our mutual friend, and I wanted to see how you were doing."

"You did? Oh, he told me about the landline thing. I'm not on a cordless phone, so you can talk."

He said, "Okay, good." There was a pause.

"I'm just freaking out a little bit, but really, I'm okay," I said, sounding bipolar. "I don't know how you guys who do this sort of thing all the time can stand it. I am not a good enough liar to pull it off. I find it very stressful."

He agreed. "It's a pretty neurotic way to live. Don't worry. I think these guys are going to blow long before you have to get used to us being around. I just wanted to call and make sure that you're not going . . . that you're handling this all right."

"That's very nice of you, but I'm fine. I just got a little creeped out. But I'm okay now. I'm going to bed. You should probably get some sleep, too. I'm going to work you hard tomorrow."

He was silent for a second, then said, "Okay, whatever that means."

"Food prep. You ever make a Thanksgiving dinner or help with one? I mean really help, not just set the table?"

"No." He actually sounded a little fearful. "You're making a Thanksgiving dinner?"

"Yeah. Mo and Ivy never get to spend the holiday together, since both sets of parents are homophobic assholes. Ivy wanted me to do a traditional Thanksgiving dinner for Mo's surprise party, since it's Mo's favorite meal. So you and Russell are going to earn your turkey. Come prepared to chop."

"Okay, I guess. We should be there around one o'clock."

"Great. Don't worry; you'll be fine. I assume you big macho cops can handle knives. See you tomorrow, Detective. Thanks for checking on me."

"No problem. See you tomorrow, Gina. Sleep well."

I wandered around aimlessly for a few moments, not seeing anything around me, wishing my life weren't so upside down. After locking all the doors and double-checking window locks, turning down the heat, and turning off the lights, I went upstairs. As I was brushing my teeth, it occurred to me that it was a nice thing for Big Bear to do, calling me to reassure me. I wanted to look tough and competent to these guys. But who was I kidding? I was completely freaked out and ultimately at the mercy of their expertise or lack of it.

Then I thought, maybe Big Bear could get a girlfriend out of all this, forgetting for the moment that he already had one. Lizzie might like him. Although, if I were honest, I wouldn't wish Lizzie on anybody nice. She was pretty in a scrawny sort of way but hard, mean, irritable. Maybe not to men, maybe just to me. Too bad he was a little young for Kay Reynolds. Maybe he and Donna would like each other. Donna was such a workaholic, apparently; Tommy certainly put in long hours himself if this case was at all typical. So they had that in common, anyway. I didn't know Donna all that well, but she had always been pleasant enough to me and sweet to the boys. I remembered John Fagin and thought, maybe I could set him up with someone else. But I couldn't see his face in my mind, just a nondescript Caucasian blur. It was hard to pair him with anyone, even mentally. Tommy's face was quite vivid, oddly, as was Russell's. All these men, I thought, fading, all these men. After setting the alarm, I thought, as consciousness faded altogether, I wish they'd go away.

chapter ten

This, then, is the human problem: there is a price to be paid for every increase in consciousness. We cannot be more sensitive to pleasure without being more sensitive to pain. By remembering the past we can plan for the future. But the ability to plan for pleasure is offset by the "ability" to dread pain and to fear the unknown. Furthermore, the growth of an acute sense of the past and the future gives us a correspondingly dim sense of the present. In other words, we seem to reach a point where the advantages of being conscious are outweighed by its disadvantages, where extreme sensitivity makes us unadaptable.

ALAN WATTS, *The Wisdom of Insecurity*

I WAS BARELY AWAKE when Stevie launched himself at me in the bed.

"Hi, Mom. Can I watch the cartoons up here?"

"Sure," I muttered. It was a familiar request. Toby would join us in about fifteen minutes. I fumbled for the remote on the nightstand

and turned on the TV. Stevie nestled in next to me, warm and wiry, taking up a mathematically impossible proportion of the bed.

The Saturday-morning cartoons the boys favored tended to a lot of "You are helpless against my superior strategy"; they were populated by lots of sensitive yet macho youths with really big eyes and impossible-in-real-life hair. At least the girls in them weren't stupid, even if they all had ridiculously small waists. After about ten minutes of this I finally shoved my sleep-soggy body out of bed, leaving the boys to watch TV, tangled in the sheets. I managed to do some yoga in the hallway, though not for as long as I normally do on a weekend, as I had too much to do. I showered and dressed in sweats, laying out a more dressy pair of pants and a long, black velvety blouse for later. I said to my bed, "Boys, I'm going down, and I'll make some waffles if you want. When you're hungry, come downstairs." Toby nodded, Stevie didn't.

I put the turkey in the oven, figuring it should be done around three o'clock. I let Sidney out and cleaned his food bowls. By noon I had things pretty well under control, although there was still a ton to do. Since I like to cook with the music loud, I had a pretty substantial boom box in the kitchen. I tend to dance a lot when I'm working like that, too. The boys were used to this; they knew if they wanted my attention in those circumstances to come in and yank on my shirt or flag me down. I could still get them to dance with me on occasion, Stevie more often than Toby, especially if Toby found the music too loud or grating. They hadn't yet succumbed to the idea that bodily movement to music was girly. (They both moved pretty well; I was hopeful that when they were old enough to go to clubs, they would be comfortable doing more than just the "White Boy.") When they were not in the room with me, I tended to work harder, bumping and grinding, exercising while cooking. In another life I would have loved to have worked for Twyla Tharp.

I was kneading bread dough for rolls, hopping around to something by James Brown that was turned up loud. Stevie came in and tugged on my sweatshirt; I grabbed his hands to join me, but he was trying to tell me something. I twirled him around and screamed as if someone had stuck me with something sharp when I saw two full-grown men in my kitchen door, where two grown men had almost never been since I'd bought my crumbly old house. I managed not to hurl poor Stevie out of the room, then hugged myself as though I'd been caught naked. My heart was threatening to crack a rib.

Tommy and Russell were both grinning like they'd just been told something really funny. Russell said, "Stevie let us in. I guess you didn't hear the bell. Sorry that we're here a little early." I was surprised he could form the words, his lips were so distended from smiling. Tommy laughed outright, looking even more disturbingly Spocklike.

I was suddenly aware of how frumpy and ridiculous I looked, hair leaking out from a big ugly clip, gray baggy sweats and a flour-stained sweatshirt, and my big toe sticking through the hole in my right sock. Oh, crap. For so long I had been proud of myself, feeling for once almost like a successful feminist, not caring much about my appearance other than being presentable and nonsmelly. But you can't escape your culture, and my hubris was biting me in the ass now. I looked like hell, and I was gasping for air. They both looked fresh in jeans and sweaters.

"You need to keep your door locked and tell the boys not to let anyone in unless they know them," Tommy said. He was still smiling.

"They know that. They know you. You're early," I said, gulping air. After a few more gasps I said, "Ready to work?"

They looked at each other, smiles slowly fading. "Uh, I guess," Tommy said.

"Coffee first," I said firmly. After that they were putty in my hands, with only the occasional snicker. I turned the music down.

I got them chopping vegetables and fruit, moving furniture, changing lightbulbs, and setting the big dining-room table. I was impressed by how rarely they took trips to the front porch for cigarette breaks. Seeing the men working, it was easier to get the little boys in on the act as well, and they were soon showing Russell where to put the forks and making sure there were enough glasses set out.

We discussed what the story about their presence was going to be. I didn't like keeping a secret this big from Mo and Ivy, but I didn't want Mo's birthday celebration to be all about my dramatic problems. To be honest, I also wasn't eager to share these problems with Lizzie. So we decided to tell all the other guests that they were in fact cops, visiting the criminology department. I told them the details were up to them; I'd just say I was asked to entertain them this particular day and introduce them to some of the locals. It was a weak story, but I hoped it would work if we got enough wine into everyone.

I was getting the potatoes ready to mash when I suddenly realized that I hadn't thought ahead and made enough ice. I almost panicked, then realized that I had two other drivers in the house besides me, an unheard-of luxury. They were in the dining room, looking proud of their work on the admittedly lovely table. I said, "Who wouldn't mind going out and getting some ice?"

Russell looked at Tommy and said, "I'll go," and grinned.

Tommy glared back. "No, thanks. I'll do it."

Russell smiled, happy. At my look he said, "Have you seen Tommy's car?"

"No."

"It's an old Mercedes sedan. He's very proud of it. He doesn't trust me to drive it."

"That's right. You wreck everything you touch. And it's thirty-five years old." Tommy didn't look like he was kidding. When Tommy got his coat on to go, Toby said quickly, "Can I go, too?"

"He's just going out to get some ice, honey," I said.

"But can I go? I really want to go!"

"Well." I looked at Tommy, grimacing in apology.

He said, "That's fine, if he wants to come."

Stevie said, "I want to go, too. Can I, *please*?"

I said, "Well, you two need booster seats. It's kind of a pain to take them out of our car, and he's just going down the street for some ice, guys. Can't you stay here? He'll be back in just a minute."

You would have thought that all the toys in the world were being incinerated and all children were to be whipped daily. The wailing, the gnashing of teeth, the tears. I was immune to this and so was preparing to banish all people under ten to the upstairs, when Tommy said, "I think it would be fun to take both of them."

Bullshit, I thought. "This is nice of you, but you're setting a dangerous precedent," I said.

"It's fine," he said. "I'm not worried. Give me your keys, and I'll get the seats out of your car."

I did so and said, "You know they're going to try to get some ice cream out of you."

"That's okay," he said, maybe smiling. It was hard to tell.

Suck-up, I thought. Or sucker; I didn't know which.

Ivy and her nine-year-old son, Trevor, arrived as soon as Tommy pulled away. She was cordial as I introduced her to Russell but was looking him over thoroughly at the same time. I thought, if they expect him to be serious about Molly, they are going to be disappointed. Trevor disappeared as soon as I told him that he could go play in the boys' room and that I'd send them up when they returned. Ivy had come with various banners and rolls of crepe paper to use as streamers. I uncharitably thought about having to clean this stuff up on Sunday but suppressed my sigh. Ivy was so happy. She chattered gaily about the fabulous antique mantel she'd found at a junk shop upstate, which would be waiting in their living room when Mo got home later that night. I told her it sounded perfect, then went back to potato mashing as she got the streamers in place. She drafted Russell, although he wasn't much taller than she was and therefore of limited use. However, I brought out my stepladder, and things went more smoothly.

By three-fifteen or so they were done, and the rest of the party started arriving. Bobbie, Clark, and Lottie arrived first; Lottie had a covered dish containing her famous green beans. Next came Lizzie, who had picked Molly up from school. Molly and Russell seemed happy to see each other, and that relieved me somewhat. Tommy returned loudly with the boys, telltale smears of chocolate ice cream around their mouths, and the ice.

When the twins heard Trevor was upstairs, they bounded up to greet him. Ivy made preparations to leave. Mo was a landscape designer and was looking over the grounds of a new McMansion for a prospective job. Ivy had offered to take her out to dinner for her birthday, really intending, of course, to bring her back to my house. As Ivy left to go get the (we hoped) unsuspecting Mo, I realized I was still in my sweats. I left Lizzie and Molly in charge of drink-getting and ran upstairs.

I told the three boys to wash up and then get their little butts downstairs in preparation for Mo's arrival. Then I ripped the clip out of my hair and went into my room. I was hurrying, and I admitted to myself that my appearance was important to me on this occasion, so of course everything went wrong. I dropped all the makeup implements at least once each. The lamp on my dresser wouldn't work, so I had to move the mirror so that my face wouldn't resemble a harlequin. I had a knot in my hair that I couldn't hide easily and so had to pick at it until it was worked completely out. I then went into the bathroom and noticed that one of the boys hadn't flushed the toilet. I did so, and it clogged. I had to spend a few minutes with the plunger before I could finish getting ready. And of course, while I was so engaged, I could hear a rousing "Surprise!" downstairs. I stared at myself in the mirror, trying to decipher my expression.

A few minutes later I made it downstairs. Mo was crying with happiness, and Ivy wasn't far behind her, with a smile so broad that it threatened to split her face in two. Mo hugged me, and all frustration was forgotten. Over her shoulder, my eyes met Tommy's. He smiled at me as well. I noticed for the first time that he, too, had nice teeth. I smiled back. I suddenly felt really good.

By this time Tommy and Russell had apparently been introduced to everyone. What they had said about their presence or their relationship to me, I had no idea. But I was too busy to worry about it and got everyone seated and fed.

It turned out to be a surprisingly compatible group. Clark was an editor for a publisher of children's books and had met Bobbie at a book fair she'd gone to. Bobbie was a librarian in the boys' elementary school and was deeply attached to kids. I supposed she wanted some of her own and hoped that Clark did as well. It seemed like a reasonable bet, given his career choice. He beamed at her every time he looked her way. I enjoyed watching the two of them; their relationship smelled like love. He turned out to be pretty funny; even Lizzie and Molly eventually seemed to like him.

The boys were competing for everyone's attention; Trevor got edged out when the twins demanded an audience for their play. I knew what was coming and was overruled by my guests when I tried to put a stop to it.

Toby: I hate you!

Stevie: I'm going to kill you!

Toby: I'm going to cut off your head with an ax!

Stevie: I'm going to cut off your head with a guillotine!

Toby: I'm going to send you to the surface of Pluto!

Stevie: I'm going to send you to the surface of the sun!

Toby: I'm going to fart!

Then Stevie ran off squealing in theatrical horror, gripping his throat and pretending to retch.

This took a long time, as it was halted a lot by the forgetting of lines and debates about which boy had which part. Ultimately, they did it both ways, switching roles. The adult audience was gratifyingly appreciative, including Aunt Lottie's surprised kudos on the boys' correct (French) pronunciation of "guillotine." The two of them were delighted that they'd gotten away with saying "fart" in company; there was clearly some danger of escalation. Ivy and I told the twins and Trevor that they could go off and play if they wanted. With that they bolted.

Ivy said, "Isn't it amazing? Someday they'll all be big and hairy and still doing the same stuff. And it won't be cute at all anymore, but we'll still have to act like it is."

It was a successful party, and the food worked out well, to my relief. Around nine o'clock I told the boys they needed to go up to bed. Aunt Lottie, Bobbie, and Clark all made noises about exhaustion and prepared to leave. I kissed them all, including the charming Clark, and they chorused their "happy birthday"s to Mo. Trevor was sleeping over, so I took all three of them upstairs after giving Tommy and Lizzie instructions for making more coffee for the remaining guests.

The boys' bunk bed was double-sized on the bottom and twin-sized on top, so there was some conflict about who got to sleep with whom. By the time we got that sorted out and teeth brushed, paja-mas on, and stories read, a bit less than an hour had gone by. I turned on the lava lamp and turned off the overhead light. After much kiss-ing and good-nighting, I left the room. I freshened up in the bath-room and then stood on the landing, listening. I heard group laughter, almost loud but not loud enough to disturb the boys. I was invaded by a sense of aloneness so profound that I couldn't walk for a mo-ment. I stood, literally frozen. How do they do that? I thought. That's my family and my friends. But not really; I don't know any of them really, except Mo. None of them really knows me. How do they do that—be social, be friendly, be intimate even? I had learned how to do it and had managed it in the past; now it exhausted me, sapped every bit of energy I possessed.

After two or three minutes I thawed enough to be able to move and went downstairs.

I found a cozy scene. Someone had lit the gas fire in the grate in the living room and pulled chairs, pillows, and cushions near the warmth. All the lights were out; the room was lit solely by its glow. Lizzie and Molly were on cushions on the floor, Russell was sitting in a chair be-hind Molly so that her back was resting on his lower legs, Mo and Ivy were entwined on my love seat, and Tommy was sitting on the edge of the couch closest to the fire, Lizzie near his feet. They all had drinks of various kinds, and everyone but Molly had a cigar. I knew that was Ivy's doing. I noticed that neither Russell nor Tommy had had any alcohol. I had forgotten that they were on duty.

I made myself a gin and tonic and brought it into the living room. After declining a cigar, I sat down in the only available seat, which happened to be next to Tommy on the couch. That spot was farthest from the fire, so I grabbed a blanket off the back of the sofa and wrapped it around me. Tommy asked if he could share it. I agreed less than enthusiastically, feeling vulnerable and odd. I said it felt like camp, although I'd never been to anything like camp in my life. He smiled and said he would have enjoyed camp a whole hell of a lot more if there'd been wine, women, and cigars there. I noticed for the first time that his front teeth were just the tiniest bit crooked. It made him look dangerous, a little thuggy. Suddenly sexy. I thought, Oh, dear, it's been too long, I'm starting to get desperate. But I was also relieved a little that I had been received like anyone else. I could pretend to be one of them, I thought. I'm a better actress than I give myself credit for. They probably think I'm normal. I'm passing.

Lizzie, who was getting drunk, said, "We're talking about sad stories. I was telling them about Donna's. You know Donna's, don't you?"

"No, I don't," I said. "I know she was married before. That's it."

"This is Bobbie's sister, right, the one who wasn't here?" Tommy asked.

"That's her, the nurse," Lizzie said. "She and Bobbie are Eberles. Our mothers are all sisters. All Lodovicos, but Lottie, or Carlotta, married Paul Eberle, and my mother, Rosa, married an Irishman."

"What about you? Where do you fit in?" Tommy asked, looking at me with a dark, almost bored expression.

"My mother is Maria. Also a Lodovico sister. She married another Italian."

Lizzie hurried on, "And Francesca Lodovico, the baby, was a nun. So she didn't marry anyone."

"But God," Molly said, piously.

"Whatever," Lizzie said. "Anyway, back to Donna Eberle." She looked at Tommy. "Lottie's older daughter." She turned to the rest of us. "Donna's ex left her for a man. I don't know much more than that other than that it could have been worse. They could've had kids."

Lizzie was not known for her tact. She looked at me. "We've started a contest. We want to see who has the worst sad romance story. Molly and Ivy and I went already. Molly's wasn't that big a deal."

Molly objected to that, but no one took her side. I didn't know her sad story, but she was only twenty-three, beautiful, and sheltered. My expectations were low.

Ivy said, "Mine's no big deal, either. Straight to gay. Have a kid, come out. It's a cliché by now."

"There's nothing cliché about you, Ivyboo," said a tipsy Mo.

"How about yours?" I asked Lizzie. This was part of my new charm campaign with her, to be more interested in her life.

"You'll have to ask them," said Lizzie.

"Awful," said Russell.

"Yes, dreadful," said Tommy.

"Terribly, terribly tragic," moaned Ivy.

"Yes, I'm the one to beat so far," said Lizzie.

"Who's next?" I asked.

Everyone else agreed that it was a man's turn, and most eyes turned to Russell.

"Oh, no," he said.

"Oh, yes," said Molly.

"Well, let me think. Sandy Kincaid dumped me in the seventh grade because I wouldn't put mousse in my hair. That was pretty bad at the time."

No amount of jollying or berating by anyone would move Russell to come up with something better. Mo went next, telling us about the summer she spent in Maine, picking apples. "It was the summer before my junior year at SUNY–Plattsburgh. That's when I met Jared, the man I was going to marry." There was much hooting at this, but she said, "Oh, I thought he was so cute, so perfect.

We really were engaged. He told me that he wanted to get married in his father's church, since his father was a preacher in Buffalo. It was time for us to drive back home before college started up again in the fall. He was going to drive me here before going home himself, and then he'd come up to Plattsburgh later, taking a term off and working to make some money while we lived together. Meanwhile, I would lay the groundwork for transferring to Buffalo, which wouldn't have been hard. We planned to leave the following morning. They actually had girls' and boys' dormitories at those orchards, and so we had a whole day off together, picnicking in the orchards, skinny-dipping in the lake, having sex in the woods, the whole bit." Ivy was looking down at this point. She'd heard this before. So had I. "Then Jared took me back to the dormitory for the evening. He kissed me, said he'd see me tomorrow. I went to bed dreaming of our future together." She took a sip of wine. "I never saw him again."

Russell said, "What, did he die or something?"

"No. He just left without me."

Tommy said, "No phone call? Nothing?"

"No, not even a letter. I just never heard from him again."

"What a shit," Russell said after a moment.

"Yes," Molly said.

"Needless to say, I didn't transfer. But that worked out well, because the happy ending is that staying at SUNY, I realized, with the help of some kind-hearted dykes, what really was good for me and what wasn't." She looked sweetly at Ivy, who grabbed her hand and kissed it. "By the way, not too long after that I came out, of the closet, I mean, and Daddy threw me out of the house and said he never wanted to see me again. I didn't have anywhere to go and no money. So I went to my groovy young cousin's happening apartment in Greenwich Village."

All eyes turned to me.

"While my parents pissed on my metaphorical grave, Gina let me stay with her for almost a year, till I decided to come back and finish college. She wouldn't take any rent; I made some money temping, and she lent me some to help with tuition. She even knew some incredible and beautiful lesbians in her profession, who showed me a few ropes, took me to some bars, helped me out. This, my friends, is one reason that she is my goombah, my buddy, cousin of the millennium." She raised her wineglass in a toast, eyes filling, all traces of sobriety gone. "Even if she isn't a Hannigan, we'll make her an honorary Hannigan."

"Hear, hear," said Ivy, beaming and toasting.

I just smiled at Mo and blushed, raised my glass back, and didn't dare look at anyone else. There was a brief silence. I wasn't sure that the honorary Hannigan thing was such a great honor but never would have said something so nasty to Mo.

"Wait," Tommy said. "You three sisters are all Hannigans? Like the big restaurant on Templeton?"

Lizzie, Molly, and Mo all nodded. Lizzie added, "Yep, that's Dad's place. That's what paid for our upbringing and college and so on. Well"—she looked at Mo—"most of college."

Tommy and Russell shared a look. I was the only other sober person there and so was the only one to notice. Tommy said, "Sorry to interrupt."

Lizzie said, "You didn't interrupt anyone. Who's next?"

"Tommy," said Mo. "Okay, Mr. Mysterious, what's your sad story?"

Tommy smiled. "Mine's pretty common, too. But it's not very dramatic or interesting, like the ones we've heard so far. Pretty boring, in fact."

"We don't care," Ivy said. "Tell us anyway."

"Yes," Mo said. "We're boring people. We like boring."

Tommy shrugged. "Okay. I lived with someone for about two years."

"Name?" said Ivy.

"Candace."

"Looked like?"

"Blondish. Slight, small, cute. Very girly, very pretty, very sexy. She was, or rather is, an artist. She's quite good and actually makes money at it, a bit, and hangs with rich and important folk."

"I thought she was a filmmaker," I blurted out.

"No," he said, looking at me with some surprise. "That's the person I'm . . . sort of seeing now. Becky Quinn. They know each other, but that's another story."

"Oh."

"Anyway, Candace and I lived together for about two years, as I said. And she wanted to get married. And when she put it to me, I really had to think about whether or not I wanted to spend the rest of my life with her, and I had to say no. I mean, it wasn't that cold; we did talk about it quite a bit. But there were some pretty big incompatibilities between us."

"Like?" Lizzie spoke up.

"Well, she didn't want kids. She comes from a wealthy family, which is how come she can afford to do what she does. But she expected me to make lots of money, too, and to be very ambitious, to want to become chief of police before I'm forty, that kind of thing. We both liked to travel, but she liked cruises and luxury vacations. I was much more a go-to-a-Greek-island-look-at-ruins-and-sleep-late kind of guy."

I thought she sounded like a lot of models I had known and not really liked, but I said nothing.

"So, anyway, we eventually broke it off."

Russell added, "She was pretty pissed at him for a while."

Tommy said, "We'd been together a long time. She wasn't ready to let go that easily. I understood that, but I knew it wasn't going to work. She eventually agreed."

"Not really. She still has hopes," Russell amended. "She knows that Rebecca is only a diversion. The question is, does Becky know it?"

Tommy ignored him. "So that's my story. Like I said, not very exciting." He turned to me. "I guess it's your turn now."

I had forgotten that I was the last one left. I was still trying to process Tommy's story. I said stupidly, "Me?"

"Yes, you," said Lizzie, clearly drunk, blinking at me.

I took a moment, figuring out what I wanted to say and what I didn't, as Sidney found his purring way onto my lap.

"There's more than one," I said, then felt pretentious and embarrassed, like I was trying to trump everyone else.

Mo helped me. "Give 'em the Scott one. It's fraught with drama."

"Okay, but it's kind of long. You sure you want to hear the whole thing, or should I just give you the first bits?"

"We'll tell you when to stop," Lizzie said.

chapter eleven

The power of memories and expectations is such that for most human beings the past and the future are not as real, but more real than the present. The present cannot be lived happily unless the past has been "cleared up" and the future is bright with promise.

There can be no doubt that the power to remember and predict, to make an ordered sequence out of a helter-skelter chaos of disconnected moments, is a wonderful development of sensitivity . . . But the way in which we generally use this power is apt to destroy all its advantages. For it is of little use to us to be able to remember and predict if it makes us unable to live fully in the present.

ALAN WATTS, *The Wisdom of Insecurity*

"WELL, I WAS IN GRAD SCHOOL in New Haven, trying to get my PhD, and I hadn't been dating anybody there, I mean, anybody in the department or any of the professors. I saw lots of people make grad school even worse than it had to be by screwing one another and then breaking up like crazy, and I didn't want any part of it." I'd been making plenty of weekend trips to New York and was having a pretty wild time during that period but saw no reason to include that. "Anyway, there was one student, a year or two ahead of me in the program, named Scott Winterburn. He was really cute, very suave, very charming." I looked at Russell. He really did remind me a bit of Scott. Russell just smiled happily. Molly and Lizzie both smirked. "He had been after me to go out with him for about a year."

"He was the Winterburn Chocolates heir, don't you know," Mo said airily.

"One of them," I corrected primly.

"Whoa. Does that mean that your sons are now the heirs to Winterburn Chocolates?" Russell said with an unwholesome interest.

"No," I said. "We are no longer affiliated with the Winterburn family. The legalities of it are weird but doable if you are very rich." I did not add that the boys were still entitled to a humongous trust fund when they reached twenty-one.

"Too bad," Russell muttered.

"We'll get by. Anyway, he finished his comprehensive exams, which were a big deal; they take eight hours each to do and are kind of this landmark in your graduate career. It was almost the end of the term, and most of the other students had gone home or wherever. Even a lot of the faculty had left for the winter break. So Scott was kind of lonely, and he had just done this really big thing, and he wanted to celebrate. I was just about the only person around."

Tommy spoke up. "You do realize that this was probably not the main reason he wanted to go out with you, right?" He was smiling that alarming Spock smile. I didn't smile back.

"Well, it was the reason I agreed."

They were all looking at me attentively, as though this was a really interesting story. Was it? I wasn't sure it was interesting even to me anymore. Tommy's arm rested on the back of the sofa, behind where I sat. I could just barely feel his fingers touching my hair, almost not doing it at all. Lizzie looked angry, but I couldn't tell if it was at me, or at the story, or at not having Tommy sitting next to her, or what. She always looked angry to me.

"I said I'd go out for a beer, since I really did feel sorry for him."

I paused, and Lizzie broke in. "Don't tell me you got drunk and slept with him? Oh my God, Gina, I thought you were smarter than that!"

Frankly, I was surprised that she hadn't heard the story already from Mo. I didn't know Mo would keep my secrets even from her sister, and I was touched. Although, I thought, it's not a secret anymore.

"No, I'm not smarter than that." I sighed. "He was sort of depressed, he had this awful family, and we started commiserating," not adding of course that I, too, had an awful family and that we really had something to bond over when we talked about them, especially around the terribly, terribly lonely holidays. "Anyway, we got sort of maudlin, and he was a pretty sweet drunk. I woke up the next morning with one of the worst hangovers I've ever had and snuck home, thinking that we'd come back after the holidays, look sort of sheepishly at each other, and that would be it. That pretty much is what happened. We were friendly in an awkward, distant sort of way. But after a little bit more time passed . . ." I waited a moment for effect.

"You were pregnant!" Molly moaned.

"It was a shocker, let me tell you. I had absolutely no intention of being a parent, so I decided almost immediately to terminate the pregnancy. No," I said. "Don't give me any shit about this, Molly. I don't want to hear it. But I went to the university gynecologist first to get all checked out, and she told me it was twins. I just couldn't abort two of 'em."

"God, with all that education, you'd think you'd know about birth control," said Lizzie.

I sighed before speaking again. I hadn't really wanted to say this, but I realized that I needed to, just to save my feeble reputation. "Well, I have to take responsibility for my actions, of course, but in my defense, Scott lied to me."

"What, did he tell you he'd had a vasectomy or something?" Russell said with a sophisticated sort of laugh.

I didn't, couldn't, answer. Mo looked pained, Ivy looked amused, and Lizzie looked delighted—then horrified.

"He didn't lie about *that*?" she said, breathy and eager.

"Yep." I finally found my tongue. "When I told him I was pregnant, he was, of course, really freaked out."

"How on earth did you get him to marry you?" Lizzie asked.

"I didn't, actually. I mean, I didn't really want to get married; I didn't want him in my life. I didn't expect him to do anything. I figured I'd have to go back to New York, go back to work—after they were born, of course—if I could still get work, anyway, and hope I could afford a really good nanny. He shocked me by saying that he wanted us to get married." I looked right at Lizzie. "I'm not even sure he liked me all that much, at least when he was sober. But he didn't want to be more of a schmuck than he'd been already, and he had terrifying parents. He told me that he wanted them to be proud of him, that he had one fuckup brother who'd had a number of paternity suits already and didn't want to be like him. He also made some polite noises about how pleased his mother and father would be to have me in the family, and so on. But it became clear to me pretty early on that his father didn't give a shit what he did as long as it didn't cost the old man anything, and his mother hated me before ever laying eyes on me. There was absolutely nothing I could do to make her tolerate me."

"So why did he want to marry you, really?" I was surprised at the level of interest Lizzie had in this sad, sordid, common little story.

"Well, my theory is that he really did want to please his parents some and not be identified with the awful Quentin, his younger wastrel brother."

"Wastrel?" Russell snorted.

I protested, "He was such a stereotype, it was ridiculous. In addition to the paternity suits, there'd been some drug busts and payoffs to several colleges to keep them from prosecuting him. He set fire to his dorm one night at Harvard. It was two in the morning or something on a weeknight. If a student hadn't gotten up to use the hall bathroom, a bunch of kids might've died. None of the smoke detectors worked, although no one ever knew if he had anything to do with that. Anyway, Scott had a lot of weaknesses, but he was a prince compared to Quentin, and Scott loathed him. But also, he really, truly hated his parents, and I think that marrying me was a big 'fuck you' to them as well. It wasn't a good idea, but at the time I thought having two kinds of useless parents for the boys was still better than one. And I definitely could use the financial help. So I married him."

"So you married him for your kids. It still doesn't make sense to me that he'd want to marry you," Lizzie said.

"Thanks," I said.

"Well," said Tommy, "you did say he married you to please his parents but also to piss them off. Which was it, do you think?"

"Look," I said, getting really uncomfortable now, "can we leave that subject for now?"

There was a brief silence in which everyone else in the room seemed to be looking back and forth at one another. My discomfort increased, then Mo said, "Tell them the rest, Gina."

I took a deep breath. "Well, for about a year after our marriage, things were actually pretty good. He continued his graduate work. I did, too, but a lot more sporadically. Having the twins together was a pretty bonding experience, and initially we were both so exhausted and wigged-out over the whole thing that I thought maybe it would have some sort of happy ending. But after a while he didn't find me very appealing anymore. I was a drone, too exhausted to be much fun, too exhausted for sex, too frazzled for intellectual talks, too drained to be sympathetic when he bitched about his ghastly family. We didn't have a lot of support from friends; most of them were childless and so were clueless about how to help, anyway. The two of us by ourselves got worn out pretty quickly. And then it became mostly just me with the twins, as he stayed out more and more and worked 'in the library' a lot of nights. The more I was left alone with the boys, the less appealing I'm sure I got, too."

"Well, duh," said loyal Mo. "Jesus, twin babies by yourself would just about kill anyone."

"Why didn't you call any of us?" said Lizzie.

"I didn't know most of you well at all, if you remember. It never occurred to me that any of you would come help me, and at that point I wasn't prepared to leave New Haven. I still wanted to graduate."

Molly said, "Was Scott cheating on you?"

"Oh, yeah. I think he cheated with a number of girls, and I mean girls. They were undergraduates. After a while he settled on one and apparently got pretty serious about her. One day when I hadn't been in the department for a while, I came in to get Scott's stipend check, and one of the secretaries was new. I didn't know her, and I asked her for it, and she said, 'Oh, I would've given that to his wife already. Do you know Nina?' I didn't know her, but I knew who she was. She was an undergraduate, as it turned out, being 'mentored' by Scott. One of the other secretaries overheard and tried desperately to give the new one some sort of signal to shut up, but she just went on and on about how sweet it was to see such a cute and happy couple working together in the department."

"God," Ivy muttered.

"What did you do?" Molly breathed.

"I just left. What was I supposed to do?"

"Well, I would have ripped her a new one," said Lizzie.

"I was too humiliated. And it wasn't really her fault."

"So Scott liked his women to rhyme, I guess?" Russell said.

"Yes, well, it was apparently a big joke in the department, Gina and Nina, Scott's two wives. Those witty academics," I said.

"So Scott's dead now, right?" said Russell. "Did you kill the bastard? I mean, you probably had grounds. You might have been able to get away with it. We see people get away with some amazing shit with juries. There would at least have been mitigation."

There was a bit of joking after this, much hilarity surrounding the gullibility of juries as well as the lack of justice in the universe for the cuckolded, and I just let it wash over me as Sidney started painfully kneading my thighs. I was hoping that with a bit of luck my story could end there. But it didn't. Lizzie again made sure that my new friends got to hear all the most embarrassing, degrading details. "Gina isn't done," she said. "There's still some more sad story to go."

"Thanks a lot," I said.

"So?" Russell said.

I took a breath. "We have some good periods where we get along pretty well, but generally we're just distant and sort of businesslike with each other. This goes on till right after the twins' third birthday. One Wednesday night Scott doesn't come home at all. I think things are just deteriorating, so I don't call the police or anyone. I'm just thinking he's with Nina or whoever at this point. Actually, I was right in that he had been with her till pretty late, but then he actually did start to come home. But he'd been smoking dope and drinking, and he was on his motorcycle, and he hit an icy patch on the road, over-compensated, went through a guardrail, and broke his neck."

"He had a motorcycle?" Molly asked. "No wonder you weakened." Russell gave her a smirk.

I didn't bother to tell her that he got that later on, when he was more interested in luring younger and more callow female students. I think motorcycles are stupid, and Scott knew it. It was also typical of him in that it gave him an unassailable excuse to avoid child transport. Leave it to Gina to have the sensible Camry.

"Tell them about the funeral," Lizzie urged. Mo had been there, so obviously she'd filled Lizzie in on some of those details. I certainly hadn't.

"Well, his mother was there, of course, thinking that I was the Antichrist. That wouldn't have bothered me so much, except she treated Toby and Stevie like Antichrist spawn. They were three years old, and they'd just lost their dad. She could have just left them alone. Instead, she was horrible to them, and to me." She kept saying, *You boys are the reason my son is dead.* She smiled and at the same time called me a whore. She said it multiple times: *whore whore whore.* I didn't say this.

"Tell them about Nina," Lizzie said.

I came back to the room and sighed silently, editing some more. "After the funeral service, I'm sitting in the great room of the funeral home, receiving people. We had two different receiving lines, by the way: the Winterburns' and mine. Anyway, I'm sitting there, hanging on to the twins, when Nina, busting out of some cheesy black Frederick's of Hollywood mail-order slut dress, comes up to me. I know who she is because, after all, she's been my husband's girlfriend for a year or so by now, and I've done some research. She's drunk as hell, reeling and sobbing louder than a drill press, and she staggers up to me and the boys. She doesn't address *me,* no, she grabs *them* each by an arm and says, very dramatically, 'I would've been your *mother*, boys, I would've been your *mother*!' "

"She sounds nuts, too," Tommy said, after a moment.

"Yep. At that stage of my life I was starting to think there were no sane people left in the universe. But I'd about had it with crazies. I took her aside, told her to get the hell out of my face and out of my kids' faces." And fell down at least one more rung on the class ladder in my ex-mother-in-law's estimation. "After the horrible funeral I holed up for a few months being obsessively focused on being a mommy, until Mo came and made me and the boys come live with her and Ivy for a while, getting us out of there so I could finish my degree and then get set up in a new place, new job, new life." I didn't mention that Ellie had reentered my life then and that it was she who had urged me forcefully to call Mo. "That's when I started to really get to know the rest of my cousins, too." I also didn't mention that after the funeral I cut my hair short for the first time in my life, almost shaving my head, in penance. I hadn't cut it since, and it had grown out rather nicely, much curlier than it had been before. So much for atonement.

Russell said, "How come you all didn't already know each other?"

"That's another story for another Thanksgiving. My sad story is over."

Mo smiled, and Lizzie rolled her eyes. Ivy was pretty drunk. "Let's go kick some Winterburn ass!" she rumbled. "Better yet, let's find Nina and kick *her* ass. She probably can't afford a good lawyer. And let's find Jared and kick his ass, too."

"So who wins?" Molly asked. "Who's got the saddest sad story?"

"I think they're all pretty sad," I said. "Who really wants to be the winner, anyway? Do we win a washing machine or something? I think I need to go to bed. You guys can come up with some happy stories for the morning."

Ivy pulled Mo to her feet and said, "Well, love of my life, time to go home. Lizzie, you're staying at our house tonight, right?"

Lizzie looked at me and then at Tommy, very deliberately, and tried to stand. Tommy helped her up off the floor. She fell into him, possibly by accident. Tommy said, "You're all walking, right?"

Lizzie swayed again. "Always the cop. Cute." I was so uncomfortable, I didn't know who to look at.

Mo looked at her two younger sisters. "I'm pulling rank as the big sister here. You gals are coming home with us. You are not going to stay here and sleep with men you just met."

I was even more uncomfortable now. Molly said, "I met Russell days ago," and Lizzie looked at me and said slowly, "Gina gets to."

I looked back. "Gina isn't sleeping with anyone tonight. I have two guest beds. If anyone is sleeping with anyone else, just please don't wake up the boys unless you're willing to explain the facts of life to them. And then pay the shrink bills." I turned, grabbed a couple of glasses, and took them into the kitchen. I wished I liked Lizzie more. It was hard to believe that Mo had come out of the same womb as all the rest of her siblings. I wondered if she felt that way herself at times.

Tommy came in the kitchen after me, carrying two dishes filled with cigar butts. The place was going to reek tomorrow, but that's what incense is for, I decided. He said, "I'm sorry if we're creating problems between you and Lizzie."

I looked at him, thinking that it was Tommy she wanted, there was nothing plural about it, and took the dishes, dumping the cigar butts in the trash. "Don't worry. The problems are not new, believe me."

He looked at me for a minute, then said, "It's got to be tough, having you for a cousin." He then looked as though he regretted what he had said. "I didn't mean that in a bad way."

I couldn't help laughing. "No, there are so many good ways to be an unfortunate relative."

"That isn't what I meant. Never mind; I'm too tired to make it come out right. I'm sorry if I hurt your feelings."

"My feelings are tough," I said.

Molly and Ivy were the least drunk of the four women and so supported the other two as they staggered out the door and down the street. Before they left, Mo put her arms around Ivy and said, "I'm the luckiest woman in the world to have a gal like this, who does this for me on my birthday. I love you so much, Ivyboo, I do, I do." Ivy was sober enough to be a bit embarrassed by this but put up with it for a moment before herding Mo and her sisters out the door. She said softly, "I'll come by and get Trevor tomorrow in the afternoon. I'll call you," then gave me a quick pat on the shoulder, and they were gone. As the door closed, Russell said, "Why does Ivy get all the thanks? The three of us did all the work."

I shrugged. "Love can blind you to a lot."

The kitchen looked as though some sort of meat bomb had exploded. The dining room was almost as bad and smelled like the aftermath of a forest fire. I said to the two men, "Leave it. Tomorrow will be soon enough to divert a river. I'm going to bed. You guys do what you want. I'm warning you, though, I don't have good cable." And I went upstairs, more tired than I'd been since the boys were babies.

That night I had a dream. This was a point in my life when I didn't remember my dreams very often. When I did, they normally fell into one of three categories: (1), I was teaching, and something about it was horribly humiliating. I was suddenly two feet shorter than all my students and unclothed. I was walking down a runway and suddenly realized that I had shit running down my legs. Something like that. Or (2), I would be trying to find a way to live with my boys in some huge ruin, or a condemned house, or a cave, places that were dark, damp, and generally unlivable.

Those dreams were usually just irritating or tension-making. They were not actually nightmares. The *real* nightmares, which I had often enough to live in some fear of them, were (3), the ones in which I lost my children somehow. I'd pick up the wrong kids at school, or my kids were drowning someplace where I couldn't get to them, or someone powerful and dark was carrying them away from me while they screamed and screamed. Those dreams caused me to wake up gasping, nauseous with fear, then stumble on shaking, ridiculously slow legs to the boys' room to make sure they were there, they were *both* there, and breathing, and not afraid, or threatened, or gone. Those were my *Sophie's Choice* kinds of dreams. They tended to ruin the rest of the night and usually the next day or two. I didn't need Jeri's expertise to know what they were about.

But this dream fit none of those categories. All I was doing was sitting talking to Big Bear, Detective Tommy. I knew that Detective Cutie Pie Russell was in the next room, although I didn't actually see him. I don't know where we were supposed to be. The room was plain, gray, no windows, totally nondescript. Tommy wasn't looking at me; he was looking over toward a door that I supposed connected to the other room. I have no memory of what we were talking about. Then he turned and looked at me. He looked right into my eyes and just kept looking. His brow lowered, and he said "Hello," his expression completely serious. That was it. It sounds like nothing, even silly, but in the dream it was neither. My insides shifted. I can't explain it better than that. My stomach tightened, my breathing grew more rapid, my heartbeat intensified. And when I woke up, it was daylight, and I knew with complete certainty that I was in love with Tommy Galloway.

chapter twelve

---

*Again, the answer to the problem of suffering is not away from
the problem but in it. The inevitability of pain will not be met
by deadening sensitivity but by increasing it, by exploring and
feeling out the manner in which the natural organism itself
wants to react and which its innate wisdom has provided.*

ALAN WATTS, *Nature, Man and Woman*

SUNDAY MORNING doesn't have good cartoons, thank God, so the
boys didn't get me up as early. Trevor being there meant that they had
other things to do, so they went downstairs to play as soon as they
woke up. That gave me a few moments to myself, to lie in bed and
wrestle with this new fact. (Religious studies people always "wrestle"
with problems. I guess it's too difficult for them to resist biblical
metaphors.) My first coherent thought was that I should talk to Ellie
or maybe make an appointment with Jeri. But I was strangely reluctant to do that.

I had my share of neuroses, God knew, but finding rejection an
aphrodisiac had never been one of them. I hadn't felt this way about
any man since I'd fallen for Riley Kupferberg when I was eighteen.

I'm not prone to infatuation, and I'd rarely thought I was "in love." So what the hell was this? I thought, there's no way this is real. This is some weird loneliness thing, you're projecting God knows what all over the poor man. The "I love a man in uniform" thing. He's protecting you, and that's sexy. Let's face it, no man has ever protected you before. That's all it is. Just hold and roll; he'll be gone, and you'll be able to move on.

I finally staggered up, showered quickly in case there were other demands on my single bathroom, and went downstairs into the kitchen. The place wasn't clean, but it was far less devastated than it had been the night before. I looked around and around. I felt like crying. It was embarrassing, and I was glad that no other adults seemed to be awake so that my sentimentality went unremarked. It was like having a couple of good elves looking after me. After making a big pot of coffee, I decided to make pancakes.

Eventually the smell of breakfast broke through the stench from the previous evening and lured all the males in the house into the kitchen. The three shorter ones showed up first and ate with great gusto. I had to work to make sure they didn't pour all the syrup onto whatever surface was near them. The adults came in a bit later, Russell first, then Tommy. Both were in jeans and sweaters. Russell looked adorably rumpled; Tommy looked much more shiny, tiny droplets of water in his dark hair from a shower. I started at first when Russell walked in, thinking he might be Tommy. By the time my heart slowed down, Tommy had walked in, and I managed not to jump more than an inch or two. Neither man seemed to notice my twitchiness, thankfully, both being too consumed by hunger and the need for caffeine. I had a hard time looking at Tommy; it was almost like he was standing directly in front of the sun and to stare right at him would burn my retinas. So I wound up being chummier with Russell, which turned out to be a bad idea.

The phone rang, making me jump again. It was Lizzie, inviting Tommy and Russell over to Mo and Ivy's for brunch. It wasn't clear if I was invited. She wanted to talk to Tommy. I handed the phone to him, thinking, I can't believe this. I had never up to that point ever, ever been jealous of Lizzie. But as I said before, it was a year of great changes for me, and not all of them were good. He was sweet on the phone, which of course made it worse. But he told her that neither he nor Russell could come over that day, which was better.

I kept trying not to look at his arms, at his neck, at his mouth, at his rear end in his jeans, while inefficiently making myself breakfast. Russell finished eating before Tommy and got up, pulling a cell phone from his pants pocket while moving into the next room. Tommy watched him, then mopped up the last of his syrup with a triangle of pancake. I finally sat down across from him with a plate and ate a bite, not tasting it, trying not to stare at him, wondering what I could say to avoid sounding stupid or besotted. He was quiet as well and seemed to be more interested in looking out the window at the thin flurries in the gray glare of a Tenway winter than at me. The silence was starting to feel meaningful, when Russell came back into the kitchen, looking at Tommy. "He drove by here last night and parked for a while. He knows your car now."

The game was afoot. Fear tickled my insides. I looked at my boys, who were playing Lego soccer in the living room. I was wondering if I should send them to Mo's with Trevor today. Now.

The pancakes had used up most of the milk, and I had to go get more. I asked Russell if he and Tommy would watch the boys while I did a little shopping run. Russell said one of them should do it. I realized that they didn't want me out anywhere alone right now and wondered if there was anything they weren't telling me.

"I'll go," Tommy said. I gave him a short list and told him where the nearest grocery store was.

"I'll be back in forty-five minutes." To Russell he said, "I have my cell." I also noticed that under his jacket he was wearing his holster. This time there was no question of Toby or Stevie going with him.

After Tommy left, I was in the kitchen, continuing to clean up. Russell came in, carrying yet another plate from last night that he'd found under some piece of furniture. He said, "Are you and Molly very close?"

I had no idea where this was leading. "Sort of. She's the baby of her family, so everybody tends to be pretty protective of her, and I guess that's catching. Why?"

He seemed edgy, and rather than answering, he paced around the room for a moment or two. He stopped, looked at me, then sort of swooped over to where I was and kissed me on the mouth. He then stepped away, looking at me and then at the floor, breathing hard. He was blushing. I stared at him. I had never been more shocked in my life.

"What the hell was that?" was all I could manage after a moment or two.

"Look, I think you're really"—he wasn't good at finding the most polite word for things, I had already learned—"hot. I mean, I think you're really hot."

"I'm sorry, but no way." My tongue felt thick with shock, and I couldn't get it to move, to articulate. "No," I finally said again. "I'm sorry."

Russell looked hurt or angry or ashamed; it was hard to tell which. I felt bad for him, then felt stupid for feeling bad. The doorbell rang before he could say anything else. Russell left the kitchen to get it, telling the boys it was better if they didn't answer the door themselves. It was Tommy, back from the store.

Later, I had a guilty conscience, although when I tried to sort out why, it was clear how irrational that was. But Tommy kept looking from me to Russell in his intense, broody way, and I was convinced he smelled something. I kept telling myself, So what?

Within minutes of Tommy's return, Josh Hepplewhite appeared at the front door. He came in to play with the boys in the dining room. Josh was hardly interested in the two men sitting on the couch in the living room; I suspected his parents would be a little keener to get some details if they knew about their presence. I'd have to come up with something to tell Patsy.

But now Russell was in cool-cop-with-a-hairdo mode again, and he and Tommy were back at work. They made me sit down in the living room with them after closing the French doors into the dining room so that the boys couldn't hear us. They both sat on the sofa; I sat opposite them on the love seat, tensely stroking the sweet and slightly dangerous Sidney as he purred and kneaded his way to sleep in my lap.

"Okay, we've established our story a bit," said Tommy. "Now we need to follow through and keep close tabs on Tim and Jason. I think we can go back to the city today, work from there till next Wednesday, and leave the surveillance to the constable and his men. Is this okay with you? Do you have any problems being left here alone till Wednesday?"

I tried to think this through, with little success. "I don't think so. If the psychos are always being watched, then I guess it's okay. Although I assume that if they head my way at all, someone will come here to save the day."

They both nodded. Russell smiled and said, "Just try to get on with your life, get back to normal, you know." I could have smacked him.

Soon after they left, the boys went outside to play, somewhat grimly. The weather was gray and awful, but there was plenty of snow on the ground, and they were building walls and throwing snowballs with Josh Hepplewhite. I was working on a lecture on the computer in the dining room; I could keep an eye on them through the window. The phone rang; it turned out to be Bobbie, calling to thank me for the dinner party. I hadn't had a chance to talk to her about Franny's baby, so I was glad for the opportunity. I told her I was sorry Donna couldn't make it.

Bobbie said, "Do you think that there's any way we could persuade *your* sister to come up here for a visit sometime? It's been so long since any of us have seen her."

"I don't think she likes leaving Florida. She really hates the cold. Or maybe she's afraid of it; I don't know. Anyway, her job is pretty demanding. She doesn't like to take time off." I decided to bring up what I had wanted to talk to Bobbie about. "Bobbie, you're sort of the research expert in the family, right? Being a librarian?"

"Well, I don't know. You're the one who got the PhD. Why do you ask?"

I told her what Jessie had told me about the girl baby. "Do you know anything about this?"

"No, I've never heard this before."

"Don't you think it unlikely that Franny's sisters would let her baby be adopted out of the family? Don't you think it's more likely that one of them adopted the baby herself?"

"What an idea, Gina! But I guess it's possible. That would mean it's one of us, which is a pretty odd thought. Do you know anything about dates or anything else that we could check?"

"No. That's where I thought you could come in. You can also ask your mother stuff a whole lot easier than I can. I asked mine, but she got pretty squirrelly. You know, after the funeral all three of them went to see a lawyer about Franny's estate. I wonder if that had anything to do with the baby."

"Like she'll inherit something?"

"Maybe. I don't know. I can't imagine that her estate is very big, but who knows?"

"Look, Gina, I'll try to find out what I can and keep you posted."

I had to cut our conversation short as the boys came slamming into the house, along with many pounds of snow and much cold wind. I had the comforting feeling that the search for information about my possible adoption was in capable hands.

After I made the boys dinner, Ivy dropped by to pick up Trevor and reminded me that the following Friday night the boys and I were supposed to go with Mo to see her in a community theater play. They were doing *Harvey,* and Ivy was playing the part of the sister. I asked her if I could get a ticket for Tommy, keeping that option open. She thought it would be fine. She had high hopes for me and Tommy, I could tell. I was surprised that they weren't higher for Lizzie instead. Molly wasn't going, so I didn't try to get a ticket for Russell.

On Monday I saw nothing to indicate that anyone was paying any particular attention to me, either law enforcement types or stalkers. Since I wasn't supposed to know about the website, I decided to live in complete denial that anything like that was going on. I managed with unusual mental control to not think about it. No one in the department had caught wind of it yet; that was obvious. I had a sign-up sheet for appointments on my office door; when I arrived in the morning, I was appalled to see that Tim Solomon had put his name down for an appointment that day right after lunch.

I called the constable's office immediately, first shutting my office door so that no one would hear what I was saying. The man who answered the phone put me through to McCandless at once after I told him my name. A hard-bought privilege, I thought, this access to the man in charge. I'd give a lot not to need it.

I told him about Tim's appointment. He told me not to worry. Tim was being watched, so if he came into the building, they'd know and make sure someone nondescript wouldn't be far behind him. Oh, great, I thought. Now I feel completely safe.

I did as much work as possible during the morning to take my mind off the upcoming meeting. However, when the time came, he didn't show. I gave him about twenty minutes, stomach tight with tension, and then left to go to the campus bookstore for a while. Since he was extremely late, I felt no compunction about leaving.

Later, after I'd gotten the boys and they'd done their homework, I took them to Josh's. I'd just come back in from delivering them, when a banging noise made me jump so hard that I squeaked. I recognized, after a painful second, Jessie's broomstick connecting to my downspout. Oh Christ, not now, I thought. But I went out.

"I got a bunch of cheese," she said. "They gave me some at the senior center, but I can't digest it. It's a lot of cheese. You can use it." Then why did you take it? I thought irritably before realizing that this was no doubt a ploy for company.

"Sure, thanks," I said with fake enthusiasm. I'm not a cheese snob; I've cooked with Velveeta more than once. But I feared this cheese.

I glanced again with mild interest at the paintings in her front hall. Jean Foxhall. Jessie Foxhall.

"Jessie, when did your husband die?" Widow to widow.

"Almost thirty years ago now." Flat affect.

"When did your aunt die?"

"She died thirty-five years ago. The anniversary was just two weeks ago."

"When were you married?" I knew I was being nosy, but I had a burr in my boot about her last name.

"Two years later." She looked away.

"So you took care of her from when she moved in with you till she died. Wow, you were a really good niece."

"Come into the kitchen. I'll get you the cheese."

The cheese turned out to be a cheap but perfectly respectable cheddar. This we might actually use, I thought. I thanked her as though we had no food of our own, wondering desperately what I could give her in return that wouldn't insult her and that she could genuinely use.

When I came back into the house, my answering machine was blinking. It was another message from John Fagin. I wondered how many times I would have to not call him back before he'd give up.

When I finally told Ellie about the weekend, she practically whooped. "Aha! Now I understand why you didn't go for Cutie Pie Boy Toy."

"Please, Ellie. This is humiliating enough."

"Why is it humiliating?"

"Because this isn't a movie. Nothing is going to happen. And Tommy has a girlfriend, anyway."

"Oh. Well, at least he's not married. Do you know anything about how serious he is about this girlfriend?"

"That's irrelevant. I don't want a boyfriend. What a stupid word. And I don't want to get married again. Probably ever."

"Hmmm. Anyway, maybe I can go after Russell. It would be so nice and symmetrical."

"As far as I'm concerned, you can have him, but I'm pretty sure Molly beat you to it. And, uh, he made a pass at me, too."

"My God, you're like some sort of superhero. Your superpower is the creation of deep animal lust in all men who come into contact with you. Some sort of universal kryptonite but aimed out at them, not at you."

"Stop. I doubt I've created any deep animal lust in Tommy. And, er, if you take Russell, make sure you do it where my boys can't walk in on you, okay?"

"Jesus, did that happen?"

"Not that I know of, but he and Molly don't strike me as the most careful couple in the world. I wish they'd abstain when they're in my house, babysitting my children, and go boink each other elsewhere, on their own sheets."

"You're assuming that they're doing it in a bed."

I moaned. "I refuse to think about that." Then, sighing, I added, "Jesus, E., I don't *know* Tommy well enough to, you know. He's not all that charming, not that handsome. But he seems *familiar,* kind of. God, listen to me."

"Pheromones or something. Have you done an Internet search yet?"

"Of what?"

"Of Tommy. See what you can find out about him."

Of course I followed Ellie's advice. I didn't find a lot, mostly archived newspaper articles relating to cases he'd worked on. Russell was mentioned just as frequently. Most of the cases were grisly in one way or another, as most were homicides. I got to wondering who Bradley Franco's parents were connected to that they could get two detectives from the big city out to dinky Tenway.

I also stumbled onto a link to something called the Auxiliary Circle. There were lots of pictures of police officers of many ranks, mostly male. The pictures were accompanied by captions and commentaries. I read for a while until I got the point. It seemed to be a fan site, with mostly women posting pictures of and stories about their favorite cops. Each had a separate page dedicated to his career and biographical information. Most of the content of those pages was from newspapers. But the bios gave their full names, places of birth and birthdays, marital status, measurements (!), favorite hangouts, foods, music, and so on. My stomach tightened when I saw with what adulation Tommy was treated, although he was nowhere near the most prominent. There was a lot of innuendo about guns and holsters. None of it was particularly well written, and neither grammar nor spelling seemed to be a priority. It made me a little embarrassed to be a female and a whole lot embarrassed that I had any feelings at all for him. I realized that I had had a small notion, hidden even from myself, that I somehow had spotted something special about Tommy, something that other women might miss. I was discerning. I could see now that discerning or not, lots and lots of other women found him attractive and were willing to admit it to the world, even if only anonymously. I wondered if he'd ever slept with any of those women. I was willing to bet Russell had.

The page dedicated to Russell was even worse, more fawning and overtly sexual, and had had even more hits. Cops as celebrities. It was both interesting and icky. If I were a cop, I would have found it alarming to be exposed in this way, maybe dangerous. Were the authors of the page crazy? Or just lonely? I thought this was especially interesting given the nature of the cases Russell and Tommy were working on, but not in a good way.

chapter thirteen

―――――――――――

*Instead of being aware of [unpleasant experiences] as they are,
we try to deal with them in terms of the past. The frightened
or lonely person begins at once to think, "I'm afraid," or, "I'm
so lonely."*

*This is, of course, an attempt to avoid the experience. We
don't want to be aware of this present. But as we cannot get
out of the present, our only escape is into memories. Here we
feel on safe ground, for the past is the fixed and the known—
but also, of course, the dead. Thus to try to get out of, say, fear
we endeavor at once to be separate from it and to "fix" it by
interpreting it in terms of memory, in terms of what is already
fixed and known. In other words, we try to adapt ourselves to
the mysterious present by comparing it with the (remembered)
past, by naming and "identifying" it.*

ALAN WATTS, *The Wisdom of Insecurity*

AFTER TEACHING ON TUESDAY, I walked back to my car, hoping to
have time to go to the dry cleaners before picking up the boys. I had
just gotten my key in the lock when I felt a hand on my shoulder,

startling the bejesus out of me. I almost dropped my satchel; when I pivoted, it turned out to be Tim Solomon, alone for a change.

That didn't help me catch my breath any faster. "What . . . ?" was all I managed to get out.

Tim dimpled and held up his hands in pretend surrender. "I'm sorry, Dr. P. Did I scare you?" This plainly delighted him.

"No, I, no, I was just startled. Can I help you with something?" He was standing too close, pinning me to my car door. I could see small hairs the color of hazelnuts sprouting underneath his chin. He didn't look like he had to shave much; they were renegades.

"I want to talk to you. I apologize for not making our appointment. I had to go into the city and take care of some family business. There's no excuse for me not calling and canceling, but I simply didn't have time, and I get hardly any cell phone service in the city. Please forgive me."

"Well, I only hold appointments for ten minutes, so don't worry, I didn't wait." I didn't want the little prick thinking he had any power over me, even though, of course, he did. He didn't need to know that I knew it. He looked irritated, which faintly pleased me. I thought, not for the first time, that he looked just like all the other wealthy white boys who came through this university, not like a psychopath at all. Vincent Capinelli had complained once that Tenway University catered mostly to dumb rich kids from upstate and from the city. That was unfair; Tenway had its share of scholarship kids and locals as well as students attracted by its stronger programs. But Vincent wasn't totally wrong; Jason Dettwiler was a case in point. Tim wasn't necessarily dumb, although it was clear that academically speaking, he didn't give a shit. But I wondered if his parents thought his problems would go away if they dumped him in a backwater school. Someday, I thought, I'm going to try to figure out what the parental lesson is in that.

"Well, I'm glad to know that." He didn't look it. "But what I wanted to ask you, Dr. P., was if you needed any help."

I hated it when people called me Dr. P. I have little-ish kids; I have no choice but to think of urine. "What kind of help?"

"You know, around the house."

"You want to be my maid?"

"No!" He didn't find that funny. "No, I mean like doing stuff in your yard, fixing things in your house, that kind of thing."

I couldn't imagine a city boy like him knowing much about yard work. "Uh, thanks, Tim, but I don't need anything like that."

"I know you paid some guys to do stuff before, you know. I just thought, like, that you'd need more stuff, and I could do it for you."

He was looking down now, looking squirmy. I said, "I paid some boys to help me move, Tim. That was all. It was just for one day." I collected myself, trying to treat him as I would anyone else. "But thanks. If I decide I need some yard work done later in the spring, I'll let you know, okay? I've got to go."

"You're a single mom, right? They always need help, don't they? That's what my dad says. You've got to let me help you, Dr. P. I can help a lot. Tell you what: Why don't I come by your place tonight? I could look around, see what I could do for you."

"No." My face felt like it was made of wood. "No. Don't do that. I don't need anything." If this were anyone else, I'd threaten him with the police. But that was complicated; I had no idea what else to do other than to be very firm. "Do not come to my house, Tim. I'm fine."

"You having company?" he said, his own face wooden now. "Is that why?"

"No," but I thought, say yes, say yes. You shouldn't have to, but he's nuts. Say it. "Well, yes. But still. You need to stay home and study. I'll see you tomorrow." I got in my car, closing the door almost in his face, locking it, and trying to get my keys in the ignition with trembling fingers. I waved idiotically at him and pulled out without hitting him or anyone else.

I took a circuitous route to the boys' bus stop, which was melodramatic of me, but I was pretty scared. I still got there early, as I hadn't stopped to run any errands. I pulled my phone out of my bag and called the constable.

TOMMY SHOWED UP at my door right before dinner with a duffel bag. I apologized as he came in, saying I was really sorry I had freaked out, and maybe I was overreacting, and so on.

He just said, "Stop. You shouldn't be here without protection. It was smart that you called, smart that you told him someone would be here."

I'd made roast chicken, figuring it was safe, everyone pretty much liked it. The four of us sat down at the kitchen table like normal people. Tommy complained, saying I didn't have to feed him; I ignored this. I initially had a hard time making eye contact with him, but the boys were thrilled he was there. Toby explained how he was the best in his class at getting the teacher to laugh, which was, I gathered, a pretty prestigious position to hold in the second grade. He was known, he said, as "the comedy guy." I hadn't heard this before and hoped it meant something good, not something about which I was going to be summoned to a parent-teacher conference. Then Toby said that his brother was known as "the science guy," which I knew. Tommy asked what that meant.

Stevie looked at him, blue eyes enormous and serious. Not the comedy guy. He said, "I know all about stars and the universe and how things work."

I waited, but Stevie seemed out of words for the moment. I said to Tommy, looking at Stevie for confirmation and "okay"s as I said it, "When Stevie was four, we were visiting at a house where there were a bunch of older boys—it was Mo's next-door neighbor—and all the boys were at least nine or ten except the twins. The older boys were talking about those rides at amusement parks, those round ones where the bottom drops out, and one of them said that what held you in was gravity. Stevie said, 'No, it's centrifugal force.' I don't remember having taught him that; at least, I never made a big point of it. He just gets stuff like that really fast." And he has such a hard time with other kids, I thought, but of course hoped and prayed that Stevie never knew I had any such thoughts, ever. Toby could charm the termites out of the walls. The comedy guy.

Tommy smiled at all the right places and congratulated both boys on their respective claims to fame. Now that the ice had been broken, Stevie started asking the appropriate little boy questions about being a policeman: Had Tommy ever killed anybody, did he have a gun, could they see it, fire it? Oh Jesus. Tommy seemed prepared for this. Yes, he had one, maybe they could see it tomorrow, but not tonight. And no, they could never, ever fire it. He dodged the question about ever having killed anyone. I flashed to something I'd long forgotten. I was younger than my boys, five or six at the oldest. My father, drunk and smelly, sitting on our patchy living-room sofa, cleaning his pistol. The closest I'd ever come to gunfire.

I took a breath and steered the conversation to Looney Tunes, about which my boys were experts. I was a big fan as well, and we talked about how dull a lot of recent cartoons were. It turned out that Tommy was an aficionado of them, too, so the boys perked up even further, and I was allowed to pretty much bow out of the conversation. I watched the three of them and felt a terrible fear, an episode of premourning. The boys liked Tommy; they would love him by tomorrow. They loved easily, and they were my sons, after all, and just as lonely in their own way for an adult man in their lives. What could I do? I couldn't keep them apart in my small house, and we needed him. I was as scared of Tim Solomon as I'd been of anyone, but I was increasingly scared, in a different way, of course, of Tommy. I could take it. But my poor boys.

Later, they wanted Tommy to read to them before bed. He said he wouldn't mind; I didn't believe him and vetoed the idea. After they were in bed, I came down and offered to make some decaffeinated coffee. He accepted, and we sat down awkwardly in the living room. I apologized again for dragging him to my house, hoping he wasn't in the middle of something when he got the call from McCandless. He assured me he wasn't but didn't elaborate. He asked me details of what Tim had said, how he'd looked and acted. I told him what I could, which wasn't much. I suddenly blurted, "Please, keep your gun somewhere else, okay, away from the boys?"

"Gina, I would never be careless about that, especially around kids. You don't have to worry."

"I can't help it." I sort of spilled over then, unable to censor myself. I told him about my father and his gun, cleaning it while stinking, droopily drunk, comically drunk, singing "Purple Haze": "Excuse me while I kiss this guy." A favorite joke. The gun went off, and my father had the ludicrous expression of someone surprised out of semiconsciousness.

"It shot a hole in the wall, and they were pretty thin, and my little sister was in the other room, taking a nap. The bullet missed her head by about six inches. It was stopped by my teddy bear, sitting on the next bed."

My father was almost sober then, shaking. Years later, after she was dead, he'd cried and cried. "Maybe it would've been better if I'd killed her then. Maybe it would've been better." Even at eleven I knew this was stupidity born of terrible grief. But I didn't tell Tommy all this, just the barest facts; I managed to keep most of the mortifying truth to myself.

"I have no intention of doing anything so asinine. Sorry," he added, realizing he was insulting my father.

I just smiled. "It's okay. He deserved it."

He inhaled slowly. "Relax, Gina."

"Not gonna happen," I said. "But thanks for the thought."

The conversation was pretty much over after that; I went to bed early, leaving him standing guard downstairs, my cat next to him on the couch.

The next day was Wednesday, so I had a night class. Tommy left in the morning when we did, making sure the house was well locked up. I gave him my extra key so that we wouldn't need to coordinate our arrivals. I spent the day working in my office, preparing lectures and seeing students. Fortunately, Tim Solomon didn't try to see me, although every time one of my advisees knocked on the door, my stomach gave a queasy little jerk. I was intensely relieved when the day ended and skulked quickly to my car, darting guilty-looking glances all around me as though I were starring in a cheap spy movie.

Tommy and Russell arrived at my house a half hour or so after I'd picked the boys up at the bus stop. As I let them in, I could see Jessie looking out her window next door, watching. Molly arrived a few minutes later and was downright excited to see Russell. I didn't know what to do about that. Should I have told her about our conversation that past Sunday? I still don't know. Russell seemed pleased to see Molly as well. I decided that for the moment that situation was out of my hands and focused on the evening ahead.

Tim and Jason sashayed into class a few minutes late again. Tommy sat in the back but was still conspicuous, and that did seem to irritate the two boys. I did my best to ignore all my feelings about what was going on and teach the class. After the break I showed a film. It was about an hour long, and Tommy and I sat next to each other in the darkened room. We kept whispering comments back and forth: nothing loud, nothing, I hoped, distracting for the other students. But if Tim and Jason really were keeping me in their sights, it should have meant an irritating intimacy to them.

The room was quite dark, with the occasional finger of light from the door if a student crept out to go to the bathroom or get some water. That happened three times, and each time both Tommy and I looked to make sure neither of our boys was leaving. But once the door closed again, it was close to impossible to see for sure who was left in the room unless the film got exceptionally brightly lit. That was not predictable, making it impossible to check anybody's presence or absence systematically. When the film ended, I turned up the lights. As my eyes adjusted, I looked around at all the blinking faces and realized with a zing up my spine that Jason was gone. Tim was still there, sitting with his happy grin, his arm casually across the back of Heather Mason's chair. She was one of the people who had gotten up and left briefly during the film. I wondered what the connection there might be; was she some sort of decoy, and somehow when she went out, Jason snuck out, too? Why would he care to be sneaky, why wouldn't he just leave? Oh God, did they know Tommy was a cop? I looked to him and saw that he was processing the situation much faster than I was.

Tommy stood up and said out loud, "Dr. Paletta, I have a personal situation that I need to resolve." He was smiling jovially, holding a cell phone. "Please excuse me and forgive the disruption." He bobbed and nodded pompously to the rest of the class and walked out the door, raising the phone to his ear as he walked out.

There was only about another half hour to get through. I did it as well as I could, mainly soliciting comments and answering questions about the film. I dismissed the class at a reasonable time and tried to gather my papers rapidly without looking panicked. I didn't know how far away Tommy had gone, either. I really wanted him close right then. Tim, of course, hung back as the other students burst out of the room. To my dismay, Heather hung back with him. Run, girl, I thought; run as fast as your purple spandexed legs will carry you. Helplessly, I watched as he strutted up to the front, where I took deep, quiet breaths, hoping for inspiration and equilibrium.

Before Tim could ask whatever it was he had in mind, Tommy walked back into the classroom. I was watery with relief. Tim's face locked down; he got a sort of a pit bull expression that didn't bode well for the rest of Heather's evening.

"Dr. Paletta, I was hoping that I could talk to you. It's really, really important. I was wondering if you had some time right now." He looked angrily at Tommy and said through thinned lips, "It's kind of personal, though."

I said, "I'm sorry, Tim, but I have a previous engagement. I have some office hours tomorrow. Why don't you come see me then?"

He was not happy; he nodded, curled his lip at Tommy, and left the room quickly with Heather shadowing behind.

"Whew," I said. "I hate this. I really wish he would just go away, out of my life."

Tommy said, "I don't know why Russell's phone isn't on. We need to go."

I drove us back, trying not to do anything stupid. Tommy kept trying to call Russell and kept getting nothing. He called the constable as well and talked for a few minutes. His worry made me feel like turning inside out with fear.

After he rang off with McCandless, he said, "The local cops have someone in your neighborhood. Patrol cars have been circling around, but since Russell was at the house, the local boys have been keeping their distance, since they don't want their presence remarked on. No one's reported anything significant yet, but McCandless will call us back when they go back around. I told him we were going there right now."

I couldn't imagine anything bad happening to Toby and Stevie, or maybe could imagine it too well and was in some kind of anxiety overload. There wasn't room for worry about Molly or Russell. I wanted to claw my skin or scream, I was so terrified for my boys. We got to the street, and I managed somehow not to clip any other cars and to slow down before turning into the driveway. Tommy grabbed my arm hard and said, "You have to wait here. I know you want to run in, Gina, but you have to stay here. Do you get me? I mean this." He then got out and, leaning low, went to the front door. The light above the door was out, which was weird, because I always turned it on when I left the house, only it was daylight when we left, so maybe I didn't; I was trying to remember. Then, the door opened; you could see light streaming from inside onto the porch. There was Tommy, face lit up by the living-room lamps. He was talking to Russell, and Russell seemed fine, startled, maybe, but fine. For the first time in the last hour I started feeling like it might be okay, like nothing terrible had happened. But Tommy was looking at something on the porch, something darker than even the shadows. He and Russell stepped out of the light, peering. I saw Russell put his hand over his mouth, and Tommy stayed low for an extra moment. I saw the beam of a flashlight come unexpectedly from Tommy's hand; he must have had it in his pocket. I kept thinking, what could be on the porch? A bomb? If so, then everyone needed to get out of there. My thoughts were retarded by anxiety, relief, and confusion. I got out of the car, my legs aching with the tension I'd been holding in them while sitting. Trying to keep my voice low, not wanting to wake up Jessie or alarm other neighbors, I said, "Tommy?"

He jerked up at the sound. His face was pale through the snow that had just started falling. His skin was almost the same color. Russell looked toward me, too, and I could see his face; he looked scared and appalled.

Tommy came down off the porch toward me and said "Gina, you need to stay away from there. I'll go in; no, Russell, go in"—turning toward him—"and open the back door, so she can go in the back way, okay? She needs to stay off the porch."

Molly was trying to come out the door by this time, and Russell was pushing her back in as well. I said, "What, what is it, Tommy? You're terrifying me."

He looked as sad as I'd seen him yet. "It's your cat. He's dead, Gina. I'm so sorry."

The news didn't take long to sink in. I started crying suddenly with sharp, hot tears. Sidney. Not my boys but still a really bad thing. Poor Sidney, poor, poor old cat. Tommy put his arms around me, and I started crying harder into his broad chest. I didn't want to see him, and my guilt almost overcame my sorrow. "Are you sure?" I said. "Are you sure he's dead? Are you sure it's him?"

"Yes, it's Sidney. Yes, he's dead, Gina. Trust me. I don't think it'll do you any good to look. It's not going to help him. Come on, come on in. Russell and I will deal with this."

He pulled me to the back of the house, his arm around my shoulders, and new lights came on as Russell presumably made his way through the kitchen. Then he opened the latch on the back fence gate, and we stepped through, our winter shoes crunching the dry frozen grass, now lightly snow-covered. I let Tommy shepherd me up the steps onto the deck and through the back door into the warm, bright room. I remembered all my stuff in the car: my purse, my satchel. Tommy said not to worry. They'd deal with that, too; sit down. He asked a practically bug-eyed Molly to make coffee and found the phone in the kitchen that had a cord and dialed. I suddenly sat up, stood, then ran upstairs. None of this was volitional. I simply obeyed my body and tiptoed rapidly into the boys' room. I leaned over them; they were sleeping, motionless. I could hear the soft wheeze from the slight congestion in Stevie's nose and watched Toby's chest till I was sure it was gently moving. Then I slowly went back down the stairs, starting to cry again as I thought about telling the boys about this to-morrow.

All three faces turned to me as I went into the kitchen. I could smell coffee and was relieved on some distant level that Molly was capable of making it. I asked, "What's happening now? What do we do?"

Tommy said, "We've called McCandless. He'll send someone over to process it as evidence. They're also watching Tim closely, and they're looking for Jason. We assume he's the one who did this. All we can do now is gather whatever physical evidence there is here and keep it for later, when we do catch the little bastards."

"But why did they do this? Why would they hurt my cat? Do they think I'll have sex with them if they kill my cat? That doesn't make any sense." I was trying not to escalate to sobs, but it was hard. I kept thinking about my poor Sidney's last moments.

Tommy said, "Anger at me. Jealousy at anything that's got your affection. Blind rage at you, displaced onto your cat. And Tim can get Jason to act it out for him."

"But how did he do it? I mean, how come no one saw anything? Or heard anything?"

Russell had been quiet and was pale and a bit trembly. He said, "It's my fault, Gina. I'm really, really sorry. I should've been paying attention. I forgot to turn on the phone. It's that simple. I forgot to turn it on." I thought that was odd. Didn't he have it on before we left? Why would he turn it off? Then I saw the squirrelly silent look that Molly gave me and got it. Russell had turned it off because they were fucking. Either all this happened while they were actually doing it, and so the phone was off, or Russell hadn't remembered to turn it back on while they were enjoying the afterglow or whatever it was they enjoyed together.

Russell was still talking. "So I didn't know that Jason had left; I didn't know Jason wasn't in the class. Tommy called me at the break, and I knew they were there then. I'm so, so sorry about your cat."

Tommy added, "It looks like the lightbulb on your front porch was unscrewed."

I had gotten Sidney as a kitten when I had the first place of my own in the Village, when I'd been away from home for two years. I'd known him longer than I'd known anyone in Tenway, longer than my sons had been around, longer than I'd been in the academic world. I didn't care about the website so much anymore. I wanted the two awful boys to pay for what they had done to a poor old cat that was, sadly perhaps, one of the best friends I'd ever had. I looked at Tommy.

"Is it so bad that I really shouldn't see him?"

"Yes." He looked right at Russell, dark eyes sharp and cold. "Russell and I will deal with this; don't worry. We'll clean off the porch, everything." Russell didn't argue.

The constable showed up later, alone. He came in, took some coffee, and told us he didn't want to make too much of a fuss outside, where it could be observed. They hadn't found Jason yet; they weren't sure he wasn't somewhere watching the place. So they didn't want to treat this with overkill compared to how something like this would normally be dealt with. "I'm gonna take pictures, though, lots of those. We can use 'em at trial later if we want evidence of malicious intent and tendency to violence. The prosecution's shrinks will love this."

I told him all that he wanted from me, mostly concerning the time line of Jason and Tim's presence in class. I alerted both him and Tommy to the likelihood of Heather Mason being drafted into things. They said they'd keep it in mind. I also told them that Jessie next door tended to see everything, so they should question her, though probably they should wait till morning. Then I said I was going to bed.

Tommy stopped me before I went up. He said, "Look, Gina. They've moved from fantasy now to real action. It's not theory anymore. This is a sign that they are willing to do very bad things. It seems even more likely now that they did something to Bradley. I'm staying here with you from now on, sometimes Russell, too, maybe. I don't know; we'll see. But tomorrow I think the boys need to go elsewhere. To Mo's, I guess. We need to make sure that Tim and Jason don't know that, though. They can't know where your boys are. Starting as soon as possible."

chapter fourteen

THAT NIGHT I SLEPT BADLY, not surprisingly. I alternated between crying about poor Sidney and worrying about what to do about Toby and Stevie. There weren't many decisions to make about that, but at two in the morning rational thought gives way to anxious scenarios, no matter how implausible. By five-thirty I was done trying to work anything out; instead, I got up, did some yoga at a leisurely pace, showered, and dressed. I then, as quietly as possible, picked through clothing, underwear, and pajamas in the boys' room. I gathered an armful, enough to get them through the weekend, anyway, and found an overnight bag in the hall closet. Tommy was asleep in the guest room; he hadn't closed the door, and I could see him from the hall, mouth slightly open, lying still and imposing. I had no idea how late he'd been up, but I knew he, Russell, and the constable had been at it after Russell had seen Molly home. I knew that had been almost midnight, since I'd had an awake episode then myself, and I'd heard them discussing things softly downstairs.

I brought the bag down to the front hallway and peeked into the dining room to see if Russell was there on the daybed. To my surprise, he was, though he was awake, sitting up and watching the morning news on TV, the sound almost inaudible. I wasn't sure why they both needed to be here, but I figured it couldn't hurt to have more protection. I had the batter ready to go into the waffle iron and was just about to go upstairs to rouse the boys when Russell appeared, teetering and pointy-headed, in the kitchen doorway. He said he'd been up for a while; he'd gotten up when Tommy finally went to bed.

"There's coffee," I said, gesturing. "You know where the cups and stuff are by now, I think."

He nodded and poured himself a cup. I was about to leave the room again, when he stopped me. He put his hand on my arm and said, "Jeez, Gina, I wanted to tell you again how sorry I am. I was a really bad fuckup last night. Really bad, really unprofessional. I mean, I even thought about resigning over this. Shit, it was inexcusable."

I was afraid he was going to go on like that for a while; I had things to do, and he had morning breath. "At least now we know how out of control they are. You're forgiven. I need to wake up my sons and tell them they have to get moving."

Russell looked like he was going to cry. It was sweet, I suppose, but in the mood I was in I found it tiresome. I didn't really care how he felt about the whole thing but had no desire to grind him through misery, either. Being nice is a hard habit to break. Before I left him, I said, "Besides, it wasn't your doing; it was Jason's."

I went upstairs. The boys were already stirring. I got them to dress quickly with the bribe of waffles and whipped cream. Tommy appeared, disheveled like Russell, in the guest-room doorway.

"Did I hear something about waffles?" he croaked. "And do I smell coffee?"

"Yes and yes," I said. "We have to leave in half an hour, but the waffles will be there for you whenever you come down. You can always heat them up in the microwave." He nodded a sleepy thanks and disappeared into the bathroom.

Before we could finally leave, I had to shovel my short walk, since the snow had come down heavily during our long night. Then I went back in and dragged the boys toward the door, saying good-bye to Russell and reminding him that Tommy had a key, since I didn't know who would be needing access. The boys hadn't yet noticed Sidney's absence. I wasn't sure when or what to tell them. Right before school wasn't the time, though.

Russell said, "I'll watch you get in, make sure no one's out there."

In the car Stevie said, "I like Russell. I like Tommy, too. I wish they lived with us all the time." Toby added, "Me, too."

"Who do you like most?" I asked stupidly, for I should have known the answer.

"Russell," said Toby. "Tommy," said Stevie. An argument followed.

I did manage to explain to them quickly that they would be staying at Mo's for a few days because I had some work to do and needed them out of the way. I had thought a lot about it in the wee hours, and this was the best I could come up with. They of course weren't about to let me get away with a useless explanation like that. But I stood firm and said don't worry, I'll tell you all about it in a few days, blah, blah. "Mo and Ivy never get to see you like they did when we were living there, and they really miss you. I told them that since I needed to do a whole bunch of work right now, this would be a good time for you to have a visit of a few days." I did some quick calculations in my head. Relieved, I said, "And this is Trevor's weekend with Ivy, so you'll get to see him more than you would normally. I thought it worked out for everyone." The thought of the more or less perpetual sleepover with Trevor did the trick. I just hoped Mo and Ivy weren't too inconvenienced by the whole thing; there just wasn't another option.

As soon as I arrived at work, I called Mo and told her what had happened the night before. She's an animal lover and gave the matter the weight it deserved. She offered to take the boys that night before I had a chance to ask; I felt enormous relief. She told me that she would get them at the bus stop but that I had to come over for dinner. She added, "Bring Tommy and Russell if they're there." I thanked her and rang off. Cindy had been walking by my office during part of my phone call; I went out to her desk and filled her in, partly, on the death of Sidney. She was appropriately sympathetic and horrified.

Talking about my poor cat's demise got me emotional again. I knew at least part of this was also sorrow at the need to have my boys live with someone else, even if it was only for a few days. They hadn't even really done sleepovers yet; I knew I had the reputation among their peers as being a bit overprotective. But I figured better that than the reverse. Maybe. I don't know.

Between morning classes, from around ten-thirty to eleven-thirty, I had office hours. I could feel my temperature drop at the thought that Tim Solomon might well visit me then. At least, I told myself as I walked back through the frozen air to the O'Henry Building, I'll be in my office. I'll leave the door open and just pretend he's someone else, someone I thought he was before last week, just some boy, any generically needy student.

I wished I could alert Cindy, could call for protection. I thought, maybe I can. I could call Tommy; maybe he could come here, be with me during this hour. Three thoughts bounced back simultaneously. (1), By the time he got here, the hour would be over. (2), I'd have to explain his presence to all and sundry. (3), I was afraid of how whiny and helpless this would make me sound. I'm not proud of the fact that number three was the clincher. Besides, I thought, getting no work done, he wasn't likely to murder me in my office, was he? He wasn't totally stupid.

I couldn't stay in my office continuously; I kept getting up and going to the bathroom. Cindy asked me if I was okay. I said maybe I was getting something, some stomach thing. After about a half hour Beverly Johansson, a student in my gender class, showed up at my door, causing my heart to leap achingly up till I saw she wasn't Tim. Whatever I told her seemed to satisfy her, but I have no memory of what it was or what the issue was that had brought her to my office to begin with.

Blessedly, it was time for my next class. I went, shuffling clumsily through notes, wondering what I was supposed to be talking about.

My two remaining classes were as exhausting an enterprise as any I've ever undertaken. By two-thirty, I was done teaching for the week, thank God, and completely sapped. Fortunately, all the other faculty members were elsewhere, so I could slip out without having to make too much small talk. I left as early as I could.

He was waiting by my car as I approached it. Our eyes met as I spotted him, so I couldn't just turn around, pretending to remember something I'd left in my office. Even then, I was aware of the absurdity of my inability to hurt the feelings of someone who almost certainly had none, at least not the kind I was used to. Of someone who was a killer, of boys and of cats.

I had the cell phone numbers of Tommy, Russell, and the constable on the speed dial of the phone in my bag. That knowledge helped me respond to Tim without quavering too badly.

"Tim, I told you I don't need any help around my house. I appreciate the offer, but you need to devote more time to your studies and less to my problems, anyway." I hadn't been aware till that moment how schoolmarmy I could be.

Tim looked confused but then recovered. "I understand, Dr. P. I need some help from you now. I still need to talk to you about my future. My grad school plans."

"I've told you, Tim. You'd be better off discussing all that with your adviser or one of the career counselors."

His face tensed. "Dr. P., I want your input on this as well. I really respect your opinion." He was blocking the door to my car nonchalantly, eyes continuously bobbing back and forth between my chest and my eyes. I was trying not to escalate things by telling him to move.

"Then, make an appointment and keep it. I've got to go now."

His brow rose. "Dr. P., I also have a personal problem that I could really use your help with." Oh God. "I'm having some problems with my girlfriend, Heather. She's a really jealous girl, Dr. P. I need some advice about how to handle that."

I'd had enough. "Tim, I don't give love life advice. Go to the counseling center if you really feel you have a problem. Otherwise, just talk to her. Or break up. I have no idea what you should do. But I need to be somewhere. Could you please move so I can get in my car?"

He hesitated, then moved a few inches to the side. "Please," he said.

"Not far enough," I answered. "You need to get out of my way, Tim. I'll see you on Monday."

He looked like he might cry. I had a flash of clinical interest in his emotional responses; then the irritation and fear returned. He moved some more, and I got my key in the lock of the driver's-side door. "Good-bye," I said as firmly as I could, and got in. I was afraid that he would try to muscle his way into the car, and so I closed the door as quickly as possible without slamming his nose in it. He backed off too slowly as I started the engine. He stepped farther away as the car started to move.

I dropped the suitcase at Mo's on the way home. The boys weren't there yet, so Mo wanted me to fill her in on the details. I gave her only the basics, promising more later, when I came back for dinner. I left as soon as she let me.

I wasn't sure who would be at my house and who wouldn't. It hit me on the drive home that this was the first time I'd left work to come home without going to get the boys unless they'd been sick or had the day off. I also didn't have to worry about getting dinner for them, or me, or anyone else. I had lied to Tim again; I didn't need to be anywhere in particular. It was both a bit exhilarating and depressing. I was so tired, however, that I was mostly grateful.

And it hit me then that Tommy was staying in my house and my kids were gone. I was appalled at the lurid fantasies that popped involuntarily into my head. I took a deep breath and pulled into my driveway. Sure enough, Tommy's car was the only one out front. That didn't mean Russell wasn't there. I got a grip and dragged my beaten, leaden body up the front steps and through the front door, wishing terribly that my boys were with me and that Sidney was waiting inside, eager to be let out, rubbing hairily against my legs. Instead, Tommy was sitting on the couch, waiting for me, and he looked up expectantly as I walked in the front door.

I had to work hard not to drop anything. He stood up and offered to help as the burdens that a second earlier had been no trouble at all now threatened to launch themselves into the air simultaneously. I'm not usually a klutzy person. Now, however, nothing that I put my hands on stayed there. My legs ceased to hold me up properly, nor could they carry me safely around a piece of furniture. I was blushing like I had the flu. We eventually got everything settled, he managed to put my satchel by the computer desk in the dining room, and I managed to get the purse and canvas bag I normally carried my lunch in to the kitchen. I thanked him, trying to keep the spate of gratitude to under a few hundred words. I finally calmed down, and he said that he needed to fill me in on what was going on. I made some tea, and we sat down at the kitchen table. I had no idea what he thought of my chaotic and confused entrance to my own home. He politely didn't mention it.

I told him about my most recent encounter with Tim and then told him Mo was getting the boys and had invited us to dinner. He said that sounded good as long as the surveillance folks could verify that neither Tim nor Jason was following us. All the time Tim was talking to me in the parking lot, someone had been close by, keeping an eye on us, supposedly. That was comforting, although I wasn't sure I entirely believed it. They had a local deputy, Jed Paley, watching Mo's house just in case. We needed to make sure that Tim didn't know where my kids were. It wouldn't be a bad thing if he knew we were alone in the house together; that might incite him to act in some way. I understood intellectually why that would be a good thing. But it made my insides icy.

If we went to Mo's, Tommy added, we needed to do it by car, not on foot, so that we weren't easy targets. Although, he said, if the police knew where both boys and now, incidentally, Heather were, then that wasn't such a risk.

"Easy targets for what? You think he's going to start picking us off?"

Tommy told me that Tim's father owned several firearms, two of which had been reported stolen in the last month. "Their apartment was supposedly broken into, but not much else was taken. If the guns are used in a crime, the Solomons can claim innocence." He told me what kinds of guns they were, but I have no slots in my mind for such things and just nodded. He also said that any time we were out of the house, in plain sight, we needed to wear Kevlar vests. They didn't want to take any chances that what happened to Sidney or, presumably, Brad Franco would happen to anyone else.

"What worries us the most," he said, "is that big hillside below you. It's steep and woody, and it's hard to patrol. And it backs onto that small shopping center down on Templeton." That was one of Tenway's main drags. "We don't have the manpower we'd like. They've got the security people in the stores there alerted, so they'll let us know if they see his car parked there. If I were him and I wanted to watch you, that's what I'd do, and then climb up on foot. I was down there earlier today. There are tons of places to hide: lots of brush and any number of places where, with binoculars, you could get a pretty good look at your front porch. I don't think he could see inside to speak of, although I think drawn blinds would be a good rule of thumb."

This was upsetting on multiple levels; the beautiful woods across the street had been one of the big attractions of our house when I'd bought it. I didn't at all like the way circumstances were forcing my view of it to shift.

I called Mo to make sure the boys were there and safe. They were. Mo said they were going to eat on the early side and suggested we come as soon as possible. Tommy checked with his colleagues; the three amigos were all accounted for. Nevertheless, we took Tommy's car just in case. The vests were in a bulky case in the backseat.

Molly was out, apparently on a date, not with Russell. I was a little relieved at this; the two of them were alike in their lack of monogamy. Ivy asked about Russell. Tommy said, "He'll be here on surveillance tomorrow. He's got stuff to do in the city tonight." When I asked if anyone had talked to Jessie, he told me that the constable had, but she hadn't seen anything.

The boys were happy to see me and ecstatic to see Tommy. Mo and Ivy had a dog named Frodo, a mutt happily rescued from certain execution. Frodo was also glad to see Tommy, although he is far less discriminating than my boys. Trevor even looked especially friendly, although after we ate some fried chicken and salad together, none of the boys stuck around us for long. They went off to play with Trevor's

Nintendo and left us to drink, except Tommy. He and I kept Mo and Ivy somewhat in the dark about the level of danger we expected, but the fact that the boys were there told them enough.

"Shit, Gina, you do attract trouble," Mo said, a glass of Chardonnay in her hand. She started to fill Tommy in on the whole Awful Bragging Man situation, but I interrupted her as soon as I realized where she was heading.

"Mo, that was a year ago, and it lasted all of two months. It was pretty humiliating."

"Well, whatever. You're considered a sort of sexual icon on campus. Tell them, Ivy."

"They don't call her anything terribly original or creative. Just the Hidden Hottie, also known as the Shrinking Violet, since you don't dress up or wear tight clothes. But haven't you noticed how many boys are in your classes? I mean, you get some girls, but it's the boys who really keep you in business." Both of them were a little drunk. I suspected that they were trying to impress Tommy on my behalf. I was starting to wonder how much Mo drank these days. I tried to cut off these lists of my "accomplishments," but Mo chimed in again. "And don't think she does anything to provoke this. I've seen it. She doesn't do anything. That's the amazing thing, Tommy. Just go somewhere with Gina and watch what happens. Men turn into these gelatinous freaks, no offense to present company. I've seen *gay* men follow her around, totally smitten."

Ivy continued, relentless. "You should see some of her student evaluations. She won't show them to me. I have to go over to the faculty assessment office and sneak peeks."

Tommy had a painfully polite smile on his face. "Please," I said, "please. I'm really exhausted. I need to go home."

Mo reminded me to extend an invitation to Tommy to see Ivy's stage debut the next night. "It's community theater, but Ivy's great. The whole cast is, actually. You should come. You'll still be with Gina then, right?"

All eyes shifted to him in one movement. "Probably. It all depends on what action our friends take, if any. If all stays quiet, I'll be around tomorrow night for sure."

I found the boys and gave them a big hug and kiss, leaving them happily doing something GI Joe–related upstairs with Trevor. I went back downstairs; Tommy made a quick phone call on his cell phone to check on the status of things out in the big bad world, and we left. As we walked to his old Mercedes, he waved at a man in an unmarked car parked a slight way down the street. He opened the car door for me; after I got in, I felt a depression that clung to me like cobwebs.

I sucked in my breath. "You know they were exaggerating for effect, to tell a better story, right?" Then I thought, you shouldn't have said anything, should have pretended like it never happened. That would have been the classy thing to do.

He sucked on his cigarette and blew a ribbon of smoke out his window, which was open a sliver at the top. "I believe that." The words were nice, but his affect was flat as a board.

We didn't say much as we went back to the house. The wind was picking up, and what had been a cold night was turning into an icy one. We had only a couple of blocks to drive, so the slick spots forming on the road weren't too threatening. But I hoped that this would keep Tim Solomon, and the now much more ominous-seeming Jason Dettwiler, far away from my little home.

chapter fifteen

[Western cultures] have been peculiarly confused by the power-ful instrument of language. It has run away with them like a new gadget with a child, so that excessive verbal communica-tion is really the characteristic disease of the West. We are sim-ply unable to stop it, for when we are not talking to others we are compulsively thinking, that is, talking subvocally to our-selves. Communication has become a nervous habit . . .

ALAN WATTS, *Nature, Man and Woman*

WE GOT BACK to the house and went in without speaking. I checked the answering machine; there was another jovial message from John Fagin that I stopped quickly and then deleted. Tommy had to have observed that, but he made no comment.

It was only seven o'clock. I decided to use some of the exercise equipment in the basement, so I went upstairs and changed into some non-revealing sweats. Tommy told me he was going to do some paper-work and asked if he could use my computer. I got him set up and went downstairs. About thirty minutes later the room was suddenly completely black. The power had gone out.

My basement was below ground, so it was literally impossible for me to see anything at all, including my hands or feet. I stood still for a minute, hoping my eyes would become accustomed enough at least to be able to make it to the steps without hurting myself. I heard Tommy calling down: "Gina, can you tell me where you keep candles, matches, flashlights?" I directed him to a flashlight in the kitchen, which he obligingly shone down the basement stairs, allowing me to come up without barking my shins.

"Thanks," I said, and together we found some candles and matches. The power went out in Tenway often; I kept an abundant supply of those items around. I had neglected the basement, though; in the future I'd have to remedy that.

We both peeked outside and could see through the fat snowfall that the streetlights were out and no other houses were illuminated. That was actually good news; we didn't have to worry that Tim had severed the electrical lines into my house with some Hitchcockian plot in mind. I checked the corded phone and got a dial tone. More good news. My stomach clenched, though, when I realized that the power might be off at Mo's as well; Toby was terrified of the dark, and Stevie always got anxious about candles burning the house down during a power outage. I called; Ivy told me that their power was on. I said good night again, apologizing for the call, very relieved.

Tommy suggested that we turn on the fire in the gas grate. That would provide a lot more light than our teensy candles as well as warming us up. I left him to do that while I went into the kitchen to make some decaf on my gas stove, which could be lit manually. I had a stove top Pyrex percolator I kept for such occasions. Within about ten minutes I brought out a tray with the coffee and fixings, along with an ashtray. I told him he could smoke inside; the boys were gone, and I was kind of enjoying the smell. Nostalgia for a type of freedom. He put up a polite protest, but we both saw it for the feeble thing it was. He lit up, comically relieved. This coziness, the fire, the tobacco, and the coffee, were reminiscent of the party only five days before. I said this, and somehow the subject of Lizzie came up and how prickly she was with me.

He said, "She's jealous of you, obviously."

I said, "I don't know why, really."

His brows came together, and he moved his hand over his mouth again, keeping himself from saying something, then removed it. "Is it hard, looking like you do? I mean, do you think it makes your life easier, or harder, or what?"

"How I look?" I was embarrassed into silence. Then I said, "I don't know. It's how I look. What do I compare it to? Is it hard looking like you look?" I couldn't stop myself from getting defensive.

"Sorry. I guess it's not a fair question. I've known a few really beautiful women, and most of them were crippled in some other way. I guess I was curious in what way you thought it might have, I don't know, impeded you."

"I'm sorry," he said again at my silence. "I don't mean to be insulting." He looked pensive and a little miserable.

My heart was banging against my ribs so loudly, I couldn't hear much else for a moment. "You're not being insulting. You're being complimentary. I just don't know how to answer a question like that without sounding like a complete drip."

"Well, here's a more neutral question. How long were you a model?"

I thought for a second. "Full-time, about seven years. I did some stuff after that, but then I was in graduate school, and I only took the occasional job for a couple of years after that."

"And that stopped when you had your kids?"

"Yep."

"How the hell old were you when you started? You must have been just a baby."

"Sixteen." He asked me about this, so I told him the story of how Mindy Stafford and I had driven to Jacksonville, two hours away, the Big Orange in our part of the world, because I had my old Chevy Nova that I'd bought with waitressing money, and she wanted to go to the big Lane-Simons department store there for modeling tryouts. Mindy was two inches taller than I was and weighed about the same. She wasn't particularly pretty, but she was skinny and determined. I was too short, I thought, too round-faced, not to mention too above it all. I had no intention of doing something so vacuous with my life.

I waited for Mindy as she stood in line with many other long skinny girls, like a field of immensely tall flesh-colored wheat. I sat at a table with a "Co-cola" in the little coffee shop at the back of the store, reading a book. I had just finished it and was worried that I couldn't afford to buy another one and maybe couldn't even afford another Coke.

A woman was having coffee at a table next to me, so understated in her bearing and clothing that I had no idea that she was rich, at least by my standards, or that she was anyone of significance. After a while, I have no idea how long, I realized that she had been looking at me. I was about to smart-mouth her, ask her if I looked like a long-lost granddaughter, which would have been a terrible insult as she only admitted, ever, to being in her (early) forties. She finished her coffee before I could get that bon mot out, however, and stood up, walking over to me with obvious purpose. She asked me my name, and when I told her, she said, "No, that sounds way too ethnic. I like the Gina part. Gina, Gina . . . Paulson. Lose ten pounds, although fifteen would be better, and be in New York by the middle of next month. I'll make you so much money, you can buy whatever horrible little dogleg you call home in a year if you want to." She handed me a card, "Mary Glenn Agency," with a New York address and phone numbers.

I smiled at him. "So I lost twelve pounds, got on a Greyhound, and went."

"Sixteen? My God, I can't imagine letting a daughter go to New York to do that on her own. On a bus?" I nodded and smiled. "What about school?"

"I was done with high school. And there wasn't any money to pay for college. So it seemed like a good idea to everybody." Except to my father, who wanted me to stay around, to work for him, to be his companion, to take care of him. Grammy saved me from the guilt about leaving him. "He's a piece of shit, Genie. Go and get the hell out of here. He's not your son, he's mine." And even he relented soon enough, when he realized what kind of money I'd be sending home. Lots and lots of money. I kept this to myself.

Tommy said, "Did you drop out?"

"No," I said. "I skipped fourth grade. I was done early."

He was silent for a moment, and I thought, Hah, surprised you on that one, didn't I?

"How big a town was Stoweville?"

"Not very. And I hadn't been out of it much before then, either."

He smiled. "So what did you think of New York City?"

"Pretty much what I think now. I'm just not woman enough for it." This elicited seriously knit brows. "I mean, it's just too much for me. Too hard. Too loud. Too expensive, too big. I was raised in a backwoods swamp, for Christ's sake. My first time there was like *Tammy and the Bachelor*. Only with Mary Glenn as the bachelor, which made the story a whole lot less heartwarming, let me tell you."

I had a stomach-churning memory of the confusion and mild panic I experienced as the bus got closer and closer to the city. I was so impatient, so terrified, so hungry, so itchy with bus filth and teenage greasiness. I saw the skyline and felt the most visceral fear I'd ever experienced. That was the first time it occurred to me with certainty that I was doing something big, dangerous, and probably stupid. I kept having little fits, a burbling hysteria that I mostly repressed but that kept escaping from me in little chirps of terror as I eyed the alien landscape, housing projects and industries and shopping centers and corporate centers and building after building after building after building, and more cars than I imagined existed in the whole United States, all out on those highways. So much concrete, it made my skin ache with the thought of touching it. The pumpkin-shaped woman in the seat next to me seemed bored, although she shot a few barbed looks my way at my tiny outbursts; I guessed she had done this before, maybe lived there, was used to the idea of such a place existing in real life.

Once I got to the street outside the bus station, I was beyond terrified, just wandering, sleepwalking out the glass doors into the hot, sweaty sunshine. It was July, and I couldn't tell you which hit me hardest upon leaving the relative shelter of the Greyhound terminal, the smell or the noise. Heat I was used to. But I'd never smelled car exhaust this intense, this concentration of urine and vomit and smog and body odor and grease and anger anywhere before. Ever. I some-times wondered if this was what drove my friend Mindy Stafford's old golden retriever, Idjit, crazy on occasion—this kind of assault of scent that you couldn't overlook, couldn't move beyond, but could only stand there, riveted and revolted, almost gunned down by the thick air.

And the noise, the roar of cars and horns and people talking and yelling, and a dull, almost choral hum that I was to associate forever after with New York City. I heard once in a class at the New School when I was getting my BA that the static that you see on dead TV channels is actually the background noise of the universe, the radia-tion that's what's left of the Big Bang. That was New York City, the screaming white noise that you'd hear on a TV set the size of Man-hattan Island, turned all the way up, just a short while after its own violent birth.

It wasn't clear to me even then how I wound up in a cab. There seemed to be lots of people yelling and gesturing forcefully at me, and I remember just trying to do what they said. The cab driver was a native English speaker, which I didn't know then was a rarity. I still thought his accent bizarre and upsetting; he sounded like someone from a TV crime drama and not anyone I would have to deal with in real life. I dug Mary's softened and crinkled card out of my jeans pocket and told him the address. I have no idea what he thought about this filthy teenage rube heading to such a posh address. Maybe nothing, maybe he wouldn't have cared if I'd been raped and killed the moment I stepped out of his cab, but I seem to remember a mo-ment, just a brief delay, when he asked me as I paid him with wadded dollar bills, do you know where you're going? Do you have some-one waiting for you? I said, oh sure, thanks. I didn't tip him; I didn't know you were supposed to. Of course, once I was out of the cab, the buildings, the sheer scale of them once you were close up, made me unable to breathe. When I got to Mary's building on Park Ave-nue, I had to look at the building number above the door from under my hand, as though I were saluting the place. I couldn't bear to look up for fear that I would be crushed by the very sight of a structure that large.

"The receptionist was appalled by me and didn't believe that Mary had ever said I could come there. I had to wait in the hall for three hours. But eventually she came and got me set up in one of the apartments she kept for yokels like me. She cleaned me up, and got me jobs, and got the legal forms to my parents for them to sign, since I was a minor."

"So why did you quit? Twenty-three is pretty damn young to retire, even for a model."

"Why would you possibly want to know this?"

"This is a universe I don't get at all. It's kind of fascinating in a grisly sort of way. No offense."

"Oh, I think I know what you mean. Well, I didn't expect to quit altogether. I expected to come back to it after a sort of academic break. I was getting sick of being treated as though I was an idiot, and being surrounded by idiots. And I was getting grossed out by myself, you know, feeling so elitist, feeling so much smarter than everyone around me. They weren't all stupid. Just incredibly shallow. But the shallowness was deep, if you know what I mean. Things like how someone had her hair cut or the drape of fabric over someone's ass was a really, really big deal. It was easy to get sucked into it, the self-importance, the surreal grandiosity of the whole thing. But I was at some party and actually met the lead singer of a famous band, Gimme It. You've heard of Pearly Benoit?"

Tommy nodded, grinning now.

"He said something about natural law, I don't remember what, and I said something like that even natural laws change because they're man-made. He was with some tube-topped girl with the body of a twelve-year-old boy who looked at me like I was incredibly stupid and said, 'What about gravity? That's *forever!*' And Pearly made some dumbass joke about gravity and threesomes. And I'm pretty sure that's when I thought I needed to do something, be somewhere where I could talk to people about something other than clothes and skin and sex and hair and diets and weight."

His smile was softer now. "I can relate. A lot of cops are pretty narrow in what they talk about, and think is important, and think is the whole world. It kind of sounds similar, though I know that's a weird thing to say. But this intense focus on one dimension of human experience, as though that's the only part of it that really counts, or even exists—that's really familiar. And just as bizarre, in its own way, if you think about it." He looked back at the fire for a moment, then at me. "So you went to college, to graduate school. Did it help? Did you find what you wanted?"

I sighed, wondering how I could get him to talk more and wishing I could stop talking so much. "Sort of. But most of the people I met in graduate school just wanted to be famous within academia, wanted prestige, and wanted to get laid and get drunk, just like the people I left in Manhattan. It was both depressing and weirdly reassuring. It helped a little. Not as much as I'd hoped. But I thought I could somehow go back and forth. But then, of course, I got pregnant."

"Do you regret it at all?"

"Of course I do. A lot of the time, actually. I mean, I love my sons, but I still regret that I was stupid enough to get pregnant in the first place. I'll obviously never tell them that. But it was my stupidity, and I do realize how many gifts I've been given, so I can't really complain that much. Most single mothers aren't anywhere near as lucky as I am, in lots of ways."

I had, to my horror, broken Grammy's Rule Number Two, which was to never, ever talk too much to a man you were attracted to. Not for any reason, especially about yourself. You had to listen to what he said, ask pertinent questions. You were not to fake inordinate interest in things you were totally bored with, but you were, as much as possible, to be sparklingly attentive and answer questions with reasonable self-control and brevity. Too much self-exposure too soon or all at once was pompous and trashy. When it came to courtship, there were few things worse in Grammy's eyes than being a know-it-all. I had no choice at that point but to say something to that effect to Tommy, making Grammy sound more prissy than she actually was. I said that this was to be the general practice around all men; in reality, Grammy expected me to do this only around men for whom I "had the nimnams." I added, "You've obviously got the interrogator touch, you know, 'Where were you on the thirteenth?' and the perp just vomits forth her life history."

He smiled, and it was a smile of such sweetness that I couldn't breathe for a moment, couldn't think of a thing to say, couldn't look away. Then air managed to squeeze back into my lungs, and I said, "So what's your story? I'm tired of being such an open book. Please reciprocate and divulge something. Please. I'm feeling boorish."

Of course, he managed self-control and brevity but still managed, I realized later, to give me a lot of information. I asked why, for instance, he'd become a cop.

"That's easy to answer," he said. "My mother was killed by a mugger when I was fourteen."

I sucked in my breath, grimacing, feeling clumsy. "Oh God, Tommy. That's terrible. I'm so sorry."

"That was a long time ago. It was worse on my older sister. She's been clucking over me and my dad ever since, trying to take Mom's place. It tends to drive me crazy, but she's really pretty sweet. Just neurotic as hell."

I turned his question around. "Has it helped? I mean, has it been therapeutic, being a detective?"

He sighed. "Actually, I think it may have made things a little worse, always seeing people at their worst, or the worst people. I'm thinking of getting out, maybe soon. I've got options. I've done a lot of different stuff. It's okay with me to change again."

"Like what else? I mean, what else have you done?"

He smiled again. "I used to be a baseball player."

"Really? I would've expected football or even basketball."

"No, I played in the minors after college for a while."

"I'd ask what position, but I'm too ignorant to know what that would mean."

The smile widened. "Center field. Then I went to China for a while, teaching English."

"Why China?"

He shrugged, lighting his third cigarette. I suddenly ached for one but resisted it. "I liked it, liked the history. I wanted the challenge of it. I figured if I could learn Chinese, I could learn anything." He stopped for a moment, then continued. "I don't think it's good for many people to deal with criminals your whole adult life. Although for some cops it's a kind of calling."

"But not for you?"

"I don't think so, not anymore." He sighed. "I was approached by an editor, someone I went to college with. She wants me to write a book on law enforcement, some case studies. She has TV connections and is interested in me consulting on some stuff. There are a number of possibilities."

"That's fabulous. You should do it, take a leave of absence or something."

"I've been thinking about it. I'm really trusting you with this; no one knows about this yet. Not Russell, not anybody. So please don't mention it."

"No problem." I felt absurdly flattered.

He shrugged again. "I'm a pretty good teacher and liked it when I did it. Criminology is becoming a big deal on a lot of campuses, including yours." He smiled again, took a breath. Then he saddened, looking at the fire. "Doing what I do makes it difficult to have normal relationships with other people. You see everyone as scum after a while if you're not careful. And you can never tell what your schedule is going to be. You work ridiculous hours."

I thought, it would be so easy, he's so close, all I'd have to do would be to scoot a little, push up next to him, kiss him right on the mouth, I could have him, I know I could. Stop, I thought then, stop. He'll hate you later. He'll know what kind of girl you are, what kind of out-of-control nut you really are. He's got a girlfriend. Not a serious one, he says. But still. Stop.

He said, "So why aren't you married again? Or involved? Someone like you must get asked out a lot, must get pursued a lot." He'd heard the phone messages from John Fagin, I realized.

I almost laughed, thinking, what if I said what I believed, however cornily, to be the truth: Because I hadn't met you yet? Instead I said honestly, "I don't get asked that often, really. Sometimes the reasons are obvious: they're married, I don't like them, whatever. I just always say no." I didn't know how to say, but I wouldn't with you. Ask me, ask me. For all I know, right then, he would have. But then the lights came crashing on.

Well, of course there was no actual crash. It was just that the lights were so relatively bright that it felt like an impact, and the refrigerator and the computer came buzzing back on at the same time, so the whole house seemed to swell with purpose. We could see each other way too well all of a sudden.

I said with false jollity, "Well, now that there's light, I realize that I'm beat. I think I'm going to turn in." Tommy didn't say anything for a moment, just looked at the fire. Then he said, "Okay. I'm going to stay up for a while. I'll turn all the lights off. I'll see you tomorrow." I couldn't read him at all. He seemed all business, polite, firm. I carried the coffee tray back in the kitchen, wondering what it would be like if I were reckless, if I still had the kind of courage that it must have taken to get me to New York in the first place.

I came back through the living room on my way to the stairs. "Sleep well, Tommy."

He looked at me then, smiled very swiftly, and said, "Sure. Good night. Sleep well, Gina." He then looked away, into the fire. I went up.

In my bedroom, changing into pajamas, I thought, looking like I do used to mean power. But I realized somewhere along the line that in order to claim it, I had to give most of it away. I had loathed it then, and the paradoxical dependency that accompanied it like a shadow. Now, I thought, it means hiding. I don't know how not to hide anymore.

Before going to sleep, I reset my clock, which was blinking irritatingly. It hit me as I was pressing buttons that I didn't need to set the alarm for the next day; the boys were Mo's responsibility the next morning. Or, rather, Ivy's, knowing Mo. I didn't have to get up. It was kind of cool but also made me feel vaguely panicky. Unstructured and unstrung.

During the night, I don't know the exact time, but after the whole house was dark, I sort of woke up. I say "sort of" because I didn't feel in control of my body at all but was conscious of what I was doing. I wasn't, however, capable of judging my actions with any of the lucidity I could when awake. I know this because I got up without turning on any lights, left my room, crossed the hall into the guest bedroom, and climbed in next to Tommy's sleeping body. I curled up on my side, facing away from him, with my rear end pressed against his hip, and then went back to sleep. I have a clear memory of doing this but no memory of why, other than that I felt chilly. I have another dim memory of turning over and feeling his hand resting lightly on my hip.

When dawn came, I did something else so unlike me, so out of control, as though I hadn't already crossed an enormous social boundary, that it scared me for weeks afterward. I was awake; I can't use being asleep as an excuse, although I certainly let Tommy think that later. But I wasn't fully lucid yet. I remember it vividly, my desire, how warm his body and the sheets under the blankets were, his face with a five o'clock shadow so dark it almost made his face blue. I looked at his mouth, feeling the heat next to me, and rolled over on top of him, putting my arms around his big chest, and kissed him full on the mouth, not caring about the sour tang of my morning breath or his, pungent and tobaccoey. I kept at it, too, kept kissing him until I got a response, which didn't take long. His arms, hot and big, came around my shoulders, and his mouth opened.

I have no idea how long this went on. He rolled me on my back in a moment, and I could feel him pushing into my belly. We both were fully clothed, in sweat pants and T-shirts, which only made our contact softer and warmer. My eyes were closed at that point, but I was not remotely asleep. I could feel the exact moment when he came completely awake. His face pulled away from mine, although the rest of him didn't, not immediately.

"Gina, wake up," he said, sleepy and low. I opened my eyes to see his brown ones peering puffily at me from about three inches away. "I don't know if this is very smart of us," he added as he watched my rise to full consciousness.

I didn't wake up; I'd known exactly what I was doing. But I hadn't been *thinking* about what I was doing; in opening my eyes, I opened my brain as well. "Oh my God," I said.

. . .

I don't know how many "I'm sorry"s I said then; I know it was a lot of them. I ran into the bathroom, staring at myself in the mirror. I can't believe I did that, I kept mouthing. I can't believe it. I took a rapid shower, compounding my offenses by not letting the poor man in the bathroom for a while. I dashed out, clad in my robe, into my bedroom, carefully closing the door behind me.

I got dressed in something safe, jeans and a sweater. I took a breath, not knowing what I was going to say, and went out into the hallway. He came out of his room at the same time, and we stood in the hallway, looking at each other. It didn't occur to me till much later that he'd probably been waiting for me to come out.

"Gina," he said, smiling gently. "It's okay. I know people who sleepwalk. I know it's a weird situation. You don't have to feel embarrassed."

"But I am embarrassed. I'm really, really sorry, Tommy. I mean, I know that if the situation were reversed, I could have you arrested for sexual assault."

"I have no intention of pressing charges." Gentle smile. He was talking to me, I realized, as he would to someone on a ledge, threatening to jump. He went on, voice low and steady, don't excite the crazy. "Soon this will all be over; you can get your kids back, get back to your normal life. I'll be out of your hair forever."

I was helpless to prevent my face from falling, to stop my sorrow from filling my eyes. This time I could see the moment, see when he read my face. His expression got neutral and inward, considering something new. I could tell the moment when it first dawned on him that I was in love with him.

He kept looking at me with that nonexpression. I tried to fill the silence, opened my mouth, but nothing came out. Then I pulled away, looking at the stairs, saying, "I'm going to make coffee."

He followed me down. I was starting to feel shaky and very fearful. He said, "Gina, is there something we should talk about? Is there stuff I should know?"

I couldn't look at him at all and busied myself with the coffee and raw eggs and bread. Finally, I said, trying to smile, "Okay, you told me stuff that I'm not supposed to tell. You have to reciprocate. You can't tell anyone I did that this morning. Please. Leave me some dignity."

He replied, pretending to laugh, "Okay. Okay. But that would have been a good one. You owe me."

I was grateful that he wasn't forcing the issue any more. So I said, "Okay, so I owe you."

After breakfast he checked in with his law enforcement cohort. He reported that both Tim and Jason were on campus. Tommy decided that he'd go with me to do my normal Friday errands but that we didn't need the vests on to do the shopping; he had his cell phone with him in case the situation changed. He also wanted to go with me to get some better locks. Before we left, I started shoveling the snow, as a lot had fallen during the night. Tommy came out the front door and took the shovel from me; I argued with him stupidly for about thirty seconds, then thought, Jesus, let him, why don't you? I went back inside to get lists and coupons for the shopping trip. When I came back outside, Tommy had also shoveled Jessie's walk. I assumed that would please her, but you could never be entirely sure.

For me, it was strange shopping with anyone, and with Tommy it was immensely so. Poor Arnie; seeing me with Tommy put the final kibosh on any little play romance we were working on. Tommy didn't touch me, didn't even look directly at me very much. But he was much more imposing than my little produce hippie, who just seemed to shrivel in Tommy's presence. I thought sadly, I'll miss our little chats, Arnie. We then visited a small hardware shop near the grocery store, and Tommy picked out a few locks, mostly for windows. I paid for them; he said he could put them in. I told him I might not have the right tools; he said he'd brought a toolbox in his car, expecting this. I resented that in a diffuse, irrational way and said so. He just laughed. Oddly, that helped break the tension between us.

The second greatest luxury of the day was the help getting the groceries into the house. He told me to put things away while he brought everything in. We both had lunch, then I left him on his own while I did what seemed to be a hundred loads of laundry. He spent the next several hours putting in the locks on the back door and the downstairs windows. I offered to help, but he politely ignored me. I then offered to wash whatever dirty clothes he'd accumulated. That got a look that indicated that I was out of my mind. I said, feeling daring, "I'm not offering to be your maid. I'm just doing laundry, and underwear holds no mysteries for me. If you want me to throw it in so you don't have to wash it later, I'll do it. It's not a commitment."

In the middle of the afternoon I called Mo and told her I'd bring sandwiches to her house that night, and we could go from there to the play. After the house was clean enough, I did some class prep on my laptop at the kitchen table, as Tommy was using the big computer in the dining room. After a few hours I called again to make sure the boys were at Mo's, safe and sound. Then I made the sandwiches and went upstairs to get dressed. I decided to get gussied up for the first time in several years. I thought about going really nuts, doing the serious glamour thing, trying to stop hiding, trying to impress Tommy in some way. But I'd always found those old movies, the ones where the girl with glasses and bad clothes gets made over into a glasses-free, makeup-wearing, hairsprayed babe, and then the hero can actually see her, can tell how worthwhile she really is, profoundly depressing. I could never suspend my disbelief long enough to stop thinking, but what about ten years from now, or two, or even two weeks, when she wakes up with her hair weird and her makeup smeared and her breath funky? Does she have to make sure he never sees that so that he'll still like her? I know this sounds ridiculous given how I used to live. But I thought, if he doesn't like you in glasses, honey, I guess you can get contacts. But make sure you never get conjunctivitis or you'll have to choose between your man and finding the bathroom on the first try.

But I still put on makeup and shaved my legs. I had reached my thirty-third year, the age of wisdom, and I was trying to adopt the Middle Path in everything I could. So I did something else that I hadn't in some time: I wore a dress. It was a nice dress but button-down, plaid, a teensy bit above the knee. An appropriate dress.

I came down a bit later. Tommy was on his phone, talking to God knows whom. As our eyes met, he stopped talking for just a second, staring at me. You'd have thought I'd painted my face green and glued turkey feathers to my head. I ignored him and got the sandwiches ready for transport. I wondered for a moment what his girlfriend, Becky or Rebecca, was doing this evening. I pushed away guilt; I hadn't asked him to be here. None of this was my idea.

When he got off the phone, I told him we needed to get to Mo's soon. He went upstairs and came back down shortly, looking about the same, if a little damper and less stubbly. He said we should make sure we had the vests with us. Right now Tim and Jason were on campus, but I lived only about ten minutes away, and we didn't want to be caught without them. That still gave me the willies, but not in a way that made me want to argue.

At Mo's the boys were sweet and clingy; it was both nice and painful that they missed me so much. Molly was gone again; I wondered if she was avoiding me, but didn't want to ask. I wasn't going to tell Mo the role Molly had played in Sidney's death. Molly could tell her sister what she wanted.

As Mo and I laid out the sandwiches, Toby yelled out, in no context I was aware of, "Suck 'em, boys!" Trevor and Stevie ignored him, but my attention of course lurched his way. Trying not to overreact and thus make the situation more interesting than it needed to be, I said, "You say 'sic 'em,' Toby." My son then explained that he'd had an idea for a story about vampire attack dogs, so you'd say "suck 'em" instead of "sic 'em." Mo and I exchanged a look. Tommy left the room in a hurry, his face averted. He came back in a few minutes, collected. We ate and rode together to the theater in Mo's van. Ivy had gone there straight from work. At the theater I was surprised to see Bobbie and Clark. Lottie would have been there, too, Bobbie said, but she was feeling a bit poorly. Donna, of course, was working a night shift at the hospital.

Now, I'm pretty easy to please when it comes to entertainment. But in this case the wooden delivery, ill-fitting costumes, inappropri-ate accents, and hammy speechifying made me hot with embarrassment for everyone involved. I looked over at Mo at one point when Ivy was lurching across the stage, screaming some conversation with the poor man (I later found out he was the third-grade teacher in the boys' school) playing Elwood P. Dowd. Mo's face was uplifted as in religious ecstasy. I thought to myself, that's love. I made the mistake of looking once at Tommy. His eyes met mine. He was completely expressionless, which made me want to start shrieking with laughter. He must have seen that in my face, for he then bit his lip. I rigidly avoided looking that way for the rest of the play.

We clapped enthusiastically during each scene change and at the end. The boys were happy because they knew someone on the stage and hadn't seen *Harvey* before in any form. I thought I'd wait a while before showing them the movie lest they realize too soon how bad this was. Mo was bubbly. Bobbie and Clark had on neutral expressions that I was trying to copy. We waited for Ivy, who eventually came out, face greasy and colorful. Mo hugged her carefully, and the rest of us gushed and applauded. Ivy said that there was to be a cast party the next night that promised to be a great bash, and we were all invited, kids as well. Tommy said that sounded like fun, a bit dubiously. Of course, we didn't know that it was going to be impossible.

We rode back to Mo's in her van. I helped get the boys ready for bed and kissed and hugged them. I could see that Toby and Stevie, while excited to be staying with the revered Trevor, were starting to feel the weirdness of not being home and weren't so sure anymore how much fun this was. I jollied them as much as I could and left them to sleep, feeling like I was bleeding internally.

Tommy was on his cell phone again. He turned to me and said, "Tim's car is in the lot below your house. We have to assume he's in the woods watching. We're going to wear the vests to the house. We're not taking chances."

This severely rattled both me and Mo, but Tommy was all business. He brought the vests in from his car and gave me a quick lesson in putting one on. It wasn't as heavy as I feared but it was heavy enough. I put my coat on over it, as did he. We went to his car and drove home.

. . .

We walked up to the porch. It was terribly cold, as it had been the whole winter so far, and I couldn't wait to get inside. It was very difficult not to turn and stare out into the trees down below the end of the street, where Tim Solomon was supposedly observing us. I was getting ready to put the key in the lock. Tommy stopped me with a light touch on my shoulder and said, "Wait, you've got something in your hair, a bug or something." I turned from the door with my key in my hand, and he raised his hand to my head, and then I heard something that sounded like the pop of an exploding lightbulb. Immediately, Tommy made a loud "uh" sound and fell into me. He was very big, very heavy, and we crashed to the floor of the porch together, with him becoming dead weight on top of me. I was completely confused and pushed him over a bit, trying to get out from under him, from under his asphyxiating weight. But he held me there, pinned me under him, grunted in a new voice, "No, stay down," and I realized that he'd been shot.

chapter sixteen

I WAS WAITING FOR BLOOD, for some oozing, draining warmth to touch me, to creep onto me from the wound I imagined in his back. He was obviously incapacitated in some way, his breathing clawing and abraded. But at least he was still breathing, I thought distantly and calmly. I had time (though how much I have no idea) to think insanely, huh, he's lying on top of me; Ellie would tell me to enjoy it. I squeezed out enough breath to say "Tommy? Are you okay? Are you bleeding?"

"Not that I know of." His voice was raspy and low. "My back hurts like hell, and I'm having trouble taking a deep breath, but I don't think I'm hurt too badly. Hard to tell. And we shouldn't try to get up till we know it's clear." His breath smelled nice; I thought, again from a planet away, that he must have had a breath mint in the car, which was possible, since I didn't remember him smoking on the ride home. Then I could hear something, rustling, car doors slamming, radios scratching and pinging. Then, "Jesus, Jesus, Tommy, Gina." Russell's voice, sounding scared shitless. Tommy got lighter, then was pulled off me altogether. Big hands lifted me as well and put me on my feet. My legs weren't cooperating, and I drooped, rag doll–like, on the arm that was offered. It turned out to be the constable.

"Hi," I said. "I think he's been shot. Is he going to die?"

"No, dear. That's why we wear the vests, you know. You been hit anywhere you know of?"

"No, I'm fine." And then I started trembling. "Is he going to be okay?" I pulled away from McCandless and dropped on my knees to where Tommy was lying on the porch, hurting one of them as I slapped against the wooden planking. Russell was already kneeling next to him, feeling parts of him and talking briskly into his radio. I could hear brush rustling on the dark hillside, could see the sweep of flashlights through the trees. There were low, grunting distant voices and more softly barking radios.

There was a sudden increase in the commotion on the hillside and then a shout, followed by another, then much crackling from the radios. Russell and the constable looked up, alert, and McCandless put his radio to his mouth, saying something that sounded like "Come on." There was an answer that sounded garbled to me but that he seemed to understand. He looked at Russell and gave a thumbs-up. "They got him."

Russell smiled a nasty smile, then looked down. "You hear that?" he said to Tommy, grin widening. Tommy answered with a weaker thumbs-up as the ambulance rolled slowly up the narrow street, careful not to ricochet off the densely packed cars on the sides.

"How did you get here?" I muttered through numb lips. Russell said he had been on surveillance. They'd been watching my house since they'd realized that Tim was there.

When people talk about events that shock as passing by in a blur, I now know what they mean. Some of what happened later is so hyperclear in my mind that I could paint a picture or describe it in such detail that no one would believe what a good witness I was. Everything else, either I have no memory of at all or my memories are distorted and fragmentary. I know that someone put a blanket around me, and I distinctly remember that I could tell it was warm, even through my coat. That felt so disproportionately wonderful, I kept trying to thank whoever had given it to me and felt intense frustration when I couldn't find the right person. But the warmth of the blanket paradoxically made me start shaking so hard, I was absently afraid that I might chip a tooth. Russell and the constable, the only comfortably familiar faces, kept floating on and off the porch, where I seemed to be headquartered. It seemed as though I wasn't allowed to go inside for some reason, although I'm not clear if I couldn't go in or just wouldn't. When the faceless paramedics unlocked the legs of the gurney with Tommy on it, I was ready to hop into the ambulance after him. Someone stopped me, and I realized that I didn't *have* rights, that it was all over, and he might be hurt, and no one would let me be with him. Or, if they did, they would be feeling sorry for me. Maybe feeling sorry for Tommy, too, for having to deal with this amorous, crazy woman. I wanted to keep saying, I'm sorry, so very, very sorry. Then the realization poured into me from somewhere far away that I didn't have my kids with me, that they weren't here, I didn't know what was going on with them. Were they safe? I almost got Tommy killed, were they dead, too? I think that was when I fainted.

I have no idea how long I was out. As I came to, I could see a ring of silhouettes floating above me, as if I were looking up from the inside of a well. Hard, wiry arms again partly lifted me up, and again it turned out to be the constable.

"I'm all right," I tried to mumble, but I was embarrassed beyond words. Eventually, I managed to stand more or less on my own. Russell put his arm around my shoulders, and the constable got one of the paramedics to take a look at me. They diagnosed shock and told him to get me warm. The first blanket had fallen off, so someone picked it up and Russell put it around me. It looked like steady, silent fireworks on the houses, the spinning lights on what looked like hundreds of patrol cars, parked jaggedly down the street. I learned later that there were only three; there were others down on Templeton, where they dragged Tim Solomon away.

I looked around on the porch, found my purse, and dug through it with palsied hands for my cell phone. I could tell Russell was about to object, but I said, "My kids. I have to call Mo and make sure they're all right." My voice was several octaves higher than normal. His objection died.

I got Ivy on the third ring. She sounded quiet, although she couldn't have been sleeping; she must have just gotten back from the theater. I told her that I needed her or Mo to check on the kids. She said they were already in bed, soundly sleeping. I said I needed her to go see for sure, anyway. She was about to get snarky with me. I told her that Tommy had just been shot, and was met with shocked silence. I continued through clattering teeth, "He had a vest on, so he's probably going to be okay. And I think they got the guy who shot him. But I'm in shock, and I need you or Mo to look at the boys and make absolutely sure that they are fine and breathing and in bed asleep. Please."

She objected no more, just murmured to Mo, who immediately got on.

"Ivy's going to check on Toby and Stevie. What the hell is going on there? Tommy got shot? Is he really okay?"

"I don't know. I think so. He had on a Kevlar vest, and I guess they work. I'm going to follow the ambulance to the hospital as soon as you guys tell me that the boys are fine."

I heard more murmuring, then Mo said, "Ivy reports that they are indeed in bed, they are breathing, they are completely safe and healthy. So you didn't get hit?" I said no. "Is whoever shot him really in custody?" Mo clearly watched as much crime drama as I did.

"Yes." I thanked her and Ivy and said I was coming over, just for a minute. She didn't object.

After I'd rung off, Russell tried to dissuade me from going anywhere. I ignored him, untangled myself from the blessed vest, which I handed to him, and headed for my car. Fortunately, Tommy had parked in front of my house, on the street, so my car wasn't blocked in. I didn't know where Tommy's keys were; presumably they were still on him, in his pocket. Russell followed me, still carrying the vest, and asked me if he could at least go with me and preferably drive. I asked him if he could drive a stick. He said sort of, and so I let him.

I told him we had to go to Mo's, then the hospital. He obeyed. I remember also thinking that I had never before ridden in any seat of my car other than the driver's. It was mildly peculiar. When we pulled up at Mo's, I burst out of the car. I ran straight for the door, then knocked quietly but with great intensity. Mo opened up, wearing green pajamas. She hugged me for a quick moment, then let me by. I ran up the stairs on soft feet, found the room they were in, and tiptoed in. There was a night-light, so I could see their dark heads in almost the identical posture, denting their pillows. I went up to them, looking closely, making sure there was breath. Making sure they weren't upset by anything, a dream, an intruder, violence.

I walked soundlessly out of the room, leaving the door ajar to let in the hall light. Downstairs, Ivy was standing between Mo and Russell, who were speaking to each other in faint voices. I promised I'd call later with more details but said we needed to go.

We didn't talk much during the fifteen-minute drive to the hospital, which was in a neighboring town, Northridge. Once there, Russell and I rendezvoused with some law enforcement types in a blue-tiled waiting room. Some were in uniform, some were not, but I knew none of them. The fluorescent lights shuddered and dimmed, and a few went out; they burned my eyes, which felt wounded. The constable found us within a moment.

Russell spoke. "Have you heard anything yet about Tommy?"

"Not really. They've got him in an examining room. I don't even know if they're going to admit him. I've already called your captain. By now he's called Tommy's family, although he's not going to have much to tell them yet."

Apparently, no one had actually seen anything. Tim's Lexus had been spotted in the parking lot of the Connecticut Deli on Templeton by the manager. I'd always thought it was one of the lamest business names I'd heard but, having no head for commerce, figured my opinion was worthless, and the place seemed to do reasonably well. The constable said through thin and colorless lips that two local uniformed officers had been sent to check it out. They didn't know how long the car had been there; the alert manager had just started his shift. His predecessor hadn't noticed anything and apparently was bored with the idea of cooperation of any kind. The constable had two cars, a total of four men, canvass all the stores in the Tenway Shopping Plaza, but Tim wasn't shopping. They proceeded to fan out, going slowly and quietly and carefully up the hillside behind the buildings. They had been in the woods only a few minutes when they heard the shot. Then stealth was abandoned, flashlights came out, weapons were drawn, and backup was called. My suspicion was that the young officers also became a whole lot more anxious as someone who'd just fired a gun was about to be cornered in the dark woods.

They found the gun in short order, some sort of rifle with a scope for sharpshooting, and a pair of men's leather gloves. Not long afterward they found Tim Solomon a few hundred feet away, panting and pale.

"He says he didn't do it. You'll love this," McCandless said, looking at me with no humor whatsoever. I'd only seen the constable so far as amiable, calm, and polite. Now, however, he was exhausted and white with a tightly managed rage. If I'd been a criminal at that moment, I would have been very nervous. "He was protecting you from some unknown stalker, he says. Someone else. He'd seen him following you around, so he followed him. He was *worried* about you. He was pissed at us, he said, because he saw the guy, the mystery man, take a shot, then drop the gun and gloves and run, and he was chasing *him,* trying to catch him for you. To *save* you. You're a lucky girl, eh, to have such a guardian angel?" The constable walked over to a metal trash can next to a bank of elevators and spat in it. He came back slowly, inhaling deeply. "I've got people going over to the fraternity house now to bring Jason in for questioning." Russell and McCandless agreed that as soon as they were confident of Tommy's safety, they would go to the municipal building, which also housed the jail, to question both boys.

I had started shaking again under the fluorescent lights, and Russell offered to get me some coffee. The constable told me to go sit down; they'd tell me when we could see Tommy.

Russell and the constable talked for a few more minutes, out of my range of hearing. Neither seemed very happy with the other, when the constable finally went elsewhere to see what Tommy's status was. Russell went in search of the promised coffee and eventually returned with two cups from a vending machine. He had just handed me one when McCandless came back, telling us that the doctor had said that Tommy was doing fine and we could see him.

I was ready to sprint through the halls, but the constable said that once we got to the room, he'd tell me when I could go in. He and Russell had to talk to Tommy first. Outside his door I paced for about ten minutes, finishing the viscous, rancid coffee and sneakily pitching the cup into a trash can in the empty room next to Tommy's. I paced in front of his door for several minutes more until McCandless came out and said, "I guess it's okay if you go in. Just don't do anything that would wear him out." He sort of smiled at me, but I couldn't interpret his look. I didn't know what he thought I was going to do to exhaust Tommy. Maybe my feelings were obvious, I didn't know or care, not then. I thanked him, and he told Russell, hovering in the doorway, that he'd see him later and left.

I slipped past Russell and saw Tommy, who was sitting up in the bed. He was almost the color of the sheets, he was so pale, and his strong face seemed slimmer, younger. He had a five o'clock shadow, yet his beard seemed lighter and softer. His beautiful big hands lay outside the covers, on the blanket. He smiled when he saw me. I practically hopped over and slowly took his hand.

I spent a moment working at not crying and then said, "How do you feel? Is it bad?"

Russell interrupted with "I'm going to the station with one of the deputies to wring confessions out of two very scared and very fucked perps." I didn't know cops actually used the word "perps." Russell went on, "Tomorrow, I'll get a ride to Gina's and get your car and your stuff and bring it back here, okay?" Tommy nodded slightly. I thought I should offer to drive him, but I had no intention of leaving. To me Russell said, "If I can't get a ride over to your house tomorrow, I might call. McCandless said I could crash at his house for a few hours later if I needed to." He smiled tautly at both of us. "I'll let you know what there is to know. Don't worry. It's all easy from here on in." I didn't believe him, but it did feel as though the worst was over. Russell didn't move or talk for another moment, just looked back and forth between us. "I guess I'll see you later."

After Russell left, Tommy said, "Gina," his voice still hoarse, "it wasn't your fault. Don't feel so bad. I've got a few broken ribs and some bad bruises, but I'll be fine in a few days. It's okay."

I had no idea what he saw in my face but figured that if I didn't actually say any of it, at least he wouldn't have to respond.

He added, "I guess it's all over. Well, except for the trial." He fell quiet as we both considered that that might in some ways be the worst part of it if the press decided it was interesting. Until now it had never occurred to me that the press might glom on to this. The blurred image of John Fagin's face zipped across my mind, ticker-tape fashion. I pushed it out. I decided to be like Scarlett O'Hara and think about that tomorrow.

I said what I'd been thinking in the hall. "Look, Tommy, you're going to need a little help in the next few days. Why don't you stay at my house for a bit longer, and I'll feed you while you're there. The boys would be thrilled to have someone to watch Bugs Bunny cartoons with, and I've got plenty of stuff to read if you get bored. That way you won't have to be totally on your own." He started to speak, but I continued. "You did save my life and take a bullet for me. The least I can do is make you some soup while your ribs heal enough for you to drive."

He squeezed my hand. "I didn't save your life. He was aiming at *me*."

"Oh God. Remind me to get Molly to light a candle for the person who invented bulletproof vests. Although I have to admit, I sort of expected them to make the bullets just bounce off. You know, 'bulletproof' sounds so *safe*."

Tommy laughed, then winced. I apologized, and we fell silent for a minute. My heart started beating a little harder. Tommy took a big preparatory breath.

"You know," he said after a few breaths, "sometimes women get a little, I don't know, infatuated with cops that have been working with them. You know, the bodyguard effect. The man in the uniform thing. But that wears off after a while."

This was terrible, and I could feel my heart dropping. I had to work hard at not letting my face sag much. I tried to raise my eyebrows in a casual, inquiring way. At least I didn't start crying. I dredged up cheerfulness from some previously unknown reservoir. "What uniform? The blue suit? I wouldn't worry about that. No offense. And I didn't feel all that safe." But I thought, I'm made of glass: he can see completely through me, and he's about to sweetly, with great regret, smash me to bits.

But he didn't get the chance, at least not right then. Before he could answer, a shrill voice sounded through the open doorway. A head carpeted with very large hair popped in. I thought, horribly, of a song sung by Katie Cameron in my New York days: I am woman, hear me roar, my hair is too big to ignore. I was afraid I might start screaming, and this woman was already looking at me as though she'd like to come after me with a vegetable peeler.

"Tommy, oh my God. Oh my God, oh my God." Pause. She swiveled the huge solid mass that was her head toward me. Not one hair moved independently. "Who is this?" said Helmet Head, hatred oozing from every follicle. Oh dear, I thought. I'm fucking doomed.

chapter seventeen

---

*[T]he function of the brain is to serve the present and the real,
not to send man chasing wildly after the phantom of the future . . . [I]n our habitual state of mental tension the brain
does not work properly, and this is one reason why its abstrac-
tions seem to have so great a reality. When the heart is out of
order, we are clearly conscious of its beating; it becomes a distraction, pounding within the breast. It seems most probable
that our preoccupation with thinking and planning, together
with the sense of mental fatigue, is a sign of some disorder of
the brain.*

ALAN WATTS, *The Wisdom of Insecurity*

"SUSIE, CALM DOWN, I'm okay," Tommy said with an unfortunately
weak-sounding voice. "Gina, this is my overwrought sister. Susie,
I'm not dying. I just have a few broken ribs, some bruises. I'll be
fine."

The big-haired Susie was sniffling pretty loudly. I was trying hard
not to find her annoying. She's his sister, I thought; she's part of the
package. Think about the family he's going to have to deal with if

you guys ever get together. If anything was likely to get me to look at her with charity, that was it.

"Who's home with the kids?" asked Tommy, with a little smile. I couldn't tell if he thought she was endearing or if he just thought her theatricality was amusing.

"Ben's got them. Dad's here, too. He's just parking the car."

"Shit, Susie, you got Dad up here, at this hour? What the hell are you thinking? He doesn't need to be here."

He slowly eased his hand from mine. I let it go, feeling suddenly embarrassed. "Susie, this is Gina," not defining me in any way.

"Are you friends or something?" she said.

"Yes," I said a bit too loudly.

Tommy smiled again. "Gina, go home and get some sleep."

"They told me you're getting out tomorrow. I'm taking you home," Susie declared in a wet voice. "The kids never get to see you, and I want you there with me. I can get a few days off work, and I'll take good care of you, Tommy. I swear, you drive me crazy with this job. People getting shot. My God, you're not going back, whatever you say."

Tommy looked inscrutably patient. He looked at me, smiled softly again, and said, "Go home, Gina."

I tried to smile back. It felt like the most selfish thing I'd ever done, to just leave him there. I reached out and quickly squeezed his hand, smiled broadly at last, and said, "Okay. I hope you feel better tomorrow. Thanks for everything, Tommy. I'll talk to you later." I turned to Helmet Head, excavating some compassion for her from somewhere. "It was nice to meet you, Susie. I'm sorry it was under these circumstances, but I'm sure everything will be fine." I was laying it on thick, but I wanted as little residue of hatred attached to me as possible. "Bye." I gave a little wave and left the room.

I consciously slowed myself down; the impulse to sprint out of the hospital and home was compelling. I had made it to the lobby of the emergency entrance, the closest to the lot where my car was, when it occurred to me to ask someone if I could find out whether Donna was working. This was her hospital, after all. I had a sudden terror of Donna finding out I'd been there but hadn't tried to find her or talk to her. And then she'd be offended and dislike me, and I didn't want to be disliked by anyone else. I told the bored nasal woman behind the desk that she worked in obstetrics and gave her my name as well; she told me that they'd page her if I was willing to wait. I also had some vague notion that she would know what to do about Tommy or maybe could help me keep tabs on him while he was there. I waited, shivering, for about twenty minutes, listening to the reception on a radio at the nurses' station tremble in and out, sounding like music being channeled at a séance, distant, high, and intermittent. Then a soft arm slid around my shoulders, jolting me back from the imaginary world where I had fled. It was my elusive cousin Donna Eberle.

She'd taken a break; fortunately, there was only one woman in labor at the moment. We went to the cafeteria. There was no hot food at that hour, but there was an elaborate array of vending machines. I treated her to some coffee while I got a diet caffeine-free Coke. They were out of bottled water, and more coffee would've sent my kidneys into arrest.

I filled her in, sparing her nothing except my heartsickness. But at that point I was pretty lousy at hiding it. Or maybe Donna was a lot more perceptive than I'd given her credit for being. She said, "So you've got a thing for him?"

What the hell. "Yeah, I do."

"You can't tell him?"

"I'm way too humiliated. He's pretty good at resisting my charms."

"Hah. I thought no man was immune to you." She said it sweetly, eyebrows raised.

"That's me, the scourge of New York. Seriously, most men do just fine at ignoring me." She raised her eyebrows farther. "What are you looking at me like that for? I'm in love with him." There, I had said it. "He's not with me. Now I'm doing the noble riding-off-into-the-sunset thing. I just wondered if there's any way you can double-check on his condition sometime tonight so I at least know for sure that he's okay and that he really checks out tomorrow."

"I can do that."

"Thanks." A pause. "So do you really use working here as a way to get out of dealing with the Hannigans?"

"Well, duh."

We both laughed. I suddenly liked Donna so much, I longed to say, Here's how to be beautiful, here's what you could do with your hair. But I didn't.

"Do you like being here so much?" Trying to get the focus off me. "Does it suit you?"

"Enough for now. I like being a nurse. I like the social life, too. Good friends." She was looking at the table, not at me. "You're nice to Clark."

"Of course I'm nice to Clark."

"Don't be too nice to him, Gina."

"What's that supposed to mean?" She looked at the table again. "No, really, Donna, do you think I'd ever try to take away Bobbie's boyfriend? I think he's in love with her, anyway, but regardless, I would never, ever do that. Assuming I even could, which is pretty ridiculous." My voice started getting too loud. I stopped and took a deep breath, heading off a weird hysteria. Donna looked kind of heartbroken. I didn't say I don't want him, anyway. "Why would you think I would?"

"I've heard all about John Fagin."

"What about him? I've spoken to him once since Franny's funeral, for about a minute and a half."

"Maggie says that he's crazy about you and that you're being heartless."

"Oh my God. Jesus Christ." All the anger I hadn't yet channeled toward Tim Solomon reared up now, zooming toward Doughboy and Maggie. "He keeps leaving me messages. I told him at the funeral I wasn't interested. I'm sorry if his heart feels broken, but I sure as hell didn't break it."

Donna just looked at me. I went on. "And I don't go after married or involved guys. Ever. Clark is safe from me."

Donna's eyes got wet, and suddenly she was crying. There was a long pause, obviously loaded, before she blurted, "I'm seeing someone here. A doctor."

I wasn't following. "Well, that's good, right? Aunt Lottie must be ecstatic."

Donna shrugged. "She doesn't know. No one knows."

"It's a secret?" She nodded. "Here, too?" Nod, yes. I had an unhappy presentiment. "He's married?" Her eyes were heavy, sad. Yes. "Oh, Donna, I'm so sorry. What's going to happen, do you think?"

"Terrible things." She smiled sickly. "That's inevitable, right? He's got kids, so no matter what, it's gonna suck. I'm heartsick, too, Gina. I can't believe I'm telling you this. I haven't even told Bobbie. I think she suspects something like this. But she's so sweet, she would never judge me." Her face was slack with misery. She was tired, too. "So that's why I'm not telling you to go for it; love is ridiculous. It kills, it abso-fucking-lutely kills you. Shrivels everything it touches. You were married once. Any fun for you?"

I shrugged. How could I argue? "Not really."

"Did he cheat on you?"

I wondered if she'd been talking to Lizzie. "Yes."

"My ex did, too. I'm thinking it's built into the goddamn Y chromosome." She let out one of the saddest sighs I'd ever heard. "Although I think my dad was faithful. You know, he was a great guy, but he died when he was fifty-four years old. My mom's going to live without him a lot longer than she had him, and she'll have no one else, because she loved him. Look at Maggie. Christ, what a gasbag she's married to. Your parents weren't the happiest couple, either, from what I hear. Your father was kind of notorious. Actually, your mom, too, kind of. No offense."

"None taken. You're right."

"We could go on and on about marriages we know. Horror stories, every one. I finally figured out that I'm doing this with this doctor only because I have no belief that I will ever score anything better, or more satisfying, or more lasting." Donna's eyes were glittering and round. "So if I were you, I'd run like the wind. Let some other masochist have him."

"There's Mo and Ivy," I said, resisting depression.

"They're both women," she said. Then she said, "Please, please don't tell anyone."

I hugged Donna, our new intimacy warming and chilling me at the same time. I wanted to rescue her, knowing the stupidity of the thought. She promised she'd get me whatever information she could by tomorrow.

Back at my house I noticed a patrol car with an officer inside parked across the street. I looked a little more closely. I'd seen too many horror movies where the poor protector cop gets whacked by the psycho on the loose. But the psychos weren't loose anymore.

The constable must have ordered this. I didn't know why, but I was grateful. After I parked in my driveway, I walked over to him. I recognized him as Jed Paley. Poor guy, having to work nights. I wondered if he had family who missed him. He rolled his window down and looked suspiciously at me. I asked him if he needed anything. He said no, he was fine. I told him I was bringing him out some coffee and something to eat. He protested. I went inside the house, brewed a pot of coffee, and put it in a thermos, realizing that I hadn't asked him how he liked it. So I found a small plastic tub with a tight seal, put some milk in it, and put some sugar in a zippered snack bag. I found a plastic spoon in a drawer, then a paper plate. I put some chocolate chip cookies on the plate along with an apple and a banana. I couldn't think of anything else. Water, maybe? I had an unopened bottle in the refrigerator, so I included that. I put everything except the cookies on the plate in a cloth shopping bag I had hanging by the refrigerator. I walked back outside and handed it all to Officer Paley through his car window.

"If you need anything else, just ring the bell, okay? I'm going to be up for a while."

He was polite but looked at me like I was insane. I'm sure I looked it. Hours of shock, tears, fear, and exhaustion tend to make you look weird. I said good night and went back in. Then, of course, the exhaustion started pushing itself on me, but I couldn't go to bed since

I'd told Jed Paley that I'd be up for a while. What if he needed to go to the bathroom or something? The fact that he was a man and that this wasn't as big a problem for him as it might be for me didn't occur to me. It wasn't until much later that I realized how all my concern might sound like a come-on. He might have thought I belonged to the Auxiliary Circle.

I made myself a cup of decaffeinated tea and decided to let Ellie know what was going on. The house seemed weird and echoey and empty without Toby and Stevie. In fact, it sort of seemed that way without Tommy and even Russell in it as well. It wasn't a particularly big house, but it felt huge now.

Ellie said, "He got *shot*?"

"Yes. In the back, no less. He's going to be fine, though. That's the main thing."

"Christ, you do have an interesting life. But it's like that Chinese curse where you wish someone will have an interesting journey. But did you tell him how you feel? Or did he say anything to you? And this is just the kind of thing that throws people together in the movies. He's bound to have the hots for you now, after spending all this intense time with you."

"That's very sweet, Ellie, but you know, there are millions, billions even, of men who are able to resist my allure. Why do I have to keep saying this? So far Tommy Galloway is one of these resisters. He has a horrible sister, too, who hates me."

"Why does she hate you? You met her at the hospital?"

"Yes. She hates me because I was there. Holding his hand."

"He held your hand? Well, that means something, doesn't it?"

"I didn't say he held my hand. I held his."

"Well, I still think he likes you."

"He does like me. I'm a likable gal. I don't want to dwell on the ways Tommy probably likes me and the ways he doesn't. What I should be focusing on is the fact that they arrested Tim and Jason. I don't know what they'll be able to convict them of. I assume they can get Tim on the attempted murder of a police officer. I just hope that my part in this will soon be over." I shifted gears. "I saw Donna at the hospital." I was proud that I wasn't even tempted to tell Ellie the big adulterous news about Donna.

"So she really is there at night. You know what, Gina?"

"What?"

"The universe isn't a giant market. A love life won't necessarily cost you two sons."

"What?"

"Think about it later and get some sleep."

The next morning I awoke puffy and disoriented. It took me a few minutes to remember sinkingly that I didn't have to feed Sidney. Some exercise and coffee later, I was almost recognizable to myself. I showered, dressed, then crept out to get the newspaper. The bag with the empty thermos was sitting by the front door. The patrol car was gone.

It occurred to me to look through the paper to see if any of this had made a media splash. Fortunately, there was nothing about it in the *Times*. Good. Maybe I would get lucky and all reporters would be bored by or at least ignorant of the events on my street last night. I decided at that moment that for the next few weeks I wouldn't read the newspaper. If reporters wanted to talk to me, I wouldn't. I would pretend that none of this existed except for appearing as a witness, however that worked. I guessed that both boys would be prosecuted both in Tenway and in New York. I had no idea but figured that I would be told by someone if I was needed. I was never so glad that I had an unlisted number. I needed to make sure Cindy knew first thing not to take any calls from the press.

I was about to call Mo to check in and arrange to get the twins, when the phone rang. I hate it when it rings under your hand; I twitched like a spooked hare. It was Russell. He told me Tommy was being discharged as we spoke, and his sister was carting him off. He wanted to come get Tommy's car and then was going to take it to Susie's. He was wondering if I would help him, follow him out to Demarest, in New Jersey, then bring him back to get his own car, which was parked at the Tenway municipal building. I quickly calculated how much time this would take, trying to figure out how long

I could bear to have my boys living in someone else's house. But this trip would probably involve seeing Tommy, so I said yes. He told me a deputy would drop him at my house in a half hour or so. It didn't occur to me till later that it would have made much more sense to have had that deputy follow Russell out to Susie's.

I called Mo and, after filling her in on what little I knew, asked if I could get the boys later in the day. No problem; Trevor was staying till the evening, so everyone was happy so far. I had just fetched myself a second cup of coffee and was about to go upstairs when Donna called, telling me what I already knew, that Tommy had been checked out. She said he had some cracked ribs but was basically fine. No need to worry. I thanked her and promised a get-together soon, and we said good-bye.

I went up to the guest room to collect all of Tommy's gear before Russell arrived. This was a melancholy task, like the aftermath of death, not a mild injury. I thought about keeping some of his effects so that he'd have to come get them later or I'd have an excuse to bring them to him. I debated it back and forth for about five minutes while I stood there, a pair of dirty socks in my hands. No, I finally thought. No ploys. I needed not to drive myself crazy anymore. I wasn't fifteen, playing teenage games. I packed up the few items I found: some clothes, an unopened pack of cigarettes, a biography of, of all people, Truman Capote. From the bathroom I got his toothbrush and razor. I double-checked under the bed. I was pretty sure I'd gotten everything. I was grateful that his gun had been on him so someone at the hospital had had to deal with it.

Russell arrived shortly, looking pretty spiffy for a guy who couldn't have slept much. Neither of us had eaten; he suggested we go out for a late breakfast before the trip to Demarest. We wound up in the same diner where we had eaten lunch together only ten days earlier. The day my universe changed. Waitress Cola wasn't there.

He told me that the night before things hadn't gone all that well. The evidence against Jason was slimmer than that against Tim. Lawyers swooped down from Manhattan seemingly within minutes of the boys' arrival at the station, and there was nothing to be gotten out of them in the way of confessions. And it looked like the gun wasn't one of the ones stolen from the Solomons' apartment in the city. "Even if it had been, it would only have helped our case a little, so it doesn't really matter." He seemed a bit worried by that but said he wasn't. Then he changed the subject, asking what I thought of Susie.

"She obviously cares about him a lot."

Russell laughed. "That's diplomatic. She's freakin' insane when it comes to Tommy's safety. He never tells her anything he's doing, because he knows she can't handle it." I wondered if he knew about Tommy's mother, but said nothing. I wasn't up to breaking confidences or sharing them with Russell. I was afraid, perhaps unfairly, that he would laugh. "This will really bring the circle into action."

I looked politely inquisitive. Obviously, he wanted me to ask.

"Tommy hasn't told you about the Auxiliary Circle?"

"No. But I saw their website. Cop groupies, right?"

He seemed disappointed that I knew about this already. "Oh, they're just women who follow big cases, who follow the careers of particular cops who get a good amount of press or who they think are cool for whatever reason. Tommy and I have been lucky more than a few times, and the papers have been pretty kind. Our pictures and names have gotten out there, and these women like it."

I found that statement disingenuous but didn't say so. I found the Auxiliary Circle itself sad and did say that.

Russell was a bit offended. He found it, apparently, validating in some way and a tribute to their—what? Maleness? Toughness? Skill? To use Tommy's words, this wasn't a universe I got at all.

"So do you sleep with these women? Date them? Give them autographs? Buy them lunch? What?"

He seemed to get that there was something unseemly about admitting this too enthusiastically. "Well, not often. I've met a few who were pretty hot, though." He didn't need to say more, and I didn't want to hear it.

He seemed to understand that he needed to drop this. "Look, I gotta ask you. Are you and Tommy, you know, hooked up?"

" 'Hooked up'? How romantic you are. Of course not." I took in a breath. "Are you done yet? I'm ready to go. I've got things to do this afternoon." I thought, Get off it, girl. You may feel sorry for these women, but you're just like them now.

I followed Tommy's car all the way to Demarest. Fortunately, the Saturday traffic wasn't particularly heavy, so we were there within an hour. I was starting to agree with Donna more enthusiastically; by the time we got to Susie's house, I was actually hoping I wouldn't see Tommy. As soon as we pulled into their driveway, however, disinclination fled, replaced by an urge to fly to him that was so strong I had to grip the steering wheel for a minute to keep myself from racing to their front door.

Susie's home was made of rose-colored brick, a large but comfortable-looking split-level with a reasonable yard dotted with the colorful signs of children. Russell was already pressing the doorbell; I got out of the car, unsure what to do. I figured that Susie wasn't going to want me there. It was cold and a bit windy, and Russell was dancing a little in the chill; it was taking a while for anyone to answer the door. The person who did was a tall man with a perfect face. I had to work not to goggle at him initially; he was one of the handsomest men I'd ever seen in my life, and I'm including male models. Not my type at all; he looked waxen. But I wasn't expecting Susie to be married to such an archetype. He smiled beautifully at Russell and then at me as I crept up behind him.

"Russell?" he said, then to me, "And you're that friend of Tommy's?" His voice was deep, resonant, a little creepy. He led us into a semiclean living room and said Susie was out getting some groceries. The kids were in the den downstairs, with Tommy, watching cartoons. He led us there over my almost inaudible protests.

The den was thickly carpeted and dark with paneling and tiny high windows. The very large television was loud and colorful, with things blowing up and people with big round eyes talking way too fast, all in blocky animation. Tommy was lying back in a recliner, sweatpants and sweatshirt on, with an afghan over his legs. He looked like himself, but not. He looked a little older than he had yesterday, a little thinner, if that was possible. He'd shaved, though, so he was pretty presentable. I was appalled at how exquisite he looked to me. He waved weakly at Russell when he saw him, then saw me. His face quite literally lit up. It was all I could do not to hop onto his lap. I smiled at him, so glad I'd come.

There were three pajama-clad children there: a boy of about ten, another boy around six, and a little girl, toddling, with an extremely runny nose. I made a mental note to wash my hands very well before picking up my boys. They seemed like nice enough kids, but they were far more interested in the TV than in their uncle's visitors.

After handing him the overnight bag that held the stuff he'd left at my house, I asked him the obvious, how he felt, how long till he was all better, and so on. He expected to be fine in a few days. Susie was out getting all his favorite foods, few of which I knew, I realized. I had had a very brief fantasy that this would be how I would find out, by taking care of him. That idea now seemed presumptuous and silly; I felt a familiar embarrassment. And then we could hear Susie upstairs, talking to her chiseled spouse, unloading groceries. I felt guilty, a little hunted, and wished there was a way to leave without her seeing me. Realizing how ridiculous that was, I resisted the urge to cut our visit any shorter.

Tommy was saying, "Now they try to get more evidence, try to find Brad Franco, and build the best case possible. Then there'll be a trial or maybe two. The DA from Tendale County will be in touch with you soon, I imagine. Probably the one from New York City, too."

Susie was coming down the stairs. I felt trapped and out of time. She saw me and looked like she was going to burst into tears. I suddenly felt sorry for her, so I smiled as sweetly as possible. "Hi, again," I said, goofy with tension. She said "Hello" with no warmth. She looked at Tommy and said, "I called Candace. She's coming over later." Candace? I had to think for a moment. This was the two-year live-in one, not the newer, less-defined one. Tommy was expressionless. Russell said to Susie, "Say hello for me." His tone was so neutral, I had no idea what was behind the bland statement. I had no intention of asking.

It became obvious within a few minutes that neither Russell nor I was wanted in the house by anyone other than Tommy, and his wishes didn't count for much. So we said our good-byes; I took his hand and told him to call me to let me know how he was doing and if he needed anything. I tried to hold his hand for a little longer, but Susie practically shoved me up the stairs.

On the drive back to Tenway, Russell was making a great effort to be charming. He was good at it, in fact, quite funny, and could even be sweet. I wanted to be by myself for a while but managed to be reasonably polite.

As I pulled into the parking lot of the municipal building, Russell said, "Look, Gina, could I crash at your house for a while? I'm pretty beat, and I'm not really up for driving back to the city yet. I could follow you back in my car."

I stared at him. He had such beautiful, wide, innocent blue eyes. Such nice teeth. Such dimples. He was so full of shit.

"I don't think that would be such a great idea, Russell. I'm sorry, but I have to get the boys and start putting my life back in order. It wouldn't be a quiet place. Maybe McCandless will let you crash there for a few more hours if you're really worried about falling asleep at the wheel."

He looked at me with those eyes, dimples deepening, so sincere, so guileless. "Couldn't Mo keep the boys for just another hour or two?" Deep look.

I had had enough. At least I didn't laugh. "Are you trying to get me to sleep with you?" He looked startled. "You've got to be kidding," I said. "Please, Russell, please don't do this again."

The blue eyes darkened. "Are you hooked up with Tommy? Is that what this is about?"

My skin was crawling. "Stop it. Talk to Tommy about any rivalry you've got with him. Leave me out of it. You need some sleep. Go home and get it."

"Is there something up with you and Tommy?"

"Of course not."

I finally got Russell out of my car and into his own. I went to get my kids.

There were a few mild protests for form's sake, but the boys were glad to be coming home. Trevor was going back to his father's house that evening, and Ivy had her last stage performance that night. She and Mo were too nice to say so, but I suspected they were glad to be able to go to the wrap party unencumbered by kids.

I had yet to break the news about Sidney to the boys and was anticipating doing it with some misery. After we'd been home an hour or so and gotten settled in, I told them that Sidney had died, lying like crazy about how. It was not easy; they were smart boys and at times could question me relentlessly. I told them he'd been hit by a car. We all cried a lot. After dinner we lit a candle and all talked about what we loved most about him. I thought that later, maybe in a month or so, we could talk about getting kittens. But I didn't want to hurry this. I didn't want them to think that loved ones were so easily replaced.

I was washing dishes, with the boys watching TV, when the phone rang. I stupidly picked it up. I think on some level I hoped Tommy was going to call. Instead, it was John Fagin.

"Gina, are you all right?" He'd heard stuff from his sources in the constable's office. He was worried about me and interested, I could tell, in getting a story out of it as well. I wished, as I had many times in the last few weeks, that Maggie hadn't given him my number. I even thought I could get it changed and not tell Maggie what it was. I didn't want her calling me, anyway. Then I thought, Mo would have to have it; she'd never withhold it from her younger sister. She'll deny her family nothing.

John was still talking. I interrupted. "I don't want to talk right now. Good-bye, John." I hung up, not feeling bad about it, which surprised me. I then unplugged the phone.

After the twins were in bed, I worked out for a while. Before I went to bed, I got some matches from a kitchen drawer, then went outside to the porch and found the ashtray that Tommy had been using. It hadn't been emptied since the day before, and there were eight butts in it, all his brand. I pulled the longest one out of the ashtray, sat on my front steps, and smoked it. I thought, this may be the closest I ever get to his mouth again. I went inside, feeling dizzy and slightly nauseous, and got ready for bed. I decided to sleep in the guest room on the sheets that still smelled like Tommy. Just this once, I thought. I'll wash them tomorrow.

chapter eighteen

―――――

THE NEXT DAY was a Sunday. I plugged the phone back in. The weather didn't improve, and Tommy didn't call me. Constable Mc-Candless did, however, and said that he wanted to come and get a statement from me. He knew that I worked on Monday and said he and two detectives from Tommy's precinct would come see me at home today if that was possible. I invited them for dinner. He declined and said they'd come in the afternoon.

I had told Stevie and Toby that Tommy had gotten hurt on Friday and was getting better. They wanted to know if they could visit him; I said I didn't know, maybe sometime. I had no idea what else to tell them. The constable and the two detectives appeared around two o'clock, after I'd finished cleaning up from lunch and was grading papers. The boys were playing a computer game in unusual harmony together, so things were quiet.

The constable looked about ten years older than he had the first time I'd seen him, two weeks before. I guessed he needed some sleep. His companions were male and female. Detective Wallace was about forty, big and very tough-looking, in a gray wool pantsuit and short, tightly curled hair. Her partner, Detective Spengler, was a little shorter than she was, slightly younger, in a suit of a similar color, thin-faced and good-looking. I made coffee, for which they all seemed grateful. I told them everything I could remember. It was little enough, since I had neither seen nor heard anything of Tim and Jason that night other than the sound of the gun. I couldn't even have sworn that what I heard was in fact a shot, just a popping sound, and then I saw Tommy falling. All I knew about Tim's actions had been told to me by the police. As a witness, I was pretty useless.

There was still no sign of Bradley Franco. They'd searched everywhere they could. The police remained convinced of foul play but had no evidence that satisfied the local prosecutor. The two detectives were wooden and silent, but the constable told me, though in no detail to speak of, that illicit substances and a number of guns were found in the room they shared at the fraternity house, enough to arrest Jason as well as Tim. The police subsequently found more drugs, mostly heroin and cocaine, in the bedrooms of both boys at their parents' apartments in the city. The more charges, the merrier.

The constable had one of the great poker faces. Now he made it, if possible, so completely devoid of expression that it was pretty expressive, if you get my meaning.

"Gina, how close are you to the Hannigans?"

"What? I'm very close to my cousin Maureen. I spend time with her sisters occasionally. I'm not particularly tight with my uncle and aunt. Why? They don't have anything to do with this."

"You're right," he said. His face didn't change at all.

McCandless and the two detectives finally got up to leave after telling me that the Tendale County district attorney would probably contact me in the next month about whether I would be needed to testify. McCandless added, blandly casual, that it would be better if I didn't try to contact any of the detectives working on the case until after the trial or trials were over. They would be in touch with me if they needed more information, but my credibility as a witness might be compromised if I appeared to have social contact with any personnel involved with this case. I wondered if that meant what I thought it did but didn't want to ask.

Later, I thought it was possible that McCandless thought I was having an affair with Russell. It was almost amusing.

That night, after the boys were in bed, I looked on the Internet and found Tim Solomon's website. It was as bad as I remembered. Oddly, it didn't bother me as much now. This would all be far in the past by the time the boys were in middle school, when something like this would be particularly icky. My mother lived in another state. My relatives here would cluck and flutter, or they would commiserate. So what? I wasn't all that worried about my professional standing. It would soon be made public that the students involved were violent and deluded; I doubted anyone would seriously see me as culpable. I looked at my pictures more closely. They were pretty damn good when all was said and done. Tasteful, even. In fact, the contrast with the other pictures on the site made it quite clear that they weren't of the same caliber, not the same kind of thing at all.

And I thought, so it gets around campus that a professor had been a *Lavish* model. If it increases enrollments for the department, I thought, they should give me a raise. It was one of the classiest, most upscale catalogs of its kind on the market, after all, even if it was a bit notorious.

This time I looked at the whole site, not just the part the police had shown me. There was another section labeled "Fiona." More stories, these about another woman, with stupid scurrilous pornographic scenarios just as unlikely as the ones concerning me. The pictures were a lot coarser than mine; they didn't look professional. In fact, some of them looked like they'd been taken through windows without the subject's knowledge. I thought it likely the police would have figured this out long before I had. Presumably they were looking into it. The woman looked familiar, although I couldn't make out her face too well; I wondered if she was also someone at the college.

I expected that the news would travel fastest on campus, given that the principals were students. The next morning, as soon as I arrived at the department, I filled Cindy in with all the details I felt advisable. She was irritated that I hadn't let her in on things from the beginning but forgave me since the story was so good and she was getting the whole thing from the source. I told her that I didn't want to talk to the general press but would give an interview to the campus paper, if it wanted one, feeling a pissy satisfaction that the *University Beacon* would get an interview with me before John Fagin did. She immediately logged on to the site herself, and when I pointed out the "Fiona" link, she squeaked.

"It's Fiona Belstein, David Renouart's ex-girlfriend. The recent one. How'd they get pictures of her?"

"Some of them look like they took them through windows."

"Yeah, but not all of them. Do you think she posed for these professionally?"

I looked at them. Even allowing for the distortion that scanning and other digital alterations could make in photographs, they didn't look like they'd ever been professional-quality pictures. I told Cindy so. She said, "Did David ever want to take pictures of you?"

I was stunned. "No. But he knew I'd been a model. And I let him see my portfolio because he wanted to so badly. Holy shit."

I also wound up talking for quite a while to Kay Reynolds about the whole business. I wanted to make sure she knew the facts before she got barraged with rumors. She was agog with interest. I was relieved that my sense from the night before was right; the publicity would only help enrollments, which was always good. Had I really been having an affair with a student, psychopath or not, things would have been different.

Vincent found the whole business quite exciting and wanted to know as many gory details as I could tell him. I expected Ida (May) Weiss to find the whole thing too sordid and to avoid me for a while. I was shocked when she launched into a long story about how her FBI file had been made public a few years ago, and she had been persecuted for it. Apparently she had been a high-profile antiwar activist in the sixties. I had all her sympathies. The difference between her past and mine, not to mention the circumstances under which our pasts were made public, was obvious to everyone else in the depart-ment. I didn't see the need to point this out to Ida; I just thanked her and gave her a hug.

The campus paper did in fact want to do a story on the whole episode and sent someone over to my office after lunch. The student reporter at first had no idea what to ask me. When it was clear that I didn't know much about the evidence the police had against Tim and Jason and that I didn't know either student particularly well, the young man asked me lots of questions about my career as a model. I told him a lit-tle, then cut him off, saying I didn't think that was relevant. He didn't bring up Fiona Belstein, so I didn't, either.

After I got home with the boys that afternoon, I tried to decide who to call about David Renouart's possible involvement with this case. I didn't seriously believe that David had anything to do with Tim and Jason's criminal activities, but they might well have gotten the pic-tures, at least some of them, from him. The cops needed to talk to him. It was a perfect excuse to call Tommy, of course. But I didn't know his sister's number, nor did I know her last name. I could have called Russell but shied away from that idea. I had Tommy's cell phone number but couldn't be sure of getting him with it. The thought of calling him made me seize up with sadness and fear, in any case. I ig-nored the three messages on my machine from John Fagin and called Constable McCandless. I was told that he was gone for the day. I was glad for him, hoping it meant he was home getting some rest. I left a message that I had some additional information that he might find helpful in the Solomon case. The woman taking it was surprisingly courteous, even offering to call him at home. I told her I didn't think it was that urgent; tomorrow would do.

I made sure the boys were happy, then told them I was going next door for a few minutes. I hadn't seen Jessie in several days and was vaguely worried. Too much going on. I didn't know what she'd heard, either. Maybe the visit was more about damage control than about concern for Jessie; I wasn't entirely sure.

I knocked on her door, waiting, shivering. After several long cold minutes, she pulled it open. She looked asleep. I immediately started apologizing for having wakened her. She dragged me in, anyway, not bothering to tell me it was all right.

She said, "I've been wanting to talk to you. What was all that ruckus about the other night? There were police and everything. I want you to tell me what's going on over there. I know you have a man coming there. I've been minding my own business about this, but you should be more careful if you don't want people to talk."

I thought the only person on the block who cared about this was probably her, but I told her, omitting the most scurrilous details about my obsessed student, the police who'd sort of moved in with me, and the shooting of Tommy. "You already heard about my cat from the constable, right?"

She nodded, now understanding the larger significance of that. "But that boy's in prison now, right?"

"Yes."

"Good. God takes care of you in the end, you know."

I thought about Bradley Franco's parents and said nothing.

Shortly after I was back in my house, the phone started ringing. Mo called, having heard from Ivy that things were heating up on campus. Then Lizzie called because she'd been talking to Mo. Lizzie was angry that she hadn't known that Tommy had gotten shot on Friday. I told her the whole story, feeling tired and frustrated. I didn't want to talk about it anymore. Lizzie wanted to know how to get in touch with him. I told her I didn't know, but she didn't believe me. I was tempted to give her his cell phone number but thought better of it. I did give her the number of his precinct; they could do what they wanted with her messages. Molly called after that, hoping I still wanted her to baby-sit on Wednesday night during my class. I said yes. She didn't mention Russell or Sidney.

The phone rang again; it was another reporter from the local paper, not John. I asked how he'd gotten my number; he wouldn't tell me. I referred him to the police, then started screening my calls with the answering machine. I wasn't planning on picking up for anyone, no matter who it was. I was in the kitchen, up to my elbows in bread dough, when I heard Tommy's voice. In my haste to get to the phone, I tripped on the Hot Wheels track that had been erected across the doorway from the kitchen into the dining room and almost fell face-first onto the floor. Between the clamor I was making getting through the room and the blood pounding in my ears, I understood nothing of what he was saying. I grabbed the receiver after hearing the word "McCandless" and, trying not to pant too hard, said, "Tommy?"

"Hey, Gina, it's actually you."

"Yes, sorry. I was trying to pick up, but a racetrack had it in for me. How are you feeling?"

"Much better, actually. Susie's making me eat too much, but other than that I'm fine. I think I'll be going back to my place tomorrow. She's pretty upset about it, but I've got to get out of here. I called to check in at the constable's, and they told me that you had called. I wanted to call you, anyway, and I figured now would be as good a time as any."

"Are you still on the case? I mean, since you were hurt?"

"Oh, yeah. I'll be back to work by the end of the week. Russell would kill me if I left all the paperwork to him. Look, Gina, if I don't call you to keep you posted on things as much as I'd like, it's because the DA here has said that we shouldn't fraternize much. I hope you don't get offended by that."

"Oh, no. No, of course not. The constable told me as much, actually."

There was a beat of silence at that. "Okay. I guess he would." Another beat. "So what did you want to tell him, anyway? Can you tell me?"

I told him about the link to Fiona, which he of course knew about already, and then I told him what Cindy had said, that Fiona Belstein was also a former girlfriend of David Renouart. It might be a coincidence, but that seemed unlikely.

"Well, we've already talked to her, you know. But she hasn't said anything about this."

"She's probably too embarrassed. It's a small campus, and her relationship with him has been humiliating in other ways as well." I gave him an abridged version of the Nedra Kelly desktop incident, trying not to find a spiteful amusement in it this time.

"Hmmm." He chuckled a bit, guiltily. "Yikes. No wonder she didn't want to mention his name. But this does sound like something that's worth pursuing, worth having a little chat with this Renouart fellow, anyway. Do you think it's likely that he's involved in anything this shady?"

"I don't know. I wouldn't have said so, but I didn't really know him all that well. I mean, I thought I did, but I didn't really." I stopped before I made more of an ass of myself. "I have no idea what he's capable of, to be honest. I just thought you guys might want to talk to him."

"Thanks. We appreciate it. Really, Gina, without you, I'm not sure if we would have gotten Tim, at least not this quickly. You've been great about all this."

A beat of silence. I said, "Well, you're the one who got shot." He snorted. "By the way, the press has started in. I got a call from the *Tenway Express* already."

"That was inevitable. It's the TV people you've got to worry about. They'll tear up your yard and catch you by surprise so that you look guilty as hell of something. If I were you, I'd figure out what you're willing to say to them and then, when they show up, say it. That way they get a talking head for the evening news, which is all they want. They'll be less likely to harass you or make you look evasive on camera. And you're less likely to be caught saying something you wish you hadn't."

"Good idea. Thanks, Tommy." I paused. "I'll let you know if I hear any more about David Renouart. Feel better." I couldn't think of any other reason to keep him on the phone, so I reluctantly let him get on with his life.

John Fagin called again shortly after we'd eaten. I told him I'd been on the phone all evening and didn't want to talk anymore. I also said that someone from the *Express* had called me earlier. That upset him;

he clearly thought he had dibs. He pressed, and I finally consented to an interview. He would come to my house the following evening after dinner. I didn't want to get a sitter for this, so I figured it would have to be at my home. But I also wanted it clear that we weren't sharing food. Nothing like a date. I wouldn't pick up the toys or clean up the general mess, either. If he was horrified at our slovenly lives, great. I didn't even care if that made it into print.

I looked at the phone after our conversation was over and thought, what's wrong with John Fagin? He's perfectly decent, he's clean, he's not repulsive, he has a job, and he theoretically adores me.

That night I said, "E., if it weren't for the twins, I'd give Tommy my liver or heart or lungs if he needed 'em, and no one would even have to tell him where they came from."

"It's a good thing you have kids, then."

"Or that he doesn't happen to need an organ. I wish I liked John Fagin. God, I knew so many girls who were attracted to adoration. I've always found it off-putting."

"Even if it was Tommy that adored you?"

"Hmmm. No, if it were Tommy, that would be okay. But it would be mutual. We'd be disgusting." I sighed. "He reminds me a lot of Riley, but bigger, stronger, smarter, better-looking, and more mature." I heard myself and groaned. "But at least I got to go out with Riley for almost a year. Even if Tommy didn't have a girlfriend"—I thought of what Susie had said—"or two, I'm too much of a wuss to go after him in some Cosmo girl aggressive way. Why can't I be like Doughboy? He doesn't seem to fear rejection at all. He courts it with every breath."

"Maybe he just fears the alternative more. You have a high tolerance for loneliness, G."

I envisioned John Fagin at my dinner table or, God forbid, at the breakfast table. My mind immediately replaced him with Tommy, and I knew my limits. I said, "But being with some people can be the loneliest thing of all."

Ellie answered with "You should call Tommy."

"But if I do," I said, "I'll get in trouble."

. . .

The next day, Tuesday, was the first time I'd been in the classroom since Tommy had been shot. It felt like I hadn't taught in six months. I figured that most of the students would have heard about at least some of what had happened. I decided to talk to them directly about everything, since rumors would only be distracting and would mostly be wrong, anyway. I told each class about the website, about the fact that I used to be a model, about how the pornographic stuff was fabricated, and about how I had cooperated with the local and New York police to catch the perpetrators, since there was criminal activity involved. I didn't mention Tim and Jason's names, of course. They hadn't been convicted, and I didn't want to be hit with a slander suit.

"Look," I said each time, "if you have questions about any of this, you can ask me. I can't promise I'll answer, since I don't know everything the police do and don't want to damage their case by blabbing too much. But I don't want people giggling in the back row, either. If we talk about it, maybe we can then get back to work."

This strategy was successful, all in all. The students asked me quite a bit about my time in New York, and I told them most of what they wanted to know. I did the same with my Wednesday night class but added that the students who had been arrested were classmates of theirs. I knew they'd figure out who they were pretty easily if they didn't know already. But at least I wouldn't have told them, and I figured that should protect me legally. I hoped so, anyway. In all four classes that week I had the best attendance of the term.

John Fagin showed up at my house right after seven that Tuesday evening. He brought a store-bought chocolate cake. I thanked him, wondering what I was supposed to do. Was I supposed to serve it to him? I asked, and he said maybe later. Seeing him, I recalled his face enough to be sure it was the same man. But I felt bad about how little his features impressed themselves on my mind even now. I was afraid I might not recognize him again if he went to the bathroom.

I expected a bit of a snit from my never responding to his calls, but he acted as though we were old pals, chatted all the time, knew a lot about each other. It turned out that he did know quite a bit about me, presumably from Maggie. Initially, he started chatting about his own life, dropping names and other references that were completely unfamiliar to me. It soon became clear to him that I didn't remember much he'd told me previously about his marriage, his kid, and his job, and I obviously hadn't pumped Maggie for any information about him. For the first time, he got genuinely peeved. He could hardly yell at me for not gossiping about him behind his back. But he, with some urgency, began telling me in detail about his life, in what ways his wife had committed various forms of emotional larceny, how his twelve-year-old daughter was perfect yet precocious and, I suspected, damaged. He used to be a reporter at the *Chicago Tribune*. Something had happened there, he wouldn't say what, that forced the move to Tenway, where his wife had family. But the marriage hadn't been able to withstand the move, the loss of money and prestige, and whatever other stresses they had had to deal with. For two years he'd been without a wife. He was ready to get another one. His circumstances had forced him to take a job at the puny Tenway weekly, trying to cover the hardest news available. At the moment, it seemed I was the answer to his prayers on both counts.

I sat there patiently, letting his dreary life story wash over me. Mine's pretty banal and depressing, too, in its own way, after all. I was trying not to get uppity or to be rude. But he evoked nothing in me but a tired urge to be alone with my sons.

When he apparently felt that I knew enough about him, he smiled rather sweetly and asked if I'd tell him about the Solomon case. I told him as little as I could without seeming to be holding out. He wanted to know, did I have a feeling about Tim, how did he act, did I know he was stalking me, and so on. The truth was boring, so I went with that. No, I'd been clueless; no, I hadn't discerned anything especially sinister about him and Jason. He was disappointed but polite about it. The boys interrupted us, telling me something that they wanted to get the next time we went on a toy run. John looked indulgent, tender, even.

"Cute kids," he said.

"Yes," I agreed.

He wanted to know more about my past, the pictures that had

played such a large role in all this. I was vague, general. I wasn't sure what he wanted to know, but I tried to make being a nascent super-model sound as dull as possible, just a job. Of course, sometimes it was. But of course, mostly it wasn't. He was a good interviewer, though, probably even better because I'd expected so little. He managed to get a few details I wished I hadn't let slip, about my friendship with Erin Steele as well as with the Van Dorens. He wanted to know details, anecdotes, insider perspectives on Dion's widely known eccentrici-ties. I thought, this is turning into entertainment news, celebrity gos-sip. I said something to that effect, trying to get him to stop. He didn't like my resistance but eventually let it go. We got back to the main story, and he asked about Fiona Belstein. I feigned complete igno-rance, wondering how all this was going to play out for her. I thought, she has no idea that she owes me now. I also wondered if anyone was asking her about me, and if so, what she was saying.

When he'd wrung me dry, I made it clear that the boys had to go to bed. He didn't seem to understand initially that that meant I wanted him to leave. I had to get his coat off its hook by the door and hand it to him before he would get out of the chair. To my relief, he didn't ask me to dinner again. Instead, he told me he'd call me later when the story was to come out and make sure I got a copy.

I was utterly exhausted when I finally got him out the door.

The next day I picked the boys up at the bus stop in the car. Fortu-nately, I saw the news van parked in front of my house before we got too close to turn around without calling attention to ourselves. I drove the boys straight to Mo's, put them in her charge, and then drove back home. As I pulled up, a thickly groomed and tightly suited woman whom I vaguely recognized from the local TV news whipped her cameraman around to get a load of me. I said as I opened the car door, "May I at least get out of my car before you turn the camera on?" She faked a smile, said "Of course," then shoved the mike in my face, the red light blinking over her shoulder.

Between Tommy's advice and my practice session with John Fagin the night before, I was well prepared. I told her the same general story that I'd told my students and feigned ignorance of everything I plausibly could. "The police have been great," I gushed. Of course, the reporter had to ask me about the website and my lurid past. I was forthright. Yes, I'd been a model, but never nude or anything like that. Goodness me, no. I helped sell clothes, for heaven's sake, not copies of *Playboy*. I didn't mention that a good percentage of the clothes I helped sell was smallish undergarments. I was a good, clean, decent woman, by God. That seemed to satisfy her.

She left, leaving only minor damage to my front yard. I braced myself for scantily clad pictures of myself on the evening news. But at least the website was down, so the actual porn was no longer available.

The next edition of the *Tenway Express* ran John's story. It was well written and detailed. But it was almost buried in the bottom corner of the front page, "continued on page 6." The main headline involved the deputy head of the Tenway town council, who had run off with a substantial portion of the town's money and gone to Atlantic City. Reading between the lines of the accounts in the local paper, I found out he had gotten the job because of his marriage to the daughter of an influential circuit court judge. His trip to New Jersey included a woman, but not his wife. He wasn't bright enough to hide effectively, and he wound up being caught almost immediately. At first I thought I was just lucky, even though it was at the expense of others. My story would be a lot bigger if the police could prove that Tim or Jason had actually murdered anyone.

I felt terribly sorry for the guy's wife and his little son. But for me the best news was that the mistress had been the centerfold of a biker magazine, so her pictures became far more interesting than mine.

But then I thought, a bit chilled, that this may have had little to do with luck and a lot to do with John Fagin. It was possible that I owed him.

part two

chapter nineteen

If . . . you are aware of fear, you realize that, because this feeling is now yourself, escape is impossible. You see that calling it "fear" tells you little or nothing about it, for the comparison and the naming is based, not on past experience, but on memory. You have then no choice but to be aware of it with your whole being as an entirely new experience. Indeed, every experience is in this sense new, and at every moment of our lives we are in the midst of the new and the unknown. At this point you receive the experience without resisting it or naming it, and the whole sense of conflict between "I" and the present reality vanishes.

ALAN WATTS, *The Wisdom of Insecurity*

IT WAS A VINDICTIVE FEBRUARY. The freezing winds picked up, then died down, then picked up again. I put off talking to the boys about getting kittens. They wanted them; I did, too, but still needed to grieve over Sidney. I thought that having a pet, a cat or a dog especially, was good training for having a child. It's not the same, obviously. But the responsibility is similar enough that if you can't handle the one, you know you probably shouldn't take on the other. I had always taken good care of Sidney, at least until the very end of his life. I'd really let him down then. I had a minor anxiety attack about what that meant about my ability to be a mother.

When I voiced this concern to her, Ellie said, "What, you're responsible for everything that happens to them? What about when they're thirty? You'll only be in your fifties, probably still around. Will they have any responsibility for their life? Where will your power end?"

"It ends," I said, "when I'm dead. Even when they're adults, I'm responsible for the tools I've given them to deal with their lives."

"Pretty grandiose, G. It ends when it ends. In fact, you only have a limited amount of power now, you know, and less every minute. They already make their own choices. There are other people affecting them. Do your best but get over yourself. What will happen will happen. What will happen *to* them and what *they* will choose. Both are almost totally beyond your control. Even beyond your knowledge."

"E., if I didn't love you, I'd tell you to fuck off," I said, sulky as hell.

One freezing Thursday I was drinking a cup of morning coffee with Cindy and Kay in the office. Vincent wasn't in yet, and Ida was teaching an eight o'clock class. They all wanted periodic updates on the case, so I always let them know anything new I had found out. I had seen the constable the day before, along with Fiona Belstein. The three of us had met in McCandless's office at his request. Afterward I had asked Fiona if she wanted to get a cup of coffee, but she winced at the thought, unable to even be polite. I suspected that she felt we had a little too much in common and didn't really want to see me again. I couldn't blame her. But for my two eager co-workers, I had big news.

"I got more dirt on David Renouart."

This immediately got their attention. "Thanks to you, Cindy," I said while she glowed, "the police knew to question him. Evidently, he took those pictures of Fiona. He denies taking the ones through the window; they think that actually may have been Brad Franco. But he also has a huge collection of soft porn and lingerie catalogs." I stopped a moment for effect. "Including, of course, lots of old copies of *Lavish,* prominently featuring yours truly. That's how he got pictures of me, but he has gotten quite a few women to pose for him willingly. He admits now to selling students erotic pictures of selected women on the faculty."

Their reaction was gratifying. "Euuwwww!" Kay squeaked.

"Yep," I said. "For quite a lot, apparently. In case you were wondering how he could afford that Beamer."

"Is he going to jail?" Cindy asked, very happy. Her status among her fellow administrative assistants was going to be golden for a while.

"I don't know. The legalities of this are touchy, since it's a question of who owns the pictures. I don't have a leg to stand on, since those of me are all out in the public domain now. But it doesn't look like he got Fiona or anyone else to sign any sort of release when he photographed them. So the lawyers are sorting it out. The students are all over eighteen, so they can't get him on corrupting minors."

"But he's up for tenure next year," said Kay. "Professionally, he's fucked."

I got a picture of Tommy off the Auxiliary Circle website. It was very small, and I printed it out and put it in the drawer of my nightstand. I thought, I'm probably in trouble here; this isn't healthy. I kept expecting to not think about him anymore and kept thinking about him, anyway. This was reminding me of Riley Kupferberg, which wasn't good. Riley had been my first real love, my first true heartache. I'd started seeing him when I was eighteen, ancient in model years. He was slender and fair, a fellow student at the New School, a poet several years older than I was. Not old enough to be mature but old enough to seem so to me. He dumped me after about ten months of, to me, ecstatic dating. It took me several years to stop pining for him altogether. Still, I remember thinking on occasion not long before this that if he showed up at my door and said, "Hey Gina, that was then, this is now. Want to try it like adults?" I probably would have said yes, assuming we were both single and he was still recognizable as himself. Sometimes my constancy was ridiculous. I was even faithful to Scott both during our loveless marriage and for several years after his death. I didn't know how to relinquish ghosts.

I didn't tell Ellie any of this, my weird internal love life, and avoided seeing Jeri. On Valentine's Day I frightened myself a little with the intensity of my expectations that something was going to happen. But it was a normal Saturday, and Tommy didn't call me. John Fagin had called three different times to ask if I'd go out to dinner on that particular evening, and I had consistently refused. On the day itself I almost relented, wondering if it would help me be less miserable, would be at least a distraction. Then I thought about how he was likely to interpret my consenting to a date on Valentine's Day, of all days, and I didn't make that stupid mistake.

I started telling myself about all the ways in which I was lucky. Thinking of my own good fortune, I was reminded, with sick remorse, of Erin. I felt terribly shallow and selfish. Christ, I hadn't even talked to her after her surgery. So it was late February, a month and a half after I'd seen her, that I dug through my address book, found her home number, and dialed it. I vowed not to mention anything about Tommy or Tim Solomon, or any of the recent events in my life.

I got her in the flesh, not her voice mail. However, she sounded funny, a little wispy, not unfriendly but like she was watching a TV show or reading the paper while talking to me. Absent. She said the surgery had gone well; she was feeling all right, although the chemo had made her a bit weak. "My agent's meeting with the *Jamais* people next week. He's hopeful that we can work something out and I can keep the account after I feel a bit better. And one thing that's great—I've lost six pounds without even trying." To my horror, I was pretty sure that this was said without irony. Then Erin said she'd call me later. I told her I'd come to the city in a week or two, come see her. She said, "That sounds great. Although I'll be busy for a while. Make it next month, okay? Thanks for calling, Gina. It was sweet of you."

· · ·

Mo dragged me to Hannigan's for lunch one Friday, against my better judgment. Mo's attempts to win her father's approval were starting to seem a bit feverish. I was horrified when, after we ordered, Uncle Frank joined us at the table. At first I thought, oh, okay, maybe all her ass kissing is working; he's lightening up on her. But he wouldn't even look at her; instead, all his attention lasered on me.

"Gina," he said, "I can't believe you went to the cops with your little problem. I don't like seeing family plastered all over the evening news."

Oh. "I don't, either, Uncle Frank. But I didn't even know I had a little problem till the police came to me."

"You can't go working with them, honey. I'll talk to this kid for you."

"The cops have him already, Uncle Frank. There's no need to do anything."

"Well, in the future, if you got a problem with some out-of-line student, just come see me. I'll deal with him directly, if you know what I mean." He rocked back in his creaking chair, considering me for an uncomfortable moment. "I'll tell you what. I'll keep an eye out. Keep an eye on things for you. Make sure you don't have another one of your little problems."

"That's not necessary, Uncle Frank. The police have dealt with things okay."

"That's not what I hear. Anyway, just leave it to me."

I hadn't known that Uncle Frank saw himself as some sort of small-town godfather. I made sure I didn't laugh at him just in case he wasn't simply being delusional. I repeated my assurances that I had no expectation of ever having such a problem again. He patted my hand, which gave me the creeps, and left us. He'd never once addressed Mo, who then polished off the bottle of wine she'd ordered. I hadn't had any.

I tried to check in on Jessie every couple of days, making sure she didn't either freeze to death or boil to death. She always treated me like a mild but necessary irritant and continued to press odd bits and foodstuffs on me no matter how much I protested: an ancient box of pallid chocolate crèmes, a stuffed yarn-encrusted turkey, a water-stained volume of stories by James Whitcomb Riley that smelled like mushrooms. With each gift she heaved sighs of taxed tolerance, but she never told me to leave her alone.

One day when I had midterms to grade, about twelve loads of laundry to do, and a freezer to defrost, I was relieved that Jessie didn't bang on the pipe. But when I came back from the grocery store, I saw the same man I had seen before, middle-aged, dark, and tall, on Jessie's porch, knocking on the door. This time he had with him a thin, too-tall teenager with a Yankees cap pulled on atop a woolen one and a beige corduroy coat that was at the same time too big around and too short for him.

I said hello and told them that if they were looking for Jessie, she'd gone that morning to the senior center by way of Access cab. "I don't know when she'll be back."

The man said, "That's okay. We'll wait inside. We have a key. Thank you."

I wondered if they'd be interested in cheese or women's clothing.

The next Wednesday, as I was approaching my house after a particularly exhausting evening class, I noticed, parked across the street from Jessie's house, a rusty blue Trans Am I had never seen before. Parking is crowded on Circuit Lane, so seeing unfamiliar cars in odd places is not out of the ordinary. There was someone in the car, a man. I had the impression of someone in the passenger seat as well, although when my headlights lit the rear end of the beat-up car, I couldn't see a second silhouette. In my former life I would have paid no attention to this. Now all my senses started tingling unpleasantly. I tried to get a better look at the man's face as I drove past, but the lighting didn't cooperate. As I pulled into my driveway, I made sure the doors were locked, then turned to see if I could get a better view of the car now that I was no longer moving, wishing I'd been able to get the license number. But the car was between streetlamps; I could see nothing useful. I gathered my belongings, then dashed from car to front porch, making sure to lock the car doors first, then locking the front door after pushing it closed behind me.

Once safe inside, I was able to talk frankly to Molly about the suspicious car, since the boys were in bed. She treated me, as usual, as though I was grossly overreacting, but I still called Mo, telling her to come get Molly rather than having her walk the two blocks to their house alone. I couldn't leave the sleeping boys to take her. The recent drama in my life made me more convincing than I would have been otherwise; Mo came ten minutes later. By then the mystery car was gone.

I considered calling the constable but thought, to tell him what? Next time, I thought, if there is a next time, I'll do whatever's needed to get a good look at the license plate.

Awful February turned into crappy March. The weather was obnoxious, pinwheeling around from blizzard to balmy and back again. The major subject on both the local news and in the department was influenza, which was taking its mindless opportunities anywhere it could as immune systems all over Tenway went into weather-related tailspins. Many students came to class intermittently, yellow-faced and miserable, and I kept my distance from them as best I could, washing my hands like some bookish Lady Macbeth.

I was home at the end of a terrible week, having shown films and given lectures for an ailing Vincent Capinelli in addition to teaching my own classes, when I got a call from Constable McCandless.

"Gina, I've got to give you a heads-up."

"About what?"

"Jason Dettwiler is out."

"Out? Of jail? Where? I mean, is he here or in the city?"

"We don't know."

"What?"

Through the legal maneuvering of his attorneys, Jason had gotten bail, which his parents had paid gladly despite its monstrous size. There wasn't much evidence against him, after all. McCandless assured me that that wouldn't present a problem in the long run; they had enough to get him convicted of some drug and pornography charges, and they were still looking for Bradley Franco or his body.

But for a month or so Jason Dettwiler had been a free man. I immediately thought about the rusty Trans Am and asked the constable if Jason had access to such a car. He said no, not as far as they knew.

The problem was that the police who were supposed to be keeping an eye on him in the city had apparently failed to do so. He hadn't shown up for a motion hearing, and no one, including his parents, seemed to have any idea where he'd gone. Once Tommy had heard about this, he'd called the constable immediately. McCandless told me that the detective had wanted to come to town or at least call me himself, but the constable had discouraged him. "Although now I'm not sure I did the right thing, because I don't have the manpower to have someone watching you and your house all the time right now. Half the department has this shitty flu that's going around. Pardon my language. I'm frankly worried about Jason coming to see you, Gina." So was I. "I want you to put the desk and my direct number on your speed dial, both on your cell and on your home phone. Anything looks funny, you see any other funny cars or, God forbid, Jason himself, you call right away, day or night. You understand?"

"But if he's free, he's not breaking any laws by talking to me, is he? I mean, how can we stop him just approaching me in a parking lot the way Tim did?"

"It's called intimidating a witness, and it's a serious thing to do. If he approaches you at all, he's doing it, and we can arrest him. If he doesn't surface after a day or two, I'm calling Detective Galloway back and telling him to get his ass out here. You call me if you see Jason, Gina. You understand?"

"I understand," I said, not feeling like this was real at all.

I was getting good at putting things that I didn't want to think about out of my mind. Instead of worrying about Jason Dettwiler, I had Bobbie and Donna over for dinner that night, just the three of us and the twins. Clark was visiting his parents, who lived in Philadelphia. I was glad that Donna had apparently come clean to Bobbie about her affair with the trauma doctor, whose name was Vijay. He had told Donna that he was preparing to leave his wife of sixteen years and his three children for her. She just needed to be patient, there was a lot at stake, and so on. Bobbie and I listened to her while she worked the whole mess out herself. She knew what she needed to do; there was no point lecturing her.

The three of us also chewed over the issue of Franny's reputed baby for the first time. Bobbie had talked to Aunt Lottie about Francesca's history and found out that she'd joined the convent when she was nineteen. We put our heads together and did some math. The only Hannigan candidates were Maggie, who was the same age as I was, Lizzie, and Molly. Molly was out, because Mo remembered Aunt Rosa being pregnant with her. The list of possibles also included thirty-two-year-old Bobbie, but Donna said she remembered Aunt Lottie being pregnant and coming back from the hospital with Bobbie. Donna was one year too old to be on the list. That let out the Eberle girls.

Then there were the Paletta girls. My sister was too old, born two years before Franny would have been in the convent. That left me, the perfect age. Franny would have been twenty-four years old at the time of my birth. Now Bobbie needed to figure out if there was any way to find birth records. We needed to know the exact year. Lottie, however, had dismissed the adoption story altogether. Either it was untrue or it was too deeply disturbing for her to be able to talk about it.

That Saturday afternoon Tommy and Russell appeared at my front door, both looking suit-free and weekendy, with heavy sweaters over T-shirts, jeans, and running shoes, and small duffel bags swaying from muscular shoulders. I swear I felt like I was going to pass out with the two of them standing on my front porch, the wind blowing icy bullets into their backs as they waited for me to come to enough to let them in.

"We're back!" Russell sang.

"We're moving in again," Tommy said.

Toby and Stevie were gleeful to see the two men; I could feel an attack of maternal anxiety grating at me. I was furious with Russell and Tommy for being so jolly; they each picked up a boy and swung him around, like happy uncles. Don't they get it? I thought, panicky. Don't they understand? They're going to break their little hearts, they're going to leave forever two boys who don't need any more leaving, who need, need, need people to stay.

I didn't understand, either, why they both needed to be here, inside the house. I didn't know what good they expected to do. But I didn't know how to ask about that; I didn't want to sound ungrateful, since they were, after all, giving up their weekend to be here. And I really didn't want to sound like I wanted to be alone with either of them. It was horribly awkward. All I wanted to do was stare at Tommy, touch his face with my hands, sit on his lap. I had to force myself to look as much at Russell, who was as grinning and handsome as ever and even less attractive to me, if possible, than he'd been before. My chest ached with frustration, and my head felt foggy. We had to order pizza for dinner, as I couldn't concentrate enough to cook.

We were eating in the living room, watching a movie, when Toby started telling Russell that he and his brother were going to be playing baseball soon. Russell pointed to Tommy and said, "Talk to this guy. He used to play, you know." Nothing could have been better calculated to get Toby to switch allegiances than that. He was all over Tommy then, asking him to tell him everything he knew about the game, about his own team, his memories, his knowledge of baseball now. I thought, I'm sorry, I can't do this for you, you poor boys, sports freaks because of your useless mother. Tommy, of course, was delighted and started telling them arcane things such as the meaning of statistics, who the big players were and why, details of certain games he'd played. Even Stevie got sucked in. They were on the couch, and Toby's little body was pressed close to Tommy's side as he talked, while Stevie crept closer from the opposite end, standing up on the cushions, leaning back against the wall, and inching over sideways. Russell continued to watch the movie, stopping it for a moment to go out and smoke on the porch. I noticed that he didn't turn on the front light; I understood, suddenly, that he was being smart. Jason couldn't shoot someone he couldn't see.

. . .

After I put the boys to bed, I came downstairs; both men were waiting for me in the living room. Tommy spoke first.

"You're obviously bent out of shape that we're here. But it's only for your protection, you know. McCandless just doesn't have any people now to keep an eye on you."

When I could talk, I blurted, "You two need to stop being so goddamn charming to my sons. I don't want them getting so attached to you." I stopped, hoping that the rest was obvious.

Tommy kept looking at me, and Russell looked at him, then at me. He fished a cigarette out of his shirt pocket. Tommy said, "They'll be okay, Gina. They know we aren't moving in permanently. They're fine." He had that tone again, soothing, liquid, like he needed to calm a maniac. It had, of course, the opposite effect on me, making me want to jump up and down and stomp and wave my arms and shriek shrilly and lose every shred of adult credibility.

"How the hell would you know?" I said, trying hard not to get gulpy and quavery and hysterical-sounding.

"Because it's obvious," he said, so reasonable that for the first time I wanted to hit him.

"Fine," I said, and went up to my bedroom, leaving them to sort out wherever they were going to sleep and whatever they were going to do to kill the rest of the evening. I closed my door, got ready for bed, and tried to read, though I was so worked up that I couldn't even begin to make my eyes and brain work together. I kept reworking my tiny confrontation with Tommy, wondering what I could do, how I could convince him to . . . what? To leave sooner or stay longer? I breathed deeply, started to cry. He was right, I thought; the boys would get over it. I was the one who probably wouldn't, or at least wouldn't as quickly. I turned out the light, lay down, and let the tears come out, muffling the sounds with my pillow so that no one, especially Tommy, could hear them.

I couldn't remember the last time I had woken up to the smell of cooking. Even when the boys and I stayed with Mo and Ivy, I usually took on the job of making fancy breakfasts or baking. I struggled to get myself together, remembering who was in my house as I did so. I made an effort not to be as bedraggled as I usually was on Sundays and put on reasonable leggings and a nice sweater, combed my hair, washed my face, put on earrings.

Tommy and Russell were both in the kitchen. Tommy was chopping various vegetables into fine pieces as Russell directed; Russell seemed to be in charge of the show. They greeted me, and Russell said that he was making omelets, a specialty of his, with Tommy's help. Being versed in Chinese cooking, he was a good chopper. "I figured I'd give you and your boys a treat in exchange for all the food we've eaten."

I thought about telling him that the boys would never eat such a thing but didn't know how to without coming across as a bitchy killjoy. I left them to it and found the boys playing a Harry Potter board game in the living room. I talked to them quietly, telling them that Tommy and Russell were making a special breakfast, and it would be really sweet of them if they could at least taste it and make sounds of pleasure and appreciation. They stared at me blankly for a few moments, then seemed to get what I was asking, and both nodded. When the omelets were ready, they made me proud, actually pretending to eat them. Stevie grinned conspiratorially at me once, right in front of Russell, and Toby kept giggling. But neither of the other adults seemed to grasp what that meant. I vowed silently to make my sons something they actually liked for lunch. I thought, am I training them to be like me—too nice, anything at all to be accommodating, never make anyone else uncomfortable for any reason? And is this a good thing? But they didn't seem particularly stressed by their polite playacting, and as I watched the four of them sitting around the kitchen table, smiling, laughing, eating, I relaxed slowly. I started smiling, too, as Tommy made some joke about eggs being cracked on people's heads.

His cell phone rang, a steady beeping, and he pulled it out of his pocket, looked at the display, and answered it with knit brows.

"Yes, Claire," he said, looking deliberately at Russell, who looked back. He listened for a few moments, said "yes" a couple of times, then left the room, phone pasted to his ear as he seemed to be gearing up to say something himself. Russell watched him leave. My first thought was, oh, another girlfriend; of course she'd be wondering where he was on a weekend. I felt flattened and lumpy at the same time.

Russell said, "This may not be good."

"Oh?"

"It's Claire Stanley."

The name rang a distant bell but not a close one, and I couldn't grasp it for the moment. "Who?" I said.

"The assistant district attorney who's handling Tim and Jason's case in the city. I thought maybe she was calling with some news of Jason. But maybe not." He followed Tommy into the living room. The boys looked at me, curious. I looked back and shrugged like it didn't have anything to do with us. But of course it did, and my stomach started tightening. I gave the boys each a surreptitious Pop Tart and scooted them upstairs to get dressed. Then I went into the living room, wondering if I was trespassing in some way, even in my own house. Tommy was still on the phone and was arguing. He was talking to her in that same reasonable, lilting way he'd spoken to me the night before, but I realized suddenly that he was angry. He said a few more gentle things: "I don't think you need to do that" and "You're making this a problem when it isn't." I thought, maybe she is a girlfriend, after all. I left, reluctantly giving him some privacy again, although Russell was there, hands in pockets, looking sullen.

I busied myself in the kitchen till they finally both came back in. Tommy said to both Russell and me, "She's coming up here."

"When?" Russell said, looking wide-eyed.

"Today. Now."

"Shit! It's a Sunday, for Christ's sake!"

I broke in, "Does she have some news about Jason?"

"Oh, no," Tommy said, nostrils flaring. He was really mad. I was appalled at myself that I found it attractive, this contained anger.

"Then why is she coming?"

They looked at each other, and I flashed back to when I'd first met them. Tommy finally said, "She doesn't think we should be here. She thinks we're compromising the case by being here at all, and she wants to talk to you. She said she might as well do it today."

"Shit," Russell said again.

Russell and Tommy went out to the front porch to smoke and to speak tensely and softly to each other. I looked around and irrationally thought I should tidy up a bit for the DA's visit. But I had a lot of work to do: study guides and exams to write, not to mention a few lectures I hadn't prepared yet. I'd been a fairly uninspired professor this term, having been terribly distracted so much of the time. If I was going to kill time, it would be better spent on work. Still, I picked up a few toys and newspapers, but then the twins came downstairs and started cooperating in the construction of a room-sized domino run. Anytime they played well together, I was happy, so I left them to it, deciding that Claire Stanley would just have to wade through our crap to get to a chair. I hadn't invited her here.

She showed up about two hours later. I heard a car engine outside and looked out the small, high window in the front door. "Jesus Christ," I said to Tommy, "there's a car the size of a city bus outside."

It was a golden SUV that blocked the sun. Tommy said softly, "That's Claire. Her husband does corporate law."

"Oh."

Claire Stanley was fortyish and very large, not fat but tall, over six feet, with broad shoulders and bad, tea-colored skin. She had long arms and bony wrists; I suspected she'd been tapped for basketball in high school or college. She had black hair done in a crisp bob and no makeup, though she needed it. She was wearing black silk pants with running shoes and a teal-colored wool sweater, bulky with pink macramé tulips all over her breasts. For the first time I sympathized with men whose eyes were drawn to chest level; between her height and her bulbous sweater, I had a hard time myself keeping my eyes on her face.

She came in with lips pursed so hard that I expected water to spurt out of them. I sent the boys upstairs, aware that they might very well spy on us anyway. I hoped that Stevie's indifference to the outside world would work in my favor this time.

Claire Stanley took coffee, never actually looking at me, then sat down after sourly removing a Transformer (the toy, not the electrical component) from her seat and thrusting it aside. Tommy was sitting on the love seat in the corner, and Russell was standing in the doorway between the living room and the dining room, looking uncomfortable. She looked at the two of them, then said, "You boys have really fucked up. You need to get out of here now before you fuck things up worse."

Neither man looked happy about being spoken to that way, but neither said anything; they merely shifted and winced. I understood that she was probably a big deal in their world. But she wasn't in mine, I decided. I suddenly became someone else, I'm not sure who, and said, as hypocritical as I've ever been in my life, "I have two seven-year-olds upstairs. Please watch your language."

She looked at me at last, nostrils flaring, eyebrows raised. She looks insane, I thought; she looks familiar. "So I finally get to see the one everyone's sniffing around. I needed to come talk to you, anyway. This seemed like a good time." Her eyebrows lowered. Her voice was rounded and fruity and sounded like it was coming down a tube and it would smell if you got too close to her. She looked back at Tommy, then at Russell. "You boys get what you came for? You done looking now? Who wins?"

Tommy's jaw was working. He was still furious, I could tell. "You don't have the right to tell us what to do with our weekends, Claire."

It took a while for me to realize what that meant; they weren't getting paid for being here. They really were using their weekend, their time off, to watch me and my house and my kids. I couldn't decide how I felt about this.

Claire spit back at Tommy, almost literally, "I do when it could fuck up my case! Jesus, can you imagine what the defense could do with this? In this day and age of defense teams everywhere saying that all evidence is planted, that the cops make everything up, you don't think that they could get a jury to look at Daisy Mae here and make them think she's boinking her own students, leading them on, then boinking some cops to get them to take care of the inconvenient college kids for her, get rid of them, make sure they don't jeopardize her job, something like that?"

"That's the most bizarre and ridiculous thing I've ever heard," I said involuntarily.

She swiveled her nasty amber gaze to me again. "Well, I'm sure with your penetrating legal mind, you know best." I flinched, feeling struck. I didn't understand why she hated me so much. She narrowed her eyes at Tommy and went on, "It doesn't have to make real sense; it doesn't have to be true. It just has to sound good to twelve rubes with nothing better to do than be on a jury. Jesus. *I'm* not convinced that there's nothing hinky happening here." She looked at Russell, who still was standing tensely in the doorway. "I realize that you're not going to tell me juicy details. But whatever's going on, it has to stop, now." She looked at Tommy, then at me again. "After seeing you, it's obvious that a trial would be a bad idea. That's a shame, because if we can ever link them to the Franco boy's death, I'd like to go for the death penalty, which I can't do if I have to offer them a plea."

I sucked in my breath, starting to feel cold prickles on my skin. "You want to give them the death penalty? They're just boys."

"Just boys?" She looked at Russell, then at Tommy, as though to say, Can you believe this idiot? "They're probably murderers. They tried to kill a cop. But it's obvious that the defense could do something"— she looked in my direction but not directly at me—"come up with some doubt that they had any defense against your charms, young hormones, that sort of thing. I'll still need a statement from you, but only after the plea agreement's been set. And after we find Jason."

My hostility against her kept inflating, and I was laboring not to start screaming at her. I wasn't sure exactly what I wanted to scream, though, and big angry speeches were not my strong suit. In movies or novels, angry outbursts in which you finally speak your mind, take some sort of stand, and ream out some nasty jerk often win people over, win their admiration, show them that you have spunk. But in real life, every time I've ever actually let loose on people, they simply wrote me off forever as a querulous bitch, as did any witnesses. It's never liberating, only costly, as I tend to feel deep shame for a long time afterward. So my mouth stayed shut, and I took her contempt with a damp sort of acquiescence. I realized right then, with a nauseous clarity, that she was way too much like my mother.

But then something else occurred to me. I actually saw her for a moment, and I had the kind of insight about people's inner worlds and motives I don't usually get until days have passed. I saw why she hated me so much. She kept looking angrily at Russell, then at Tommy, and very little at me. She was jealous. I wondered which of them she had a crush on. Both of them, perhaps. Or maybe it was more than a crush, maybe some sort of midlife crisis; I almost certainly would never know.

Then I was filled with an unwelcome compassion. She was a woman with a lot of money, a lot of power, a prestigious job, but obviously not enough to make her happy or at least pleasant. I was distantly glad I hadn't exploded at her. It would have eaten at me for days.

"I don't really need your statement now," she said, standing up, still not exactly looking at me. "I know what I have to do." She looked at Tommy. "I'll wait while you two get your stuff. As much as I want to leave, I won't till I can follow the two of you back to the city."

Tommy opened his mouth, but she cut him off. "It's the local cops' job to watch out for her, Tommy. Not yours. You both have to get back. Now."

I went into the kitchen, loading the dishwasher with trembling hands while the two detectives packed up their few things in their duffel bags. Claire Stanley stood silently in the living room. I heard the rumble of voices briefly upstairs: Tommy saying good-bye to the boys. Tommy followed Russell downstairs and said something to Claire, then something more strident. I then heard "Goddamn it, Claire, I'm leaving, but I'm going to talk to her. Don't fuck with me anymore. I mean it. Russell, would you take her outside?" I heard mumbling, then the front door open and close. Tommy came into the kitchen. I wanted to touch him so much, my whole body hurt. "I'm really sorry, Gina. I'm really, really sorry." He stuck his hands in his pockets, and I had an intense if impotent desire to rescue him in some way. He pulled a card out of his right pocket, got a pen from the counter, and scribbled on the back of it.

"They're going to keep me busy for the next few weeks, but if you see Jason or if you're worried about anything at all, please call me." He handed me the card. "There are all my numbers. I don't know if you still have them. Call the constable, too, but call me. I'm really, really sorry."

I told him it was okay and tried not to look bereft at his leaving. I walked him to the door, and we stood awkwardly facing each other. "Good-bye, Gina," he finally said, patting my arm. I lifted my hand like I was saying the pledge of allegiance and worked up what was probably a grotesque smile, and he left.

Later that week, on Thursday, the boys and I were walking home from the bus stop. We were about two doors away when I saw a tall thin figure get up from where he'd been sitting, on our porch steps. My heart lurched; at first I thought it was Tommy. I quickly registered that he was too thin and nowhere near tall enough. It was Jason Dettwiler, and he had seen us.

chapter twenty

I GRIPPED BOTH BOYS by their small shoulders. I said, "Go to Josh's. Tell his mother to call the police right now and have them come to our house. Go." As they scampered obediently away, I reached into my bag and grabbed my cell phone.

"Dr. Paletta. Gina. Please. Please."

He was so young, his voice still cracked. His Adam's apple was the size of a golf ball, poking out from a neck as bony as a chicken's. "Gina, please," he said as he walked toward me on the sidewalk, greasy-haired and pale. "I just need to talk to you. Please. I wanted to say I'm so sorry. I'm so fuckin' sorry about your cat." Then he burst into tears.

This sodden and pathetic boy seemed as dangerous to me as a dandelion. I walked the few steps to my house; he followed and sat down on the front steps again, sobbing into his hands, noisily sucking in greats gusts of air, letting it all out in a kind of tenor honking sound. Eventually I sat down, too, as far away as possible.

His sobbing slowed. He said, "I didn't want to do it. Tim made me." He let out another sob. There was a line of snot about a half inch long dangling from his nose and a large whitehead at the corner of his thin wet lips. "He said we had to show you, you know, how we both felt. Tim said you loved him, but if I could do this one thing, you would love me, too. Tim said it. I didn't believe him, really, but he kept saying it till I thought, I have to do this, maybe he's right. Maybe she'd let me, you know." I thought I did. He wiped his nose with the back of his hand, wiping that in turn on his knee. "I'm really, really sorry. I just love you so much. I just wanted you to know." He finally turned his head to look me in the eye. Poor crazy boy, with swollen eyes and disordered brain and no sense of reality at all. Or maybe he simply saw how unlikely it was that someone like him would get a reasonable girlfriend in the normal way. Maybe he saw reality in all its grimness perfectly well, after all. Poor boy. He looked away quickly, maybe ashamed, maybe just unable to sustain eye contact with another human being. "I'm really sorry about your cat." He put his face in his hands again, quietly now.

I said, "Jason, I have to call Constable McCandless now." I pulled out my phone and hit the constable's number on the speed dial.

"Who?" He didn't look up from his hands.

"The cops."

"Oh. Gina, I love you so much. I'd do anything for you. If anyone bothers you, you just let me know." He turned for another brief look.

The constable answered his phone. "Gina?" he said. Caller ID, I thought. I could see Jessie peering out from behind her curtains. I thought, I'll have to tell her everything later. She'll enjoy hearing all about this.

"We're here, Constable, on my front steps," I said to the phone.

"Jason and you?"

"Yep."

"You okay?"

"Yes. I'm fine. We're just chatting."

"Someone's on their way. I'm right behind them."

"Okay."

"I love you so fuckin' much," Jason said again. "I helped Tim pick it out. He wanted something in red, but I said jade was good. Like China, you know. You teach stuff about Buddhism in China and shit, you know, like in the intro class we took."

I hadn't expected him to make much sense, anyway, but this was, initially at least, even more nonsensical than everything else he'd said. Then the image of the jade heart I'd received anonymously in the mailbox on my birthday jabbed into my memory. Understanding cut me. Oh my God. I had a bizarre, confused moment when I thought I should thank him for it.

"You wouldn't ever wear it. It really pissed Tim off. That's one reason why he thought, you know, we needed to make, like, a statement. You know."

I didn't, and then I did. They killed Sidney because I hadn't worn their gift. The heavy, ugly heart.

That Jason might have a weapon on him had never occurred to me, so when he pulled a Swiss Army knife out of his pocket, I felt no sense of increased danger. But when, sniffing loudly, he pulled a blade out from the array of tools that were neatly folded together, my mouth opened. I gathered myself in impotently, preparing to stand, to try to run. He looked at the blade for a moment as my muscles spasmed and clenched uselessly. Jason positioned the knife in his thin right hand, then stretched out his left wrist, so scrawny I could easily have circled it entirely with my thumb and forefinger, skin the color of bread dough. He brought the knife down on the baby-white skin and cut and cut. The blood was dark, more maroon than red.

I wanted to reach out and stop him but couldn't; the same dream-like paralysis that kept me from getting to my feet faster also retarded my ability to do anything else useful. There was no liquid in my mouth, so the noise that came out of it was foreign and low, something like "no," but far less specific.

He cut a third time, watching his own skin part and his own blood creep out of his wounds with a dreary concentration, face dripping. I finally said around a thick tongue, "Jason, stop."

I have no idea if he heard me; or if he had, if that flabby excuse for a command would have had the slightest effect on his behavior. But I saw movement behind him, cars with jolly swirling lights but no sirens coming carefully closer and closer down Circuit Lane.

The uniformed deputies looked far more dangerous than Jason ever would. But they treated him as though he were armed with something more serious than a camping tool and as though he were violent. But he relinquished the knife with no more than another sniff and a vaguely tortured look, his favorite toy gone. They handcuffed him and pulled him away. He gave them no resistance and held his arm out passively when one of the men wrapped it in gauze from a first-aid kit in one of the cars. He looked at me again before he was put into a backseat. "Remember, Gina," he said, "I love you. I'd do anything in the world for you. I could find you another cat. Would that be good?"

The constable showed up briefly; with no smile at all, he told me he'd be back to take my statement personally once Jason was processed. After everyone was gone, I went inside and changed my clothes; I'd found some of Jason's blood on my sleeve. I wasn't sure how it had gotten there, but I wanted it off me as fast as possible.

The constable came back shortly after I had gotten the boys home and reassured them about my earlier alarming behavior. He made sure they were playing in another room, then proceeded to berate me in a low, noncarrying voice: didn't I know better than to engage young psychopaths in conversation? Jason could have had a gun; he pulled a knife, for Christ's sake, he could have raped me, killed me, cut me, pick a nightmare image. All I could say in my defense was "He was just such a pathetic little boy. Crazy and terribly unappealing but really, really sad."

He shook his head, grunted in disgust, and finally left, promising to keep in touch, to keep me in whatever information loop was swirling around Jason and Tim. "Don't be so trusting," he said as he left.

That night I went through my jewelry boxes, trying to remember where I'd put it. I finally found it, opening the bright box, touching the cold jade, thinking, poor Sidney, poor, poor Sidney, I'd wear this goddamn horrible thing every day for the rest of my life if it meant you got to die of old age warm and comfortable in your own house, in my lap even. I debated calling Tommy. Ellie thought I was a fool not to. But I thought, the constable will tell him whatever he needs to know. I was terrified at the thought of talking to him again, of revealing something.

I wondered, of course, whether I should hand the necklace over at once to the constable. But I thought about what Claire Stanley had said about the likelihood of Tim's defense lawyers painting me as an academic harlot. Would anyone believe I had simply forgotten such an expensive present, given anonymously? I couldn't explain it myself; I could imagine what Claire Stanley would make of it, let alone a hostile defense attorney. I suddenly couldn't bear the thought of any more antagonistic scrutiny. A plea bargain had been struck; they didn't need any more evidence.

The next day after school I went next door and told Jessie everything she didn't already know. "That boy is probably possessed," she said, then gave me a small glass candy dish in the shape of a duck.

"Wait," I said. "You have to, for once, take something from me." I handed her the purple box. I told her where it had come from. She had a right to know, after all, and some people believe that objects have auras. But its provenance only seemed to enhance it in her eyes. I said, "I know you like green, and this would go really well with your green dress. I don't have anything to wear it with. And I really don't want it in the house. You'd be doing me a big favor if you took it." She said nothing as I put it in her hands, but she never took her eyes off the box, almost smiling.

That evening Toby decided that he no longer spoke English but instead only spoke cat language and spent the whole night mewing at me, becoming genuinely frustrated when I couldn't decipher exactly what he was trying to say. Stevie, meanwhile, kept muttering, "You want a piece of me? You want a piece of me?" while determinedly pressing keys that made things explode on the computer monitor. This military ardor confused and annoyed me. But I knew so little about normal boy behavior and I didn't want to turn them into freaks. I knew there was a line to draw but had no idea where to draw it. I watched them in their parallel universes, both seeming perfectly happy, and felt a surge of love and completeness so profound, I found the necessity for any other human in my life bizarre and laughable. I have everything, I thought. I have all I could want.

But this shimmering contentment faded after a day or so, and I returned to my old sore numbness, a kind of easy ache where I could function perfectly well, where I could recognize and observe my own misery, but at a comfortable distance. I was okay, I was functioning, I wasn't out of control. I had a grip on reality.

My control slipped a little when Lizzie called one evening, sounding like she'd been crying, maybe drinking as well. We had the most acrimonious conversation of our strange relationship. She asked about Tommy, if I'd seen him or heard from him, how he was doing, and so on. I said I hadn't and didn't know anything. She asked me if I thought she should call him, would I mind? I was so surprised by this, I couldn't answer for a moment. What could I say? I stammered that I didn't know. She started challenging me: didn't I think she was good enough, didn't I think someone like him might like her, was I the only one who was allowed to try to interest a man? This escalated quickly; she suddenly spit out, "It's all so easy for you. Must be nice to be so goddamn *perfect*." She went on for a while longer in this vein: how I'd had everything so easy, handed to me, I was so lucky. I took it for a few minutes, figuring she was drunk, she was miserable, I *was* lucky, after all, in lots of ways, and she just needed to be heard. But then she started in on Tommy: how I'd probably fucked him and dumped him—after all, that's what I did—and now he probably wouldn't want anything to do with her because she was my cousin. This was so odd and so unfair, I couldn't just sit there anymore.

"I haven't gone near Tommy. Stop telling me how perfect I am. I've failed at most things that matter to me; my love life has been pathetic for years."

"Stop with all that 'aw shucks' stuff. Everyone just fucking *loves* you."

This was news to me. I thought few of the Hannigans, for starters, liked me at all.

"And all these men just go all melty for you and will do anything you need. Must be great."

"What the hell are you talking about? People usually see me as some sort of Amazon who doesn't need anything at all. I'm lousy at getting help."

"You've got to be kidding me! Are you blind or stupid? You don't even notice what men do for you. You take it for granted; it's your goddamn *due*. I guess you've had it your whole life. Have you ever had a mechanic really rip you off?"

"Of course."

"When?"

I thought. "In Stoweville, I know Kenny Guthrie sold me used tires as new."

"Oh, for crying out loud. You were how old? Sixteen?"

"Yes."

"That's the last time, right?"

I couldn't think of another one, but I was on the spot.

"I could go on and on, I bet. Men open doors for you. That produce guy gets you the freshest stuff; I've seen him. Guys ask *me* for your number."

"That only happened once."

"And you have those two great kids. Of course, you're the perfect mom, baking bread, taking them to museums, perfect house, perfect mom car, perfect mommy job where you can be home when they get there, no day care for you, oh, no."

"My house is eighty years old and looks it. Day care is expensive. For Christ's sake, Lizzie, don't you understand that all that stuff is overcompensation, anyway, because I didn't want them in the first place?"

My voice had gotten strident, so this rang out, suspended in the air like a cloud of noxious gas. I desperately whipped around, looking to see if either boy was in earshot. I had moved into the kitchen;

they were in the living room watching TV. I didn't think they'd heard my last comment, but you could never be sure, especially with Stevie. You never knew what they picked up.

It had the effect of shocking Lizzie into silence for a moment. Then, in a smaller voice, slushy with wine, she said, "I dare you to go around and ask single moms if they get the kind of sympathy you do, the kind of breaks. I'll bet you a million dollars they don't."

I couldn't come up with an answer to that. My mind scurried away from everything she said, then froze somewhere else. My tongue felt thick. Finally, I forced out, "I'm sorry."

"No you're not. Why would you be? Just don't get all sanctimonious on me."

"Am I being sanctimonious? I'm sorry." It was all I could think of to say.

Large, wet sigh. "Stop it. It's okay. You can't help being perfect, I guess."

"Stop saying that. That's ridiculous. If I were perfect, I'd know what to say to make you feel better." To make you like me. My head was hot and felt twisted, and words erupted from me. "Lizzie, I'm in love with Tommy. I'm sickeningly, ferociously in love with him. But he doesn't care; he's not interested. This is why I'm not so wild about helping you get together with him, all right? I'm jealous. Are you happy with me now?" I thought, you stupid, stupid idiot, what are you telling her this for? Dumb, dumb, dumb. But it shut her up. She muttered something about needing to go and how men were jerks. I think she was crying a little.

The next day she came by the house. She offered to take the boys for ice cream and let me have an hour to myself. I think for her it was an apology.

I tried not to feel guilty about Lizzie when Tommy did call the next night. After establishing that he'd been to a law enforcement conference in Washington, DC, he got down to the business of yelling at me for a while, apparently angry that I would let Jason get near me, especially with some sort of weapon, even a pathetic one. I tried to joke my way out of it, saying that I couldn't exactly imagine Jason as one of those tough-guy marines or soldiers of fortune or whatever who could eviscerate you with a spoon from fifty yards away before you had time to blink. He didn't laugh. Our conversation was short and he was grouchy, but Ellie saw it as a sign of deep romantic feelings on his part. I wasn't so sure. The irritation had sounded pretty genuine, and he had made no noise about ever speaking to me again.

On Wednesday of the following week I got home with the boys, very tired, and made instant macaroni and cheese for their dinner (organic and with whole-wheat noodles). There was a message from John Fagin on the machine, which I ignored. There was also one from Mary Glenn in New York. I think I had some vague idea that she wanted me for a shoot, though why now was puzzling.

Toby started asking me when we could get a cat; we needed a new kitten, maybe two, maybe three. I said we weren't ready, meaning, of course, that I wasn't. Stevie looked at me, blue eyes cold, brows lowered, as angry at me as I'd ever seen him.

"You didn't want him. I heard you. You didn't ever really want him."

I thought it was very likely that Stevie had heard me right when I'd said that to Lizzie. He didn't misinterpret much. He was changing it for his own reasons, I knew, to keep it tolerable.

I swallowed, breathed, and said, "Everybody I love most in the world, I didn't ask for. They just dropped into my life like big unexpected gifts." It's a relief sometimes how sappy you can safely be with seven-year-olds. "Like you guys. I didn't plan to have two boys, but the Universe gave me you, and I love you both so much, it practically drives me crazy sometimes." This was familiar talk to them. "I think we should do the same with a cat. Sidney came to me; I didn't go looking for him. Let's let a cat or kitten find us. Or kittens. It might take a while, but I think it's worth it."

This seemed to satisfy them both, even steely Stevie. I snuggled with them both till they fell asleep that night, worry slowly seeping out of me.

The next day, in my office between classes, I called Mary Glenn. Her receptionist put me through immediately. I was pleasantly surprised.

When Mary picked up, she didn't waste a word. "Erin's dead," she said.

Jeri squeezed me in the next day. We ignored the checklist and focused on Erin. I mostly talked, she listened and didn't say much. She did ask finally, "Are you sorry you left that life? Have you missed it?"

"I honestly don't know. I really don't. Of course I had lots of fun, lots of money, lots of freedom, of a sort. And a lot of attention, lots of sex, at least when I wanted it, and a few times when I didn't." She raised her eyebrows at this, and I shook my head. I said, "Nothing so melodramatic as rape. Nothing like that. Just acquiescence when I shouldn't have, didn't really want to. It's a habit I've mostly broken, at least when it comes to my body."

She nodded, brows knit, then said, "Why haven't you talked to her more over the years, do you think? This is someone you were very close to, after all, right?"

"Yeah, well, you have to remember, it was mutual. She could've called me, too, and didn't."

Jeri was silent. I thought, trying to be honest. "It felt humiliating, like I slunk away in shame."

"Going to graduate school was shameful?"

"Well, kind of. To that crowd. And I was always sort of . . . marginal, anyway. And then having the boys, well, that tore it. I mean, I became a freak hippie earth mother. The kind of person they constantly ridiculed. I couldn't bear it. I know I shouldn't care so much what others think of me, especially shallow people, but I can't help it. Their scorn is painful."

"At least, the scorn you imagine them feeling. And it's natural to want some validation from others. None of us is totally self-sufficient, after all. But you've never told me what pushed you away from New York to school. Was there a precipitating event?"

There were lots of things, of course. But I said without thinking, "Valerie Kinney."

Valerie was pretty in an ethereal, crystalline sort of way. Blond like Erin but wispy, far less substantial. I'd known her for a year before it occurred to me that she was getting smaller and smaller. Wispier and wispier. Mary said over and over, Valerie is so beautiful. She's got it, or, rather, It. She is perfect, she is the paradigm. *Harper's* loved her; they wanted her in every bathing suit shot, no matter how bony she got, no matter that she was clearly dying. In fact, the dying part was her appeal. She became famous; she was talked about as the most beautiful of everyone Mary represented. She was doomed, had doomed herself. But even as she was dying, starving herself to death quite literally, heavy-lidded with a heroin addiction, vacant, empty, even the *doctors* commented on how much she resembled an angel. They made pilgrimages to her room just to look at her.

"She killed herself so that she could be photographed in underwear for *Harper's Bazaar.* And the horror of it all is that if that's what you want to do, that's often how you have to do it. At those shoots, the only way to tell the junkies from the anorexics, when there was a difference, was by their smell. Junkies sweat a lot. Anorexics don't, because a lot of times their glandular systems are on the verge of shutting down altogether."

I had to stop for a breath, as I was panting, my voice starting to get strident. I put my hand in front of my mouth. Jeri just looked at me, her face expressionless. I squeezed my hands together in a double fist, looking away from her.

After a short silence she said softly, "So Erin's the second colleague of yours to die."

"Yeah." I found Jeri's use of the word "colleague," which I associated with academia, amusing in a disturbing sort of way. "But modeling didn't kill Erin like it did Valerie." I paused in thought. "Well, maybe it did, in a way. She probably waited too long to treat anything." I started to rub my face with my hands, then reflexively stopped. Mary Glenn had practically beaten that habit out of me. The acid in the sweat on your hands does terrible things to the thin, delicate skin on your face.

Jeri said, "So does this scare you? Like it could happen to you?"

I shook my head. "No, I mean, I think death scares me the normal amount. But I take pretty good care of myself these days. And I was never anorexic. I was lucky and naturally pretty thin. I didn't need that much control."

Jeri's brows rose at that. Then she said, "Yeah, well, people do a lot of shit to themselves in the name of control."

That night I had a dream in which I was trying to talk to Erin. We were on my front steps, and she was trying to speak but couldn't. I finally figured out with a horrified jolt that her lips were sewn shut. Her cheeks had several parallel slashes on them, darkly oozing, and she was holding a bloody Swiss Army knife, and she looked scared to death.

chapter twenty-one

There is the woman who, having suffered some deep emotional injury in love or marriage, vows never to let another man play on her feelings, assuming the role of the hard and bitter spinster. Almost more common is the sensitive boy who learns in school to encrust himself for life in the shell of the "tough-guy" attitude. As an adult he plays, in self-defense, the role of the Philistine, to whom all intellectual and emotional culture is womanish and "sissy." Carried to its final extreme, the logical end of this type of reaction to life is suicide. The hard-bitten kind of person is always, as it were, a partial suicide; some of himself is already dead . . . If, then, we are to be fully human and fully alive and aware, it seems that we must be willing to suffer for our pleasures. Without such willingness there can be no growth in the intensity of consciousness.

ALAN WATTS, *The Wisdom of Insecurity*

FOR REASONS THAT WILL FOREVER remain mysterious to me, Erin's funeral was to be held on a Monday. That worked out well, however, since I had few appointments that day and all were easily canceled.

Patsy Hepplewhite, bless her, had offered to get the boys from the bus stop with Josh that afternoon and keep them for dinner if need be. I promised her truckloads of reciprocal babysitting, especially during the summer. Before getting ready for the week, I took a few minutes to look through my books. I found one that suited my purposes: Timothy Miller's edited volume, *America's Alternative Religions.* I ordered another copy online as it was one I used a fair amount.

After taking the boys to school, I went home, showered, and got ready to go into the city. I knew that no matter what I did, I was going to look hopelessly blodgy next to the New York fashionistas. I had a lot of clothes, but the new ones were almost all dowdy or way too casual, and the old ones had been passé ten minutes after I'd worn them years and years ago. I can't say I didn't care, but I didn't care enough to do anything drastic about it. I had had a momentary fantasy about going to Bergdorf's first thing in the morning to get something new but found the execution of this plan too exhausting. I had a black silk suit that I'd given a paper in at a conference the previous fall; it would do. I dressed with as much care as possible. I made sure I had the book I had chosen in my bag, along with my charged cell phone in case anyone needed to contact me about the boys, another book to read, a well-stocked makeup bag, and the journal Mo and Ivy had given me for Christmas. I drove to the station and took the train in.

I took a cab from the station to Tommy and Russell's precinct house. I got out of the cab and stood for a moment at the double glass front doors. I wasn't sure why I was doing this or what I expected to get out of it. But now that I had started this mission, I was compelled to finish it. I breathed deeply several times and went in.

At the desk was another man whose body seemed to be expanding beyond the boundaries of his uniform. I thought it likely that they had a gym somewhere in the building. I knew better, however, than to point this out. I managed to get his attention, then asked in a nervous, croaky voice if Detective Galloway was in. He seemed surprisingly friendly after he heard my name. I had a very bad feeling about this but it was too late to slink away. He made a phone call, saying in broad, deliberate tones, "Is Detective Galloway available for a

Ms. Paletta? She's down here and would like to see him." He listened, grinning happily, then said, "Thank you so much, Detective." He was smirking at me, no doubt about it. I was becoming miserably uncomfortable. He was listening to someone on the other end. After a few minutes of silence interspersed with "uh huh"s and "okay"s, he hung up. I was on the verge of telling him not to bother, I just had a book to leave him, and I'd be on my way, but again it was too late.

Bloaty Boy said, "Detective Galloway will be down shortly. Please take a seat."

I sat down on a polished wooden bench by the door. The desk sergeant continued to smirk at me. He made another couple of calls, voice low. I kept telling myself that they couldn't be about me, that in New York City the desk sergeant in this precinct had many more important things to do than call his friends to say I was there. Who was I to these people, after all? I wasn't anyone interesting, wasn't a criminal.

But I had been the star of a pornographic website that highlighted a scantily clad past that the detectives had all no doubt pored over; the fact that I managed not to think about it anymore, the fact that all interest in it had blown over in Tenway, didn't mean anything here. It was down now, but for all I knew, everyone in this building might have gawked at it at some time or other. My cheeks started changing colors. I started sweating, feeling stupid and reckless. I didn't need this today of all days.

My wait was brief. Tommy was coming down the central stairs from the upper, mysterious reaches of the station house within minutes of the desk sergeant's announcement. At the sight of him, my body began producing all sorts of chemicals and my knees went soft. I'm sure I looked hunted. I stood up, hoping my legs didn't go wiggly. He didn't look happy to see me, which made all of this worse.

I licked my lips to help my mouth work. I said, "I'm sorry to bother you, Tommy." I then almost choked, thinking I shouldn't have called him by his first name. "I just wanted to drop something off, no big deal. I could've left it at the desk; you didn't need to come down." I was filled with a deep, blood-red self-loathing.

Tommy looked expressionlessly at Bloaty Boy, then back at me.

Taking my arm, he led me over to a corner of the suddenly tiny room. He said softly, "It's fine, Gina. It's good to see you." He didn't look like he thought it was good at all.

"I just had an extra copy of this book," I lied, "and I had to be in the city, so I thought I'd drop it off. Really, I should go. I have to go, anyway."

"Wait," he said. He looked at me and looked angry, which I was starting to realize was what his face did when it wasn't doing anything in particular. He said very quietly, "Look, it would be better if we didn't look like we had too much to say to each other. Here's the thing: There's a Chinese restaurant about five blocks due east of here called Chung Win's. Do you think you could meet me there for lunch in about half an hour?"

"Sure," I said, befuddled.

"I'll take the book." I gave it to him. "It's just better if we don't let anyone here know this."

"Okay. Shall I slap you or something?"

"No." He smiled but suppressed it. "That would actually be worse." Than what? "I'll see you there in half an hour. Okay?" With a bored air, he left me standing empty-handed in the lobby. I smiled gaily at the desk sergeant, who was watching every move we made, and waved a perky "thank you" as I sashayed out.

I got to the restaurant about ten minutes early, thinking I'd have some time to compose myself, but Tommy got there only about five minutes later. I had to consciously tighten my muscles to keep from launching myself at him. He looked a little thin, pale, overworked, but really good. I wanted to get a good meal into him. I was horrified that I couldn't keep more of the joy off my face.

After we ordered, I managed to relax the gaping grin on my face as I slowly calmed down. I said, "Okay, spill the beans. What the hell was all that about? I know the DA hates me, but does she expect me to avoid New York City altogether? That seems a bit extreme, doesn't it?"

"Well, sort of. It's just not a good idea, you being seen at the station and having anything much to do with me. I know Claire was pretty objectionable, but she had a point, you know. The defense at-

torneys in this case are extremely well paid and extremely desperate."
He was talking unusually fast and wasn't meeting my eyes. "They'll
use anything they can to discredit the witnesses. They don't have much
of a defense other than that." He changed the subject. "But what
brought you in on a Monday, of all things?"

"A funeral."

"Jesus, Gina. I'm sorry. Who died?"

"A model friend of mine, Erin Steele."

"Close friend?"

"Yeah, a hundred and sixty years ago. She was my closest friend of
that whole bunch."

"What did she die of?"

"Breast cancer. Occupational hazard. You let it go too long, because what female in the fashion industry is in a hurry to cut off a
breast, you know what I mean? Although chemo's usually good for
some weight loss, the hair loss negates the benefit of the nausea."

"Yikes."

"Yeah, well, that's reason number three hundred and twelve why
I'm no longer in the biz." I waited a beat, trying not to start talking
too much again. "I pretty much abandoned her while she was dying.
That's the main reason I'm doing this. Penance."

He asked for details, and I gave them, mindful to have some restraint this time. He absolved me of guilt, saying that she could have
called me, I did try, and so on.

"I knew she had breast cancer, Tommy. It wasn't like she had the
measles." I sighed. "So I figure I'll spend a few hours either being ignored or being told how fat, old, badly dressed, and ugly I've become.
Either way, I'm hoping some mortification will cleanse my conscience
a little."

"When do you have to be there?" he said.

"Not until three o'clock. The fashionable types don't get up till
noon at the earliest and take at least two hours to get ready to go anywhere."

He told me he didn't need to hurry back. The privileges, he said,
of being a detective, this flexibility. He asked about those he knew in
my family, asked after the boys. Our food came, and I returned the

favor. How were his sister and his father, what weird cases did he have, how was he doing physically, were there any repercussions of being shot, and so on. He was physically fine now, he said, but it had ruined an expensive camel-hair coat, which he missed. We talked about some of the articles in the book; I pointed out particular ones that I thought he might find of use, about cult activity and the law. Very friendly.

Then, after I'd drunk a second and final cup of tea, I suddenly couldn't stand it. I blurted, "So is there something else going on at the station that you don't want me walking in on? The desk sergeant was way weird to me." I was proud that I'd at least managed not to sound whiny or accusing. It came out sounding like I was simply interested.

His head jerked back slightly. After a long breath he said, "Well, yeah, there is."

At least he didn't treat me as though I were insane. I raised my eyebrows in inquiry.

He slowly continued, "I didn't want to tell you this. I know you're going to be upset."

I was alarmed and imagined he was about to tell me how much he knew I loved him, but it was not to be, he had gotten married last week, he was feeling sorry for me, but he loved his wife too much and couldn't hurt her by being friendly with someone nutty like me.

"There's a bet on at the station."

"What?" This took a minute to register, for me to put what the words meant together in my brain. "A bet?" I repeated stupidly.

"Yes. It probably doesn't surprise you that lots of the other guys at the station house have seen the Solomon website, right?"

"Ye-es. I mean no, it doesn't." I didn't like the sound of this at all.

"Well, they knew that Russell and I were working the case, of course."

"So?"

He sighed heavily. "There's a bet on in the precinct that one of us, either Russell or me, will wind up . . . having a fling with you."

"A *fling*?"

"I told you that you wouldn't like it."

"You're goddamn right I don't like it. What's the bet exactly? I mean, who wins if what happens?"

He licked his upper lip, an obvious delaying tactic. He breathed in deeply. He finally said, "Some people have money on me, some on Russell, some on both, some on neither."

I couldn't respond at first. Then I looked him in the eyes. "Well, what's the smart money saying?" Real anger was starting to build now. "So who's favored to win, or however you say it."

He blushed and looked unhappy. I knew I wasn't being fair, but I was sick of trying to be fair. He said softly, looking at me with what seemed like anger, "Russell. Okay? Look, I didn't start this stupid fucking thing, and I haven't ever participated in it. That's why I said we should meet so far away from the precinct, so that no one would see you and no one would bring up the goddamn pool. I hate it, too. You asked, so I told you."

I looked at him for a minute, not speaking. Then I said, also quietly, trying not to throw my anger at his relatively innocent head, "Here's the inside track, or insider information, or whatever. Russell seems to me to be about the age of my sons. Not being a pervert, I don't find children sexually appealing." Oh God, that was what Claire Stanley meant. *Who wins?* Humiliation burned me. I stood up, keeping my voice low. "Thanks a lot for lunch, Tommy. I'm really glad to have seen you. And I really do appreciate you telling me about this. But I have a funeral to go to, so I'd better leave."

"Gina, come on. And I should tell you that this isn't Russell's doing, either. Please don't go just yet."

"It's okay, I'm not really mad. I'm just tired and feel like shit. You guys didn't start it, but you haven't ended it, either. I understand that you probably can't. But I need to be somewhere not embarrassing for a little while. I'm sorry. I'll see you later." Or I won't, I thought, sinking further. "Thank you again for lunch, Tommy." He was standing by this time. I hesitated, then gave him a quick peck on the cheek. I figured even if someone was watching us, it hardly looked like some passionate lip-lock. Tommy certainly didn't look happy. "Bye."

I did a fast walk out of the restaurant. Poor Tommy tried to come after me, but a determined-looking man cornered him, worried that we were trying to run out on the check. I hoped it hadn't been too expensive. I hoped I hadn't been too rude. I hoped I hadn't hurt his feelings. But I had to be by myself. I wished I could call Jeri or talk to Ellie. I would've loved to have had a prefuneral martini and a cigarette, but the last place I wanted to hang out now was a bar. I wanted to be left alone, not be endlessly harassed. I walked and walked through the snowy, windy, blowing cold, through the stinking city, knocked around by foot traffic, feeling like I shouldn't be there. I've never belonged here, I have to leave, they'll eat my flesh and crush my bones.

I finally found a dingy but anonymous-looking coffee shop, bland with booths, not too crowded to get a seat, not so empty that I would be conspicuous. Half the lights overhead had blown out. I got a soy cappuccino and sat down. I checked my cell phone's display to make sure the boys' school hadn't called and I'd missed it for some reason. I got out a handkerchief and blotted my eyes, I hoped surreptitiously. That was when I realized that I had pretty much told Tommy that he'd win his stupid bet if he gave it half a try. I got out my journal and began to write.

Erin looked like a giant sleeping Barbie doll in her casket. It was one of the most distressing things I'd ever seen in my life. I've seen my share of dead bodies, how fake they look after embalmers get hold of them, how plasticky. But Erin was so blond and beautiful and so perfect-looking. So deadly thin. It was horrible. I was fine, quite collected, till I saw her. Then I started hyperventilating and had to find a restroom. I was able, however, to come out in time for the service. It was short, nondenominational, and full of hyperbole. I saw no familiar faces at first, at least not personally familiar. There were a few that were almost famous. Fortunately, I didn't see much media, therefore no one who looked to be there for the publicity. Sometimes grief shots can be really good press. Icky but true. Her rock star ex-boyfriend wasn't there; I found out later he was on tour on the West Coast. I hoped that if I were ever involved with someone again, he'd take off work long enough to come to my funeral, even if we'd just broken up.

As the minister mouthed meaningless, impersonal nothings about our journey back to the spiritual patriarchy, I kept thinking about Tommy. It occurred to me that he might have been hinting that he could come with me; he had such a flexible schedule, plenty of time today. I wondered if I'd been a jerk. He didn't have to tell me about the bet. He was trying to be honorable, for God's sake. I owed him an apology, and I decided to give him one later. Maybe I could call him or even drop by the station house again. That would prove that I didn't care about it, the bet thing. He could claim the winning slot or not, whatever the hell you called it when you were the winner. I could pretend that I needed to let him know something about the case; it would fool no one there, but maybe it would keep the DA from becoming apoplectic.

I mentally apologized to Erin for having a wandering mind during her funeral service.

I spotted two good-looking middle-aged people who had to be Mr. and Mrs. Ladislaw, her parents. Erin really was her first name, but Steele sure as hell wasn't her last. There was a pretty, younger brunette with them. I guessed she was a sister; Erin had mentioned one occasionally, Amy. They were all from Poughkeepsie.

After the service I approached them, identified myself, and held both parents' hands while the mother had a good restrained cry. I told them that I loved Erin and that she was one of the best people I knew. That was close enough to the truth that I could live with myself. I eventually moved away, realizing that I'd cut ahead of everyone in the receiving line. I had forgotten about funeral etiquette; that was inexcusable given how many I'd been to and how recently. There were quite a few beautifully made up and resentful faces in the line. I took a deep breath and decided to let it go. I reminded myself I didn't need any of these people, and incurring enmity over social gaffes simply didn't matter. Grieving parents take precedence over everything, and I had no idea if anyone else there genuinely gave a damn about them.

I approached the coffin again with great fear. I didn't want to hyperventilate again. I was also afraid of starting to bawl all over the place, causing a scene. I'd never done that at a funeral, but these days I cried so easily, I had no faith in my ability to keep a grip on myself.

I looked at her empty shell and wondered what was left of her consciousness. Had it simply evaporated, like fog? Was she part of the great universal consciousness, as I said I believed, and so was the question itself of where she was, meaningless? Because she was everywhere, here and over there, just as we all were, right? We just couldn't remember it all the time. I started crying then, saying good-bye.

I looked around, drying my face with the handkerchief I'd brought, trying to be discreet about it. I saw a few faces I recognized, people I had known fairly well once, had socialized and worked with: a photographer, a set designer, even a few models who had risen to some prominence. The gazes of those few, however, glanced off me, not seeing me or pretending not to. Penance, I thought, penance.

A weight fell on my shoulder. I heard a soft "Gina" and turned around to face someone I hadn't seen in eight years, someone I'd known well, known better than I knew any of the Hannigans or Eberles now, including Mo. It was Dion Van Doren. We literally fell all over each other, both crying. I said, "My God, Dion, it's so good to see you." I meant it. He said, "What in the name of all that is holy are you wearing?"

He held my hand like I was his high school girlfriend, weeping gently. He didn't leave me even when Mary Glenn, looking like a well-made bed of uncertain age, marched over to me and gave me a painful peck on the cheek. "Gina," she said. Then, "Call me. You need to work. You're getting soft, and I have some clients that could use you. Do it for Erin." She then left, going off to terrorize some six-foot, ninety-four-pound eighteen-year-old who was looking too longingly at the coffin. I hadn't really missed Mary, even though she'd given me an entire life. A great one by most standards. Dion summed up why: "Mean as a snake. But hoo-hoo, she wants you back. After how long?"

This I knew I would have to process later. Do it for Erin? Oh, please. I briefly imagined an issue of *Lavish* dedicated to their former, fallen model; it was so bizarre a concept, I almost started burbling in insane, macabre laughter.

DeVonne, Dion's frightening sister, appeared at his side and saved me from indulging in that unseemly fantasy any longer. She was looking ageless and fabulous in one of Dion's filmy gray creations, very

Morticia Addams, trailed by some creamy boy in wrinkled gray linen. D and D told me I had to come to the wake. I said okay, but I had a call to make first. I went into the hall of the funeral home, dug out my cell phone, and called Tommy. I was frustrated by electronics and got his voice mail.

"Tommy, it's Gina. I wanted to apologize for leaving you like that. I was really rude to you, and I'm sorry. The funeral's ending, and I was wondering how flexible your schedule really is. Would you be willing to be my, uh, bodyguard at the wake? I wasn't planning on staying there long, but it sure would be nice to have the company. If not, I hope I talk to you soon." I gave him my cell number even though I was pretty sure he had it and told him the location of the restaurant where the wake was happening. I hung up, wondering what I'd just done. Was this asking him out? If so, it was a downer of a first date. And I still had no idea of his status re the girlfriend(s). I could almost hear Erin say, "Life's too short. Do it anyway." Okay, I thought, okay.

The restaurant was an easy walk from the funeral home. My shoes were black Dansko Mary Janes, comfortable and flat, so this was not a problem for me. Not so for many of the other mourners, in stilettos so thin and high that the March wind threatened to topple over their owners, most of whom weighed little more than the shoes. I wondered for no real reason how many of those reedlike women had had their feet surgically modified to fit better into their strappy little numbers. Ah, the advantage of mostly modeling lingerie; your feet didn't come into it all that often.

I accompanied Dion and DeVonne, who were shockingly warm to me. I thought how weird a procession this was. We should have had those little "funeral" flags they attach to cars, I thought, and we could have held them up so that pedestrians could part for us. But this was Manhattan. Pedestrians parted only for those brandishing firearms. I lost everyone in the afternoon crowds. It was only a few moments before I arrived at Bozo's.

Bozo's was actually Beaux Eaux, and it catered to the very thin who wanted to stay that way and spend gobs of money doing it. It was starting to be a big deal when I left the city; apparently it had established itself as The Place to not eat. It was about as far from the faux-Irish pubbery of Hannigan's as you could get. When I had last come here, most of the crowd had stopped smoking and was vocal and self-congratulatory. Now I saw more than half the assembled mourners wandering in and out of large, edgeless glass doors leading into a central outdoor courtyard to smoke. I went outside awhile with Dion, who had never managed to give up his Kools, no matter how many times Carlton told him they'd kill him in horrible and aesthetically grotesque ways. Blue-gray clouds of tobacco smoke hovered over faces with cheekbones so prominent that it looked like you could cut meat with them, until updrafts carried the fumes gracefully away. The smell didn't bother me; it smelled in a way like home, but tinged with Eternity. I wondered if Tommy would come. I wasn't sure I wanted him associating me with this crowd, but I also wanted to apologize in person. Mainly, I just wanted to see him again.

Dion told me that Mary had booked the whole place. It was all done in silver and green with mirrors everywhere. The mirrors, I was mildly interested to note when we went back inside, were *not* slimming.

"The food is fabulous here, Gina. My God, it's been how many years since I've seen you? You look great. Maybe just a tad too prosperous, but great."

"You look great, too, D. You look like Prince. It's so fabulous on you." I slid into the speak like an old suit. I knew Dion couldn't help commenting on my body. It was a professional reflex. Now that I had been legitimized by Dion, other people started drifting our way. A few were strangers who simply wanted to know who I was, if I was anyone worth schmoozing. I met a few editors and writers for magazines, people I used to have to be nice to. I spotted Katie Cameron, who pretended to have just seen me, and she came over to say hello with a hearty jollity that made no sense in the circumstances. She was joined shortly by Tandy Collins, whom I'd known slightly. Tandy, several years my senior, by the way, made a comment about how I would look good in a flour sack. I thanked her and said that was great since I had a whole closetful. I was relieved that I didn't care more. Katie was grimacing in a disturbing, lockjawed way; it finally dawned

on me that she had probably just snorted about a half pound of cocaine.

My eyes kept returning to the front of the restaurant, just in case.
I was starting to accept that it was a long shot that Tommy would
come. Betting hadn't been too good to me these days. But within a
few minutes his familiar silhouette filled up the doorframe. I spotted
him the moment he walked in in a blue suit that he might have slept
in. A few big heads on flamingo necks swiveled around to look at him
even before I practically sprinted over to where he stood, looking at
me with the beginnings of a smile.

"Hi," I said, breathing a little hard, almost running into him.

"Hi," he said. "I got your message."

"I figured," I said. We grinned stupidly at each other. "Am I forgiven for being such an ass earlier?"

"You weren't even remotely an ass, but sure," he said. "What the
hell is this place? Bozo's? Are they serious?"

"As serious as an eating disorder. Come on in. I'd introduce you
around, but I don't know many people, and most of them are terrifying. You can smoke in the courtyard if you want to." Looking
through the wide glass wall out at the enormous stick figures puffing
mightily away, I added, "I guess, being an ace detective and all, you
figured that out. There's one designer named Dion Van Doren who
is apparently still a friend of mine, and his sister still likes me. Other
than that, I'm pretty much a leper because I weigh nine pounds more
than I used to. Please don't leave me."

Tommy's entrance created a bit of a stir, partly because he was too
big not to notice. The question was, of course, was he so rumpled
because he wasn't One Of Us, or was he so important that he didn't
need to care? Some folks were clearly wondering the same thing
about me. I dragged Tommy back to the relative safety of Dion. De-
Vonne zoomed back to us when she spotted Tommy, wanting an in-
troduction. I wasn't worried; Tommy was at least fifteen years too old
for DeVonne, but I found it strangely flattering that she looked at
him. DeVonne was not remotely subtle in her passions. She got way
too close to him, sniffed his shoulder and then his cheek, and looked
him in the eyes from about six inches away. She squeezed his biceps,

then his forearm, checked out his rear end, then looked at me and said, "Not bad." Then she floated away. I had to hand it to him, he took it gracefully and just looked at me with eyebrows slightly raised when she was done.

Dion said to Tommy, "Aren't you a big fellow? You a friend of Gina's here? She always preferred her men less . . ."—I could feel a wave of searing embarrassment coming on—"substantial." There it was, my skin burning. I licked my lips, trying to think of something to say. Tommy just smiled, raised his brows again, and looked at me.

"We're friends, Dion," I said.

"Oh, so your tastes haven't changed?" Dion was enjoying this way too much.

"Never mind. Let's talk about you. Where's Carlton? I hear you two are still together."

"Yes. He's at home with the flu, but he will be devastated that he missed you. Raphael will also be miserable not to see you. He's on vacation in the Andes. No one's been able to reach him, so he doesn't even know yet about our poor Erin. Doesn't that suck terribly?"

"Yes, it does. Where's Philippe?"

"You'll love this, sweetie. He's in L.A. Doing films."

"Films?"

"Yes, he met some woman who's some sort of producer, and she got him a job working for someone, some studio, doing set design or something like that. He'll be back. He pisses off every woman he's involved with so thoroughly that he'll never be able to work in that business again if she's as powerful as everyone says. Anyway, he couldn't make it back here for the funeral. But let's talk about you. You live in some ghastly suburb now, right?"

"I live in Tenway. It's not that ghastly."

"Is that where you're from?" Dion looked sweetly at Tommy.

"No, I live in Manhattan."

"Oh?" Dion's face lifted. "Are you bringing our Gina back to civilization?"

He said, "She's living a pretty civilized life now from what I can see. You know that she's a university professor, right?"

"Oh God, Gina, that sounds so good coming from his mouth,

but my image of you teaching a bunch of farmers about something dusty makes me so sad. You're so exquisite, even now. Even though you've so let yourself go. Your skin is still good; you don't have too many wrinkles. Your hair isn't too bad, though that's a terrible cut. I assume you're getting it colored." He put his hand on my ass. "You're still working out, thank God, although your belly pooches just a bit. You had a kid or something, right? That explains that. A little tuck here and there and you could be right back. You are *so* being wasted. Do the teaching thing when you're old and wrinkly and Botox won't work anymore. Not while you're still so fabulous." He turned back to Tommy. "Did you know that she had the most magnificent natural breasts of any model I've worked with? Just ask Mary; she'd agree. Gina was famous for it."

My hands involuntarily flew up to cover my face. My elbows were also covering my breasts. I thought I was going to faint, so swift was the rush of blood from my brain to my cheeks. Dion kept on. "She never had any work done. It was all natural, and you could really tell. The camera loved her body. Not always her face, and her hair could be a nightmare. But her body, oh, lordy." Tommy started laughing while Dion kept assuring him earnestly that it was true.

I finally gathered my wits enough to say, "Dion, will you please stop talking about my parts? I am not an old car."

Dion looked at me briefly, then back at Tommy. "You know, she could be a problem to dress. Her breasts were too big, so dresses didn't always hang right. See, I'm remembering this now. Erin's were a bit smaller; she looked better in a lot of things. And Gina isn't so tall, sometimes in clothes she looks a little chunky. But in the lingerie, now, no one did it better than our Gina. She looked great in garter belts; it was like her trademark, right, Gina? And she always looked so sad and so beautiful when she was sad, we called her the Queen of Pain. Do you remember that, Gina? I don't think you liked it that much, as I remember, but you were, oh, you were, you always looked so sad. You looked better sad than anyone, and Erin always looked like she was laughing. I remember thinking in those pictures Raphael did of the two of you, it always looked like she had just stolen your lover, she was so happy, and you were so brokenhearted. It worked, though.

We sold so many of those teddies that one year that DeVonne and I could have retired then, gone to live in Fréjus, and just relaxed. Now all the girls are beanpoles with these awful silicone tits that look like they glued tan baseballs to their collarbones, just awful. You were really, really pretty. And so sweet; it showed in all the pictures how sweet you were."

He swiveled to Tommy. "She would bake cookies for the people on a photo shoot. Did you know that? Fucking *cookies*. Low-fat and no sugar, of course. Everyone loved her. Although a lot of the girls were jealous, it's true. That beautiful wavy brown hair, those chocolate brown eyes, just slightly slanted, you looked Welsh or Polynesian or something—those lovely breasts, great long legs, nice tight ass, perfect, perfect nose, and you were one of those that get more and more beautiful as you get older, as long as you take good care, lots of sunscreen, and you look really good now, but then, you were so perfect, so gorgeous, but you were just so smart, you had to leave to go be smart, and that was the saddest, dumbest thing you ever did. We would have done anything for you, to keep you here. Why did you leave us, Gina? Why did you do that? We were such a happy, happy group. I wish you hadn't left. That was very bad. And now Erin's gone and died, and what's happening to all of us?"

Poor Dion was crying, and Tommy wasn't laughing anymore. I hugged Dion and pulled him off to a corner. Bozo's had many alcoves for God knows what purposes, and the three of us hid in one for a bit while Dion sobbed and I held him. Tommy stood guard, terrifying anyone who tried to peek in. It wasn't long before DeVonne found her way to us, and no one, not even a menacing giant, was going to keep her from her baby brother. She put her arms around him, gently replacing mine. She said, "He needs his meds. I've got them; don't worry. Erin's death's hit him really hard. Come see us, Gina. Don't abandon Dion. Please keep in touch."

I said of course, I love you guys. I kissed the top of Dion's head, still shaking but cradled now in DeVonne's arms, and left the alcove with Tommy. People were at various tables now, and there were toasts being offered up, much drinking and tasting of tiny colorful bits of food on very expensive plates as we fled.

. . .

"Wow." Tommy looked like he'd been hit in the head with something big and porcelain. "Are you okay?" We were walking aimlessly down Fifth Avenue, sort of looking for cabs.

"Yeah. I had no idea it would get that maudlin, even if it was a funeral. Dion is one of the sweetest, most generous people on earth, but I think seeing me freaked him out. I guess Erin's death hit him pretty hard. I can't imagine that he really misses me that much."

"Is he bipolar?"

I looked at Tommy with respect. "Just a touch, if it's possible to be a little bipolar. It's usually pretty well controlled with meds. Poor Dion. Once he gets those conversational rivers going, they're pretty hard to dam, if you know what I mean. Dion's still a great designer, in spite of or because of, who can say?"

"I had a roommate in college who was bipolar."

"Did your roommate's life turn out okay?"

"Nope. He killed himself, actually."

"Jeez." I heaved a huge sigh. "I'm sorry to hear that." I looked at him. "This has been a weird day. Thanks a lot for coming, Tommy. I'm sorry you didn't even get a meal out of it."

"It would be hard to eat there, anyway. Those were the skinniest people I've ever seen in my life. Almost all the women looked anorexic."

"Many of them were, or bulimic. If you see anyone like that actually eat, never follow them into the bathroom. I speak from bitter experience."

"Yikes. Do you miss that at all now that you've revisited a little bit of it?"

"Are you kidding? The only thing I miss is the chance to travel. But with the boys, I can't do that much traveling, anyway. The money was good, too, of course. But money isn't everything."

We were silent for a minute. My tongue thickened; I could think of nothing okay to say.

He said, "I need to get back to work, Gina. I still can't be seen with you, you know. It was pretty stupid of me to go to something where there was likely to be press. They might have taken my picture just because I would have been so out of place there. The DA would eviscerate me slowly if a picture got in the *Voice* of me partying with you and a bunch of models." He grinned happily, and I grinned back.

"Well, I'm even more grateful, then. It was getting pretty surreal there."

We parted at a corner, shaking hands, sort of. It was ambiguous as always, at least to me. I stood on tiptoe and kissed his cheek finally. I said, "Thanks again, Tommy. I'll see you." He patted my arm, smiled, and walked away. I thought, You want a kidney?

Ellie whooped. "You guys will be Romeo and Juliet, just you wait and see."

"Romeo and Juliet both killed themselves, E. And they were only fifteen or something. I'd be much happier being like Paul Newman and Joanne Woodward."

"What's their story?"

"They're old and they're still together. Raised kids. Lived through tragedy. Are still doing great and worthwhile things. Seem to still like each other. That's what I want."

"At least now you know what you want, G. Before Tommy, you didn't. Or you didn't want anything. And, he came to your *rescue.* This is *huge.*"

"*Social* rescue. He didn't exactly risk his life."

"Whatever. Those people are pretty scary." I snorted at that, but she went on. "He's a really smart guy, which is what you like about him, let's face it. He knows *you* merit a little caution."

"What's that supposed to mean?"

She dodged the question. "Do you think it's really love?"

"Oh yeah. I'd do anything for him. I want him to be happy, even if it's not with me. It's love, all right. Masochistic shitty fucking love."

"Yikes," Ellie said.

chapter twenty-two

Every form is really a pattern of movement, and every living thing is like the river, which, if it did not flow out, would never have been able to flow in. Life and death are not two opposed forces; they are simply two ways of looking at the same force, for the movement of change is as much the builder as the destroyer. The human body lives because it is a complex of motions, of circulation, respiration, and digestion. To resist change, to try to cling to life, is therefore like holding your breath; if you persist you kill yourself.

ALAN WATTS, *The Wisdom of Insecurity*

I KEPT EXPECTING A PHONE CALL, some kind of summons, something having to do with Tim and Jason's trial. After hearing nothing for weeks, I finally called the office of the Tendale County district attorney, Mark Rodriguez, not wanting to volunteer, not really wanting any part in any of this, but not wanting to be blindsided by some precipitate scheduling. I figured I was a witness to some stuff; they must want me. One of Rodriguez's clerks got back to me a day after my call, telling me that there had been a brief jurisdictional battle between New York and the locals over who got to prosecute Tim and Jason. Since the primary charge was for the attempted murder of an NYPD homicide detective, mighty Manhattan won. The clerk couldn't tell me why no one in Claire Stanley's office had contacted me. I tried to forget about it, telling myself that there was nothing I could do; I would be told what I needed to do when they decided to tell me. Of course, I could have called Claire Stanley's office myself, but to be perfectly honest, I didn't want to.

March ended with spring break for both the boys and me. The university had for once admitted that there was a town around it and had made arrangements for its calendar, in this one instance, to line up with that of the area's public schools. The three of us took advantage of the time off to do some stuff together. We went to a small amusement park near Tenway called Lavaland on Monday, which the boys thought the height of fun; on Tuesday we went swimming at the Y.

On Wednesday we planned to stay close to home. It was a beautiful day, and it was relatively easy to get Stevie off the computer and outside right after breakfast. I had a lot of work to do but decided it could wait. The three of us went bike riding, seeing no suspicious lurkers anywhere. That changed after we came back; there was a small white BMW sports car parked in front of our house. As soon as we got to our steps, a small woman with an immaculate blond bob got out, her Jackie O sunglasses obscuring most of her face. When I got a better look at her, I still didn't recognize her. She was wearing a mauve Donna Karan suit and had a model's bearing in spite of her lack of height.

"Are you Gina Paletta?"

"Yes."

"I'm Anita Solomon, Tim's mother."

"Please, Mrs. Paletta," she said in a voice that sounded like it belonged to Boston, "Please, may I talk to you?"

"I'm Dr. Paletta. Or Ms. Paletta. But I'm not Mrs. Paletta. My late husband's last name was Winterburn." I was babbling at her out of nervousness; I was relieved that at least I wasn't swearing. "I never changed my name. What do you want?"

"I just want to talk to you. Please. May I come in?"

I got the boys inside, got them a snack, and was about to make some chitchat about children and how they are so demanding, then stopped myself when I remembered that her child was about to be prosecuted for serious crimes and was suspected of murdering someone else's child. So I got the boys squared away in the living room, letting them watch a movie, and drew Anita Solomon into my kitchen.

I offered her coffee; she took it, stalling. Then she said, "Look, Dr. Paletta, I'm sorry to be bothering you in this way, but I had to come here and actually see you and talk to you face-to-face. I mean, I don't want to excuse what Tim did; it really isn't excusable. But you have to admit, he had some provocation when he took classes from you. Really, I mean, it's too much to ask of a boy, all hyped up on hormones the way they are, to ignore the kind of past that you have and to ignore the kinds of things you used to do while you're parading around in front of a class and all. I'm hoping that you can see that."

I stared at her, not getting her point or knowing how she expected me to respond.

"Tim is a troubled boy, I know. But he was pushed over the edge. He really was. He never did anything that extreme while he was at home, before he went to that university. I think things happened there, things that weren't so good for him."

"Like what kinds of things? What are you talking about?" I finally said, trying to be gentle and calm. Trying not to incite the psychotic killer's mother to anything like her son's violence.

"Like . . . like influences. You know. Other kids, some of the classes, some of the professors. I don't want to blame you, Dr. Paletta. May I call you Gina?" I almost nodded automatically but did nothing when I thought about how bizarre any chummy familiarity between the two of us was. She didn't seem to notice my nonanswer. "Tim always liked you. I knew that, but I didn't realize in what way he liked you till after he was arrested. I wish he had come to talk to me. We could always talk about everything; we've always had such a good relationship. But when he went to college, things really changed, our relationship got strained, he got more secretive. I can see now that he didn't want me to know about you, because he knew I'd see through you, that I wouldn't like it, that I'd want him to keep his distance from you."

I said, having had enough but trying for some compassion, trying to not be simply hostile, "I was his teacher, Mrs. Solomon. I didn't have a personal relationship with him. I wasn't even his adviser. I'd barely ever seen him outside of class, and that was in my office to discuss an assignment or two. I can't imagine how horrible all this has been for you, but you've got to understand, I didn't really have all that much to do with it. Whatever went on in Tim's head about me, it was only in his head." I thought all this would have been clear to her by now but had underestimated the ability of a mother to delude herself about either her son's good qualities or her own good mothering or both.

"Maybe you didn't mean to. I'm willing to believe that. But you can be honest with me now, you can say. It's time for that, don't you think? Now that the trial has actually started. Soon it will be too late for you to make things right, to tell the whole truth. I'm sure you think you've been doing the right thing. Maybe you have, I don't know, but you've got to come forward now. I told Kip that you need to testify. I don't know why you're not there right now; I thought you would be. Maybe this isn't all that important to you, I don't know, but it's my son's life we're talking about."

This sounded almost like a word salad to me, but a few bits stuck out and gelled enough to provoke a few questions.

"There's a trial? I thought they were going to do a plea bargain."

"We refused it. Kip told us that Tim's chances would be better at a trial."

"And the trial's going on now?"

"Yes. You didn't know?"

"No, I'm sorry. No one told me. I thought I would be called. I'm confused, too." I refocused. "Who's Kip?"

"Our attorney. Kip Condon. Tim's attorney. I can't understand why

he won't put you on the stand. The prosecution, I can understand."
Presumably, they wouldn't want a perjurer like myself, I thought.
She started again. "You must have done something. Some little thing,
maybe, to give him that idea, that you and he had some kind of special connection. Please, you had to have known something. My God,
I mean, how could you not know something like this was going on?
You don't seem like a stupid or blind woman, and he was so, so attached to you. How could you not be aware of feelings about you
that strong? Don't you talk to your students? Don't you look at them?"
She was starting to cry now, starting to lose her perfect control. Even
the tight blond hairdo was starting to unravel slightly as she ran her
hands through it, disturbing the carefully lacquered locks. "They think
he murdered that boy. Which is so ridiculous, so unfair. But you have
to have felt *something*."

I sat in mute horror. Then I said softly, "I'm so sorry. No, I didn't
know anything, and I can't believe it myself. I don't know why I didn't
know. But I didn't. I'm so, so sorry. Other than a death, this is every
mother's worst nightmare." Or will be if they ever find Bradley's body,
I thought. "I can't imagine what you must be going through."

She looked at me then with shiny granite eyes and said, "I wish he
were dead. That would be much, much better than this."

She left shortly after that, hugging herself but with a return to perfect
posture. I wondered if she was leaving a broken woman or if she was
somehow unbreakable. All I knew was that I hoped to never see her,
or anyone else in her family, ever again.

Patsy Hepplewhite called, desperate to get rid of Josh for a few hours;
neither Josh nor his mother was weathering the structurelessness of
spring break very well. I told her to send him over; the boys would
be thrilled. I was also well aware of how fortunate I was to have a
neighbor who could be called on to babysit at a moment's notice
without much fear of undue imposition, and so was happy to be able
to accrue some karmic points by doing the same for her whenever
possible.

After Josh appeared at our door, all four of us went outside. For a few minutes I watched the boys play a dysfunctional game of hide-and-seek in the backyard. While they ran around and yelled at one another and made up all sorts of rules I had never heard of, I sat with a glass of iced tea, watching the leaves on the maple that shaded the rear part of our lot. I thought, The trial is going on right now. I knew nothing about it. Why not? I'd been in an unconscious news black-out, I realized, not liking to read, even accidentally, any stories by John Fagin. This was not only irresponsible, it was unfair. He was a good reporter and a good writer. I just found all associations with him distasteful. So, I thought, my petty prejudices have kept me from being informed about anything, including the trial of my former student/stalker for the attempted murder of the man I love.

I had a panicked moment in which I wondered if I was supposed to be there, anyway, if I was somehow supposed to know when and where to go, and I was right now in some sort of trouble, contempt of court or something, because they'd called my name and I hadn't been there, had been oblivious, at home cleaning a toilet or reading *Captain Underpants* to my boys. It was like those anxiety dreams most of us have from time to time in which you go to class and everyone else knows about the test but you, and you're not prepared, or you've never even been to the class before, you aren't even in the right room, the right school, the right planet, and so on. But then I thought, the court system can't be that rinky-dink, can it? They'd *want* you to know the right day to be there. It's not like it's a casual sort of process.

So neither the defense nor the prosecution was interested in my testimony. I was both relieved and irked. I guess I shouldn't have been surprised that Claire Stanley didn't call me; she'd made it pretty clear that 'Daisy Mae' wasn't much use to her. I thought, be glad that you don't have to be questioned by Tim's defense attorneys. Who knows how they'd portray pretty much everything about you? Still, I felt aggrieved. Someone could have let me know something. In other words, I sulkily translated my own thoughts to myself, Tommy could have called me, filled me in on how things were going.

After a few fruitless minutes of this I went inside. I called the constable, a bit irate, and left a message on his voice mail, asking about the status of Tim's trial. He called me back only about five minutes later and said he'd make some calls for me and find out. He was pretty nice about it, actually, so I managed not to take out my irritation on him.

Silently grumbling, I went back to the deck, back to the unprepossessing job of grading papers. The three boys were playing something involving lots of yelling and pretend shooting with plastic ray guns. My backyard was surrounded by a sturdy fence made of unpainted wooden slats about eight feet high. The fence was strong but aged, and many of the slats no longer met tightly. I lifted my head at the sound of a particularly bloodcurdling shriek, which turned out to be Toby's victory cry, although his methods for achieving this victory were unclear to me. But as I watched this violent display, I caught something, some slight movement, through the gap between the boards of the fence.

There was nothing behind the fence but a dirt path between my backyard and that of my rear neighbors. It was used only occasionally by a few locals, usually when dog walking. And I knew what that sounded like: the padding of sneakered feet and the tinkle of dog tags as responsible pet owners made their rounds. The odd thing about this was that it was accompanied by no sound at all. That was only an impression; there was no way to get a real look at what lay on the other side of the fence. But something or, rather, someone had been there, had been still for some period of time, maybe only a few seconds, maybe a few minutes, I couldn't say, until my gaze fell on the suggestion of a form beyond the fence. And then there was the unmistakable sense of movement, of the kinescopic effect of a body quickly running past. But so quiet, though not absolutely silent. I heard something, some small disturbance of air and grass as the person left. The overwhelming impression from those few seconds was that someone had been spying on me or my boys and had run when he was about to be caught. Reporter? I thought. Nosy neighbor? Private eye for the Solomons' attorney? Or even for Claire Stanley? Unlikely; what did they care about my day-to-day movements?

Bradley Franco?

Again I debated calling the constable back. Tim and Jason were in custody. No one had ever physically threatened me, including those two. Someone had gotten curious about the sounds in our yard. The fence was sound, and the gate had a stout padlock on it, which I typically kept secured. And, I admitted to myself, I didn't want to come off as a quivering ninny to McCandless, especially after having fainted the night Tommy was shot. I was tired of appearing so helpless and rabbity. So I thought, I'll wait.

Instead, the next afternoon the constable called me. "I'm sorry, Gina, but you've missed the whole thing. The jury's out. They expect them to come back with a verdict tomorrow."

Patsy said she'd be happy to keep the boys on Thursday. She didn't mind having Josh around, she said; she was just tired of him being bored and underfoot. In this case three was definitely better than one. I hoped she wasn't just being nice, deposited them with her in the morning, and took the train into the city.

I took a cab to the courthouse. By the time I got there, it was after eleven. I asked a guard where the Solomon case was being tried, and he led me personally to the room. It was empty; after conferring with another guard, he told me that they had adjourned for lunch and everyone should be back around one o'clock.

I found a dark and unprepossessing coffee shop and ate a bowl of soup; I wanted to keep a low profile. At twelve-thirty I made my way back to the courtroom. There were plenty of spectators now, though none of the principals seemed to be there. I sat as far back as I could, deep in a corner next to a tiny elderly black woman with an enormous red purse. It perched on her lap like an alert grandchild and partially blocked my view. I liked that; if I couldn't see everything, at least I would be somewhat hidden myself. I asked her what was up; she said that everyone, including the jury, was due back at one.

At about ten till, various well-groomed people in suits started entering, making their way to the front of the room, taking their places. Tim and Jason were brought in from a side door, accompanied by bored guards. Anita Solomon filtered in, accompanied by a thin white-haired man with a tennis tan and an expensive haircut. There was a middle-aged anorexic woman with them, very dark, very grim, in a tight gray suit. Perhaps, I thought, Mother Dettwiler.

My whole body twitched when Tommy came through the set of double doors at the back of the room farthest from me, followed by Russell. They were both in work clothes, suits that hadn't yet been too wrinkled by the day. I hung back behind the scarlet handbag.

The jury found Tim guilty of the attempted murder of a New York City police detective. Jason was found guilty of conspiracy to commit murder, and he and Tim were also convicted on a small array of drug and weapons charges. The news caused a lot of noise, comments, and expostulations from most of the people in the room. Big Bag next to me said "I knew it!" and nodded wisely. Tim's hands fisted on the desk in front of him; that was all the emotion I could register from my distant seat. Neither his mother nor his father touched him; Jason's mother, if that was who she was, remained motionless, while in front of her Jason collapsed like a popped balloon, shoulders starting to pulsate in sobs. The judge dismissed everyone finally, and guards moved to the two criminal boys, no longer alleged, to take them away.

Claire Stanley stood up, shaking hands with various suits around her. I decided it was time to leave. I didn't need to be treated in some comradely manner by Tommy. Maybe it had been a mistake to come. I could have gotten all I needed to know from the constable. I thought, get out, get out, before you're seen.

I looked around outside the courtroom door, lingering for just a moment. I spotted Tommy in the crowd of lawyers and onlookers, even a few reporters, but he wasn't looking my way. He was talking to Claire Stanley, who was as close to eye to eye with him as any woman was likely to be, even in spikes. She was talking forcefully to him; I imagined she was congratulating herself. Russell was with them, talking as well, hands working the air. Tommy looked back and forth between them, smiling slightly, looking more hit man–like than ever. Then his attention was diverted by someone else, a small person in the crowd, so much shorter than the three in conversation that it was almost comical. The crowd parted enough for me to see that it was a tiny blond woman with a tight-waisted blue dress and a darker blue shawl, good legs in black tights and blue half boots. Very fashionable. Very tidy. Sexy. He didn't seem unhappy to see her, although he did seem surprised; it was hard to tell if he was just being polite or what. I realized I'd been peering at them from behind a pillar; I wasn't even aware that I was hiding. I thought, Stop being insane, you need to go home now, and I turned to leave. I had gotten a few feet down the hall, trying not to scurry, when I heard my name called. It was too close to pretend I hadn't heard; I turned, and it was Russell, running up to me, smiling breathily.

"Hey, wait. I didn't see you before. Have you been here before today?"

"No, just today," I said, moving away. This is exactly what I didn't want to happen, I thought.

"Well, you picked the right day to come. A few of us are going out for a drink to celebrate. You want to come?"

The thought of sharing a drink with Tommy and his girlfriend, Russell, and Claire Stanley made me nauseous.

"No, oh, no, I have to get back, you know, to get my kids."

Russell knew he couldn't get past that excuse but said, "I have my car here. Can I give you a ride back to Tenway?"

This was also way, way more than I wanted to deal with, and I was firm in my refusal, saying he needed to go celebrate with his buddies, they'd earned it, and so on. He was fairly persistent and wanted to at least give me a ride to Grand Central. I was trying to figure out how to refuse this, too, when I saw Claire Stanley's face over his shoulder. She'd spotted us, spotted me talking to Russell, and by the miserable look on her wide face, I knew which one of the detectives her crush was on. I thought, I guess I should be glad it's not Tommy, but I wasn't, really. I wanted to tell her, don't hate me, I don't want him. And, I reminded myself, she's married. All of this, oddly, allowed me to refuse Russell's offers more forcefully, though I thanked him as pleasantly as I could.

He asked me out then, for a date. I said, "Russell, I'm sorry, but I always say no. That's just what I do."

I turned to go find a cab, but Russell took my arm, causing me to turn back. Over his shoulder, at last, suddenly, I could see Tommy, still talking to Tiny. His eyes finally moved to mine and caught them. He stopped talking and stared at me for a moment; it felt long but was probably more like a second, maybe two. Looking at Tommy caused me to hesitate long enough that Russell got a good grip on my arm, and he led me enthusiastically away, toward his car. I couldn't get away graciously then, and I was forced to turn away from Tommy, forced by the demand for social pleasantness to go with Russell. I did manage to get a ride only to the station. He asked again for a date; I refused again. I wondered if he knew about Claire's feelings for him as I said a resolute good-bye.

As I watched office parks and highways ripple past the window of the train, I thought, It's over, it's over, Tim's in jail, you can relax again. I thought about what jail must be like for twenty-year-old boys. Or anyone, for that matter. Unimaginable, gray, bleak, deadly. I had a pretty good idea of what jails were like in the small-town South. They were bad enough. I imagined they were like summer idylls compared to the Fritz Lang nightmares you heard about here.

Then, of course, my brain wouldn't let me focus on any topic other than Tommy, had to pick at it and worry it, since the subject was so nicely fresh and sore. I thought about how in a lot of books you're supposed to fight for your man. You're supposed to work to keep someone or win someone. If the books are old enough, you're supposed to do anything, using guile and deception to reel him in as though he were some sort of romantic marlin. But fight what? I thought. Fight whom? If he doesn't want me, it doesn't matter how much energy I throw at the problem, how much wanting I have for him. It won't magically melt his heart. He knows how I feel, or close enough, I thought. Of course, if Russell tells him anything (and will he? I wondered. I had no idea), if Russell tells Tommy anything true, anyway, he'll hear that I always say no. Maybe he'll think that would include him, too, even if he was interested. What do I do about that? Who do I fight? The tiny blond Kewpie? I could certainly take her in a fight, I thought, but I didn't think that would help me much. He'd just have to go to her rescue. I'd never encountered a heroine in fiction who appeared more appealing to the man of her dreams by bullying smaller people.

But I felt increasingly heavy and horrible, as if I'd somehow lost something big. I had to remind myself over and over that I hadn't lost anything. You're not the one going to prison. Celebrate that, at least.

I had told Toby and Stevie enough about the Solomon affair for them to know that the end of it was cause for celebration. I had downplayed the potential danger to us, of course, instead focusing on the drama of the whole thing. We had police staying at our house; we were involved in a sting. Cool, right? The three of us went out to dinner that night to a Chinese restaurant where they had a buffet, so that the boys could eat as much rice and as many egg rolls as they wanted. I couldn't eat much but found that I could still smile and joke and feel love for my kids. I was supremely grateful for that. It took a lot of effort to listen to them the whole time, to respond with enthusiasm when required, to understand all their anecdotes, but I did it.

It was still early when we were done with dinner, so we stopped at a bookstore on the way home. I treated them to a new book each, which made them less happy than a new toy would have. But the nearest good toy store was thirty minutes away, and I wanted to get home. Later, I promised them. Toby got a book on cats, and Stevie got one on robots. I wanted them to get actual stories, but they weren't interested in what I wanted.

We read the books that night before bed. I had to work especially hard to get them to calm down. Toby finally slept, and Stevie was nodding off when he said, "When's Tommy coming back?" I said, "He's done here, I think, honey. I don't think he's coming back." I didn't cry then, which was good. Stevie has always been a little psychic and weirdly prescient, and he knew to leave it alone for the moment.

The next night my mother called. She said she'd heard that I was involved with some reporter, and what was I thinking?

"I'm not involved with anybody, Mom. You can relax."

"Well, I should hope not. You have your sons to think about."

"I don't get why this is a problem. I wouldn't have sex with someone in front of them."

"Gina! Goodness, you're getting a mouth on you."

"Who told you I was seeing someone?"

"Rosa."

"She doesn't know her butt from her hand on this one. And since when do you care so much about Toby and Stevie?"

"I just hope they don't forget about their father."

"Of course not, but Jesus, Mom, they were three when he died." I tried to inhale more deeply; I had been having trouble breathing. My trachea felt shrunken and hard. "They've forgotten most things about him. I've tried to keep pictures around and stuff, but you know, there's not much else I can do."

"You could keep in better touch with his family."

Ahhh, now I could see what this was about. "Mom, the Winterburns don't want anything to do with them. They don't want anything to do with me. They made that very clear. I can't force them to be family if they don't want to be."

"Well, what have you done about this lately? That was a long time ago. Things change; people change their minds about all sorts of things, especially important things. Have you approached anyone lately? Called them or anything?"

This seemed bizarre to me, even for her. "What are you talking about? The boys will be fine. If what you're worried about is that somehow I'll be expecting you to contribute any money to their education or something, there's no problem. It's covered. They'll be able to go to college. Otherwise, I don't know why you're concerned about this." I'd never told my mother about their trust fund.

"I just think that the boys should be attached to that family." No, *you* want to be attached to that family, I thought. "There are all sorts of opportunities and advantages that they would have that they don't have now. I don't think you should dismiss that so quickly, and I don't think you've done enough to see if you can reconnect with the Winterburns."

"Mom, they're horrible people. Scott's mother and his one brother are seriously crazy. This is the brother that tried to incinerate some of his classmates."

"I don't believe any of that. I never saw anything in the papers about the incident you're talking about."

My mother was not good at letting go of things. When I bought my first car, the ancient Nova, it was a stick shift. That, to her, was a bad idea. I didn't know why. But she nagged me about it for three solid months, every single day. She wanted me to sell it and buy another car, an automatic. She couldn't drive a stick herself, but I couldn't imagine she would ever drive my car, anyway. I think now it was a class issue; in her mind manual transmissions were associated with country folk and low status.

"And his mother didn't like you, but you can hardly blame her, under the circumstances," she went on.

I was trying hard not to lose my temper. I breathed in and out once to regain some patience. "There's not much point in discussing this, Mom. I'm not approaching the Winterburns for anything. You might as well let it go. Okay? I'll call you sometime later, but now I'm tired. Good-bye." I hung up.

The following Sunday was Easter, and the Eberles coerced me and the boys to eat Easter dinner with the Hannigans. I wouldn't have set foot in the Big House, but Aunt Lottie had agreed to go there this year, and that meant that her daughters and Clark were committed as well. I asked the boys how they felt about it. Stevie shrugged, unconcerned either way. Toby, bless his loving little heart, said he was willing to give his cousins another chance even after the horrible cross-beating incident. The Eberles said they needed allies. It was flattering, but it was a weight I didn't want. I agreed to go, anyway.

The big sloppy Sunday meal was another typically miserable family occasion. Maggie and Stu were there, of course, with their cluster of children. Mo was there without Ivy, as usual. I wanted to ask where she was but knew I'd be doing her no favors if I did. Mo and her father were the big drinkers, and I saw with some tension that when Frank was good and drunk, he seemed more likely to at least acknowledge his oldest child's existence. More specifically, he'd grunt at her when she said something directed at him.

"You want some more ham, Dad?"

"Uh." (Yes.) The most horrible thing about all of this was the way Mo's face lit up when he made this guttural, almost barnyard-level contact with her. Poor Mo, I thought. Poor Ivy, too.

Before dinner Clark managed to sneak off with Toby and Stevie, keeping them, for a time, anyway, separate from Maggie's children. The twins had taken a great liking to Clark; it was almost too cute to watch them together. He had lots of violent boy books, which he liked to read to them while making loud, sometimes vulgar sound effects. They clung to him as to a raft in a sea of adult boringness.

Everyone else was either working in the kitchen or drinking in the den. No one seemed to need my help, so I joined Aunt Lottie, who was sitting on the couch in the living room, watching Clark and the boys. I asked her if she remembered Jessie from her childhood in the Big House.

Lottie said, "Jessie Foxhall? You mean Jessie Hays. Foxhall was her aunt and uncle's name. She lived next door to us for years, till her aunt died. Then she moved away. I don't know what happened to her uncle, either, but I knew she bought a smaller house somewhere else in town. She was fairly close to Mama when we were kids, but Mama sort of lost her taste for her after Jessie's mother died."

"She said they kept a lot of foster kids."

"Oh, yes, well, Jessie's father was gone. I don't know if he died or left or what. But they didn't have any other way of making a living."

"Yeah, she said her mother was sickly."

"Well, depressed is more like it. I don't think there was much wrong with her that a handsome husband wouldn't have cured, but I can't really say. Widowhood, or whatever, suits some people better than others." She winked at me.

"It seems to suit Jessie all right."

"Oh, I don't think she ever married. She had a hankering for a black man that she met one summer out of town. Her parents wouldn't have any of it."

"A black man?" That would have been a big deal then, especially in a small town.

"Oh, yes, and no one would have much to do with her after that. I'm ashamed to admit it, but even Nonna, my mother, thought Jessie was a little, I don't know, tainted after that." She tsked. "Nonna wasn't always a very nice person. She was a pious person but not very nice."

After the big afternoon meal, Donna, Lizzie, and Mo collaborated on setting up an Easter egg hunt for the kids. That was especially generous of them, as none of the parents, neither Maggie, Stu, nor I, had lifted a finger. Donna had to leave, and then so did Bobbie and Clark, pleading something feeble and work-related, making sure that Lottie could get a ride home with me. That was irritating, but Frank hadn't let up for the whole meal on the "beauty tips" I could give them. I couldn't blame them for wanting to get the hell out of there.

Shortly after they left, the weather cooperated; it was cool but sunny, uncertain in the way April weather always is in the Northeast. The children exploded outside, baskets flying; even two-year-old Ewan disconnected from Maggie's dress long enough to go hunt for a few eggs. Toby and Stevie had had less experience at this kind of thing than had Maggie's kids, so they were taking a bit longer to find the colored plastic eggs hidden in bushes and behind flowerpots in the big hilly yard. Toby was cackling with laughter; he had found three in a row and now had more in his basket than ten-year-old Adam, who had been bragging that he was the finest egg finder in the universe. I wasn't proud of his delight, though I certainly could understand it. I took him aside and said quietly that it wasn't nice to make people feel bad, even if they were nasty losers who would make you feel bad in a heartbeat if it suited their evil impulses.

Maggie started talking to me pointedly about John Fagin as we stood on the lawn. She was wearing a yellow sundress cut for advanced pregnancy, and it billowed in the slight April breeze. I was distracted by the gooey wet spot on the hem left by Ewan's oral fixation; I was trying to make sure it didn't caress my calf as it blew gently around. All the other women watched the children from the front stoop. Uncle Frank staggered from the house, leaning against the doorjamb sloppily, watching the kids with a vaguely irritable expression on his face.

In the speckled shade of the big oak in the front corner of the yard Adam started screaming at Caitlin, then hit her hard enough to make her stagger. I didn't know what had set off their fight, but it escalated quickly, with Caitlin hitting Adam back even harder. She was almost a head taller and quite a bit thicker all around; Adam clearly got the worst of it. Maggie said something small and thin that had no effect on their behavior. Stu was inside watching something to do with sports on TV. Frank just stared, jaw working, getting more and more peeved but not doing anything. Everyone else fell silent for a moment, trying to figure out how to intervene in front of Maggie while not offending her. I quickly grew weary of the ineffectual adult dithering and went over to the feuding children. I grabbed each of them by an arm and said, "No hitting. Hitting is always bad. Stop it right now." I've developed a pretty good adult-who-will-tolerate-no-more voice over the years. It worked, sort of. They both stopped actually hitting, although Adam twisted and pulled away from me, stomping off in a blue fury. Caitlin kept screaming at him, "Loser! Loser! I'll make sure Daddy whips your butt for this, loser!" I was surprised; usually Caitlin was sneakier.

Adam tore off into the rose garden. On a reflex, I looked for the twins. Toby was off under an oak tree with little Kelsey, wrangling over which one had found a blue egg. I didn't see Stevie anywhere. I looked harder; Lottie, noticing my growing anxiety, looked around, too. I heard a high scream, recognized it as Stevie's, and ran into the walled rose garden. I followed the sound of another scream and came upon Adam, who was shoving Stevie headfirst into Rosa's prized La Dolorosa della Vecchia rosebush. He had Stevie by the collar of his green flannel shirt, pulling him out, pushing him in, while Stevie screamed and bled as the thorns tore little rivers in his face, in his neck, on his hands.

I must have made some sound, but nothing stopped Adam, engorged with rage. I grabbed him for the second time that day, yanking him hard, then pulled Stevie to me gently, slowly, trying to assess his wounds. Poor little boy, I kept thinking, poor little wounded boy.

I left a deflated, defused Adam, who was saying in a small nasal voice how Stevie had provoked him in some way. Saying that Stevie deserved it because he'd found more eggs, he'd hogged them, he was the loser. I didn't even look at him, just carried all fifty-two pounds of blue-eyed boy out of the little walled garden, Aunt Rosa's pride and joy.

I carried him to the Big House after saying to a pale Lottie, "Please keep an eye on Toby." Frank was still in the doorway. He was smiling, a weak, jolly smile. "Got into a little fracas, hey now?" I waited for him to move, then carted Stevie to the powder room off the kitchen. I cleaned him up with damp pieces of toilet paper, blotting as gently as possible as he wailed and flinched.

Then he said the thing that broke my heart, finally, in two. "I'm sorry, Mom. I'm sorry."

I could feel my whole body pulsing, swelling with outrage. "It's not your fault, honey. None of this is your fault. You have crappy cousins. I'm sorry. It's not your fault that you have such crappy cousins." I heard a noise behind me. It was Mo, checking on us.

"That's a terrible thing to say, Gina." She looked hurt. I just stared at her. "I can't believe you'd talk that way about your own family." It was like she was speaking a language I'd never heard before. Or we were watching a murder and she was dickering over whether it was going to rain.

In the yard I said, "Toby, we're leaving. Come right now. Don't argue," I added, as I could see Toby wanting to get back his rightful booty from Kelsey. "Grab your basket. We're going home." Lizzie watched, very pale. Neither Molly nor Rosa was anywhere to be seen.

Maggie tried to talk to me. "Really, Gina, you make such a big deal out of things." But her heart wasn't in it. I didn't know if she was bothered by the behavior of her children or was just glad to get me out of there. I found Stevie's basket and got both boys into the car. Aunt Lottie joined us without comment.

From inside the little walled garden I heard Aunt Rosa's shriek tear through the rest of the day. "My rose!" she cried. "What did you boys do to my rose?"

. . .

Lottie asked me if I wanted to come in. I said no, the boys needed to get home. She sat for a minute, looking at me, then said, "They're not particularly wonderful people, but I swear they seem to have it in for you, sweetheart." I burst into tears, and she let me cry on her warm shoulder for a few minutes, the boys silent and watching in the backseat. I finally said a moist good night to my nicest aunt, waited till she was safely in her house, and took my sons home.

The next day after school the weather was reliably nicer, no clouds, no breeze suggesting imminent meteorological changes. So I made the boys go play outside, pulling out some new water guns from a secret stash I kept in the basement for just such occasions. I watched them through the kitchen window while I made some bread dough, shaped it into rolls, and left it to rise on the counter next to the stove. I was momentarily smitten with sadness at the thought that I no longer had to worry about Sidney getting on the counter and licking the dough or leaving black hairs stuck to it like lint.

There wasn't much I needed to do yet for dinner, so I grabbed some notes I needed to go over for two of my classes the next day and went out to the deck overlooking the backyard, off the kitchen. After making a loud and solemn rule about not squirting me or my papers, I sat at my garage-sale patio table and opened my notebook. I'd been working for about a half hour or so, the boys in my direct or indirect vision the whole time. They tired of their game, though not of refilling the water guns at the spigot, and so started an informal contest as to who could shoot the farthest, which deteriorated into them both shooting the fence at close range, methodically soaking one board at a time. They were both doing this with great concentration when I heard an unmistakable yelp from the other side of the fence, the sound, as I later reasoned, of someone getting shot in the eye with a blast of water.

It took me a second or two, of course, to figure that out, but as soon as I did, I hollered at the two of them to get in the house. They tried to argue, but I said firmly, trying to calm myself enough to sound rational, not terrified, go ahead and watch something on TV, play on the computer, do whatever, just get inside the house. I know I scared them, but I was so scared myself all of a sudden that it was all I could do not to scream at them.

As soon as I'd gotten them in the living room and double-checked the locks on the front door, I ran out the back again, this time with the key to the padlock to the back gate. Before opening the gate, I tried to peer through the slats in the wet wood where I'd heard the noise. It was alarming how much I could see when I put my eye close to the opening; everything going on in the yard of my rear neighbor, across the path, was clearly visible. I could also see into part of their kitchen through a set of double glass doors that opened onto their back patio. No one appeared to be home.

I opened the lock with unsteady fingers, then creaked open the gate. I knew that the peeper was gone, but I was hoping to find some evidence that he'd been there, assuming it was a he, in the hope that I wouldn't sound insanely paranoid or needy to the constable. I had a fear of him thinking I was just eager for the attention, and a shame-filled fantasy in which the constable called Tommy, saying that I was asking for help again, and could Detective Galloway come help him out, as he didn't have the resources to constantly keep coming to this hysterical ninny's house. I knew the constable was far too gentlemanly to do any such thing; in fact, he had always been perfectly kind to me. But I hated the idea of calling him again, telling him about some other vague or possibly nonexistent threat.

So I looked beyond the fence for cigarette butts or footprints, dropped candy wrappers or beer bottles, anything that might confirm that a person had been hanging out in that spot or near it recently. Something that crime scene people could get fingerprints from, or spit (and therefore DNA) or anything like that.

There was absolutely nothing. I wasn't that surprised, really. How much of an idiot do you have to be to drop litter somewhere where you intend to commit a crime and people can easily spot you? Nevertheless, I am not a total fool, so I called the constable, anyway.

He told me he was headed home, so he'd come by himself and take a look around. I explained that there wasn't anything and that I knew there wasn't much he could do. He said that was okay. "You never know if something bigger might happen later, and then it might help us both if there's a record that you've seen stuff before." That didn't make me feel better at all, but at least he wasn't treating me like I was completely wasting his time.

He looked around exactly where I had and said he'd ask the neighbors if they'd noticed anyone they didn't know on the path. Beyond that, he said, there wasn't much to do but make a record of the call. He said, "Probably curiosity. A nosy neighbor. You've had some publicity lately, you know." I said I did know. He smiled, something unusual for him. "Well," he went on, "keep an eye out. Could be a Peeping Tom, and we like to catch those if we can." I didn't mention Bradley Franco, although I'm not sure why not.

After dinner the twins had happily forgotten my tyranny earlier in the backyard and were watching a movie. My arms were deep in dishwater when the phone rang. It was Maggie.

"Gina, I was talking to Mama, and she thinks it would be fair to split the cost."

"What are you talking about?"

"The rose. It needs to be replaced. I thought we could split the cost."

"I'm supposed to help pay for a new *rose*? First of all, was it killed?"

"No, but it was pretty badly mangled. It's ruined. Mama thinks we should replace it."

I took a few deep breaths. I was trying so hard not to start screaming at her.

"Gina, are you going to answer me? I think splitting the cost is fair. These roses are expensive. This way neither of us will go broke paying."

"So the fact that your eighty-pound son broke the branches by shoving my fifty-pound son into them makes us equally responsible, you think?" I was keeping calm. I was pretty proud of myself.

"Hey, they're kids, they got into some stuff, that's what kids do."

"When no one ever tells them to stop."

"Oh God, here we go. I knew you'd pull this. Just because you're so goddamn overprotective; you're raising a couple of sissies, that's what Stu says. You've got to learn to let go, Gina. My goodness, I have five children; you don't see me having a hissy fit every time one of them gets a bruise. You have to let them go their own way. How else will they learn anything?"

"Take the damn rose money out of Adam's allowance. If your mother has a problem with that, she can call me herself." I hung up, shaking so much, I had trouble getting the receiver back into the cradle. She didn't call back.

That night I had a dream in which my father was sitting in a chair in my living room, with a single light on. He looked sick and yellowy, sicker than I'd ever seen him. He just kept shaking his head, saying, "*What* have you *done*? *What* have you *done*? You're not a credit to your kind, not your kind at all." His voice was more like Dion's than the way he actually spoke, but it invoked the same old helpless sadness in me. "It's a good thing you haven't had kids. That would be very, very bad. We'd have to pay for them, and we can't, Gina, we can't. We don't have it, not at all." I kept trying to tell him that I had sons, it was too late, but he just kept shaking his head, repeating himself, and I lost my nerve and couldn't say anything.

chapter twenty-three

WITH APRIL, the boys began Little League baseball, the "Slow-Pitch League," which I gathered meant that they didn't shoot spitballs and fastballs and other deadly missile-type projectiles at tender young heads. I got them both baseball pants made out of the most miserably scratchy and nonbreathing polyester I personally had ever come in contact with. I miscalculated sizes and wound up having to wind the drawstrings twice around skinny little waists to keep the too-balloony pants from routinely falling down. The T-shirts that they got were also a bit big, however, which was good; the extra length hid their waistband travesties, and they managed to look more like the other kids.

I sat in the stands, camera in my lap, stomach clenched in an anxiety like no other, watching as each of my tiny boys approached the plate at his turn, swinging wildly and seemingly without any aim at all at the small ball, never making the slightest contact. Other boys approached the act of batting with some assurance, some swagger, and gripped the bat with authority; if they didn't hit home runs, they usually managed to hit the ball after a few tries. I realized that all the other boys on the field had been coached by some eager parent, usu-ally a hopeful dad, and at least had at some point before in his life touched a baseball and bat and glove.

The difference between Stevie and Toby and all the other boys on their team and all the other teams, for that matter, was so obvious, I might as well have put sandwich boards on the two of them that said "freak boy" in giant Day-Glo letters. Toby was so demoralized after the first Saturday practice that I pretended to be convinced that they both had stomachaches the following Monday and let them stay home from school. I couldn't decide which was better, making them stick it out or allowing them to quit something so quickly. Which was worse to be called on the playground, a loser or a quitter? I decided I'd make them stick it out till after their first game, figuring that at least they would have actually, really and truly tried it before they gave it up altogether.

I regretted this later; the first game in which they actually had to pit their skills against those of another team was a bloodbath. Their fielding was even worse than their hitting. Both boys stood like blocks of wood every time the ball bounced by them. Then I watched in impotent angst from the bleachers as they sat on the bench, taking their turns at bat. One boy, an eight-year-old named Gentry Howard, walked up into the stands to get a drink of juice from his unseason-ally tanned mother, a woman with fingernails like scarlet shivs, and said, "Those brother boys are really weird. That Stevie one is such a nerd. I hope they get kicked off." I waited for the mother to say something Golden Ruley like you should be supportive of others on your team, help the younger, less-experienced players, and so on. But she smiled at him and said softly, giggling, "Oh, you." My own stubby nails were digging into my thighs, trying to keep myself under some sort of control. She knew they were my sons; we'd just had a conver-sation about which kid belonged with which parent. She also knew I could hear Gentry; I was sitting within two feet of them, and his voice was clear and carrying. Her husband was one of the coaches, and as much as I hated Gentry, it was clear that he was a well-trained player already, even at his age.

Still, their team lost by a lot, and my boys contributed more than their share to that loss, and everyone knew it. Gentry said something ugly to Stevie as the boys left the bench to come find me, something about being losers, about being nerds, about being "spazzes." A distant part of me was amused at the persistence of certain schoolyard epithets, but mostly I was swamped by a sick pained love. I tried to ignore it and focus on what they needed from me. Toby started crying; Stevie just looked surprised and, finally, hurt. They didn't want to ever go back. I heaved a mighty sigh and told them they didn't have to.

I managed to get final exams over with by mid-April, thus ending one of the most tension-fraught academic years of my life. Unfortunately, it had competition, as I had been teaching in graduate school when my ill-fated connection to Scott Winterburn began. I thought, when I get my student evaluations back, maybe I'll dig out the ones I got eight years ago and compare them, see which ones were worse.

Russell called me several times early in the month. I treated his calls with a little more respect than John Fagin's, since I actually had had some sort of relationship with Russell rather than the surreal pretend bond that Doughboy had called into existence between the two of us. In other words, when Russell called, I picked up and told him that I didn't want to see him socially and that he needed to give it up. I was far more direct than I usually was, and eventually he stopped calling. John Fagin never stopped, although the frequency of his calls decreased. He was now down to one about every ten days, and his messages were always chirpy, like I'd be glad to hear from him, good old reliable John, persistence would pay off eventually, right? Since directness had worked so well with Russell, I thought I'd try it with John. When he called on a Monday night after I'd turned in my grades, I finally picked up and said to him, "John, I will never, ever go out with you. Please stop calling me."

"Oho, this is progress. I got a human being! It's about time! I have tickets for this show in the city, it's a real Broadway thing, they fell into my lap. Would you like to go? I'd feed you, too!"

"John, no, I don't date. I told you."

"Oh, well, this doesn't have to be a date. Just a night out between friends, you know."

"We're not friends, John. I don't know you." And I really don't like what I do know of you, Doughboy, I thought.

"Well, we can change that. This is how people change that, you know; they share meals and shows and so on."

"No, thank you. I've got to go, John."

"Now, what I need to ask you is, Do you have someone else in your life? I mean, are you seeing anyone?"

I was not expecting this, though I couldn't have said why. It was an obvious enough question. "Well, no. Well, sort of." I thought, What answer would be the most likely to get him to leave me alone? "Well, yes, kind of. Sort of." I was such a terrible liar, so I kept thinking of Tommy, trying to make myself believe it. "Sort of," I said lamely again.

"Ah, but I thought you don't date. You're holding out on me!" I'm doing a hell of a lot more than that, I thought. "So if it's only 'sort of' and you're not dating anyone, then there's still a chance. I mean, it doesn't sound serious. So I'm going to keep calling, keep my hand in; you just never know."

"No, your hand shouldn't be in at all." That came out wrong. "Stop calling me, John. How else can I say this? Nothing that will ever happen in the universe, in all the universes of possibilities, will ever result in me going out on a date with you. How much clearer can I make it?"

April ended cool, with a bright, prickly sort of light. The boys were still in school, restless and cranky, but I was done for the year. We were encouraged to teach the stray class or two during the summer term. But the pay wasn't that good, especially if I had to pay for child care, and the winter had taken so much out of me, I needed to repair things. For one thing, my house needed lots of work, mostly little stuff I could do myself or learn to from books or websites. But mostly I wanted to hole up with the twins as much as possible. Baseball had been such a terrible washout, I knew I'd have to think of other ways to get the boys outside and involved with the world. This didn't come naturally to me, so I knew I'd have to give it a lot of attention.

I had been honest with Kay Reynolds about my reasons for not wanting to teach in the summer, at least to the extent that I thought she should have to be bludgeoned with my troubles, and she went easy on me. Being junior faculty, I was the least entitled of anyone in the department to dictate my schedule. But Kay needed the extra cash, however meager, to help with her daughter's graduate school tuition, so she didn't mind doing the summer classes herself. I didn't go into the fact that I was also pretty well situated financially, having been careful with what I'd earned in my previous life. I kept that information pretty close, of course. I knew that Lizzie, for one, would see this as another way in which I was a privileged and sheltered single mom. She was right. I knew this and wondered if I felt enough guilt to satisfy her, or the universe, or whoever might care.

Though I had no interest in being more like Rosa in most ways, I did have an interest in gardening. I had the will but not the skill. However, I had no intention of talking to her, possibly ever again. Fortunately, it appeared that my colleague Vincent Capinelli had transplanted what looked like an Elizabethan kitchen garden into his backyard, all beautiful fat cabbages and plump beans on glossy vines, lovely even mounds of black composted dirt, tall tomato plants in neat cages, chives and onions and pepper plants with waxy white flowers. The tomatoes he'd brought in from the last summer's garden looked like they'd been inflated with bicycle pumps. He had a small two-bedroom stone house only about five blocks from mine, on a large wooded lot. He dragged me, Kay, and Ida to lunch there one day when the boys were in school, and we all *ooh*ed and *aah*ed appropriately over his horticultural skill. Not only was his vegetable/herb garden something from a Merchant-Ivory film, the flower beds in his front yard were so dense and fragrant with purples and yellows, it made something inside my chest hurt with its beauty. It was perfect, too, in that it wasn't so perfect. There was a certain wild sloppiness to the flowers that made you completely relax around them. I had no shame; I flattered him up, down, and sideways and begged for his help with my own feeble efforts. He seemed eager, so a Friday in the last week of April found us in dirty cutoffs, T-shirts, and kerchiefs, digging in my small front yard with flats of various annuals and vegetable plants tumbled in the uneven grass, ready for a new home.

As we dug out weeds and overturned dirt, we talked, and I found out more about Vincent than I had learned in two years of working in the same academic department. He was an only child from Wilmington, Delaware, and had known he was gay since he was thirteen. His parents were embarrassingly supportive, marched in gay pride parades, tried to set him up with boys from the neighborhood, that sort of thing. It was a foreign world to me in more ways than one. But he was sweet and funny and generous, and I was genuinely glad for the opportunity to get to know him better, if a little ashamed that the only circumstances under which I'd been willing to do this were ones in which he was helping me. I at least managed to let him do most of the talking. I learned something else that had, not at all to my credit, never occurred to me. Vincent was lonely. He was single; it turned out he'd had only one long-term relationship, and that had ended when he'd finished graduate school in Illinois and come back East for the job at Tenway U. Tenway was a fairly liberal little town, so he was grateful that he hadn't felt a lot of hostility or distaste from most of the locals, but the pool of eligible men was even more minuscule than it was for someone like me.

I immediately thought I should introduce him to Mo and Ivy, then thought, is this a form of discrimination as well, this assumption that being homosexual is enough in common to create instant bonds between people? Well, no, I decided, but it's always good to know more nice people who understand some of your difficulties. It's not like they'd know every gay person in town, but then again, they knew more than I did. In the end I told Vincent about Mo and Ivy, and he seemed interested, if for no other reason than to have a slightly larger social circle.

I had made some sandwiches and iced tea, and we had taken a break to eat them, sitting muddily on my front porch, when a car came down my otherwise empty street and stopped in front of my house. It was a dark blue SUV so large that my little Subaru wagon could have fit inside the passenger compartment, possibly twice. After the engine died, Maggie's husband, Stu Lindsey, got out, wearing a gray suit that fit him beautifully, hiding his slowly expanding girth. At least it had been slowly expanding in the two years I had known him.

He came up the porch steps with a false happy smile. I suddenly wished I had on more clothes, even though it was very warm. I offered him some iced tea, trying not to sound as reluctant as I felt, and introduced him to Vincent.

"Well," said Stu, "I guess I'll have to tell John that the rumors are true, that there is someone else."

I decided to leave it to Vincent to disabuse Stu or not, as he saw fit. Stu said he wanted the tea, to my disappointment. I went inside and got him the smallest glass I could find. I handed it to him and tried not to sound too short when I asked, "So, Stu, what's up?"

He sat down, took a slow sip, and said, "Well, now, Gina"—he looked from the glass to my legs and finally up to my face—"Maggie's a little upset, you know."

The rose. I managed not to swear, but it was work.

"I'm sorry to hear that, Stu. But I'm not giving you or her any money. If Rosa wants money from me, she can talk to me directly. This isn't between me and Maggie; it's between Rosa and whoever she thinks damaged her rose."

Stu proceeded to talk to me in a way that I was getting alarmingly used to, as if I were a loony child who needed to be gentled and told things in very simple and nonthreatening terms. I said nothing for a while, trying to breathe away my anger, wondering if I was treating myself the same way Stu was. Vincent looked understandably puzzled, so Stu interrupted himself to give a watered-down version of the Easter events in question. I decided that if Vincent wanted more details about this, I'd tell him the real story later, after Stu had gone.

Stu was just getting to the part where Adam ripped chunks of Stevie's flesh off with the thorns of the rose when I heard another car coming down the street. It wasn't anywhere near the time when people drove much, not near school getting out or people getting off work, so it was noticeable, and I idly looked toward the sound. I saw an ancient silver Mercedes cruising carefully toward my house.

.   .   .

I suddenly realized how much I had to go to the bathroom. "Excuse me," I said, and left the two men on the porch, running inside, running into the bathroom, looking at myself in the mirror, saying, "Oh my God, I look like hell, why is he coming here? Don't get so wound up; he's probably only serving you with a subpoena or something or arresting you for putting your boys in baseball." I was working myself up into a burbling sort of hysteria, so I looked myself in the eye again and breathed. "Calm down," I ordered, and wiped the mud off the end of my nose.

I heard his voice before I saw him through the front screen door. I couldn't believe my physical reaction to the sound of his voice could be this strong, especially after how long, a month? Everything in my body simultaneously clenched and bubbled and oozed, and I thought, Jesus, I hope I don't act like an idiot.

He looked up when he heard me at the door. His smile was big and made his face warm and not scary at all. He was wearing jeans, running shoes, and a short-sleeved button-down cotton shirt, tiny black-and-white checks, slightly open at the neck. His arms weren't tan but were muscular and hairy, and he looked handsomer than I'd ever seen him.

"Hi," I said, but the breath didn't make it all the way into my lungs first; there wasn't much force behind the word, so it was almost inaudible. "Hi," he said back, his smile getting even bigger.

Stu looked puzzled, and Vincent looked interested. I introduced the three of them around, sloppily identifying the relative positions of each of them in my life to the others. I asked Tommy if he'd like some iced tea; after he said yes, he said he'd help me get it and followed me inside to the kitchen. My heart was beating like I'd been running, and I kept biting my lower lip. I was humiliated to see that my hands were shaking as I got him a glass for the tea. He had to have seen that, but of course he didn't comment on it. He just looked at me with a sweet expression, like he was really glad to see me. I kept wishing I could just return the look, but I was so freaked out, I couldn't even meet his eyes. I thought, I just look furtive, like a criminal.

He said, "You don't have to be nervous on my account. I'm not here to arrest you. Or to give you any more bad news."

I was about to ask him why he was here, then, when the phone rang. We both stood frozen in that awkward social pause when your machine is picking up, and you're both listening, and you have no idea if someone is going to say something embarrassing on the machine, but to run over and turn it down so your guest can't hear it would be odd and paranoid-seeming, but to just answer it outright would give your guest the rude impression that an unknown caller took precedence over him or her, so there's nothing to do but for the two of you to stare politely and blankly at each other till it's clear who it is and what they want and whether you're going to pick it up.

It was a man's voice, though not one I recognized, and I missed his self-identification at the beginning. He was saying something about practicing with the boys; I had no idea what kind of practicing he was talking about. Then the pieces joined, and I understood all at once; it was Gary Howard, the boys' baseball coach, father of the objectionable Gentry. He was offering to come over some evening after work or maybe a weekend afternoon to help the boys with their sub-par baseball skills.

I said to Tommy, "Excuse me," knowing I needed to nip this in the bud right away, and got to the phone in the dining room. "Hi," I said into it, trying not to sound as dismayed as I felt. "I caught most of that. Look, I appreciate it, but there's no need. I decided that the boys are too young for baseball. We'll try it next year, maybe. But thanks."

He hemmed and hawed and wanted me to reconsider and kept making offers of help. It was so tiresome, I wanted to bellow at him, but I merely persisted in my polite refusals and finally got him off the phone. I walked back into the kitchen, where Tommy was still standing, trying to look as though he hadn't heard the whole thing. I over-explained, telling him about the boys' awful sports experience and how their coach was willing to help them, but he had an awful son, and I wasn't interested. Then I remembered Tommy's baseball-related past and realized that he might think I was trying to give him a message as well about not being interested in sports help for my boys. So I backpedaled clumsily, turning hot and so, I assumed, bright pink. His eyebrows had risen slowly during this mortifying spiel and stayed that way for a while; he was smiling very slightly. He opened his mouth as though he was about to say something in his slow way when I heard another set of steps clunking onto my wooden front porch through the open screen door. I looked that way, down the front hallway, and saw a neutral-shaped male figure silhouetted by the spring light.

He pressed his face close to the screen, peering in, and said loudly, "Gina? It's John." Oh, no, I thought. Please God, not Doughboy. Not now.

The Universe clearly has a sense of humor, if often a cruel one. I often felt as though She laughed a lot at my expense. This was one of those times. My boys weren't anywhere near puberty yet, so the testosterone-fueled displays in my house had been limited to playing with toy guns and swords and the cartoony violence of computer games. Now there were four adult men on my porch, two of whom I wanted dead and a third I now wished would decide to just go home despite his gardening help. None of them would move. The place reeked of male weirdness, and I didn't know what to do with any of it.

I introduced John all around. I didn't know how to define him, so I just told everyone his name. Stu of course knew him well and raised his brows and smirked at me for reasons known only to him. John looked at Vincent, then at Tommy, and said loudly, "Well, which one is it?" I didn't answer, horrified at his tactlessness, and said, "Why are you here, John?"

He shrugged. "I talked to Stu earlier, and he told me he was coming over here. I thought I'd drop by, see if he wanted to play some golf later." The thought of my home being used as a casual meeting place for these two goobers made me feel creepy and vulnerable, then irritated. I was about to tell them to go ahead and tee off, when John interrupted me by asking Tommy if he could get an exclusive interview about the Solomon case. Tommy looked vaguely uncomfortable, but John continued, saying that I'd given him one, and it would be a great companion piece, an interview with the lead detective on the case. Tommy said that he'd think about it but wasn't sure and that he had to go. He was in the area because he had to question someone who lived near here for an investigation. He couldn't say more, but he needed to go before it got too late.

I felt panic oozing through me. Shit, shit, shit. No, Tommy, please, I thought, please don't go. How could I explain, I thought, that it's not normally like this? It's *never* been like this, ever before. And never again, if I can help it. I couldn't think of a way to say out loud Vincent's gay, Stu's an interfering in-law, John's just this pesky guy I barely know. In fact, I might need to consult law enforcement about him, he's so persistent.

But Tommy started for his car. I followed him, and as he reached for the door, I said, "Tommy, please, do you really have to go?" I thought desperately, then said, "The boys will be home soon. They'll really be sad to miss you. Why don't you stay for dinner or something?" There, I thought, that's about as bald as I can make it. If he doesn't take me up on this, I'll know he really was just in the area, isn't really interested in me in that way.

He looked at me for just a moment, no longer almost smiling. "Gina, I can't do this kind of thing. I'm not Russell, you know."

I said, not thinking first, "Are you angry?"

He leaned back a little, then lied, "Of course not. I just dropped in. I can't expect you to just be sitting waiting to entertain me." A short, fake smile, then he looked down, reached into his pocket, got one of his cards out, and handed it to me. As though I hadn't kept each one he'd already given me. "I'm going out of town for a couple of weeks, starting on Monday. I'll be in Chicago." Brief smile. "So if you need to get in touch with me, leave a message or call me on my cell phone. But I just wanted you to know that I wouldn't be in the city in case you needed to talk to me."

This made no sense to me. It seemed that he was blowing me off but was making himself available. Stalling for time, I said, "So, what's in Chicago?" then was horrified at myself, thinking, what if it's because of a girlfriend?

"Law enforcement conference. I'm actually presenting some cases. It's academic stuff again, believe it or not." He smiled briefly, touched my shoulder, then opened the car door. I thought, he couldn't really think that Stu and John were possible suitors, could he? But maybe Vincent. I wasn't really thinking rationally, but before he could close the car door, I held it, leaned in a little, and said, "Vincent's gay. He was helping me with my garden when all hell broke loose." He looked at me blankly, then quite deliberately not at me, at the street in front of him. I felt incredibly stupid and crass as well. I thought, I've blown it somehow, and I didn't even really do anything. My heart started hurting. I've done it, I thought, I've done it.

He finally looked at me again, not smiling. He looked sad and tired and said, "I'm sorry, Gina. I've got to go. Call me if you need me. I'll see you." I had no choice but to step back, and he pulled the door shut and started the car, not looking at me till he actually went to pull away from the curb. I could feel my face sagging with sadness, couldn't fake a smile or anything. And I thought, What difference does it make now if he sees how miserable you are about him going away? Maybe he'll feel relieved that he got out of here before you did something insane again.

I went back to the porch and told both Stu and John to leave. I'm not sure I was even polite about it. Vincent made noises about leaving as well; I said no, you don't have to go; you were the only invited person here all day. I thought he might be curious about Tommy, might want to chat about it after the other two had left. But he was ready to go home. It was getting near time to pick the boys up at the bus stop, and I realized, not for the first time, that Vincent didn't have much use for kids. That was one reason, I remembered, he and I hadn't bonded too much before.

"E., I'm finally done. He made it pretty clear." I was crying, trying not to but failing.

"It doesn't sound all that clear to me. For crying out loud, G., why the hell did he come see you in the first place?"

"He said he had to interview somebody."

"Oh, please. He wasn't wearing his suit. He wasn't working. G., for a smart girl, you can be a doofus sometimes."

"I'm done, Ellie. I'm done. This is killing me."

. . .

On Saturday the boys and I went to the library. When we got back, there was a message on the machine from Tommy. He said he wanted me to call him back. The phone rang later, but I turned off the machine and the ringer on the phone and went to bed.

For the next week I was an archetypal Great Mom. I baked brownies from scratch, I let the boys ask Josh Hepplewhite to a weekend sleepover, I rented all their favorite movies. I made my own chicken nuggets, and I played games with them, including some computer games. The phone and the answering machine stayed turned off. Eventually Ivy dropped by, a little worried that she hadn't been able to get hold of me. She got Lizzie to come over and give me a massage. Lizzie shocked me by not charging me. Ivy tried to take the boys out for the afternoon on Saturday; I wouldn't let her. I told her that Trevor could come to the house, could join the boys in their sleepover, but I couldn't let them out of my sight this weekend. Just for now.

With Josh and Trevor at my house over the weekend, I had to turn the phone back on, but I screened my calls. John Fagin called again on Sunday. So did Tommy, but I didn't pick up.

After school on Monday, Patsy Hepplewhite asked if she could take our three kids to the playground near our house, a good-sized one that the boys were still young enough to find exciting. I agreed, finally relaxing my grip on them, deciding that while they were gone I could try to meditate, try to breathe away at least one or two of my neuroses. It didn't work, of course. Then Patsy came back with them about an hour later, and I could tell by her pallor that something weird had happened. There had been a man at the park, a stranger to Patsy and the other parents who were later asked about him. The consensus was that he had been maybe thirty or so, dark hair, nondescript jacket and jeans. The day was nice and the park was full of relaxed parents, so at first he blended in completely. Patsy was in happy conversation with our newish neighbor Yvonne Corbin, there with her son Derek, who was more or less the twins' age. Stevie and Josh were taking turns going down the big slide, and Toby and Derek, striking up a new friendship, decided they wanted to get on the swings, which were only ten feet or so away.

Patsy and Yvonne were talking about the local schools, a favorite topic of many mothers, when Patsy noticed that Yvonne's son was swinging by himself. Stevie and Josh were happily sliding, but Toby was nowhere to be seen. I'm sure she had no interest in having to tell me she'd lost one of my kids. Everyone began searching; Derek was the one to spot him, talking with the strange man by the water fountain about forty feet away. Patsy and Yvonne called to Toby when they saw him; the man looked up and then ran. He was gone before anyone registered just how unsettling all this was.

Toby said the strange adult just wanted help working the water fountain; it shoots straight up from the middle and has an awkwardly placed foot pedal on the side. Patsy assured me that Yvonne had called the police on her cell phone; they had arrived promptly and gotten a description. They looked for him, but he was long gone.

Toby didn't understand why there was such a big fuss surrounding this boring encounter with the strange man, and no one wanted to frighten him or the other kids more than necessary. But still, Patsy and Yvonne put out the word that there might be a pervert watching the kids at our local playground.

I wondered and wondered in between bouts of relieved horror. I wondered if our pervert had a beat-up blue Trans Am or a bloodshot eye.

chapter twenty-four

---

*The more a person knows of himself, the more he will hesitate
to define his nature and to assert what he must necessarily feel,
and the more he will be astounded at his capacity to feel in un-
suspected and unpredictable ways. Still more will this be so
if he learns to explore, or feel deeply into, his negative states
of feeling—his loneliness, sorrow, grief, depression, or fear—
without trying to escape from them.*

*It is curious to speculate upon the consequences of civilized
man's refusal to be eaten by other forms of life, to return his
body for the fertilization of the soil from which he took it. This
is a significant symptom of his alienation from nature, and may
be a by no means negligible deprivation of the earth's resources.*

ALAN WATTS, *Nature, Man and Woman*

AT ELLIE'S URGING, I called Jeri the next week. She had an early-
afternoon opening, so I could go while the boys were still in school.
She said, "I know a lot's been happening with you. I was wonder-

ing if you'd call. I've been following the story about your psycho student in the papers. We can talk about that if you'd like, but first things first."

She did the checklist again. When she got to my love life, I hesitated. She waited very patiently.

"I don't really have anything new in my love life, really. I mean, there's no real person I've gotten involved with, at least not really. Not physically. Not emotionally, either. At least, not in a requited sort of way." I was sweating.

"I'm sorry, Gina, but I don't know what any of that means. Have you met someone?"

"Yes, but he doesn't have any feelings for me. I have some for him, but he doesn't know that. Besides, I don't really see him, anyway."

Jeri blinked a few times. "You like someone, but he doesn't like you?"

"I think so, yes."

"You think so? You don't know so?"

"No. I mean yes. I know so. I think he has a girlfriend, anyway. It's probably for the best. It doesn't tend to work out with me, as you know."

"By 'work out' you mean men don't tend to love you the way you want them to."

"You know that."

"Do I?"

I hated that answering-things-with-a-question crap and told her so.

"Sorry. Give me examples," she said.

"Easy. For starters, Awful Bragging Man."

"Didn't he tell you he loved you?"

"Yes! Case in point!"

"How do you know he didn't?"

I was silenced by this. Then, "I know because it was obvious."

"Because he spread your sex life all over campus?"

"Yes, you know the story."

"Does that mean he couldn't have had any real feelings for you?"

I thought for a moment, too rattled to put my mind in good order. "I don't know."

That brought a slithery, slightly shameful memory: we were in a hot tub at his cabin, and he was kissing my shoulders and saying, "You're like a jewel in a dung heap. You radiate like no one I've ever met, but you radiate for whom? This place can't stand the kind of light you give off." I was slick with shame that such crap made me feel good in any way, made me feel so appreciated. Then later, "Oh God, Gina, forget that, that's stupid bullshit. I'm so sorry, but please let it go, please. It's just that those children have nothing better to do than to talk about people like you and me. It's just the price you pay for being so outrageously different, special, so . . ." Christ, I'd been mad.

It had never occurred to me that his remorse might have been genuine. I felt almost vertiginous with memory. I had started finding him repulsive *before* I'd heard about the tale-telling nonsense from Ivy. I remembered suddenly my feelings when she told me. Anger, certainly. Intense humiliation. And relief.

I started feeling physically cold. I hugged myself.

"What about Scott?" said Jeri.

"What?" I was lost. "What about Scott?"

"Why did he marry you?"

"Well, because he wanted the kids."

"Would you have kept him from them?"

"Of course not."

"Did he know that?"

"Yes. I told him that."

"He had no reason to think that you wouldn't do what you said, did he?"

"No, but . . ." I was starting to feel panicky. "Scott didn't even like me by the time he died. I've told you about the affairs. I mean, it wasn't really a marriage, you know? Not in the normal, fall in love sense, at all."

"Not to you."

My teeth started chattering.

Jeri wouldn't let this go. "I've always wondered about this. I think we should explore it for a minute. You got pregnant. How?"

I resisted giving the easy, snotty answer. "You know how. A one-night stand."

"And he lied about being . . . infertile."

"Yes."

"Why on earth would he do that? Was he a stupid guy? Did he not get where babies come from? Could he not afford a condom?"

"I don't know. He was really irresponsible! He lied about a lot of things."

"Like what, besides the vasectomy? Or lack of it."

"Well, he had girlfriends, for Christ's sake."

"Did he lie about that?"

"What? Well, I don't know. Not very well, I guess."

"Would you still have slept with him if he hadn't said he'd had a vasectomy?"

"Yes, almost certainly."

"So he didn't say that just to get you into bed with him? He didn't need to lie about that?"

"No."

"Then why would he risk getting you pregnant?"

"He was drunk. He wasn't thinking. He didn't really like condoms."

"Couldn't it have been up to you?"

"Well, yes, but he said he'd had a vasectomy, so I didn't bother. That was the whole problem."

"Yes. So he didn't have to use a condom, and he still could have been reasonably well protected against a possible paternity suit or worse."

"I guess. Some guys like it bareback, you know." I was very hostile and freezing.

"You slept with him again, right?"

"Of course. We were married for almost four years."

"Did he prefer it 'bareback' all those times?"

I couldn't answer at once. "No."

"Did you ever have unprotected sex again?"

"No."

"Did he seem to mind?"

"No. I used a diaphragm."

"So he didn't mind a diaphragm later."

"We were drunk. You're overestimating both of our powers of reason that night."

She looked at me for a moment with her fist in front of her mouth. She lowered it and said, "How many girlfriends did he have in all? Do you know?"

"Lots, from what I heard later."

"Quantify 'lots.' How many do you *know* about?"

I thought. "Two."

"So that may have been it."

"I guess. But so what? Does the number matter, really?"

"Did you want to sleep with him after you were married to him?"

That question made my skin crawl. Eventually, I couldn't not answer her steady look. "Not really. I mean, I put up with it for a while. We were married, after all. I thought it would be okay. I mean, I thought, sex is sex. I like it, he's okay, he's good-looking: How bad can it be? We were both so lonely. I mean, his family was even worse than mine. I thought we could help each other out. I wasn't really romantic, I didn't have great expectations for marriage, I thought it would be okay, I really did. We had two little babies together." I paused and took a shaky breath. "But I didn't want to after a while. Have sex. With him, I mean. I didn't love him. I felt like a hooker, just sleeping with him because he was there."

"So again I ask, why do you think he married you?"

"*I don't know.* To piss off his parents." I was so mad at her, I could have hit her. Hard.

"It wouldn't have pissed them off for him to have illegitimate kids somewhere or live with you and the boys without getting married?"

Of course it would have, but I didn't need to say it.

"He had plenty of money, right? He could have afforded to support you separately, without you having to get married, right?"

"He had a huge trust fund."

"By getting married, you had rights to it?"

"Yes. That really horrified his parents after his death."

"Would he have been kicked out of school? Or would you?"

"Of course not."

"So what would have been the consequences of *not* getting married? Either for Scott or for you?"

"I don't know. I haven't really thought about it, at least not lately."

Her next question took me by surprise. "How long had you known Scott before you first slept together?"

I thought. This seemed reasonably neutral; this was a fact. I could reason this out. "Two and a half years, I'm pretty sure."

"Taking classes together, socializing, that sort of thing?"

"Yeah."

"So, he knew you pretty well before that night."

I just looked at her.

"Enough to be in love with you, maybe."

No, no, no no no no.

Aw, *shit*.

The hour was up pretty quickly after that. I felt like I had been hit in the head by a concrete block. I had just bought a new watch; it had stopped.

Two days later I did a quick Internet search for a hotel in Mayfield, Connecticut, that had a restaurant, cable, and a swimming pool. I packed a couple of overnight bags and then took the boys out of school an hour early. They weren't happy that we were going for a two-hour drive instead of getting to play on the computer or with Josh Hepplewhite. We drove to Connecticut, out to the little cemetery outside Mayfield where Scott was buried.

The boys didn't say much as we walked to the grave. It took a few minutes to find it; I hadn't been there since his funeral. It was flush with the ground and was covered in dogwood petals; that was one reason it was so hard to find. On the cold gray rectangle that covered his coffin and whatever remained of him, it read, "Stephen Scott Winterburn. Born June 10, 1967. Died April 19, 2000. Beloved Son, Beloved Father." I had had no say in anything about his burial. I was lucky they acknowledged that he had children. I let the boys read the simple inscription. Then I started talking, hoping I was sounding matter-of-fact.

"You know, Dr. Silverman told me that lots of times, when little kids lose a parent, they might think things like somehow they made it happen, they killed their dad. But you know what? No kid has that power, even if they feel like they do." I paused and looked at them. They looked back with large, dark eyes. "Neither one of you had anything to do with Daddy dying. Do you get that?"

They both nodded. "Do you believe it, is the next question. You're both smart, but this is stuff we haven't talked about enough. I guess I didn't want to because it made me sad. But I'm pretty tough, and I can talk about it now, if you want."

They looked at each other in a twin sort of way. Toby said, "Do you miss Daddy?"

I lied without a blink. "Of course I do. Do you?"

Neither one answered right away. I tried with all my energy to imagine what they must think about all this. I'd done this exercise before, but never with as much intensity as in that moment. "Look, guys," I said finally. "You two were three years old when he died. *I* have trouble remembering some stuff about your dad. It's okay if you don't remember much about him. That's one reason I keep pictures of him around, because you know, it's one of the hardest things to remember, how people look."

Stevie said, "I've been having some trouble remembering what Sidney looked like, even."

"I know what you mean. Me, too, sometimes, and I knew Sidney for a lot longer than you did. Maybe we can remember some stuff together.' "

We found a cool stone bench near the grave site and talked for an hour. The boys bloomed with questions. Sometimes I lied, and sometimes I didn't. I told them what Scott's favorite thing to do with them had been, dancing with a tiny boy in each arm to the O'Jays' "The Backstabbers."

We talked for a while, gently and slowly. Toby eventually admitted that he sometimes had nightmares in which Scott was a monster, some kind of living dead creature, trying to bite Toby to death. Few things in my life have been harder than in that moment not reacting with a scream of lovesick horror. But I managed to just nod and say yeah, that's normal, it's okay, I'm not worried about you. "But you both need to know"—I stopped, looked at one and then the other, put my arms around both sets of narrow little shoulders—"your dad loved you both so, so much, he would never, *ever* come back to hurt you or scare you in any way. The nightmares are from your own head, your way of being sad that you don't have a dad. They're not real. And it's okay to be sad about that. It *is* sad."

We talked about Sidney, too. Stevie said, "I really miss him lying on my feet in my bed." They both started crying, and I held them, two big satisfying armfuls of boy. I kissed each fragrant head.

After a little while Stevie said, "Daddy's in the ground over there? Is his body, you know, all gross?"

Whew. I had been preparing for that one. "No, he's not gross. His body's kind of dissolved, you know." I saw no reason to go into our culture's need to pickle people and put them in big concrete crates. "His body's now part of the ground, and the grass, and the flowers, and the trees. We're all part of everything on earth, you know. We're all connected. So we're still connected to Daddy by the air we breathe, the food we eat, the ground we walk on. And he's partly in you, just like I am, because he's your dad."

Toby said, "Josh says he's with Jesus."

Stevie snorted. They tended to take opposite roles: Mr. Piety and Mr. Skeptic.

"Well, some people think there's an actual place that you go to, to be with God, who's like a nice old man. But when you think about it, we come from the earth and everything else there is in the universe. We're all part of the same thing. We just don't remember this, usually, while we're alive. So I think what Daddy did when he died was remember and sort of say 'Yippee, I'm back!' But of course, he never was away; he had just forgotten that he was already home."

Toby looked like he had something to chew on for a while. Stevie said, "It's like string theory and how everything's made out of the same stuff, like energy."

Yes, I said, exactly like that.

It was starting to get dark. I said, "Okay, let's have a very quick game of hide-and-seek, and then I think we should go."

After about fifteen minutes the boys were willing to continue, but I was not. They protested riding in the car for another two hours. I said, "Well, how about we go swimming before dinner?" There were a few moments of extremely gratifying "Mom, are you crazy?"s and "What are you talking about?"s; then I told them we were staying in a hotel with a pool.

After a good swim we ordered burgers and fries in our room. The boys fell asleep on either of my shoulders in the queen-sized bed while watching cartoons on the hotel TV. After they slept, I took my Walkman, went into the bathroom, and shut the door. I put in a tape I'd dug out from my desk drawer that morning. It had been made by a fellow grad student in the religious studies department at Yale, a woman a few years older than I was named Chelsea Dunning. I hadn't seen or spoken to Chelsea since Scott's funeral, although she had tried to get in touch with me numerous times. The tape was a compilation of songs, sweet quiet songs, good for helping restless babies sleep.

I listened and had a memory so intense that it was almost hallucinatory. The song was by Alex Chilton; it was called "Blue Moon." It was simple and beautiful, and I had heard it many, many times, sitting in a rocking chair in the second bedroom of the town house Scott and I shared, the town house was so much larger and more comfortable than the homes of many of the other students I knew, because Scott had so much money that he could afford a place that was really nice. The room in this memory, the boys' room with the oversized crib, was lit only by a night-light the size and shape of a small box turtle. I would rock and rock, a little baseball-sized head resting on each of my arms, warming them. It was to this song that I first felt my heart swelling, larger than my body, so large that it ached and ached. With great silent ferocity I promised them then absolute unconditional love, eternal vigilance on their behalf, and that I would never, ever let them down. And the memory spilled on, not just that one time, no, several times, I remembered Scott opening the door, silhouetted in the bright hall light, standing there, watching us, not leaving, just watching, while I rocked and the babies' eyes slowly shut and the beautiful song played.

Now, here, sitting on the edge of a cold narrow bathtub, sorrow speared me so forcefully that I had to bite on a bath towel to muffle my sobs. I cried so long and so hard that I vomited hot bile and burger bits into the toilet, having to pull the headphones off and slap them on the small white counter by the sink. But all sound was muted, almost silent. "I'm sorry," I whispered again and again. "Scott, I'm so sorry, so sorry. I'm sorry, I'm sorry."

The next morning we had breakfast in the hotel dining room and then drove home. There were, for a change, no messages on the machine, which filled me with a bleak relief.

That Monday, after I saw the boys off to school, I received a registered letter from the Winterburn family, demanding my sons.

chapter twenty-five

One can be less vulnerable by becoming less sensitive—more of a stone and less of a man—and so less capable of enjoyment. Sensitivity requires a high degree of softness and fragility— eyeballs, eardrums, taste buds, and nerve ends culminating in the highly delicate organism of the brain.

ALAN WATTS, *The Wisdom of Insecurity*

THE LETTER WAS FULL of legal jargon, and it took me a good forty-five minutes to comprehend the important point. When I finally realized what it was, I collapsed into a sort of terrified jelly for a while. Then I thought, I have to get help. I need a lawyer. They can't possibly win this. No way. This is a nuisance suit of some kind because they really want . . . what? What could they possibly want from me? Revenge for Scott's death? What?

The first person I called was Ray Damita, the attorney in New Haven who had handled my severance from the Winterburns in the first place. I was told by a nasal and bored woman that he was deceased. His partners had possession of his papers, but that wasn't helpful. She didn't want to put me through to a partner, didn't want to speak for anyone, barely wanted to take a message. This was not good. I needed an attorney who was ruthless, fabulous at family law, able to deal with cases in Connecticut as well as New York. I knew no one. I made a few babbling phone calls to Ivy, to Kay Reynolds, to Vincent. Vincent said it made more sense to look in Manhattan for someone like that than in dinky little Tenway, no offense to the legal community there.

I realized I did know people who knew people in the city. I called my former agent, Mary Glenn.

She was out of her office. I told her secretary, who had no idea who I was, that it was urgent. I'd never asked Mary for anything after leaving the business, and I was hoping she remembered that now. It's not like she really owed me, either, but I hoped that the idea of getting me in her debt would appeal to her. The only other person I could think of to call in the city was Dion, but I couldn't imagine that he or DeVonne would be of much use. If Mary didn't call me back within a few hours, however, I decided I'd try them, anyway.

Mary got back to me in the middle of the afternoon. I told her briefly what was going on, trying to keep my emotions under control. She gave me a name. "He's the best attorney in the city. He handles all sorts of litigation. If he doesn't want it or can't do it, he'll know who else to get. Tell him who you are; tell him you work for me."

"But isn't that a bad idea, since I don't?"

"No, because technically you still do. I never took you off the books, and if you ever do another shoot, I still get thirty percent."

"It used to be twenty."

"Not anymore. Let me know what he says."

I told Mary that I owed her, which was unnecessary. I then called the attorney's office. I told them I was Gina Paulson, an associate of Mary Glenn's, real name Gina Paletta. I was shocked that Bill Koerner got on the phone with me almost immediately.

The attorney was able to fit me in on Wednesday of that week, early in the day. On Tuesday I tried to do things around the house and tried to avoid getting on the phone with anyone. But it kept ringing. No long-distance calls from Tommy from Chicago, about which my feelings were mixed. But others were relentless in their attempts to talk to me: Donna, Bobbie, Mo and Ivy, Kay and Ida and Vincent, as well as Patsy Hepplewhite and Yvonne Corbin, who dropped in together to offer their help. They all eventually succeeded in getting me to talk; even Aunt Lottie called one evening and made me tell her everything about my legal woes. Lizzie was uncharacteristically supportive. I'd known for a while that she loved my boys rather fiercely; I wasn't sure why. This genuinely freaked her out. Dion heard about the situation from Mary and contacted me immediately, suggesting that he and DeVonne mount a smear campaign against the Winterburns. I discouraged him, but with gratitude. John Fagin called, wanting a story on my dilemma. I was appalled that he knew anything about it and told him I wasn't interested in talking to him.

As I rode on the train to see the lawyer in the city, I spared a minor thought for how much this was likely to cost. But I had no choice; if it meant good-bye to their college fund, to my stocks, to my house, even, so be it. I couldn't believe how practical I was being. It was a sort of shock, a defense against dwelling on what the stakes actually were.

Bill Koerner was jolly, a joker, tall and broad with a spongelike mass of black hair perched on his head. I was in no mood for his brand of charm. He reached out with enormous hands covered with hair while telling me he was a fan. Then he started talking about all the clothing he'd bought his wife from *Lavish,* especially outifts I had modeled. It was as peculiar a compliment as I'd ever heard in my life. I didn't care. I just wanted to be convinced that he knew what he was doing. He had some work left to do in that regard.

We went over the letter and all the papers I had pertaining to the Winterburns and Scott's death. I could feel panic licking me around the edges. I told him that my attorney had gotten Leona Winterburn to sign a document agreeing to relinquish all claim to my kids on the condition that I make no claim to the family's assets other than the trust fund the boys were entitled to as Scott's sons. They had no access to that until age twenty-one. I told him every sordid detail of my dealing with the Winterburns in case anything could help.

Bill, as I was commanded to call him, read over the letter. He said, "This is strange. They are asserting that you have been in contact with them, demanding more money, and thus have broken the agreement. So they're declaring it null and void. Have you?"

I assured him that I hadn't.

His eyes still on the paper, he said, "They actually say 'your agent.' Do you have any idea who they mean?"

"No. Nobody's contacted them with my knowledge." I couldn't imagine that my mother would be calling them up to chat about money, and she was the only person I knew who would care.

"There's also some mention of impropriety on your part that would make you unfit. They're throwing some pretty serious charges at you, of moral turpitude, associating with felons, corrupting minors, among other things."

I filled him in on the recent case. "Assuming that's what they're referring to, they have absolutely no grounds. You can contact the detective in charge of the case if you want." I gave him the number of Tommy's precinct. I couldn't imagine that Tommy would mind talking to him.

He made me sign a letter that gave him permission to discuss the case with someone else, namely Tommy. That made me squirm a bit; I didn't really want Tommy knowing that I was a damsel in distress. My pathetic hope that it might make him come to rescue me was unpleasant. Besides, there wasn't anything he could do. It didn't occur to me until about a month later that it would have made a lot more sense to suggest that the attorney contact Claire Stanley's office or Constable McCandless.

Bill said, looking out the window at an impressive river view, "The Winterburns may not care whether or not there's anything to these allegations. It may not be about winning. It may be about making your life miserable."

He said to come back in a week. By then he'd know what we had to do.

. . .

On Saturday I worked up the courage to let the boys go over to the Hepplewhites for a while. Josh had just gotten a puppy, and it would have been downright abusive to keep them at home. Both boys, especially Stevie, were getting more and more sullen with me. I figured the problem had to be me, but I had no clue what to change or how. I hadn't told them about what was going on and had asked Patsy to keep it from Josh as well. I didn't see any benefit to them knowing that someone rich and powerful was trying to snatch them from their mother. It was way too much like my nightmares, and so I could rarely sleep. That didn't help my mood any and didn't make me a more cuddly mother.

I was contemplating old toothbrushes, trying to decide which one to use for scrubbing the grout in the bathroom, when a familiar rapping on the downspout startled me.

Jessie said with her typical air of resigned charity, "Here's something for you. I'm in the craft club at the senior center, and we make things. I thought you could use this next year."

It was a Christmas tree about the size of a pineapple. It was made out of cut-up egg cartons, the cup-shaped parts, glued together atop a cone-shaped base. It was pink and white, the colors of the Styrofoam the shapes had been cut from. At the top was a star, bought intact, I think, from a craft shop. A faded red ribbon was wound around the "branches," which were also dusted with gold glitter. It was the saddest little creation I'd ever seen in my life.

"Wow, Jessie," I said. It sounded like someone else's voice. "It's really beautiful. You made this?"

"Yes, me and my craft partner, Geraldine. We made a bunch of them. I thought your boys would like it."

I didn't even want to think about their reaction to it. "Of course they will. It's really sweet of you, Jessie. What can I do for you? You keep giving me all these nice gifts. Is there something I can get for you, run some errands, something?"

"I'm just fine on my own, thank you." This was prim, a little miffed. "I don't need anything. But I imagine it's tough being a single mother." She was a bit scolding. "Take this home now. Put it away until Christmas." I noticed she was wearing the jade necklace, but made no comment.

Later that day Donna called me. We talked on the phone for a long time. It seems she'd ended things with the doctor and was feeling pretty awful. In fact, she was avoiding the hospital, a first for her. She asked if the boys and I would come over for dinner that night, which we did.

Bobbie was out with Clark, and Donna and Aunt Lottie were home together. Aunt Lottie sat at the dining-room table with the boys, showing them how to play Uno, while Donna and I talked in the kitchen, washing dishes. The doctor couldn't leave his wife right now, she was sick with something and needed him desperately, even though it was really Donna he loved, blah, blah, blah. She knew it was a crock. She just needed to have someone besides her mother hear her say it. A witness. I put my arm around her. I said, "Do you have any idea how beautiful you are?"

Later, when Stevie and Toby had exhausted Aunt Lottie, Donna switched places with her, and I chatted with Lottie over coffee in the living room. She asked me if I'd seen Jessie Hays lately.

I said yes. "We've become pretty friendly. She keeps giving me things she wants to get rid of. I don't know what I can give her back." I didn't mention the necklace. "She obviously doesn't have a lot of money; I hate to keep taking stuff from her."

"Is it stuff that costs her?"

"No, or at least not much. I get the feeling she wants something back from me, but I don't know what. She doesn't eat sugar, so I can't bake her stuff. She doesn't like kids, so I can't have her over. I don't know what to do."

"She probably just wants some company once in a while and someone to listen to her."

"You're probably right."

"After her mother died, her aunt was sweet enough. But her

uncle was a piece of work. He was very stern, thought very well of himself. I heard that he'd been considered handsome when he was young. I thought him a big gargoyle of a man. Very scary. But I was only about twelve or so when the Foxhalls moved in."

"Wait. The Foxhalls? Was he Jessie's dad's brother?"

"No, no. John Foxhall was married to Jessie's aunt. Jean was the sister of Josephine Hays, Jessie's mother."

"Do you remember their maiden name?"

"No. Maybe Pelham, or Grenville, or something very British. I couldn't tell you."

So why would Jessie have the same name as her aunt and uncle after being married? I wondered if she'd taken their name for some legal reason later, to pretend to be a daughter to make inheritance easier or something. Did they adopt her? But she was well into her thirties when they moved in. I wished there was a tactful way to ask about this. I was being inexcusably nosy. But there it was.

On Monday, after getting the boys, I sat with them for a while, helped them with their homework, tried to engage them in conversation. Toby cooperated; we had an interesting interchange about a bad kid in his class, a kid named Justin who would never be quiet and kicked anyone near him when the mood struck him. Stevie was harder, though. He wouldn't look at me directly and squirmed away when I asked him questions.

Finally I let them go play; they did it separately. On an impulse, I looked in my pantry and found a box of whole-grain crackers. I told the boys I was going next door, making sure to lock the front door behind me.

It took Jessie a long time, maybe ten minutes, to answer her door. She looked more tired, older, than she had only a few days before. She was dressed in an aqua housecoat, blue mules, and a graying white sweater with blue balloons embroidered on one shoulder. She smelled of dust and lemons. She was clearly disappointed that it was me. I didn't know who else she expected.

I said, "I bought way too many boxes of these crackers. I was wondering if you'd do me a favor and try them. I hate to see them go to waste, and I thought you might be able to eat them, since they're whole grain."

Her expression didn't change, then she moved aside. I took this to be an invitation.

"Where's that big fella that was at your house so much a few weeks ago?"

"He's gone. He was a policeman; I told you that."

"Oh, yeah. I'd forgotten. I'm not good at remembering things much these days."

"Me neither."

I saw that the photo album was out again on her small cluttered coffee table. It was open to a different page than before. "May I?" I said, pointing to it.

She nodded. There were several very glossy black-and-white snapshots of little girls. Two identical little girls in fancy dresses with bows and big, pleated skirts, little boots with lots of buttons. The dresses were obviously colorful, there were so many different shades of gray. Two little horse-faced girls in doomed finery. "How beautiful you and your sister were," I lied. "How old were you?"

"We were seven in this one," she said, yawning. I didn't want to hear this. Ann had three years to live. Jessie had at least another seventy-nine. I didn't want to hear about how long you might have to live without your other half, didn't want to contemplate loneliness on that scale. Just keep them with you for now, I thought, get them into college. Then you can kill yourself, you can troll the waterfront for sailors, you can start smoking again, drink yourself to death like your dad, whatever. Just eleven more years. Wait, get them through college first, maybe. Okay, fifteen years.

Jessie stood, took the crackers from the coffee table, and swayed for a moment. I hopped up and caught her arm, trying not to grab her so hard that it would hurt. She looked at me, eyes slightly filmy. "I have something else for you." I tried to protest, knew it was hopeless. She freed herself from me and went to a china cabinet on the far wall. She pulled open a slightly stuck glass door and took out a pair of small porcelain objects, one black and one white. It took me a moment to understand what they were. It was a pair of salt and pepper

shakers in the shape of cats. "You lost a cat. Give these to your boys."
I started crying then, couldn't stop. I wanted to hug her, which was
clearly not okay. I said instead, "They'll love them," and this time I
meant it.

She harrumphed, looked angry, and said she needed a nap. I took
the cats and left.

I was again lucky; Patsy Hepplewhite didn't have to be out of town
or at a doctor's appointment. She said she'd be happy to pick the boys
up at the bus stop with Josh, since I had no idea if I'd be back from
the attorney's in time. She extracted a promise from me, though, that
I would let her know as soon as possible what was going on with the
case. I appreciated her empathy and said so.

Bill Koerner stood up when I walked into his office and shook my
hand again. Fortunately, he understood that I was pretty eager for an
update, and he immediately told me about his meeting with the
Winterburns' attorney.

"They're pretending to be all in love with your children, but it's
apparent that they want the money."

"But it was Scott's. The rest of his family isn't entitled to it. Scott
very clearly wanted his sons to have it. I don't even have the authority
to give it to them, do I?"

"Yes, as the boys' guardian, you do. But your *sons* could sue you
later for doing it, when they reach a legal age. So you're at some risk
either way. The Winterburns probably wouldn't win a custody case
for your children, but it's always possible, especially if they get a sympathetic judge. They were a wealthy family, so that's a possibility."

"Were a wealthy family? Is that the problem?"

He nodded. "Some really bad investments by the living son. The
mother apparently relies on him, and that wasn't a wise decision."

"What about the old man? Kenneth?"

"He died three years ago. Things have pretty much gone down
the toilet for them since then."

"I hadn't heard. I guess I've been in a kind of news blackout concerning them. Someone may have even told me; I might not have

registered it. The boys' trust fund is a lot of money, close to half a million dollars. Is that a lot to them? They always seemed so hugely rich to me. And four years ago I thought that it wasn't the amount of the trust so much as the gesture that made them so angry. They didn't want me or my sons to have anything from the Winterburns, on general principle."

Bill sighed. "These are some nasty people. I understand why you went to the lengths you did to protect yourself from them. But they're still powerful enough, desperate enough, and vindictive enough to give you a lot of sleepless nights."

"So you think I should give it to them?"

"How bad off would you or your boys be without it?"

"We'd be okay. Actually, your fee is my biggest financial worry at the moment."

"Well, I'm sure we can work something out without your having to sacrifice the trust fund to pay me. But you may have to sacrifice it to get them off your back."

It was their last real connection to their father other than his name. I'd debated many times changing that to Paletta, making the break clean and complete. Except that that is never possible with your past.

For a little while we bandied other options back and forth as I clung to the trust fund, the idea of it, the security of it. But it was clear ultimately to both the attorney and to me that there was really no choice. There was no point in any more dithering or delaying. The Winterburns knew what they were doing. I supposed there should have been some gladness in it, that Leona Winterburn would know at last that I hadn't been after their money at all costs. But all I felt was regret and a deep anger.

"Okay," I said, sighing. "If that's what I have to do, then that's what I'll do. But before you make it official, let me tell the boys so that in fourteen years I can tell them that I really did ask their permission. Maybe they'll remember that. I just hope they say yes."

He smiled. "Regardless, I'm not going to call their lawyer too soon. Let them think that they had to fight a bit, that it hurt you more. Then they'll go away happier and faster." He said there were papers to draw up for me to sign and suggested I go away, shop, get coffee, whatever, for an hour or so, then come back for them.

I found a coffee shop, got a cappuccino, and looked out at the beautiful spring day. Warm, clear, a day that made the city seem like a place I could like again. The news from the lawyer was terrible and terrific. Maybe a blessing; who could know? If we had been living in our car, things would be different. Now they'd just have normal opportunities, not abnormal ones. That would be all right. I hoped.

I thought about all the calls I would have to make when I got back home. The Eberles, Patsy Hepplewhite, selected Hannigans would all want to know that most likely the boys were staying home. None of them knew about the money in the first place; it would be quite a surprise, a deus ex machina solution. I thought, I'll have to send Mary Glenn some flowers, some really nice ones.

I let myself fantasize: what would you do if you were on your own, no kids, no dependents, no one but yourself to worry about? I'd live in Italy, I decided. Take my savings, buy a small villa on the Amalfi coast, go back to modeling, if possible, just for a few years. Start writing, novels, essays, anything. Maybe a memoir about modeling, if someone would publish it, to pay some bills. Take time to meditate and swim in the ocean every day. Walk everywhere. Get even healthier. Eat fresh pasta and fruit, learn to like wine again. Read novels and books about Zen. Talk to no one. See no one.

I had a small table by a window. A man in a suit, fortyish, chubby, with shiny curls and a nose that was too small for his face, sat down in the other chair. The place wasn't crowded; I was momentarily confused. He smiled pseudo-apologetically. "Hi," he said. "I hope I'm not intruding. You looked lonely." What to say? I saw no ring, didn't care, a reflex only. "I'm not," I said. "Please let me be alone. Please." I thought I was being as polite as the circumstances allowed. He didn't seem to think so, seemed angry, hurt. I thought, What do you expect? What did you think was going to happen? Don't you know you can't expect the world to act out your fantasies for you? I felt sorry for him but not enough to do whatever it was he wanted. "I just wanted to chat, to share a cup of coffee," he huffed. I doubt it, I thought. "I'm sorry," I said. "I really need to be by myself."

As I walked back to the attorney's office, I thought about calling Dion or even Mary. I had my cell, I had their numbers, I was in the city, it was early, before lunch. I couldn't do it. I just wanted to go home as soon as possible.

I stepped into the lobby of Bill Koerner's offices, and the first person I saw, standing talking to the receptionist, was Tommy.

chapter twenty-six

In almost every culture love is an intimacy between two particular people in which conventions that govern other relationships are set aside. In this respect it already suggests, even if only symbolically, the sacred rather than the profane, and the lovers' removal of clothes in one another's presence is already a sign of taking off the personal mask and stepping out of role.

ALAN WATTS, *Nature, Man and Woman*

THE WORLD RECEDED to a pinpoint. I could feel the blood rushing to everywhere in my body other than my head. He saw me, walked quickly to me, and grabbed my hand. He didn't talk, just looked at me.

The receptionist said, "Detective Galloway, you can go into the conference room on the right, down the hall. Ms. Paletta, would you like to join him? Mr. Koerner will be right in."

He didn't let go of my hand as we went to the small walnut-paneled room. I tried to pull it out of his when we were alone. He wouldn't let me. He said, "Why didn't you call me?"

I could feel a sharp pain right underneath my breastbone and a small tic developing under my left eye. My anger came from no-where, sour and hot. "Why should I call you, Tommy? What the hell for? I just gave the lawyer your name so you could tell him that I wasn't a felon. I don't even know why you needed to come here. Besides, you were out of town."

He looked hurt. That made me feel bad, but anger fought the guilt and won, so I didn't apologize. He said, "I had my cell; you have the number. I got back from Chicago last night; I just got the mes-sage from Koerner this morning. I called, and they told me you were going to be here today, so I came down rather than talk to him on the phone. When did you last eat anything?"

"What? I don't know. This morning."

"I'm taking you to lunch when we're done here."

"I'm going home after this."

"Please, Gina. Please, will you talk to me?"

"About *what*? Talk to you about *what*? I don't want to be friends with you. I don't need any more friends."

He breathed in deeply. "I don't want to be your friend." He looked momentarily confused, shook his head. "Well, of course I do, but that's not what I want to talk about."

Bill Koerner walked in, looked at us, and seemed at a loss for a moment, reading our body language. He looked at Tommy and ex-tended his hand. "Detective Galloway? Thank you for coming down in person." Tommy let go of my hand to shake the attorney's. Koerner's attention came back to me. "Gina, here are the documents you need to sign. Detective Galloway, I have some for you as well, although I also need to get a statement, if you don't mind. I'll get Minnie in here to take it down."

An enthusiastic clerk named Jacob took me into another room, where he guided me through the massive array of documents that needed my signature or my initials. Jacob called in the receptionist, who apparently was also a notary, to apply her seal to various pages. Young Jacob took his job seriously and explained each line to me. I understood everything he said as he said it, then promptly forgot it all. I was at their mercy, knew it, had surrendered.

It seemed to take hours but actually took only one. When I was done, I wondered distantly if I was going to have any savings left once I paid for all this.

Back in the lobby Tommy was waiting for me.

<hr />

HE INSISTED ON LUNCH, and I didn't have the will to break away from him. He held my hand, not letting go, gently dragging me to a cab, then pulling me out twenty or so blocks uptown. We went into a small, dingy Szechuan takeout place. He got me to make some choice from the menu, paid, took the bags in one hand, and grabbed my hand with the other. We walked that way for two blocks, stopping at a small brown building. I numbly let him pull me up three flights of stairs and into an apartment. It turned out, not surprisingly, to be his.

It was a compact one-bedroom, though good-sized by New York standards. No dishes lying around, no dirty clothes on the floor. But everywhere piles and piles of books. Bookcase after bookcase, crammed full. Here and there there were piles of CDs, some tapes, even stacks of vinyl against one wall. I didn't know much about Tommy's tastes. I walked around for a few minutes while he set out lunch things and got stuff to drink. The food smelled really good, and I started to feel hungry for the first time in days.

The music was predominantly blues and old jazz, with a large dose of classical, none of which surprised me, for some reason. He had books on all subjects: fiction, nonfiction, biographies, books on science, history books, psychology, true crime, textbooks on forensics and biology. The novels were equally wide-ranging: science fiction, Westerns, hard-boiled detective stuff, horror, and lots and lots of classics. Mark Twain and Dickens and a surprising amount of Hawthorne and Kafka, Shirley Jackson and Flannery O'Connor. There was an entire bookshelf dedicated to books on philosophy as well as religion. There were several books by Alan Watts, my favorite philosopher. None looked in mint condition; he was a reader, not a collector.

The place smelled of cigarette smoke, paper, and Chinese food. I asked him where the bathroom was; after I shut the door, I looked quietly through his medicine chest. No womany products, no sign that a woman hung out here a lot. I've known men to be really stupid about this, leaving tampons, pink disposable razors, diaphragms, or birth control pills in the bathroom when trying to seduce someone. I don't know where they should put them; maybe under the kitchen sink.

When I came out, he took my hand again and led me to the small table in his respectable kitchen—again, by city standards. It was a third the size of mine. "Eat" was all he said.

I admitted between bites that it was fabulous. I was about to make some comment about his knowledge of Asian restaurants in the city, then remembered he'd lived in China for a while. I was embarrassed at how comforting I found it to be fussed over, even in this angry, macho way. He drank a ginger ale; I had water. He asked me about my current legal fiasco. I told him everything. He might as well know that I didn't have access to a half million dollars. His expression slowly, gradually softened as I talked. His brow relaxed, his mouth loosened, his breathing deepened.

When I'd finished my latest sad story, he commiserated, told me he was glad there was a solution. The loss of the money didn't seem to jar him at all. I thought finally to ask him how his presentation went over in Chicago.

"It killed. Sorry, cop convention humor."

I was done eating. "Why am I here, Tommy?"

"I needed to talk to you in private," he said, lighting a cigarette. I waited. "First, I wanted you to know the bet's done."

"What?"

"It's over. The bet at the station. About you. And Russell. And me. It's been stopped."

"How?"

"I stopped it. Russell helped."

"But *how* did you stop it?"

He paused. Lips tightened. He didn't want to tell me. I waited. Finally he said, "I told everyone involved that they would never know if anyone ever won. I got Russell to agree we'd never tell them anything. We made sure it was known."

I couldn't say anything. My body started heating up.

"I also wanted to ask you if you were planning to ever start seeing Russell, or that John fellow, or anyone else."

My eyebrows raised. "What about Rachel or whatever her name is?"

"Becky. That's over."

"She knows that?"

He looked puzzled. "Of course she does."

We were both keeping our faces carefully expressionless. He took my hand, took a deep breath. He looked at me, and I realized in absolute terror that his face was flushed. "I have to spend almost my whole professional life with Russell. I didn't want to get into one of these stupid macho competitions with him."

We stared at each other. Then he looked carefully at the cigarette between his fingers, waiting for me to do something. I thought, he's finally being straight with you. Be an adult. Return the favor.

It took me a few minutes. I had to breathe and breathe, then I swallowed, and said, "You don't have any competition at all," and leaned over and kissed him on the lips, smoke and all. Not a coy smooch, not a demure peck. Then we were stumbling to our feet, lips locked, his arms crushing me to his chest and mine thrown around his waist.

He lifted me somehow, my feet dangling, hands clutching him, mouths still connected. We wound up on his bed, breathing heavily, openmouthed, foreheads touching. I said, "If you don't have a condom, the deal's off. I'm completely unprepared."

"I am prepared. Don't worry."

An hour or so later, after I noticed that his bedroom clock no longer seemed to be working, he brought up what I'd come to think of as the ugly porch incident. Tommy said, "I suddenly thought that I was just like all those poor schmucks who were sniffing at your hem. I'm not proud of this. But I'm not very good at chasing someone, competing with other guys, pushing ahead in line to get a woman's attention, that sort of thing."

"What line?" I said.

He smiled. "Come on, Gina. You know what I mean."

"No, not really. Who do you have to shove aside? You're the only one on the field." I touched his face, afraid I'd start crying and then be a terrible cliché. He kissed me again.

He said, "I got over it about halfway back to the city. It finally dawned on me why you told me Vincent was gay. I didn't know what to do, though, since I had to get back; I couldn't just turn around. That's why I kept calling. I fucked up. I'm really sorry."

"Oh. Well, that's okay."

"You're way too nice, Gina."

"I know. But partly I'm being nice about this because I was scared to death of being another Auxiliary Circle honey."

"Oh Jesus, you know about that, huh?"

"Yeah. Have you, er, mined that particular lode for company?"

"No. But don't be too hard on them. It's hard not to be lonely in the city."

"Hmmm. So I hear. But the 'burbs aren't always a whole lot better."

His phone rang. He let his machine pick up.

"Hi, Tommy. It's Candace. I don't want you to forget about next Saturday. It's really, really important to me that you don't forget. Wear a tux. I'm so nervous. Call me." Of course, his answering machine had to work.

We avoided the subject of the message for a while. Then he started laughing.

"It's funny to you?" I said.

"I'm sorry, Gina. You have a very expressive face."

"I'm about to have a very expressive fist."

"Would you come with me?"

"To what?"

"To Candace's art opening. It's a big deal, at a fancy-schmancy place in Soho. The Cornerstone Gallery. Have you heard of it?"

"Yes." It *was* a big deal.

"She's known about this for almost a year, and she wants all the support she can get because it's her big break. I felt really guilty about things back then, so I promised her I'd go, for moral support. She knows I might bring a date. When she asked, there wasn't anyone in particular to bring. Now there is. Will you come with me?"

I decided to be a big person about it. What else was there to do, get all snitty and stay home while he went alone? I don't think so.

"This is Two Year Candace we're talking about, right?"

"Yes."

"Almost-got-married-to-you Candace."

"We were never engaged. There was no 'almost' about it."

"Oh. Okay."

"Russell may be there, too."

"That'll be just dandy."

"I can't stay here tonight, Tommy. I have to go home."

"I know, I know," he said, his breath hot on my neck, his hands warm on my back. Real life, I kept thinking. Real life.

At three o'clock I called Patsy Hepplewhite from my cell phone, telling her I'd be a bit late but would collect the boys for dinner. She said no problem and asked how the meeting with the lawyer was going. I said fine, things were looking much better. She invited me and the twins to stay to eat. I assumed, correctly as it turned out, that this meant her husband was working late and wouldn't be home for dinner.

An hour and a half later Tommy put me on a train to Tenway. On the platform he kissed me hard, on the mouth, in full view of all the other passengers. He said in my ear, "You have no idea how sorry I am I have to go back to work tonight." I said, "Yes, I do." I watched him through the window as the train pulled away. I could see him standing there until the platform was out of sight.

I hadn't told the boys anything about the pending case with the Winterburns. After we got back to our house from dinner at the Hepplewhites', I made them sit down to talk. I told them that their father had left them some money in a bank for when they were older, but now his family wanted it back. They'd become poor somehow. Stevie and Toby knew nothing about the trust fund; this wasn't how I wanted to tell them. I tried to make it sound as though the nicest, best thing we could do for their father's memory was to give the Winterburns the money. Toby was all for it. Stevie was worried that we, too, would be poor when he grew up. I promised him that that wouldn't be the case; we would be fine. They needed it far more than we did, and so on. But I said that the two of them had a right to know about it. I mentally aimed great obscenities at the Winterburns for making me twist the truth this way just so the boys wouldn't be more soured than they needed to be by a world full of grasping and deranged kin. Sweet, generous boys that they were, they said, ultimately, of course, our poor relatives need the money more than we do, we're so fortunate to be so comfortably off. Let them have it. I thought vindictively, let them have it, all right, and let them choke on it.

I didn't tell Ellie anything that night, nor did I call anyone else. Tommy called as I was putting cream on my face where his five o'clock shadow had burned my skin. I needed a shower but was reluctant to take one. I wasn't ready to wash him completely off me. I knew this was childish, but you never know when it's the last time you'll ever see someone. On the phone we didn't say much and didn't talk long, but the conversation was extremely soothing. After we hung up, I took the picture I had of Tommy out of the drawer in my nightstand and looked at it. I kept thinking, this is real, this is real.

chapter twenty-seven

Sexuality is not a separate compartment of human life; it is a radiance pervading every human relationship, but assuming a particular intensity at certain points.

ALAN WATTS, *Nature, Man and Woman*

TOMMY AND I had our first date that Friday. Mo and Ivy volunteered to babysit. I figured that Lizzie must not have confided her interest in Tommy to Mo, or maybe Mo just wasn't holding it against me; I didn't know and didn't want to bring it up. That day I cleaned the house fanatically and changed my mind about what I was going to wear at least six times. I've been nervous for dates before, but never to the point of psychosis to which this one sent me. I had to go back to the attic and dig out some of what Ellie and I called my Sunday-go-to-meetin' clothes. I hadn't been out at night for a while, and I have small closets. I had a large number of things that were not current at all; they would have sent Dion screaming for his drawing board, but they worked fine for a dinner date in Tenway. I finally settled on something red, not black, something a little short but not too tight, showing a little back but not too much cleavage. I used to be quite skilled at conveying exactly the information I intended through clothing. I guess I could still do it, but the message I had been sending for years was simply "Leave me alone." My other chops were pretty rusty.

Mo got to my house around four, bringing Frodo, as there was no feline impediment anymore. I had told her only that Tommy and I had seen each other in the city and now had a date. I'd been as matter-of-fact about it as I could and felt a little like I was cheating her somehow, not giving her any juicy details, but I hadn't given them even to Ellie; my afternoon with Tommy felt more private than anything else I'd ever done. As soon as she arrived, I jumped into the shower and started trying to remember how to prep for a real date, shaving and plucking and all kinds of things I'd sort of let slide over the past few years except for my primping spike with Awful Bragging Man. I'd begged and pleaded and bullied and had had an emergency gynecology appointment and gotten myself a new diaphragm. There was no way I was being careless about birth control for any reason, ever.

I was still getting ready, dropping things with shaking hands, when I heard Tommy arrive about ten minutes early. I could hear Mo teasing him about how spiffy he looked; I wondered if he was half as nervous as I was. I came down the stairs about five minutes later, wondering if I should keep him waiting a bit, then deciding that that was ridiculous. We grinned dopily at each other after a quick awkward peck on the lips. Mo was smiling like a benevolent Buddha. Tommy had on a tweedy sports jacket, a nice shirt, no tie. He looked fabulous. The boys were momentarily ecstatic to see him, whooping and jumping on him before repairing back to their toy motorcycle race. Toby spared me a second glance and said, "You look nice, Mom. I haven't seen you dress like a girl very much."

Tommy had asked me to make dinner reservations since I was a local. We ate at the best that Tenway had to offer, a little Italian place off Templeton called Amico's. The next best restaurant was Hannigan's;

I had no intention of going anywhere near it. A movie was a possibility, but neither of us was stressing over it. After we sat down, the subject of the art opening came up.

He said, "Some friends of mine, the Lowerys, will be there. I'd really like you to meet them. He's a cop, she's a riot." I smiled. He added, as if I wouldn't really notice, "Susie and her husband are coming, too."

"*Now* it's a party!" slipped out before I could cork it. "Sorry." I regrouped, then asked, tactfully, I thought, what the story was on Susie and Ben, her frighteningly handsome husband.

"You wouldn't think it to look at him, but he's really funny. And he loves Susie like crazy. He works at a top-forty radio station in Demarest. They play the shittiest music ever made, but he's a great newscaster. He's got a great on-air presence, you know; he makes you think either that the world is coming to an end or that God has made everything all right. He used to have fan mail that you wouldn't believe, with women sending obscene pictures of themselves. They lurked by his car, called the station all the time. All that stuff made him miserable. He just wanted to get married. He met Susie, and that was it."

"Did you introduce them?"

"Sort of. He worked for a station in the city then, and I knew him as a reasonable news guy, someone who wasn't too stupid or careless about facts. He had dropped by the station for a quickie interview about a case I was working, and Susie dropped by to tell me about a birthday party she was planning for my dad. He asked her out right then. They were married less than a year later."

"Sweet. Why is she going to be there?"

"She and Candace are pretty good friends. That's how we met. Susie took an art class from her at the New School." He looked at me very directly. "Susie wanted me to stay with Candace. You'll get that soon enough."

"Why?"

"She knows her already. She's safe."

"I'm not?"

"I guess not."

"She hates me, doesn't she?"

He smiled. "No. She's terrified of you."

"Why?"

"She thinks you'll hurt me. Now, don't give me that look."

"What look?"

"That Queen of Pain expression. I'm not worried at the moment. Let's just do what we do and let Susie work it out for herself. There's nothing we're going to tell her that's going to stop her fretting about this. Only time will do that."

He told me about his mother, who sounded suspiciously saintly. I didn't comment. He asked after my immediate family, my southern childhood. I told him about Grammy. "My most vivid memory of her is from when I was staying with her when I was about eleven. She mostly left me alone while I was in her house, so I was doing some solitary thing, and then I walked into her den. She was sitting in her Barcalounger with her feet elevated, red stilettos, black fishnets, pancake makeup, filterless Camel bobbing on her lower lip, a martini in one hand and the remote in the other." I suddenly realized how indelicate this story was and had a moment of storytelling insecurity. Tommy urged me to finish it. I thought, oh, what the hell. "She was screaming at the television. 'Fuck the pope! Fuck God! He just wants your money! Assholes!' I never knew if she thought the money-hungry one was God or the pope. My father hated the Catholic Church, and it's pretty obvious where he got it from."

He laughed, thank goodness, and said, "This is the one you take after?"

"Supposedly. You can imagine how I felt about hearing this when I was eleven. She really liked to show off her cleavage, which was considerable. There's a story about her wearing a green sequined cocktail dress to some hotel bar in Atlanta and picking someone up and taking him home with her two days before her death. I have no idea if it's true or not. I wasn't living at home then."

"She was how old?"

"Eighty-six."

"Jesus. Well, at least you can look forward to aging well."

"Hmmm. I guess you're a glass-half-full kind of guy. She did give me really good advice on some stuff, though. Like she always said, 'If you have a man that other women want, the thing to do is to be nice as pie to the women who are circling. It's a lot harder for them to betray women who are nice to them than women who are all snooty.' I call it Grammy's Rule Number One."

"There are worse ways to be old."

I thought of Jessie. "You're right," I said.

He sat there for a moment, just smiling, his chin in his hand.

"What?" I asked finally.

He smiled wider, eyes shining. He said after a moment, "I was thinking that you're delightful."

I had no idea what to say to that. I opened my mouth and was trying to form some appropriate words, but Tommy stopped me, still smiling.

"You don't have to say that I'm delightful back, Gina." He seemed to think that that was funny.

"Oh. Okay." My head and neck and shoulders were all terribly hot. I had no idea what to make my face do.

After a brief silence I changed the subject back and said, "So at this big art hoo-ha, what do you want on your arm?"

"What?"

"Big guns are going to be there, right? Captains of industry? Political bigwigs? The artsy-fartsy elite?" Ex-girlfriends, I thought.

"Something like that."

"Well, I guess I am objectifying myself, but what the hell, I used to do that for a living. I still remember a thing or two. Do you want class or skin? I mean, I won't wear anything that says twenty-dollar-a-night hooker, don't worry." I was enjoying the expression on his face. "I won't wear anything too Hollywood or too slutty." I couldn't believe I had used the word "slutty" on our first date. But I'd already blown any pretensions to being ladylike by my "Grammy yelling 'fuck the pope' " story. "Do you want Come Hithery or Ice Queen? Think about it. Just let me know by midweek so I have time to get it together."

"Come hithery. Skin. Definitely," he said.

"I know! I'll call Dion. He really liked you. DeVonne liked you more, which is what really matters. I'll bet they'll lend me something."

"Skin," Tommy said.

I asked him about his most interesting or bizarre case to date. He said, "The murdered clown. We, of course, called it the Clownicide Caper."

"A murdered *clown*?"

"He was beaten to death with his own floppy shoes. It was a hard one to solve. He'd made a lot of enemies."

We closed down the restaurant, having missed the movie by over an hour. I suggested a bar I'd heard about from Vincent Capinelli. It was an after-hours place called Sonny's, an old-man kind of bar that he loved. They played almost nothing but Sinatra on the jukebox, and you could slow dance if you wanted to. I ordered a martini, of which the seventy-something bartender approved. It was only my second drink of the night. Tommy ordered a Scotch on the rocks, a nice manly sort of drink. I beamed at him.

"We're being such adults," I said when he looked a question at me.

He went to use the men's room, and within a couple of minutes two boys who couldn't have been much past the drinking age slid into the circular booth on either side of me. "Oh, jeez, fellas," I said, "I'm on a really great date. Y'all had better leave." They said the kinds of things boys say in situations like that, joking, flirting. Tommy came back, and they gaped up at the wall of him. He looked angry, and they practically dissolved, they left so fast. I beamed at him again.

"You're pretty useful," I said.

"Hmmm," he said.

We got up to do a slow dance to "Witchcraft" and then "It Was a Very Good Year." I'm a tepid Sinatra fan, as, I later found out, was Tommy. But it was the perfect music for the place. He pulled me closer and closer until our cheeks were touching. I could feel his breath in my ear and his thighs against mine. I kept reminding myself of Toby and Stevie. I was a mom, moms have to be careful about being slutty. After we sat down from the last dance, looking at each other from under sleepy, swollen eyelids, I told him this. How can I do this, how can I sleep with you in my home, Tommy? What if they hear us, what if they come in? This isn't something they know about, their mom dating, what do I do?

Poor Tommy. He took a deep breath. Then he said, "I'll wait. We'll wait. We'll get them used to us. And we'll put a lock on your bedroom door. Tomorrow."

By the time we got back to the house, it was raining the way it does sometimes in late spring, thick, heavy, and merciless. Ivy had come over after work, so she, Mo, and Frodo left us to slog home through the blotchy wetness, both humans smirking. Tommy used the weather as an excuse for staying overnight in the guest room.

I brought him a clean towel so he'd have one handy in the morning. I knocked, he said okay, come in, and I saw him with his shirt off, eyes heavy-lidded. He was very pale, not overly buff, but big with big arms, some hair, just startlingly male after so much abstinence, not counting David Renouart's effete stringiness. The memory of our afternoon was hot and sharp. I had to leave the room. I ran to the bathroom, looked in the mirror, breathing, breathing. I didn't think, just put in the diaphragm with unsteady, slippery fingers and went into the boys' room to see if they were really, really deeply sleeping. They were frozen in sleep, small snores from Stevie, mouths slightly open. I went back to the guest room, where Tommy still stood. I grabbed his hand and pulled him across the hall to my room, pulled him in, closed the door, and whispered in his ear, still holding his hand, my other hand on his naked arm. "Can you be absolutely quiet?"

He looked in my eyes from inches away. He said, with barely a breath's volume, "Yes. Yes, I can."

In the morning the boys found us in separate rooms. They jumped into my bed to watch cartoons. Tommy heard us and came in to join us. Our eyes kept meeting over their heads, and we grinned goofily at each other. Later we made pancakes for breakfast, and as the boys watched even more cartoons, Tommy made a run to a hardware store and bought a hook latch for the bedroom door.

The rain stopped by midday. We took the boys to the nearby playground, bringing their bikes. There we saw Yvonne Corbin and her son. Derek Corbin had a set of Rollerblades, so the three boys went off together. I'd never thanked her for foiling the possible plot of the mysterious pervert; I did so now. She waved it off and explained the story to Tommy. He went into cop mode for a moment, asking about further sightings, descriptions, and so on, but no one had heard or seen anything since that one conversation with Toby. We all agreed it was likely that he wouldn't return, that he'd gone to terrorize some other community. Then Yvonne Corbin asked if Tommy was the twins' father. I said no. She said oh, a boyfriend. I could feel my face burning enough to dry the wet pavement. Tommy just nodded and grinned, wrapping a loose arm around my shoulders.

The next day, Sunday, Tommy had to leave to go back to the city, to his life there, his job. He stayed till after dinner, but then we said a long sloppy good-bye by his car, out of view of the boys. He said he'd come back next Friday, and he reminded me to get a sitter for the dreaded art opening on Saturday. After he left, I felt like I was stepping back into my normal empty life after a mind-blowing journey to an alternate universe, like going to Oz and then coming back to a drought-ravaged Kansas.

Later, Ellie said, "So he likes the fact that you're going to be just like Grammy, eh?"

My mother called on Monday night. She got right to the point.

"Now I hear you're dating a policeman, Gina."

"This time your sources are more accurate. How did you know this? Rosa again?" God, she was quick.

"Yes. She keeps tabs on all you girls." This was a little distressing, actually. I guess I had Mo to blame. "Frank is really unhappy about this. Unless it's serious, I think you should reconsider."

"What the hell is it to Frank? Why would he care?"

"Well, I thought you should know."

"Why? Why doesn't Rosa call me herself, or Frank, for that matter?" Although I was glad they hadn't.

"Well, she thought it would be better coming from me."

"Well, she was wrong."

"You haven't been seeing him long. It can't possibly be that serious."

"How would you know? Why do you, or anyone else, care?"

I didn't get a real answer till much, much later.

I called Dion and filled him in on what we needed. Tommy would pick the dress box up on Friday to bring to me. Dion was delighted, at least partly, I think, because it meant that he got to look Tommy over again. Tommy called me the next day, Tuesday, saying he'd landed a case in which a woman was murdered, seemingly at random, in a shooting. She had three small children and a young, bewildered husband. He probably couldn't come to Tenway till Saturday afternoon with Dion's dress. I could hardly complain about such a cause and said come when you can.

So I wasn't expecting him on Thursday night. At around midnight I heard movement downstairs. With a sort of hopeful terror, I walked downstairs to see Tommy standing in the hall. He had let himself in; he still had the key I had given him and Russell so long ago. His face was pale, slightly sagging. He came toward me, and I went to him, putting my arms around him, wondering if there'd been a family tragedy. I got him some tea and some soup, dragging him into the kitchen. He ate a little, still gray-faced. I waited, pressed him only a little about what had happened.

Finally he said, "Just another shooting. Just a high school kid with his daddy's handgun, robbing a little grocery store, one not far from me, actually. A Vietnamese mom was shopping there; she always went there. She was just getting some milk, some toilet paper, some celery, for fuck's sake." He stopped and pressed his eyes with his long, pale fingers. "It was a shitty thing, but it was normal, you know, it's what we do. I was fine till I talked to the six-year-old, who still had some of her mom's brains on her dress."

Tommy's hands were supporting his face, elbows on the table. I didn't say anything, could think of nothing adequate. I put my arms around him again, then his came around me, his heavy head on my shoulder. I thought it didn't take much insight to figure out why this was worse for him but didn't say so, imagining that it wouldn't be very helpful then. I thought, it's so much easier for women to cry.

Eventually I took him upstairs and rubbed his shoulders till he fell asleep. He woke up an hour or so later, disoriented. We lay in my bed, him on his back, me on my side facing him, lips on his shoulder, gently running my fingers up and down his arm. He said, thick with sleep, "Thanks for taking care of me, G."

My hand came to a full stop for the smallest second, then resumed. "My pleasure, T.," I said.

I let Tommy sleep in a little after I got up, then gently roused him for breakfast, since he had to go back to the city. Our conversation around the boys was necessarily elliptical, but I was firm about him not apologizing. He left soon after breakfast, resisting the boys' plea to stay. He had, he said, to go back to endless paperwork, endless loose ends.

Tommy hugged me a long time before he left. Then the house felt cold, and Toby cried that he was gone as I took the boys to school. Later, he called me to apologize for falling asleep. I said he had looked very tired and terribly sweet. "Great," he said. "That's how every man wants to seem when he's in bed with a really sexy woman, sweet and tired."

During the little over a week in which things had shifted so dramatically in my love life, I hadn't talked to Lizzie. I figured she'd know by now, since Mo, and apparently Rosa, did. Her answering machine had been broken for months, so I couldn't call when I knew she was gone and leave a message. Frankly, I was afraid to tell her directly, feared another venomous outburst. It was cowardly, and I'm still ashamed of it.

I did call Cindy in the department office and tell her about it, of course, and she was all atwitter. Cindy loves a good romance as much as a good scandal, just like the rest of us. I was her favorite person on campus at that point; I'd given her both.

chapter twenty-eight

Role-playing is so automatic that we seldom notice how deeply it pervades our lives, and readily confuse its attitudes with our own natural and genuine inclinations . . . Love itself is frequently an assumed emotion which we believe we ought to feel . . . Lovers are expected to be jealous of one another. The man is supposed to act protectively and the woman a little helplessly. The man is supposed to take the initiative in expressing love and the woman to wait longingly for his attentions. Certain types of feature, voice, and figure are supposed to be peculiarly lovable or sex-appealing, and the intimacies of sexual intercourse are governed by rituals in which the man is active and the woman passive, and in which the verbal and symbolic communications of love adhere to an extremely limited pattern.

ALAN WATTS, *Nature, Man and Woman*

I WAS GOING TO ASK Debra Corbin, Derek's sister, to babysit for me on the night of the opening, but I didn't know how late we were going to be and didn't want to make a sixteen-year-old stay up till all hours her first time sitting for me. So I asked Donna. To my surprise, she said she'd do it. I was flattered that she didn't take a shift at the hospital to avoid it.

I had stupidly suggested that we eat with Tommy's sister and his friends before the opening to try to ease into the evening's social pressure cooker. My logic was extremely flawed, I know, and I paid for it later. The restaurant was a tiny Indian place in the West Village, near the gallery. When Tommy and I walked in, Susie and the perfect Ben were already there at a large round table. Ben greeted me with great jollity; like Tommy, he wore a tuxedo. Susie was a great deal more reserved. No surprise. She had picked a bad color, an orange dress that made her skin look yellow. I swore that I would take some of these women in hand. I'd find a way to do it without them feeling insulted, I vowed silently to Grammy.

Within minutes, we were joined by a handsome black couple, Dan and Hazel Lowery. He was tall, slender, and very good-looking, though not as flawlessly so as Ben. Hazel was stunning, voluptuous, with big Bambi eyes and vast tresses of beribboned hair. Now here was a woman who knew how to dress. She was all in revealing silver, but Hazel Lowery had the most beautiful skin I'd seen since I'd left the biz, not to mention a fabulous décolletage. I almost said so, then realized not everyone liked being picked over like this, even in a complimentary way. I loved Dion, but I didn't want to be him.

I tried to be as nice to Susie as I could. I asked about her kids, if she did any gardening, her house, her job, everything I could think of. She could barely be civil. This made even Ben uncomfortable; he was without a doubt the most gallant man I'd ever met. Every time some female even moved her chair, he stood up.

After our food came, Susie lightened up some. I had ordered some really good lamb. I arranged for a doggy bag, since I couldn't eat all of mine and it wasn't cheap. Susie looked mortified, and I wondered if I'd committed some sort of faux pas. I had developed this habit over many years, because no one in the fashion industry ever ate everything on her plate and many models were pretty poor. Not to mention graduate students. Now I was just thrifty; I couldn't help it. There seemed to be nothing I did that didn't infuriate Susie. Ben tried to make up for her impoliteness by chatting with me, but I was as monosyllabic as possible with him without being downright rude. I could just hear it later, that I was flirting with her freakishly handsome husband.

Eventually I gave up on Susie and concentrated on Hazel Lowery. She seemed as friendly as Susie was cold, and we chatted like old buddies. It turned out that Hazel was from Atlanta. We discussed the merits of living in the South versus the North, bemoaned how huge and impossible that city had become, and I quizzed her on how she compared living as a black woman in New York versus Atlanta. According to her, it was better in Georgia. I wasn't surprised. People who think that the South is a more racist environment than the North haven't lived there lately or have terrible illusions about the North. In my experience, the latter is true only if they're white.

Hazel said, "Maybe afterward we can go to this club Dan and I've been to, called X Minus One. Lots of cops go there, believe it or not, but it's a good place to dance, and it's pretty close to here. Man, I never get to dance, and I don't want to waste an opportunity. Even if the guys won't, I'll just do it by myself if I have to. Are y'all in?"

"I don't know about Tommy. But I'll dance with you, if you want. I haven't been to a club in years."

"If we tell Dan and Tommy that you and I are going to shingaling together, I'll bet you a hundred dollars they'll both want to go."

After we finished eating, I stowed my little foil-wrapped package of lamb in my small shoulder purse, further annoying Susie. We walked to the gallery. I had to shake a reluctance to take Tommy's arm; his sister's disapproval hovered over me like a stinking halo. I was having enough trouble accepting that I was part of a couple this evening. I alternated between feeling like showing off by flamboyantly grabbing Tommy's hand and feeling like a fraud who should keep her distance from everyone male. I tried to follow Tommy's lead; he offered me his arm, so I took it.

The Cornerstone Gallery was your typical high-end chic Soho art establishment, money pretending not to care about money. Lots of new white paint over old gas pipes and tin ceilings, gleaming hardwood floors and fat mothy chairs. There was nothing fat or mothy about the people, but you could easily find ways to work the words "paint," "hard," and "gas" into sentences describing them. I had been mildly concerned that Dion's dress would be overkill; it was one-shouldered (*very* Wilma Flintstone) and black, laced with strategic holes. It was tight, too, but flexible and surprisingly comfortable, the perfect weight for the mild June night. It was threatening to rain, but I had a light raincoat in Tommy's car. I had also brought my black Mary Janes in case we decided to do a lot of walking later. Dion had provided almost nonexistent stilettos to go with the dress. I wouldn't have worn them had Tommy been short; as it was, I still couldn't look him in the eye. It was the first time I'd worn shoes like this in years, and I was relieved that the ability to walk in them seemed to be coming back to me. I was also relieved that I hadn't talked Dion into something more plain or demure. This was a milieu in which, at least in terms of clothing, it was eat or be eaten.

It took a while for the crowd to dissolve itself into individuals. Russell was there with a nervous, very fake blonde named Melissa. Her gaudy yellow dress made me want to take her outside and explain the purpose of foundation garments. I would never have said this to anyone, of course, with the possible exception of Ellie, but I could calculate almost to the dollar how much those breasts had cost her. Russell treated her with a casualness that I found irritating on her behalf. I never warmed to her, but I still kept wishing she'd backhand him and walk away with someone taller. Russell was stiffly polite to me, nothing more, which was a relief.

Another blonde soon joined us. This one had a much more reined-in fashion sense, dripping in bright pastels. On her tiny, pale frame it worked beautifully. It was Candace; I recognized her as the woman who'd corralled Tommy at the courthouse while I skulked behind pillars. Her smile at Tommy was wide and warm. Her expression changed not a bit when her gaze moved to me as Tommy made introductions. But her face somehow seized, and the warmth that had been there seconds before fled. Or perhaps it was my paranoia. I decided then and there that I needed to obey Grammy's Rule Number One as I'd never obeyed it before. I let rip with my sweetest, toothiest smile (thankful that Raphael Priazzi was nowhere in sight, lest his presence turn me into some sort of piranha) and gushed. Her art, which I hadn't had much chance to look at yet, was inspired, the gallery so prestigious, what a privilege for little me to get to bask in such greatness. I'm from Florida cracker country; I know how to play Lulabelle even if my acting skills are otherwise limited. Candace looked dumbstruck. Tommy was trying not to laugh as I got more and more Deep South by the second. Blame Hazel Lowery, I thought, for the inspiration. My accent broadened as it hadn't in years.

Eventually Candace was carted away by Susie for some reason, underscoring the fact that they were pals. Tommy and I walked around the main rooms of the gallery, inconspicuously hand in hand, looking at the admittedly good, if pretentious, work. Lots of female figures, lots of red, very menstrual. I liked it fine, but my respect for Tommy rose as I thought about his ability to be with a woman like this even if it wasn't, for him, permanent. I wondered if she felt about him the way I did. I suddenly felt bad for her.

I stopped suddenly in front of a large piece; it was a male figure for a change, so it stood out. But what had caught my attention was the little card with the title on the top of the stone pedestal on which the piece stood. It was called *Tommy*.

The statue was a nude; his privates were impressive, his shoulders stylized and strong, but his head was enormous, cradled in his oversized hands. It was immensely sad, the weight of the head more than the rest of his straining frame could carry. I was thunderstruck. Was this how she saw him, how he was with her? He was watching me, not looking at the sculpture; clearly it was familiar to him. He said, "I should have warned you. I'm sorry. Does this bother you?"

I wanted to ask, did you *pose* for this? Afraid of the intimacy that a yes would imply. But of course he'd lived with the woman for two years; did I think their intimacy hadn't surpassed ours, at least so far? For the first time in the few weeks that Tommy and I had been together, I thought, Am I being an idiot? So I had to ask. His response was a sharp "God, no." Then I wondered if this had been part of the reason for the breakup in the first place, her insistence on using him in this way or the fact that she saw him like this.

"Is this how you were with her?"

"I guess she thought so," he said.

"You're not like this with me. At least not now," I said.

"Aren't you glad? I'm a lot happier now."

We stayed face-to-face for a few minutes, and I could feel my own heat rising. Then we moved on, gazing at more Candace art. I was examining a female figure with a face that vaguely resembled Elvis when we were interrupted by another short woman, this one also fair, a strawberry blonde tightly wrapped in black and gold. Not so Nordic as Candace. She got Tommy's attention by yanking on his arm; I couldn't believe it when he introduced her, a thin sheen of sweat forming on his brow, as Becky Quinn.

"Where did you find *her*?" she said to him, snorting. "Did she come with instructions?"

I don't normally deal all that well with rudeness that forceful and so just stood there, awkward and mute. Tommy was about to say something, I hoped in my defense. But the endorphins my body had been cranking out just seconds before ebbed; I could feel bile rising, resentment, against Susie and Candace and now this bitchy little person. I said to myself, to hell with Grammy's first rule. I turned to Tommy and said exactly what was on my mind. "Was she this awful when you two dated?"

Tommy was again about to talk, but the little woman gave him no chance.

"Oho, it speaks. You look like a model or something." She was angrier now. "I'm surprised at you, Tommy."

"A lingerie model, in fact. Past tense. Now I've got a PhD. Go fuck yourself." I seemed to have lost the restraint I'd mustered around Claire Stanley; I was terrified about whatever else I was about to say. I had to get away from her. Voice mortifyingly tremulous, I said to Tommy, "I'm going to get a drink. I'll see you when you're done," and semisashayed away. Grammy always said show no fear, and I always wished I could obey her more convincingly. But then, Grammy had been insane; I was trying hard not to be.

I was shaking a little in anger and misery and some shame that I wasn't better able to rise above and stay civil. My dress felt transparent, and I felt like a fraud. And of course it was always possible that Tommy wouldn't come find me anytime soon, that he'd feel like spending a while apologizing to Bitch Queen for my behavior. A quick survey of the room revealed few faces that were both familiar and friendly, so I went to the bathroom. Once safe inside, I took a few deep breaths, fixed myself up, took more breaths. I girded my mental loins and went out again, heading for the bar. No gin, only awful wine. I got some anyway, trying not to look like I was looking for Tommy. A thirtyish, well-suited handsome artsy type accosted me softly, asking some fake question: did I know the artist, what did I think about her bold use of texture? I said I'd met her and it seemed okay to me, but I preferred more classical uses of form, blah, blah, blah. A tall shadow materialized next to me, and Tommy gently put his hand under my elbow.

"Excuse us," he said, smiling ferally at Mr. Art. I smiled happily and let myself be led away.

"That was interesting," he said. "Where'd you disappear to?"

"The bathroom," I said, too truthfully. "I'm pretty ashamed of myself but not enough to apologize."

"Honey, she had it coming. I haven't seen you be that, I don't know, Foxy Brown or something." He smiled and put his arm around me. "Now you know why we only dated for a few weeks. She's kind of a horrible person. You don't have to bear any guilt for breaking us up." He pulled me a little closer. "You're not. Horrible, I mean." He could tell I was still a little rattled. "You were goaded beyond all possibility of civility, Gina. But let's get out of here before it happens again."

We went to find the Lowerys. Hazel, Dan, Russell, and presumably Melissa wanted to go to X Minus One. I was agreeable; Tommy went to find Susie and Candace to say our good-byes. I hadn't practiced dancing in spikes in a long time, so Tommy went to the car to fetch my other shoes and our raincoats.

As we left, I saw Candace again, very briefly. I couldn't resist: I gave her a hug. "I'm so glad I finally got to meet you," I chirped. She responded vacantly at first. I think by then she was quite drunk. Then she grabbed my arm with alarming force; she had a grip like a pair of pliers. She pulled me away from him and almost whacked her head against mine, leaning in. "Good luck getting him to decide anything," she hissed in my ear. "Don't wait up. You'll grow old alone if you do." She grimaced blearily and let me go. It felt like some curse from *Macbeth*.

On the street Tommy whispered to me, "What did she say to you?" I said, "You don't want to know."

At the door to the club, Tommy said, "This is okay with you? Being outed?"

"Let 'em collect on their stupid bet," I said.

We walked into the club and were hit by the volume, the heat, and the smell. Oh, yeah, I thought, I remember this. The doorman/bouncer was a huge fellow, bigger than Tommy by at least fifty pounds and three inches. He smiled and winked at me. I wondered for a split second if I'd known him in my previous incarnation, then realized that was unlikely. I mentally dubbed him Conan the Friendly Bouncer. Tommy, Dan, and Russell kept high-fiving other men, mostly young-ish. It was a weird permutation of a cop bar.

We found a table and got drinks. Russell and Melissa wandered away to the dance floor. Hazel leaned over and said, "Dan won't dance. Will you go out there with me?"

"Sure," I said.

I hadn't done this in eight years, danced in a New York club, with anyone. I realized that even though I was a lot older than I had been when I used to do this all the time, I was in some ways in better shape. I didn't drink much, and I hadn't had a cigarette in a long time. After two songs we came back to the table. We had our arms linked and were giggling. I was breathless and a little sweaty, and as I sat down, I pointed at Dan Lowery and said, "You should dance with your wife." Dan was smiling at Hazel with an embarrassing amount of lust and said, "You gals make sure you use your powers for good."

I looked back at Tommy, who just stared at me as though I had something purple hanging from my nose. "What's wrong?" I asked.

"Nothing's wrong," he said.

After a few minutes Tommy and Dan went to get more drinks,

and I asked Hazel why they had gone to Candace's opening. "Are you friends with her?"

"Well, sort of. Dan and I are good friends of Tommy's, you know. They were together for . . . a while, and we socialized with them some; you know how it is. After they broke up, they both tried not to make it nasty. She asked us a long time ago to come to this thing. She was pretty nervous about it. But we're not really close. She's a little, I don't know, tense about things. She always made me kind of tired. She's perfectly nice, though. I don't mean to be ugly about her." She seemed to remember what my position was in all of this, and her brow knit. "Oh, shit, I'm not making you uncomfortable, am I?"

I assured her that she wasn't, even though of course she was. I could see our two swains on the horizon, heading back to the table. I saw a hand from nowhere poking Tommy in the shoulder. He stopped, looked behind him, and there was Susie. She stood on tiptoe and said something in his ear, gripping his arm. She dragged him, glasses still in hand, over nearer to the door of the club. He waved Dan on, who came back to our table and gave Hazel her wine. I asked him what was up; he shook his head in puzzlement.

Ben was by the door and was waving his hands in the air, as if he was trying to semaphore to Susie. Tommy looked frustrated and maybe in the early stages of anger. But Susie didn't seem intimidated; she seemed irritated about something. I hoped it didn't somehow have anything to do with me; I had done nothing but try to be sweet as pie to her all night. I thought that if I ever got to know her well enough, I'd tell her about Grammy's Rule Number One. If she thought I was some sort of evil slut, the rule would be even more important for her, given her handsome husband.

It was getting embarrassing watching this tense family scene, so I turned to talk some more about whatever came to mind with Hazel Lowery. Hazel understood Grammy's rule, consciously or not. She could not have been nicer to me all evening, and I appreciated it.

I was prattling on about something clothing-related and then felt Tommy walking up behind me even as Hazel's eyes went to him over my shoulder. I turned.

Deep sigh. "I have to go with them," he said, placing drinks on the table in front of me.

"Why?" I blurted, then thought again. "Okay. But what do you want me to do? Can I come?" I said, trying to sound upbeat and casual, as opposed to panicky and bewildered.

"Their car won't start, and it's started raining. They need a jump. I'll be back soon, okay?" He quickly kissed my cheek. "You'd better stay here. Hazel, would you and Dan keep her company while I'm gone?" Hazel nodded, of course. What else was she going to do? "I should be back within a half hour."

I gave what I thought was a brave little soldier kind of smile, but it probably looked pretty crumbly. "Okay," I said, the good sport. Of course, no one else in a city of eight million people could possibly jump-start their car on a Saturday night. No, I thought, it had to be Tommy.

He walked off to where his snooty sister and her pussy-whipped husband stood waiting by the door to the club. Susie was holding the door open, looking crabbily at him, obviously impatient. She looked at me not at all, although her ultramoussed husband did. I hated them both right then as much as I've hated anyone in my life.

Tommy herded them out the door. I watched and gave him a wave as the door closed. He noticed me just before they shut it, and so I saw the beginnings of a feeble wave back.

I was suddenly furious at Tommy for putting me in this awkward position, and more furious at Susie for dragging him into the night, transparent in her desire to get him away from me and back with artistic Candace. My head didn't think Tommy's sister was likely to succeed, but the rest of me wasn't so sure. I grew hot with anger and anxiety. A small but venomous part of my brain whispered that both women could have him.

I made the most shallow of small talk for a while. I had another martini. I tried hard not to keep looking at my watch. Hazel wanted to dance again, but I made Dan dance with her. Melissa returned to the table without Russell. She told me he'd gone to get more drinks. Great. I would be stuck at a table with Russell's girlfriend of the hour. We discussed clubs we had known. Melissa was current and I was not, so there was little enough to talk about after five minutes. I asked her how long she'd known Russell, what she did for a living, and so forth. She was a pet groomer, and she had met him through a case. A liquor store next to her shop was robbed, and the manager killed; Russell and Tommy had worked the case. She asked me how Tommy and I had met; I was dismayed that it was going to sound similar to her story. Before I had to admit that, Dan and Hazel came sweatily back to the table. I'd been good about not checking my watch obsessively but managed a glance now. It had been almost an hour. I swallowed and turned to Hazel. "I need to go to the restroom. Can you show me where it is?" She took my arm and led me to the women's room in the back.

I washed and fixed my face and combed my hair. I was doing pretty well, I thought. I wasn't crying. This was good. Hazel tried to cheer me up.

"You know, I've heard Dan talk about how good Tommy is with female suspects, questioning them and stuff. He gets all that charm on him, you know how he gets, and he can get them feeling like they're the only woman in the world, and they'll tell him anything. He's so smooth, the way he talks." I thought, He is? "But you know, with his girlfriends, he sometimes doesn't know his dick from a shovel."

If this was supposed to make me feel any better, it wasn't working. So much about this was disturbing, I didn't know where to start.

"How many girlfriends are we talking, Hazel?"

She looked a little appalled at herself and backpedaled so hard that you could smell the rubber burning. "He hasn't had that many since I've known him, really. Only two or three. Or four, maybe, maybe five. Or six. But he really likes you. You can tell."

"He didn't like the other ones?"

"Well, yeah, of course he did, but not like he likes you. For one thing, he didn't show the other ones off like he's showing you."

She obviously remembered the bet and verbally skidded to a stop. I could almost feel my heart dropping in my torso, sliding as if greased. I didn't want to take anything out on Hazel, but she was making herself into a tempting target. "You think he's showing me off?"

"Well, I don't mean it like that, like you're a new car or something. More like he's not ashamed of you or he doesn't mind talk about the two of you." She was getting a little more frantic, talking faster. "I don't mean what any of this sounds like. I mean like you're more serious, like he might stay with you, so it's okay if other folks know about you. Because he's not expecting you to be gone in the next ten minutes."

"Like the others?"

"Yeah. Well, except for Candace."

That was it. I knew she meant well. But I didn't want to be baby-sat or be a charity project. It was their night out, too, after all. So it wasn't total selfishness that made me decide to go home.

When we got back to the table, Dan was still there alone with Melissa. She asked us, "Has anyone seen Russell? I seem to have lost him." Sad fake laugh. I was trying to feel sorry for her; if I'd liked her more, it would have been a lot easier. I added, mainly to Hazel, "I think I'm going to go. I need to get back for the sitter." I thought quickly: I had my wallet, my cell phone, and my keys in my little purse. Some meat in case I got stranded without food somewhere. My spiked heels were in the pockets of my raincoat. Okay, so I could get a cab to the station, and then maybe I could afford another one to my house from the station in Tenway. Maybe. Hell, the station was only about three miles from my house. I could walk. Thank goodness I'd brought walking shoes. It would be okay.

Dan and Hazel were looking at me weirdly, very serious. I said, smiling tautly, "It's fine. I just need to go." I was even being sort of chirpy about this, which I'm sure was scary to see. "Listen, if Tommy comes back, tell him I'll call him tomorrow, if you don't mind." I wished I had said "when he comes back" instead, but it was too late. They made some polite noises at me, but I managed to get away without too much work.

I serpentined through the crowd to get to the door. Conan the Friendly Bouncer smiled and winked at me again as I walked past. I automatically smiled back. The sudden relative silence felt wonderful as I stepped into the cool, damp night. Cars hissed by on wet streets, but the rain had stopped, leaving the air sweet. The door cracked open again behind me. Before I could turn around, my arm was grabbed. It was Russell, swaying in the streetlight and stinking of way too much Heineken. His hair wasn't as perfect as normal, but it looked even better all mussed up. He had a little five o'clock shadow. He looked like an artfully tousled movie star. He was hurting my arm.

"Gina, where you headed? Where'd Tommy go?"

I saw Conan in the doorway, readying for attack. I dragged Russell, attached to me, as I took a few steps toward Conan, leaned over to him, and said as quietly as I could, "It's okay. And he's a cop. You don't want to get in any trouble, honey. But thanks for the thought." Bouncers often have records. I didn't want the poor guy getting busted for trying to be chivalrous. He nodded and sort of melted back, but I appreciated the fact that he was still watching us. I turned back to Russell.

"Russell, go back to your date. She's missing you."

"I don't give a flying fuck about her. Where's the fucking brainiac?"

His meanness didn't bode well. "Tommy had to go. I have to get home, too. My cousin Donna's sitting for me, and she needs to get up in the morning." That was not true, but I didn't care. "Please let go of me."

"God, the man's an idiot. I'll take you home," he said, swaying some more.

"Thanks for the offer, but you're drunk. You shouldn't be driving anywhere. I'll get the train."

Two or three men started leaking out of the club during our conversation. They kept their distance, but all were watching with great interest.

"You shouldn't be taking a train at this hour. You can't even get a train."

"Yes, I can. The last one leaves around eleven-thirty. It'll be fine."

"Gina, honey, don't go away. The night's just started. I bet if you call Donna, she'd be glad to stay overnight." I thought, how the hell would you know? "Let's go somewhere else where we can talk." He still had my arm. His face was sweaty and pleading. I thought, Christ, are *all* men assholes?

"Look, Russell, I just need to go home. Let me go, okay?"

"Tommy's not here, Gina. You gotta give me a chance, gotta let me talk to you." I was afraid that this stupid encounter would continue until I missed the train, even though I had over an hour before it left. "Tommy's gone, babe, and I'm here. You've got to see that this is way better. Come on, honey, come on. Come on." His voice was low, sweet as he pulled me closer. He was wiry and very strong.

The men were watching us closely now as it started raining, a slow spitting from the sky. Russell saw them and nodded. He knew them. Christ, I thought, fellow cops. His friends. I wondered if they were friends of Tommy as well. I said, trying to keep my voice low, just between him and me, "Russell, we wouldn't be together no matter what. Even if I'd never met Tommy. I'm sorry if I hurt your feelings. But you're hurting my arm. You need to let go. We're both going to get soaked."

"No, you need to talk to me." His eyes drooped for a minute. My arm was starting to pulsate with pain. I looked at his motionless friends and suddenly was searingly angry. I thought, What are those dumbasses just standing there for? I was tired of everything, of men, of being a woman, of being a mother, of being nice.

"Let go of my arm, Russell, or I swear I'll hurt you. I will, I swear to God." He let out a big breath through his nostrils like a charging drunken bull and squeezed my arm so that it hurt more. I jerked my arm down the way I had learned in a self-defense class once. Pull your arm away against the thumb of your attacker. The thumb is too weak to hold out against the force of a whole arm. Russell's hold was broken, but he only got madder and grabbed both of my arms and pulled me to him. He kissed me wetly on the mouth, blowing stinky-sweet beer breath all over my face. I jerked my head back, tried to pull away, but his grip was hard, bruising my arms. I looked him in the eye and raised my knee as hard as I could. I couldn't get full force behind it, but I got enough to hurt. If he had been sober, I never could have pulled this off. But, of course, if he had been sober, we almost certainly wouldn't have been in this position. He screamed incoherently, deafeningly in my ear, then screamed again, *"Bitch!"* as he doubled over onto the sidewalk again as the rain picked up, starting to be serious, to be soaking, to mean business. Finally his buddies moved. I was half-afraid they were coming to help him do whatever it was he wanted, to beat me, to rape me, to kill me, or whatever. But two of them were both lifting him and restraining him as he was still trying to come at me, murmuring things I couldn't understand, in an attempt to calm him. He wanted to hurt me. I thought, I've just made an enemy for life. I had almost liked you, Russell. Too late, too bad. I was shaking so hard that I couldn't talk very well, but I managed to say as the rain started streaming in my eyes, down my cheeks, into my mouth, "I'm done with all of you. I'm leaving." Then I couldn't help adding, "I'm sorry if I really hurt you."

Conan was suddenly at my elbow. He said, "Hang on, sweetheart. You need a cab?" When I nodded, he found one for me, flagged it down, and helped me in. I was appalled by the fact that I needed the help, my knees were shaking so much. I thanked him, hiccupping, and he patted my shoulder and closed the door. "Grand Central," I said.

chapter twenty-nine

It is commonly thought that, of all people, lovers behold one another in the most unrealistic light, and that in their encounter is but the mutual projection of extravagant ideals. But may it not be that nature has allowed them to see for the first time what a human being is, and that the subsequent disillusion is not the fading of dream into reality but the strangling of reality with an all too eager embrace?

ALAN WATTS, *Nature, Man and Woman*

AT THE TRAIN STATION I found that the last train for Tenway left in about forty-five minutes. I bought a ticket with a credit card and then went to the bathroom to dry off, wash my face again, and try to collect what I could of myself. In the mirror I looked like I was haunting the room, like I had risen from death by drowning. Fluorescent lights, trauma, and a deluge don't mix if you don't want to look like hell. I swear I was purple and white; you could see my entire circulatory system at work through my skin. The lights flickered, making my appearance even more zombielike; half of them buzzed and died as I dried my hands. I buttoned my coat up completely to hide my body as much as possible in my holey and provocative dress.

I left the bathroom and bought a cup of coffee from a kiosk, dangerously reducing my cab-fare fund. I tried to find a bank of chairs that were inconspicuous and then slunk down in a hard molded seat, sipping the nasty coffee. I started shaking again. I kept breathing. In, out, in, out. I checked my watch, saw that it had stopped, and was grateful that there was a huge working clock looming above the travelers in the station.

I suddenly very badly wanted to be home with my boys. I started worrying irrationally that the Winterburns might change their minds and decide they really did want my children and that some court might be so impressed by their money, what was left of it, that the cops would come and take my boys. My screams would scandalize the neighborhood and maybe even get me some sympathy, but ultimately there would be nothing anyone could do. My boys would be crying for me from the back of a police cruiser, and I would be running after the car, bare feet on asphalt, shrieking, shrieking, big blue and brown eyes staring helplessly at me from the back of the shrinking car.

I came to from my horror trance. Jesus, I was good at making myself feel as bad as possible. I told myself I needed some perspective. I pulled my legs up onto the seat so that I was in an upright fetal position, careful to tuck my raincoat around my legs protectively. I put my mouth on my knee and started sucking on the damp cloth very gently. It was strangely comforting. Maybe somehow this would all work out, I thought, we'd laugh about it later, it would make us closer in the end, blah, blah, blah. But within seconds I started to feel that I had made a big mistake, that I had run out too soon. What was poor Tommy supposed to think when he came back from dealing with his pain-in-the-ass family and found that his girlfriend had run off in some sort of neurotic snit? And how were Russell and all their cop cronies going to paint the whole knee-in-the-groin assault? I could imagine the spin Russell could put on it: *"Tommy, man, that chick is hot to trot, you know what I mean? I mean, she went after me, man, that's the only way I can describe it, and man, I tried, you know, but she does* not *take*

rejection well, you know? I'm your buddy, man, I gotta be honest with you."
And I could also imagine his pals on the force, the witnesses, uncomfortably but silently nodding, solid, true to the force. At that moment I completely and totally loathed all men, especially cops. I started to cry again, softly and quietly, just a few tears; I hurried to rub them off my cheeks with my palms before I started publicly blubbering in earnest.

I was shocked into complete dryness when a man suddenly dropped himself in the cold, vaguely butt-shaped seat next to me. He was long and very dark and looked almost mummified. His aromatic clothes seemed a lot fatter than he was: billowy raincoat and lots of plaid scarves. "Are you okay?" he said softly, slurring only a little. He seemed a lot less drunk than Russell had been.

My first reaction was a start of muted terror, and I quickly glanced around to scope out potential help. I was nowhere near as confident of being able to protect myself from this stranger as I was from Russell. There was no handy Conan nearby. I remembered that I had a spiked-heel shoe in each pocket of my raincoat. My left hand worked its way in to close around the strapped front of my weapon, and I felt a little less vulnerable.

Floppy Man said, his voice scratchy and thin, "Relax, sugar. I'm a sad man, not a bad man. I'll move on, I'll move on." He looked away from me, at nothing, and I had a sudden resurgence of sadness, as if his own had drawn mine out, closer to the surface.

He turned back, still not having made a move to leave. "I was gonna ask you for a few bucks. If you want, I'll trade you a few bucks for some sympathy. What do you say? I saw you cryin'."

Still shaking a little, I said, "What do you mean by sympathy?" What I imagined wasn't pretty.

He turned his yellowy, watery eyes at me. "I'll listen, sugar. That's all."

I suddenly believed him, although I couldn't have said why at that moment. But I was all at once tired of social maneuvering, of working so hard to do the things you were supposed to do, to avoid the people you were supposed to avoid. I thought, So he hurts me. So what? I could imagine the constable shaking his head at me angrily, another grouchy phone call from Tommy. I suppose I should have been imagining two motherless boys, or two boys with a more obviously damaged mother, at least. But I just felt a wave of sorrow, of fellow feeling. This guy had it a whole lot worse than I did, I thought. I remembered reading a story on the homeless in the *Village Voice* many years before; the reporter had interviewed a bunch of men who avoided shelters and instead camped under the higher and more accommodating bridges. Their most tragic complaint, other than the obvious, was that no one would talk to them, that they were treated essentially as monsters or as lepers, as, at best, invisible people, even though most of them were harmless. Living gargoyles, an inert part of the urban landscape. They were some of the loneliest people on earth.

"I don't need an ear," I said. I fished out a five from my tiny purse and handed it to him. That left me with another five-dollar bill. Not enough to get a cab home from the Tenway station. "Here's some, anyway."

He smiled at me. "Thanks." He had beautiful teeth. I was beginning to wonder if I was on some karmic path where teeth were significant in ways I hadn't yet learned to interpret. I could see myself from the outside, knew that if Lizzie or Maggie or Molly or even Erin could see me, she would be screaming at me right now. Oh my God, he's homeless, he's gross, he's smelly, he's a psycho killer, leave him, you can't talk to him. But my fear of him had gone. His face was so, so sad, and I thought, give me this old wino over Tim Solomon any day.

"You want some lamb?"

"Huh?"

I pulled the little foil-wrapped pouch out of my purse. "Here," I said. "I know it's weird, but it's meat. Perfectly good. It was really tasty, from a meal I had earlier. Is it insulting of me to give it to you? It's cooked, it's good. You want it?"

He took it, looking at it as if he'd never seen foil before. It quickly disappeared into some pocket in the mountain of fabric he carried on him. I said, "Be sure to eat it soon."

He raised his eyebrows at me as if to say "No, really?" I knew I deserved it.

"So," I said, "you got a sad story?"

He looked surprised, understandably. "Ain't it obvious?"

I waited.

He looked away again. After a few minutes he said, "Well, it used to not be so sad. I used to teach high school math."

"Really?"

"Algebra, trig, even calculus. I was the first black math teacher in the district. This was in Mobile, Alabama. I was a hero." This was said with a gapped smile that suddenly broke my heart. "I can tell by the way you talk that you're a southern girl yourself. You know Mobile?"

"No. I'm from Stoweville, a dinky little town in north Florida. Mobile was the big city."

"Well, I sure miss it. I hate the winters up here."

"I know what you mean. My name's Gina." I extended my hand. He took it. His hand was dry and hard and rough, like emery paper.

"Mine's Wendell."

"I don't like the city very much, anyway. People are awfully rude up here." I could feel my language slipping more deeply into the childhood rhythms. The South was everywhere tonight. "I don't miss Stoweville; hell, I don't really miss the South. Or the heat. But I miss the basic courtesy. Here it's too hard to feel like you belong any-where. People are so full of themselves."

"You said it, Gina. The city's a hard place. You want my sad story, here it is. I'd still be in Mobile, but my wife took my three girls one day. She just up and took 'em. Left a note: She had no love left for me and had to go looking for it. We'd worked for twelve years to get our house, to get our girls in a good school. She just up and leaves one day. I took a leave of absence, went looking for them, hired a private detective because the police couldn't have cared less. She told some women that I hit her, which as God is my witness I never did, and they helped her get the hell out of Dodge, forever."

"You never found them?"

"Nope. I lost my job, lost the house, lost everything. I let her kill me, or worse than kill me. My brother lives up here, works for the parks department. He offered to help me get another job up here, but by then I was drinking, and here I am. That's my sad story. You got kids?"

"I've got two boys."

"You don't look old enough or settled down enough for that. They got a daddy?"

"A dead one."

"Sometimes that's the best kind."

We sat for a bit, silent and thinking. I wondered, unworried, if his story was true. I suspected that at least some version of it was, but I would never know what the wife's take would be.

After another moment he pulled a small, crumpled brown bag out of his pocket. He held it out to me. "You want some of this here fine wine?"

"No, thanks. I can't drink wine anymore. Now I'm strictly a gin girl. You don't happen to have a bottle of Tanqueray stashed anywhere, do you?"

"Nah." He sipped quickly, then the bottle disappeared. "So tell me your sad story. You were cryin'. You got one."

"Oh, it's not as interesting as yours. You could write that one up, get it made into a movie or something. Might help you deal with it. Make you a bunch of money, anyway."

"Yeah, right. You're not answerin' me."

"Oh, all right. Let's see. I didn't kill my husband, but I feel like I did. You know what? You know what I felt when they told me he was dead? Relief. That's all. He was a messed-up guy; I might've been his only chance at having any kind of good life. We had two little boys who needed their father, and all I could feel was relief. I might as well have killed him myself."

Wendell sat up straighter. "That's crazy. You didn't do nothin'. You're way better off than if you'd done it. You'd be in jail, and your boys wouldn't-a had nobody."

"Good point."

He wasn't done. "Lots of boys don't have a daddy. Kids do okay." I'd insensitively forgotten that his daughters didn't have a father, either, unless his wife had gotten them a new one.

"I'm real sorry about your kids, Wendell. I hope you find them someday. How old would they be now?"

No pause. "Twenty-six, twenty-four, and twenty."

I was impressed. "If they wanted to find you, could they? I mean, do they know about your brother? Does he know how to get in touch with you?"

"Sometimes." He smiled.

"Well, you should get in touch with him. Make sure that if they do come looking for their daddy, they can find him. They might, you know."

He just looked at me for a moment, no expression. Then he said, "You're right. You're right." He looked off at the signs above us. "You know, I could try again, ask a few people I used to know in Mobile. Write 'em or something. I bet Father Paul over at the kitchen would help me."

"Of course he would," I said, having no idea what I was talking about. But you'd think that something like this would be right up the alley of someone named Father Paul who worked at a soup kitchen. "Let's face it, Wendell, you don't have anything to lose."

"So you cryin' over that dead husband?"

"No. A living boyfriend. He ditched me at a club."

"Whoa. He couldn't have ditched you for another girl, honey. You're as pretty as they come, if you don't mind my saying so."

"Well, thanks." I resisted the impulse to cross my eyes or suck my cheeks in like a fish. "He ditched me for his sister." Wendell laughed. I started laughing a little, too. I gave in to an impulse. I dug into my purse and pulled out the last five. I was walking home, anyway; it didn't matter anymore. "Here's the last I got," I said, handing it to him. "Wendell, promise me you'll get at least a little food and then maybe a decent bottle of wine. Eat that lamb. Okay?"

He took the five and smiled. "You're okay. Next time you're in the station, I see you, I treat you to a drink at the bar. Something with gin."

"Sounds great."

"Unless you wanna go somewhere and cut the mustard."

This was the first jarring note in our otherwise chummy conversation, and I said only "No, thanks" and decided it was time to get out of Wendell's company in case things got weird.

That was when I saw a tall dark shape shift position as it came through the doorway and head toward me with what looked like purpose. It was a tall, tall man. It was Tommy in his long drapey raincoat, his face as dark and hard as I'd ever seen it. His jaw worked, and he came toward me quickly, then started almost running in his long, loping way. He looked wild, angry, hard, his hair beaded with raindrops. My heart started flopping around painfully inside my chest, pounding harder and harder, till I thought I wouldn't be able to take a breath and would pass out right there on the frigid tile floor. I thought, Is this how he looks at criminals? How terrifying for them.

Wendell saw him, too. I turned quickly to him and said, "Wendell, you might want to get out of here. He's a cop, and he looks mad. I don't know what he's going to do."

"He's not gonna hit you, is he?"

"No, that's not the problem."

Tommy stopped a couple of feet away and looked at Wendell, then at me, puzzled. He was breathing hard. I said, my voice only slightly quavery, "Tommy, this is Wendell. Wendell, this is Tommy. You'd better go now, though." Wendell nodded and said, "Pleasure to make your acquaintance," then, "Thanks, Gina. I meant what I said about that drink. See you later." Then he bobbed off.

We stood there for a fraction of a second, staring at each other. Then he took one large step, grabbed me by the shoulders, lifted me up, and hugged me harder than I'd ever been hugged in my life. His mouth went to my neck, and through my hair he said, "I'm so sorry, I'm so sorry, please, please, I'm so sorry." I hugged him back without a pause, and of course I was crying and saying, "Tommy, you didn't do anything wrong, I'm sorry I left," and he kept saying, "I should never have left, I shouldn't have, but you had to know I would come back. You didn't really think I wouldn't come back, did you? Oh God, Gina, I would never leave you there. You can't believe I was gone for good. I'm so sorry, honey, I'm so sorry. But you have to stop running away from me. Please don't run away from me anymore." We kissed each other, over and over, and then I'm not sure, actually, who said it first, but we exchanged our first "I love you"s right there in the middle of the train station.

We walked back to his car, which was parked crazily on the curb, clinging hotly to each other. He put me in the passenger seat, then closed the door as if he wanted to make sure I was shut in there and wouldn't get a chance to run again. Once he was in, we started kissing each other again, so it was a while before I noticed his right hand. It was encrusted with little scabs, and two knuckles looked slightly swollen.

"Oh God, you and Russell had a fight. You hit Russell?"

"Of course I hit Russell. Didn't you expect me to hit Russell? I don't think we're partners anymore."

"God, Tommy, I'm sorry about that."

"You know it's not your fault that he's both a prick and a shitty drunk."

"I shouldn't have kicked him. I should've defused the situation somehow. I'm really sorry—"

"Stop it, Gina. It's not your fault that some men are assholes." He sounded tightly furious. "None of this is your fault, okay, but let's face it, you bring out the worst in a lot of guys. That's something I'm going to have to learn to live with, just like you've probably had to your whole life." He turned to face me directly and put his hands on my cheeks. He looked me in the eye. It reminded me of my first dream of him. "Are you ready for this, Gina? I'm serious. I'm ready for this, but are you ready for me? Or are you going to run away from me again?"

I said, "I don't know what you mean, but I love you, Tommy. I don't know what I'm supposed to be ready for, exactly. And I ran because I thought you ditched me. I can see now that I was just a teensy bit paranoid. I'll try not to be so paranoid."

He smiled, although it was a tense one. He said, "Me, too."

His sheets were clean, he said. I looked at him, predatory and very large, and I thought how unfair it was. My house was neutral ground, no memories of real men there that interfered with anything at all.

You couldn't call Doughboy's transient presence interference of any kind. This was different, his territory; presumably there was still a whiff of Candace, of Becky, of God knew who else in his mattress, his bathroom, his couch. I said this. He reminded me that Candace had never lived there; they'd lived together somewhere else. Small comfort. Before he could say anything more, I asked him what happened after he left the club. He was silent for a moment, then told me. He had gotten Susie's car started with a jump from the Mercedes. But Candace had been there as well. He wouldn't say much about that. I gathered a proposition of some kind was made.

I said, "I appreciate you resisting temptation so you could come to my rescue."

"Gina, there wasn't any temptation. At all." He grabbed me and said, "I shouldn't tell you this." He pressed his forehead against mine and closed his eyes. "She said to me, 'How can I compete with that?' Meaning you. All I said was, 'You can't; you need to stop trying,' and I left. There's no whiff of anybody, anywhere, for me but you."

We got back around three in the morning; Donna was asleep in the guest room. I went upstairs to check on the boys, who were fine and sound asleep. Tommy was right behind me. He asked if he should go to the daybed in the dining room to sleep. I whispered no, it's okay, and for only the second time we actually got to sleep together.

Around five a.m. Toby came into the room and snuggled down between us, never quite waking up. An hour or so later Stevie joined him, gradually levering me out altogether. I left the three unconscious males and slept another couple of hours in the bottom of the boys' bunk bed. When Donna got up a bit later, I'm sure she was confused at how the sleeping arrangements had sorted themselves, but she said nothing. She left after a good breakfast and an edited version of the evening before. The boys hugged and kissed her good-bye very sweetly and seemed completely unconcerned that Tommy had been in my room overnight.

Later, after they'd had lunch, Tommy asked Toby about their experiences playing baseball. It took a while for Stevie to join in the conversation, but eventually he did, amplifying Toby's complaints about how mean the other players were and how humiliating their lack of skill had been. I was in the kitchen, putting together dough so that we could make pizzas that night. But then the three of them clomped past me, out the back door, and were in the backyard, doing something that I'd never actually seen in real life. They were playing catch. Watching them through the kitchen window, I saw Tommy toss a slow ball along the ground at Stevie. The twins were next to each other, each with a glove on his hand, low to the ground, ready to scoop up the ball. Stevie managed to stop the rolling ball with his glove, then picked it up with his right hand and awkwardly but carefully threw the ball with a gangly overhand motion while putting his right leg forward. It was a completely graceless display, but Stevie's grin showed that he was inordinately pleased with himself.

Tommy yelled something encouraging and congratulatory and then, with brows knit at the seriousness of the moment, threw a slow ground ball to Toby. Toby caught it right in his glove. This had to have been the first time in all his seven years that Toby had caught a ball of any kind. The glow on his face could have lit the neighborhood. Tommy clapped his hands in a show of understated masculine appreciation. I found my insides tightening up suddenly and realized that I was about to start bawling. I didn't even know what emotions were percolating in me; they were just big, so big that I thought I might pass out. I took deep breaths in and out, closing my eyes, counting my breaths, to keep from crying.

Over dinner Tommy explained things about baseball that might as well have been in Aramaic for all that I could understand them. Not the rules; those I mostly get. Things about statistics and the history of the game, who the big players are, and all that sports arcana I've never even thought about. Both boys were as happy as I'd seen them since Christmas. It was hard getting them to bed later, they were so wound up.

We hadn't really talked again about the events of the previous night. I'd been working hard at not blubbering all over him about the game of catch and so had kept the conversation frighteningly light.

Tommy had followed my lead, no doubt puzzled at my vacuous gaiety. But that evening, in bed, I brought it up.

"How did you find out about the . . . thing with Russell? I mean, who told you?"

"Howard Beckley, one of the guys there, saw the whole thing. He felt pretty bad that he didn't step in earlier, but he didn't really know what he was seeing at first. Randy told me, too."

"Randy?"

"The bouncer, Randy Katilius. You made a big impression on him. He actually told me to get my ass to the train station to catch you. He's jealous as hell of me; that was obvious. He told me that you looked out for him, which he thought was really funny but sweet. He wouldn't tell me what that was all about." His eyebrows rose.

I told him about my brief warning to Conan/Randy, and Tommy actually laughed. When I got a little huffy, he explained that Randy was a moonlighting off-duty cop from a different precinct and had absolutely no fear of other cops.

"Oh," I said. "Well, it seems like an awful lot of bouncers have shady pasts. I didn't want him ending up in jail because he was trying to be nice to me."

"He was right. It was sweet."

Out of nowhere I said, "Poor Candace."

He was silent for a moment, then said, "I was a real shit to her, though I didn't mean to be. I was trying to be nice and wound up being sadistic. I wish she'd quit being so nice about it and move on, tell me to go fuck myself."

"She still wants you back, Tommy. She thinks that if she loves you enough, you'll catch it from her." I thought for a nanosecond about talking to her, trying to help her. It instantly occurred to me how horrendously obnoxious that would be from her perspective, and I dropped the idea. "But that doesn't work all that often."

Tommy was lightly rubbing my back. "I promise I won't ask you again what she said to you, and I won't keep talking about her. But we lived together, as you know, for a long time. I liked her, respected her; I was attracted to her. But I wasn't in love with her. I tried; I just couldn't. That's why we were together for so long; like an idiot, I just kept trying." He turned on his side to look me in the eye. "It's already different with you, you know. When I met you, it was weird. I swear, I just thought, Oh, *there* she is." He returned to lying on his back, looking at the ceiling. "To tell you the truth, I wasn't all that happy about this at first."

I almost told him that I'd said much the same thing to Ellie, then thought better of it. Instead, I said, "I'll bet you weren't if you thought I was a child-molesting porn queen slut. Just what every man wants in a girlfriend."

"Well, just like every woman wants a moody smart-ass oversized cop"—he paused—"with an enormous head." After I stopped snorting, he went on. "I didn't think that you were whatever it was you just said once I'd known you for twenty seconds. You just seemed like . . ." I waited, tensing, a little. "Like a lot to take on."

I thought about Candace and her edgy bloody paintings and sculptures and wondered if I qualified as more or less to take on than that, but I said nothing.

Tommy and I slept together in my bed all night through for the first time. It was weird, having a man in my bed, like it was a normal thing.

The next morning was a Monday, and Tommy had taken the day off. I left him sleeping as I got the boys up and out the door and to school. When I got back to the house, he was awake, in the kitchen, a cup of coffee in his hand, still in his nighttime sweatpants and T-shirt. We stood there looking at each other for a few moments, then I practically jumped on him, and we dragged each other upstairs, freed from silence.

Much later, after we had showered, we were sitting in the kitchen, eating various things for lunch: grapes, cheese, crackers, a cut-up apple, some leftover spaghetti, coffee. I had on my terrycloth robe; he had on jeans and yet another T-shirt. We were sitting on one of the benches side by side, outer thighs pressed tightly together.

I had my mouth way too full of a wheat cracker and a hunk of smoked cheddar when Tommy said, "You know, I think we should get married."

The food in my mouth prevented any response and in fact almost killed me, trying to lodge permanently in my throat.

He was very carefully not looking at me, stirring his coffee. The cream was extremely well integrated into it already, but he kept at it. "I just think maybe it would be a good idea." He kept stirring. "I'm ready to do something else. My job's been soul-killing for a while now; I told you that. I'd be sacrificing my pension; that's the downside. But the stress and the hours would probably kill me too soon to draw it, anyway. Although, I guess if we got married, you'd get it." Quick smile, a fast glance at me. "I could see if I could teach some classes at the criminology school here. I could do some consulting for the department; I wouldn't have to burn bridges. Or I could work for the constable." He shrugged. "Anyway, I have prospects. I'd kind of like to leave the city, and what the hell do you think?" He finally looked at me, expressionless.

I looked back, managing to swallow everything without choking, but even then I couldn't talk. My mind exploded with all the considerations, the discussions we needed to have about money, where we'd live, kids, mine and future ones, religion, maybe, who knew what else. Only people who are very stupid or very young make decisions like this so quickly. Worries skittered around my skull like a bunch of crazed monkeys, but none could really gain any purchase; without much of a pause at all I said, "Sounds great."

After a bit I managed to think, poor Candace. She's going to be so miserable when she hears about this. I even managed to spare a thought for John Fagin.

After a while I said, "You know, this should be partly up to the boys. You have to propose to them, too, you know. I can't marry you if they won't."

"Do you think they'll say yes?"

"I can't imagine why not. But you never know. They're pretty inscrutable sometimes."

. . .

Over dinner that night, Tommy proposed to the boys, sort of. They understood, I think, and jumped up and down. Toby said "Yahhhh!" the way he does when he's really happy about something. What Stevie does is execute a little hopping dance. That night he hopped all the way to the computer. It was the first thing they'd agreed on all week.

Tommy had to leave later that evening, since he had to be at work early the next morning. As we said good-bye, he pulled something small out of his pocket. He wouldn't look me in the eye at first as he handed it to me, a first for him. Then he did, saying, "I have yours, you might as well have mine. You never know when you might find yourself in the city." I took the ring with the two keys attached and looked at it, not sure why I was so stunned. Then he left. I made him promise to call me when he got to his apartment so that I would know for a fact that he hadn't died on the way. You can only tempt the Universe with so much positive energy at once. You don't want to fuck with Her.

chapter thirty

I KNEW that in circumstances like this it's customary for most women to do things like tell their girlfriends or their relatives, especially their mothers. I, of course, first told Ellie, who was, in good sisterly fashion, very happy for me and relieved that I wasn't living the gloomy unrequited life any longer. Then, I thought, it's time to call Mom. I owed it to her to tell her before Rosa gathered it first from some psychic insight. I couldn't begin to imagine what her reaction would be. She had been pretty happy when Scott and I got married because of his family. I wasn't sure how she'd feel about Tommy or about me getting married to someone who wasn't a millionaire.

She picked up after the third ring. "Yes?"

"Hi, Mom,"

"Gina?"

"Yes, Mom. How are you?"

"I'm fine. What's going on?"

We didn't generally call each other just to chat. "Well, Mom, I have some news. I'm getting married."

"Married? When?"

"I don't know yet exactly. Maybe this summer. We haven't set a date."

"Who on earth could you possibly be marrying? It's not that Frenchman, is it?"

"He wasn't a Frenchman, and no, it's not him."

"Didn't he have a French name?"

"Yes, but he wasn't French."

"Then why did he have a French name?"

"Because some ancestor must have been French. His family was named Renouart. Just like your family was named Lodovico. An Italian name."

"I know Lodovico is Italian."

I sighed.

She went on. "So who is this person you're marrying?"

"His name's Tommy Galloway. He's a police detective. He's the cop you were probably talking about when you called me a while back. He's going to quit the force, though, when we get married, probably."

"And do what?"

"Well, there are a number of possibilities. Anyway, that's not important right now. I just wanted to let you know. I haven't told anyone else yet."

"Well, you'd better keep it that way until you know for sure that you're going to do it."

Sigh again. "Why do you say that?"

"Well, you have children to think of. You can't just uproot your life like that. And it doesn't sound like he'll be much of a provider."

"I'm not going to uproot my life much at all. We may not even move from this house. I'm not quitting my job. The boys are staying in the same school. The boys, by the way, think he's great. They're really happy."

Silence. Then, "But what about the Winterburns?"

"What about them?" I had no intention of telling her anything about my latest issues with that family.

"I can't imagine that they'll like this."

Goaded, I said, "Who the hell cares what they like or don't like?

Give the goddamn Winterburns a rest, Mom. I just wanted to let you know about me getting married so that you wouldn't hear about it from someone else. I'll let you know the details later."

Oddly, I felt it important to tell Jessie as well. I knew she'd been monitoring our relationship from her window and probably had a pretty good idea of the way things were hanging. I went over and knocked. She looked as though she'd been sleeping, but she gruffly let me in. I told her the news, told her that it didn't necessarily mean that too much was changing that would affect her, but there would be a man around more now if she needed manly things done around the house. Poor Tommy didn't know I was volunteering his services. She didn't seem impressed and got slightly agitated when she realized that she didn't have anything to give me. I assured her that was all right and went home.

Mo was so excited, she could hardly contain herself. She wanted to treat Tommy and me to a special Saturday lunch at Hannigan's, inviting other members of her dreaded family. Molly was interested in coming, as was Lizzie. I didn't hear much about Maggie; I was hoping she would be too busy with her difficult children. Ivy was apparently not even in the equation; I wondered how Mo was dealing with Ivy's inevitable hurt feelings but didn't have a chance to ask. Neither Donna nor Bobbie was able or willing to come, but Mo somehow persuaded Lottie that we needed her support. Guilt seemed to work well on Lottie. I was preparing alternate ideas, trying to figure out how I could get out of eating at Frank's, but as it turned out, Tommy was oddly interested in seeing the restaurant and even in meeting Frank. That was completely surprising to me.

"The food's not that good," I said when Mo wasn't around.

"So? I'd really like to see it. It's your family, right?"

"A really horrible part of it, yes."

"Exactly how bad is your uncle?"

"Bad enough that I'd rather you didn't know he's related to me, even if it's only by marriage."

. . .

I had never told anyone but Jeri about my first encounter with Uncle Frank. I was thirteen; it was only the second time I had left the state of Florida. My mother dragged me and my sister, who was briefly home from college, up to Tenway for Thanksgiving against the wishes of my father. He loathed the whole lot of Lodovicos, mostly because they didn't consider him good enough for one of their girls, and he didn't tolerate not being good enough for anyone. The Eberles still had a father at this visit. I gather he didn't like Uncle Frank, either, so they kept to themselves that holiday. I met them briefly, too, for a grim lunch, but they were pretty quiet around the loud and bossy Hannigans; I developed no real sense of them then.

The three of us stayed with Aunt Rosa and her family in the Big House. Molly was an angelic-looking and demonic-behaving four-year-old, Lizzie was a brooding and sullen eleven, and Mo was an impossibly angry fifteen. Maggie was my age; my mother had great hopes of us bonding. But Maggie took one look at me and made it clear that she loathed me with every nerve, every follicle in her lumpy little body. I didn't know why. But I looked older than thirteen; that year I was beginning to look like my adult self. As an adult Maggie would be attractive if she wasn't such an unpleasant person. At thirteen she was not pretty, was not slim. Her skin was a minefield. I didn't have a clue that this would cause problems between us. I was so hungry for connections, I would have given her all my hair and a skin graft and been bald and bleeding if she would have liked me. I practically turned myself inside out trying to be nice; it still amazes me how often that just bites you in the ass.

After Thanksgiving dinner Aunt Rosa wanted us all to gather in the great room of the Big House for a family photo. It was, after all, a historic occasion in a way, even if the Eberles weren't there. I was trailing along after everyone, trying to fit in, trying at least not to gum up anything that needed to happen. I was tall even then, the tallest of the kids and taller than my mother and Aunt Rosa, so I was shoved to the back, next to Uncle Frank. He put a hard and heavy arm around me, pulling me tight to his side in familial joy. I was looking directly at Aunt Rosa's head between the heads of my mother and Mo, when Uncle Frank reached his hand under my arm and quite thoroughly grabbed my breast.

I didn't get that it was intentional at first. I just shrugged, embarrassed, assuming that he would be, too. But his grip stayed firm throughout the shot. I have replayed this incident in my mind several times since then, of course, and wish I'd been able to make a stink, preferably one that involved physical injury to Frank. But I was thirteen, socially crippled, and totally aghast, a stranger in a strange land. I just kept wriggling, trying to get him off me, till the shot was done and he finally let go. The picture, a famous one that hangs on many a Hannigan wall to this day, shows most of the family with more or less successful smiles looking at the camera. My face is brown and bug-eyed, peeking over Mo's curly hair. I look miserable, and Uncle Frank has a hearty leer next to me. Of course, our bodies are hidden by everyone else's. I don't know how many times my mother has told me that I ruined that picture by not smiling.

We had a big table in a private part of the restaurant, a back room you could reserve for special events. Mo apparently thought this qualified. There were shamrocks everywhere: on the wallpaper, in the faux stained glass of the high windows, on the tablecloths, on the light fixtures. It was all very green. Jessie would love it, I thought. Maybe this was even where she had gone that night in her green dress. She would have been in bliss.

There were abundant bottles of inexpensive wine, and beer and ale were served practically the way water was in normal restaurants. I opted for a martini. I knew, however, I'd need to nurse it. Mo was paying, and mixed drinks were expensive. She was trying so hard to be a good relative; I could at least try not to bankrupt her.

"So you're a cop," Frank said, in the same tone you'd say "So you sell crack to ten-year-olds." He was doing what he liked best, I gathered, dining in his own restaurant. From what I could tell, he always enjoyed jovially throwing his weight around. His servers didn't seem to hate him, which surprised me. But then, he seemed to treat them somewhat better than he treated his family. He was at the head of a long table, having just finished telling everyone what to order. Earlier he had supplied a huge tray of slippery and shiny slabs of fried potatoes, which sat, corpselike, in the middle of the table. Its weight made passing it around impossible, so Rosa stood, taking small hors d'oeuvre plates from Lizzie as everyone passed them along and transferring soggy, heavy masses of potato to them from the platter with a thick metal spoon. She then handed the plates back to Lizzie, who distributed them. I stared at the shapeless brown mass on my small plate. It looked like something Sidney had once brought home. It didn't smell much better.

"Yep, I'm a cop," Tommy said.

"So how's that pay?" Frank continued. The two of them squaring off in this weird big-guy sort of way made me even less inclined to eat the substance on my plate.

"Enough. Good pension."

"So you can support our Gina here?"

"Sure. If she wants."

"What's that supposed to mean?"

I broke in. "It means that you don't have to worry that in a few years we'll be trying to live off you." This came out snottier than I'd intended it.

"I'm not worried about that," Frank said with a potatoey grin. "But I do like to see my girls doing well for themselves. Your late father, may Jesus take his soul, didn't do so well by your mother from what I understand. Just didn't want you making the same mistakes. Marrying a cop and all."

Tommy looked puzzled. Then Frank laughed in a hard, sneaky sort of way. "She didn't tell you about her womanizing drunken daddy? The soused sheriff of Nottingham or whatever the hell the shitty little town was that you grew up in."

"Stoweville. He was sheriff of Stowe County," I said, wondering why I was bothering.

"Yep. That was it," he said, as though I'd needed his recognition of the fact. "His affairs numbered in the hundreds from what I heard. Handsome bastard, I'll give him that. That's where our Gina here gets a lot of her looks, from the Palettas. A bunch of good-looking losers. He wanted to be a painter. Can you believe that? The sheriff of a tiny shithole, with pretensions to art." His smile faded away. "But he was a son of a bitch to Maria and to his daughters and spent all his money on God knows what." It was poker and Scotch and paint, actually, but Frank didn't know that. I wasn't sure how grateful to be about that. "I know almost nothing was spent on clothes for you!" He laughed as though this was the funniest joke ever. "The few times Maria escaped up here to get a good meal for a holiday, her kids looked homeless."

The fact that he was right didn't ameliorate his nastiness in the slightest. Neither Tommy nor I knew what to say, for different reasons. Frank enjoyed another gulp of Chianti. My insides hurt, and I had to fight a ridiculous urge to start crying. I noticed that a few of the small bulbs in the chandelier overhead weren't on. I hadn't noticed if they had been working when we sat down.

Aunt Lottie broke in finally, blessedly changing the subject.

"How is the restaurant doing now that the renovations have been completed, Frank? Have you noticed any change in business?" She couldn't have cared less, I imagine, but I inwardly thanked her. There weren't too many interveners or peacemakers among either the Hannigans or the Eberles; no one really wanted Frank's attention turned on him or her for any reason.

Tommy asked some seemingly inoffensive questions about Frank's restaurant, information about size and capacity and things that seemed completely boring to me. But Frank started getting a bit huffy, I thought, and started evading Tommy's questions. He usually offered people freebies or special treatment when they expressed an interest in the restaurant: "Come on down; I'll cut you a deal on the specialties of the house," that sort of thing. But Frank changed the subject, offering nothing.

The conversation and ambience at the meal deteriorated as Frank drank more and more. So, I was alarmed to see, did Mo. She was getting increasingly sullen, no doubt missing Ivy. I didn't know where Ivy was; I wanted to ask but knew I wouldn't be doing Mo any favors by bringing it up.

. . .

Later, when we were alone at home, Tommy asked, "Why didn't you tell me about your father?"

I thought for a second, then said, "There's lots of things I haven't told you, Tommy. We haven't known each other all that long. And how much of my grotesque family history do you really want to know or know all at once? I have to admit, I haven't been eager to give you all the lurid details lest you run screaming from me."

"Give me some credit." I raised my brows but said nothing. "He's dead, your dad?"

"Yes. Hepatitis. He was fifty-two."

"Why didn't you mention that you're from a law-enforcement family?"

"My dad was the sheriff of a backwater county. He didn't enforce many laws; he barely obeyed any. He wasn't a good sheriff. He was a drunk and miserable one." Trying to be fair for a moment, I added, "The saddest thing is, he was a pretty talented artist. But there was no way, in that place, with his personality, that it was ever going to work for him. For one thing, Frank was right; he was a terrible drunk." I didn't know why I was getting so irritable. "I didn't tell you because I'm not particularly proud of this and don't like talking about it. Do you feel closer to me now?"

He looked at me, remarkably patient. "Believe it or not, yes." I started crying, humiliated that I couldn't stop, and he let me, hugging me on my couch as though we'd been together for a long time and this was the comfortable, normal thing to do. Every time I tried to apologize, he told me not to be a nitwit. It was the most peculiarly comforting experience I'd had in a long time.

What I didn't tell him till much later was that I hadn't been there when he died; I was starting graduate school at Yale, thinking I was hot shit, too hot for my crooked father. He died in pain and misery, his deputy determinedly told me later, crying out for me, distraught that I wasn't there to tend to him. My mother was as angry at me as

Deputy Buddy was, but it was less clear why. Grammy died only six months later. She knew I needed her to stick around, although she couldn't have known how much I'd need her not too long after that, when I'd have ill-conceived babies. But she couldn't; she told me her heart had been at last finally, irretrievably broken by her youngest, and oddly favorite, child dying before her. Grammy loved me, but she wouldn't stay alive for me. At least I made it home for her dying. After I came in and sat down next to her, I was waiting for some piece of wisdom, some gem, some rule, some joke, even an obscenity. Instead, she patted my face, closed her eyes, and that was it.

Later on Tommy said, "Gina, your uncle is . . . known to the constable."

"Known how?"

"The only reason I'm saying this is because I really want you to stay away from there. Now that I've met him, I want that for lots of reasons."

"You didn't answer my question."

"I can't. I'm already in an awkward position. And you shouldn't say anything to your cousins, either. That's one reason I can't tell you more. How much do you know about the restaurant? The day-to-day stuff, the staff, and so on?"

"Practically nothing. I avoid going there at all costs. Is Uncle Frank in trouble? With the law, I mean?" Silence. "Now that you mention it, he did get all godfathery about the Solomon case, after the fact, of course, and he seems pretty unhappy with you. I just thought it was posturing, though. Was it?"

"I can't say. But how would you feel if I were involved in . . . getting him in trouble?"

I thought for a moment. I thought of Mo and Aunt Rosa and had a pang. Then I thought of Mo and Aunt Rosa again. "Go ahead and nail the bastard."

He smiled at me. "Remind me to stay on your good side." Then he placed a quiet call to the constable.

. . .

The boys had their last day of school that Wednesday. Toby was upset that Tommy wasn't there to share the joy. He said, "Doesn't he live here now?" I said, "Only on weekends."

Tommy called me every evening when he wasn't there, and so I pretty much knew his every move. He'd phone around dinnertime, when he took a break. It was obvious to me, and becoming so to him, I thought, that he worked too much. It was the kind of job where you didn't have much choice about that. The heat and misery and anger of a city that swollen, that compressed, caused more violence than someone like me could imagine. More, too, than someone like Tommy was really suited for wading through every day. And the Universe isn't always kind to those who try to fix the unfixable.

I was careful not to ask for this consistent contact, but he cheerfully volunteered it; it seemed to him to be the normal stuff of intimacy. He'd want to know about my days, too, although I was mostly doing mommy/housewifey things that were not interesting to talk about and trying to continue the writing I worked on from time to time, basically turning my dissertation research into a book for publication one day, I hoped. Tommy was, to me, shockingly supportive, said he wanted to read it, seemed interested. I felt I was drifting paddleless on a completely alien sea.

And when he was at our house, when he was with me, it felt thrillingly strange. I could touch him. Anytime. I could just reach out and run my hand over his arm, pat him on the shoulder, kiss him on the cheek. If the boys were in bed, I could explore more intimate parts of his body, too, as long as I was prepared for the response. I wondered to myself about this over and over, wondered at the liberties I could take with his person. I could, if the boys were not in the room, walk up to him and kiss him on the mouth. In the past I knew that I could have done this with any number of people, but it was never under circumstances in which the consequences of that would have been a good thing for me or even tolerable. And frankly, the desire hadn't been there for the most part. I literally couldn't remember the last time I'd experienced this degree of freedom, of true comfort, with another human being.

Each night Tommy spent at our house during those first weeks, I would wake up next to him, several times a night sometimes, and look at him. We always had some sort of clothing on because the boys tended to burst into the room first thing in the morning and the situation was already shrinkworthy enough. I'd think, he's a good person, he loves you, just look at him. I would feel overwhelmed with what was probably happiness mixed with gratitude. But it would have been hard for me to label it as such at the time. It was all going too well. I knew that and feared I'd gotten off too easily.

Still, most of the time Tommy was at work, and I had to carve out a summer routine with the boys. The first day of their summer vacation they wanted to lie around the house all day, eating pretzels and watching *Tom and Jerry* cartoons. I indulged them, warning them, however, not to expect the rest of the summer to be this decadent.

Jessie banged on the downspout as I was trying to figure out what to give them for dinner. I wasn't feeling overly excited about having to make that particular decision, so I was actually a little relieved at the distraction.

"In the kitchen," she said.

At least now that the temperature outside was high, the heat inside didn't come as such a shock. She was wearing a housecoat covered in faded purple pansies. To my surprise, she was wearing the jade heart.

"Wow," I said involuntarily, then, to cover my rude amazement, "That looks really good with that pattern." It didn't, but I'd already blurted it out and couldn't think of a less absurd comment. Then I thought with horror that she might think I was trying to get more gratitude from her, so I changed the subject, a little desperately.

"You moved the dolls, didn't you? They look nice over there." I pointed to the two disturbingly lifelike figures, frozen in a frilly childhood, by her gas grate, which thankfully was not lit.

"No, they've always been there." She was looking at me oddly, and I weakly admitted, "Oh, yeah, I guess you're right."

"Look," Jessie said, and led me into her crowded kitchen. The room wasn't that small as kitchens go, but all the countertops were covered in crockery and ancient appliances, and the center of the room was filled by four metal chairs with cracked yellow seats and a round Formica-topped table that was too large for the space. I had to scoot sideways around it to get to the opposite counter, on which sat another of Jessie's brown paper bags. This one was too small for clothes.

Jessie had gotten there before me. From the bag, she pulled a huge dark bottle decorated with gold finery around the cork.

"It's Tiger Lily champagne," she said.

I thought for a bad moment that we were going to drink it then and there, toasting each other's widowhood or maybe my upcoming nuptials. The thing was huge, a magnum, and the idea of drinking it made my face pucker.

"For you and your fella to celebrate." Thank God, I thought, as a vivid picture of me emptying it down the kitchen sink spooled through my mind.

"Thank you, Jessie. That's really sweet of you. But where'd you get this? And don't you want to keep it, maybe for New Year's?"

She looked grim, but that was a pretty normal expression for her. "I'm not going to be here for New Year's."

I made all the noises you're supposed to make: She'd outlive us all, and so on. But in truth I suddenly believed her. She'd been looking more and more tired each time I saw her lately. I'd suggested echinacea and vitamin C, but she and I both knew that if they were enough to protect you from the inevitable decline of age, they'd cost a whole lot more.

In spite of my disclaimers, she made me take the frightening bottle of champagne. She'd gotten it as a prize at the senior center, she said, and her friend Geraldine was a teetotaler. Jessie, being diabetic, couldn't touch the stuff. I told her I'd bring it over on New Year's myself, and maybe she could have a thimbleful.

I took the thing, which easily weighed fifteen pounds, to my house and tucked it away in a dim corner on the kitchen counter, thinking I'd pour it out someday when I was sure Jessie would have forgotten its existence.

. . .

Later that afternoon Tommy called, early for him. He'd made arrangements to take off early from work on Friday, the next day. The boys and I were going to go to the city to meet him for lunch, go to the Museum of Natural History, and ride back together in his car.

"Gina, something's happened. You need to be careful, lock up, keep your eyes on the boys, maybe even send them back to Mo's for a while. In fact, it might be a good idea for you to go with them this time."

"For God's sake, Tommy! What's going on?"

"Tim Solomon's out of jail."

"What?"

"His lawyers won his appeal. There are still some drug charges pending, but they're pretty small potatoes. The attempted murder charge is the one that went away." He sounded tired, even bruised.

"How . . . ?"

"Claire Stanley fucked up. Goddamn it, she fucked up the case by being in such a goddamn hurry. The police never investigated Tim's version of the shooting, no one called you as a witness, I don't know what the actual issue was. I didn't hear the judge myself, but I told you the Solomons got really sharp, really motivated lawyers. Whatever their strategy was, it worked."

"Shit."

"You said it."

"Does this mean that Jason is out, too?"

"He will be shortly. I can't do anything with you and the boys in the city tomorrow, partly because I want to check into what's going on with Tim and Jason and partly because I'm also supposed to talk to some guys from the FBI. I shouldn't even have told you that much, but the point is, the shit's hitting the fan from all sides here. The three of you could still come in if you want, and I could probably drive us all back around three or four, but no earlier, and I couldn't hang out with you at all. It probably wouldn't be a good day to give the boys a tour of the station, either, under the circumstances."

"Well," I said, trying to find a bright spot in all this, "we'd all be safer there than anywhere else."

"Not if Claire Stanley shows up for any reason. She's got a bad tendency to blame other people for her problems. I'm sure she'd love to lay some on you."

Disappointment was mingling with terror, making an unpleasant stew in my stomach. "God," Tommy continued, "I wish I could come tonight, but I can't. I've got to get some shit done here tonight. But you see anything weird, anything at all, you call McCandless, then me. Immediately. Right?"

"Right."

He paused, "I'm serious. Think about staying at Mo's."

I was on the cordless phone and so was pacing in a jittery sort of way around the first floor of my house. As he said this, I was in the living room, where the boys were sitting on the couch, Stevie sitting absently in Toby's lap. They were watching a video we'd gotten from the library. "Maybe so," I said.

I called Mo but got her machine and didn't want to leave a recording of the details of what was going on. I had a vague memory of Ivy saying something about their anniversary. Their fifth, I thought; pretty good these days for any couple. Inconvenient for me, though, and it also confirmed my feeling that Trevor was with his father that weekend. I had a key to their house; we could have gone there uninvited, I supposed. But for no rational reason that felt less safe than battening down the hatches in our own nest, which after all had been reinforced of late lockwise.

Tommy called me again after dinner, checking in. His anxiety was pretty well masked, but I'd learned to read some of his signs. He didn't like us being there without him at all. I thought but didn't say, But you're the one who got shot. Ultimately, isn't it you he wants to kill?

After we said good-bye, I looked at the boys, who were arguing naked in the bathtub, told them Tommy would be back late tomorrow, and made them get out and into pajamas. I'd already let their disappointment at the canceled trip tomorrow wash over me. Now I took deep breaths, trying to relax, and checked all the locks for the third time, after taking an irrational peek outside to see if any miscreants were doing any obvious lurking. I had a desperate fear that something was going to mess up, that the Universe was turning its freezing, radiant eye my way.

. . .

That night, I sat straight up out of a sound sleep, remembering that Tommy and I had talked on a cordless phone. I couldn't remember what we had said, whether it had been anything that Tim Solomon would care about. Did it matter? I told myself no a few hundred times before I could get back to sleep.

The next morning Tommy called early, making sure nothing awful had happened in the night and telling me to expect him between four and five in the afternoon. I told him to relax, but it didn't take. After breakfast, the boys had been invited to Josh's; I walked them down, thinking that I'd finally been on the verge of letting up on the parental worry. I had anticipated that at this age I'd be letting them walk the few doors to the Hepplewhites' by themselves. But not now, not now. Oh Jesus. Maybe never, I thought. When will I not have to worry about bad guys anymore? I guess the bad guys will never go away; it just won't be my job to protect the boys from them anymore, when they're older. But not until they are older. Much older. Never old enough, I answered myself. Never old enough not to worry. Too much evil in the shape of regular people, I thought.

But maybe not evil. That's too easy. Sadness, misery, misguided attempts at power and happiness. Big, big mistakes. Lost people who take some of the rest of us down with them. Compassion, I thought; that's the appropriate response. That and watching your back very carefully.

On the way back from Josh's, I stopped in at Jessie's. She was still looking a little more pasty than usual but seemed more energetic than she had in a while. I told her that Tim and Jason, whom she knew as the bad boys, were out of jail. I carefully described both of them. If she saw anybody who looked like that hanging around, call the cops and then call me. She nodded, interested. Almost happy.

I got back in the house and immediately noticed that the light on my answering machine was blinking. John Fagin had finally stopped calling after Tommy had gotten on the phone with him one night, so I was no longer expecting his chubby baritone on the incoming messages. I thought it might be Tommy and hit the button immediately. It didn't take more than a second or two for me to understand who it was, even though he didn't leave his name.

"Dr. P. Or can I call you Gina now? I need to talk to you. My lawyer says it's okay now. I wanted to let you know a couple of things. First, I don't hold you responsible for the arrest and stuff. I know you didn't have anything to do with that. The second thing is that my dad's going to hire some private detectives, since the police have done such a shi—ridiculous job investigating the shooting. I promise, Gina, I'm going to do everything I can to find the person who was really stalking you. You and that boyfriend of yours. Hey, you can do better, though, you know? Anyway, I'll talk to you soon. You can call me on my cell if you want."

He left the number, then hung up. He sounded like an old pal, perfectly sane, reasonable, a good friend. My buddy, Tim Solomon.

chapter thirty-one

[*To children*]

Now when God plays hide and pretends that he is you and I, he does it so well that it takes him a long time to remember where and how he hid himself. But that's the whole fun of it— just what he wanted to do. He doesn't want to find himself too quickly, for that would spoil the game. That is why it is so difficult for you and me to find out that we are God in disguise, pretending not to be himself. But when the game has gone on long enough, all of us will wake up, stop pretending, and remember that we are all one single Self—the God who is all that there is and who lives for ever and ever . . . You may ask why God sometimes hides in the form of horrible people, or pretends to be people who suffer great disease and pain. Remember, first, that he isn't really doing this to anyone but himself. Remember, too, that in almost all the stories you enjoy there have to be bad people as well as good people, for the thrill of the tale is to find out how the good people will get the better of the bad. It's the same as when we play cards. At the beginning of the game we shuffle them all into a mess, which is like the bad things in the world, but the point of the game is to put the mess into good order, and the one who does it best is the winner. Then we shuffle the cards once more and play again, and so it goes with the world.

ALAN WATTS, *The Book*

I CALLED THE CONSTABLE and left a message on his voice mail. Curiously, I wasn't as terrified as I would have expected, but was rather oddly twitchy. I took my time calling Tommy because he couldn't leave any sooner than he could leave, and I wasn't sure it would be very kind to make him more worried than he already was. However, I knew he'd be really mad if he found this out only after he got here. As I was dithering, the phone rang, causing me to jump a foot or two. It was the constable, who told me that if Tim bothered me anymore, I should call back. But he wasn't breaking any laws by calling me, even by showing up on my street or knocking on my door. He'd never been charged with stalking and hadn't been convicted of anything serious yet. There wasn't much they could do to keep him away from me; there weren't even any grounds for a restraining order.

After talking to the constable, I called Tommy, who, as I feared, was even more irritable, though not with me. "I'll be home as soon as I possibly can." That shows you how freaked out I was; the fact that my house counted as "home" didn't register with me till much later.

Patsy then called and said she'd been trying to reach me for a while. The boys were hungry, and Toby had decided that all he would eat was his mother's macaroni and cheese. I went to get them, brought them home, and fed them. They were sulky and out of sorts, especially with each other. I threw them out in the backyard, as it was a balmy, sunny day and there was a good, strong, high fence around it. "Play," I ordered, then made sure the padlock on the gate was secure.

I decided that for dinner we'd have soup and bread and started cooking. I was far too distracted to write anything, didn't care if the house was clean, and figured that both things could sit for a while and be ready whenever we wanted to eat. Tommy had some issues with me cooking for him so much; I patiently explained that, one, I was good at it, and, two, as long as it was summer and I wasn't teaching, it wasn't unfair and sexist for me to do that part of the work. Later, we'd see.

I took a quick peek out the window, reassured by the sight of the boys running around happily and violently with plastic swords. I turned back to get some more flour out of a canister on the counter behind me and almost jumped out of my skin at the sight of a large man standing in my front hallway. It took only a second or two to register that it was Frank, but it was an excruciating second. I made some loud incoherent noise, then said, "What the hell are you doing here?"

He smiled at me; it didn't look friendly, but neither did it look particularly menacing. "Hey, Gina. Didn't mean to scare you, but your front door wasn't locked."

The front door wasn't *locked*? Oh my *God,* I thought, remembering dazedly that I hadn't actually turned the bolt. My brain ranted at me, silently screaming, my house is like Fort Fucking *Knox* now, I am being stalked by a possible homicidal maniac, I have rude and sinister relatives who apparently like to wander into my home uninvited, and I forgot to lock my miserable *fucking* front door while my children and I were oblivious prey in our backyard. Idiot, I thought, idiot, idiot, *idiot.*

Frank continued, "You need to watch that. Stu says this neighborhood's kind of, you know, iffy. A woman alone like you needs to be more careful." He was sweaty, as if he'd been running. He was quite heavy, at least two hundred fifty pounds or so, on a frame that was designed for about eighty pounds less than that. He wheezed a little, too. As I tried to bring my mind back to the present, I wondered what he had been doing before coming here.

"You're right." I had rarely, I realized, ever called him anything to his face. Somehow calling him "Uncle Frank" seemed much more cuddly and affectionate than was warranted. I thought for a moment that maybe he was lending his support relative to Tim Solomon, then realized that he was unlikely to have heard anything about this yet and that it was even more unlikely that he was actually trying to help me at all. I inhaled, trying to get my shaking heart and spasming lungs under control. "What brings you here?"

"Where's your boyfriend?"

"Tommy's in the city."

"He coming back here soon?"

"Later today."

"When?"

"I don't know, around dinnertime. Why, did you want to talk to him?"

"Mmm, yeah." He swayed a little. I got a whiff of alcohol and sweat. He hadn't shaved in a day or two, and that made him even less pleasant-looking than normal. His color was bad, too, red veins stark on bluish-white skin.

He said, "Hey, can't I even get a beer in this house?"

I said I didn't have any, which was true. I didn't know what to do and kept nervously looking outside, making sure the boys were still there. I couldn't break the hospitality habit—take your shoes off, y'all come back now—of my youth. I couldn't connect the big ugly jerk in front of me with terrible criminal things, but I was starting to be afraid of him, not because of what Tommy had hinted at but because of some smell, some right-brain synthesis that traveled down from my brain and lodged in my lower belly and made me want to start begging for mercy. This was a side of myself that I wasn't happy to discover, this cowering before big masculine brutality. I later wondered why it hadn't kicked in when Russell had grabbed me.

I said he could have some iced tea if he wanted something to drink, hoping desperately that he wouldn't want it and would just go. Unfortunately, he said, "If that's what you got, that's what I'll take." He looked around, then sat down at the kitchen table. "This is a nice little house even if Stu doesn't much like the neighborhood."

I got the tea from a dark refrigerator, trying to make a mental note to replace the bulb as soon as Frank left. "Stu just doesn't like that some of my neighbors are black," I said, putting the glass in front of him.

"Hey, look, he's just concerned about your resale value." He looked at me, eyes narrowing. "After you and the cop get married, you going to stay in this house?"

I thought, Why the hell do you care, Don Corleone? "I don't know. We haven't decided yet."

He took in a deep breath. His nose was large and roomy, so it surprised me that the breath whistled, as though there were only tiny, twisting corridors in there. "You sure about this guy? I mean, I thought you were like, you know, being like a nun. My girls tell me you don't go out, you don't play around. So nothing for a long time, then you have to go for a cop?"

"I don't understand."

"You could have any guy you wanted, Gina. Any guy at all."

"No one can have anyone," I said, trying for joviality. It didn't sound convincing to me, but I could see now that Frank was very drunk.

"Look, Gina, your aunt is real upset about this rose thing. I thought I'd come by to try to get it straightened out."

Not the goddamn rose again. "What's to straighten out?"

"It's only fair if both sets of parents pony up, you know."

"Adam attacked my son and used him as a battering ram. It wasn't like my son was at fault here. I'm not making Maggie pay for the bandages and Neosporin." I was going to add shrink bills to the list but thought that would add to the general perception that my boys were overly swaddled.

"Oh, come on, Gina. You know that boys do this kind of shit to each other, pardon my French. You need to take responsibility for them."

"Wait, I thought you all thought that I took too much responsibility for them. I'm overprotective, I don't let them make their own mistakes, that kind of thing. Now I'm supposed to take responsibility for their actions. Hmmm. You folks need to make up your minds." This was a weak argument, and I knew it. But I was pissed and tired and missed Tommy and wanted Frank out of my house. I wished, not for the first time, that I was an orphan found adrift on the ocean and raised by kindly Tibetan Buddhist monks. Hell, they didn't even need to be that kindly to be a big improvement over the reality. "What do you want from me, Frank?" There, call him by his first name like an adult. "Do you think you can talk Tommy into making me pay up?"

"You need to think about this, Gina. This is the kind of little thing that can create bad blood for a long time. Is a few dollars worth it to you?"

"Look," I said, weakening, worn down, "I'll think about it, okay? I don't want to argue any more right now."

Frank smiled. He touched my cheek with a raspy finger even as I flinched back. He looked a little hurt but said, "Good girl." Then, "You have any beer in the house?"

I didn't remind him we'd done this already. "Uh, no. Sorry, Frank."

"You know," he said as he rocked to his feet, "I know you love those little boys. But you got to think of their future. No cops. Cops aren't what you want. I'll do you a favor. A fucking *favor*." He swayed toward me, grabbing. I was suddenly pressed against his round and stinking body. I backed up, but he kept half walking, half falling into me till I was pressed into the counter. His erection was evident, and I swear my gorge was rising, a combination of disgust and terror. He said, "You're so freaking beautiful, such a pretty girl. I've always loved you like a daughter." His meaty hand touched my cheek. There were sudden stomps of small feet on the back deck, and the storm door rattled. Frank pulled back, swaying, almost falling in the other direction. The door banged open, and Stevie flopped in.

"Mom—" he began, then stopped at the ungainly sight of his uncle tottering in our kitchen.

"Uncle Frank was just leaving, honey. Say good-bye," I said in a voice I'd never heard before.

Frank stumbled toward the door, making noises about me and the boys coming to the Big House for dinner the coming week, not including Tommy, I noticed. I made noncommittal noises back, having no intention of ever going there again.

After he finally teetered off the front porch, I locked the front door with every bolt and chain on it. My hands were shaking so badly that it took a few minutes.

I had never wanted to see any man more than I wanted to see Tommy that day, but by late that afternoon I still hadn't heard from him. I knew that it was always possible that he'd gotten delayed at work. But he would have called if he knew he was going to be late or a no-show. Out of nowhere, I distracted myself from worries about Tim and Jason by thinking of Mo and Lizzie, wondering what they would think if they knew that their father might go to prison and that

Tommy might be somewhat responsible for putting him there. I couldn't imagine anyone weeping for the loss of Frank Hannigan in her life, but none of the Hannigans seemed to feel the way I did, including Mo. I had never subjected Mo to my real opinion of most of her family, but I was surprised how loyal she remained to a bunch of people who barely tolerated her. I started feeling a mild panic, queasily mixed with relief, at the idea of Tommy succeeding at whatever it was he and the constable wanted to do with Frank. Would Mo forgive me? She was one of the few good relatives I had. She had practically saved my life. What would I do without her? And frankly, I wasn't sure what she'd do without me and the boys. And poor Ivy. I knew she needed us, too, at least as much as we needed and loved her. What a mess. However, I didn't know what Frank was supposed to be guilty of. Theft, murder, what? In some ways it didn't matter, I supposed, but of course in other ways it did. I sighed. Thirty-three years of almost no involvement with the wrong side of the law. There was some underage drinking in my youth. Some tepid and limited drug use. Extramarital sex in some positions that were illegal in a few states. But that was it. It was like I'd been saving it up.

I had held off calling the precinct, having some pride and not wanting the other cops to think I was some neurotic, checking up on him. But I wanted to, and by five-thirty I said to hell with it, and called. I got the desk sergeant, who told me that Detective Galloway had left some three hours ago. I breathed away panic by telling myself that that didn't mean he had left the city then. I called his apartment but got the machine. I left a painstakingly casual message. I called the precinct back and asked to talk to Dan Lowery, who, it turned out, was gone for the day. I said to myself, "Fuck it," found the number in my evening purse, and called Dan and Hazel at home. I got Hazel, said hello, tried not to scream through social pleasantries, and asked to talk to Dan. She was puzzled but got him to the phone. I said, "Forgive me for freaking out, but I know Tommy left the station hours ago. Did he say if he was leaving the city right away? He's not here yet, and he said he'd be here by now, and he's never ever not been here when he said he'd be here, and we talked about the case he's working on, on a cordless phone, and I'm really scared someone heard something, and my creepy uncle was here earlier, and I'm starting to wonder why. I'm sorry. I'll let you answer me now."

I was waiting for Dan to laugh at me, tell me I was being ridiculous, a hysterical girlie civilian, but instead he said, "He's not there yet? He said he was going right from the station. I know something about the case. Let me make a few calls, and I'll get back to you, okay? I've got your number. Keep the lines clear."

Ten minutes later Lizzie called to ask me if she could borrow a boom box of mine; hers was broken, and she needed the music for three massages she was doing early the next week. She was being unusually chatty; I wanted to shriek at her to get off the phone. I didn't have call waiting, so it felt absolutely vital to cut her off. I said yes, yes, yes, and started to cry when she asked me what was wrong. I told her briefly. She said, "I'll be right over," and hung up. I stared at the phone for a precious second in amazement before hanging up.

Lizzie, bless her, said she'd take the boys to a movie after reminding me to feed them. She made sure I had her cell number handy so I could call her when I knew something. I hugged her and thanked her, grateful for what seemed to be the new Lizzie.

The three of them had been gone for about twenty minutes when Dan Lowery called. "Gina, he's alive, okay? That's the first thing you need to know. He's alive, and they think he's going to be fine. He's had a bad knock, but he's okay. Maybe a broken leg, though it's too soon to say."

I collapsed on the couch, shock making it hard for me to write down the important stuff. He was in Northridge Hospital again. He didn't have me written down as an emergency contact in his goddamn wallet. They didn't even know that he was a cop at first, because they had to use the goddamn *jaws* of goddamn *life* to get him out of the goddamn *car.* It wasn't clear what had happened yet, but it looked like he'd had a blowout or something else made the car go off the road, down an embankment. All I could think was he's okay, thank

God he's okay, Jesus, I'll become a Christian or a Muslim or a Jew or an actual devout, practicing, disciplined Buddhist, or whatever the hell the Universe wants if he's just okay.

As soon as I was coherent enough, I called Lizzie and told her about the accident. She offered to stay with the boys. I was getting my keys, wallet, and cell phone, was almost ready to go, when the phone rang again. It was the constable. I irrationally thought at first that it was a coincidence and started to tell him about Tommy. He interrupted and said, "Gina, we don't think it was an accident. I'm sending a deputy to escort you here."

"What? What do you mean, escort me? Why?"

"We'll talk about it when you get to the hospital. You know he's at Northridge, right?"

"Yes. I was on my way out the door."

"Please wait. My deputy will be there in just a few minutes. Please. Humor me."

There weren't many people on earth right then whom I would have listened to, but he was one of them. "All right," I said.

It was a nightmarish replay of the last time I'd done this. Russell wasn't there, but everything else looked the same: the ashen constable, the same staff. I was pretty sure Donna was working. They also told me that Susie had been called; her number was still in his wallet as an emergency contact. I didn't have it in me to be irritable about that. I was identified to key medical people as his fiancée. I had never been referred to as someone's fiancée before. I wasn't sure how I felt about it, but it seemed to have more clout than "girlfriend." I got shown at once to his room by Jed Paley. "Oh, hi," I said vacantly as soon as I recognized him.

Tommy looked a lot worse this time, not just pale but bruised and cut and bandaged, an IV in one arm. I ran to him and held his hand as before, but this time I did kiss him, again and again. It was better and worse. He was awake and able to kiss me back. He said, "It's not as bad as it looks, really."

"Quit being such a brave little soldier and let me be hysterical about how wounded and heroic you are."

We kissed a bit more, with me standing up because it didn't seem like a good idea to lean on him anywhere. He said he wasn't in too much pain, at least not physically. "I loved that car, Gina. I've had her for eleven years and have taken better care of her than anything else in my life. No one will give me a straight answer about her condition, which makes me think it's really bad." Poor Tommy. I told him I'd try to find out more details, but I, too, had a sinking feeling about his beautiful old Mercedes.

I patted him, kissed his cheek, trying to comfort him. Then I said, "I don't care what your sister says, I'm taking you home with me this time."

He said, "Okay. I'll tell you a secret." He whispered, "I like your cooking better. And your kids have better taste in cartoons."

Fortunately, Susie came in a moment or two after that remark, and so I'm pretty sure she didn't hear it. But she did see a replay of her own previous nightmare, me holding her invalid brother's hand and smiling as though everything in the world was just peachy after he was injured in the town where I lived, in some way because of his association with me. I knew she hated me in that moment, and I couldn't blame her. I tried to greet her with warmth; she wasn't warm in return. I left them alone together and went in search of the constable.

I found him in the waiting room, talking to Dan Lowery and Russell Barnes. Tommy thought Russell owed me an apology, but I was happy he hadn't pressed assault charges against me; I figured we were, karmically speaking, about even. I said, "Okay, what's up? What's the 'not an accident' thing about? Have you talked to Tommy about this?"

The constable said, "Yes. That's how come we're sure. We've also done a preliminary exam of the car. It's been towed to our facility to be checked out more thoroughly tomorrow, but it looks like Tommy's tire was shot, then his windshield. He's one lucky SOB that he didn't get hit by a bullet himself and that the crash didn't kill him."

I said, stupidly, "Oh my God, Tim must have followed him or something."

The constable shook his head sadly. "No, Gina. We've already arrested the person who did it. His name's Kenny Kelly."

The name rang no bell.

"He's a short-order cook at Hannigan's."

He wasn't, apparently, a very bright guy. Kenny and his girlfriend Brenda had waited for an hour or so at the first major intersection into town from the expressway. Tommy's car was pretty distinctive. As soon as they saw it, they started to follow him. Brenda had done the clumsy driving while Kenny aimed a rifle out the passenger window. They had waited until the traffic had thinned, but there were still plenty of witnesses who saw them do it, plenty of physical evidence of foul play. They shot him at a red light, so people had time to get a good look. Ballistics no doubt would put the gun in Kenny's hands. The police were pretty confident that they could get him to rat out Frank. It was just a matter of time.

The constable then asked, "Guess what kind of car Kenny has." I looked at him, confused. "A blue Trans Am. Really rusty, lots of dents. It's not like it's the only one on the road in these parts, but coincidences aren't really all that common, you know? I'm willing to bet that Kenny was the one playing peekaboo behind your fence. Checking up on you for your uncle."

After chewing on this for a few horrified minutes, I confessed my probable role in all this to the constable, telling him about Frank's horrid visit and my spilling the beans about when Tommy was likely to be coming to Tenway. I felt sick. I thought, I'd better make sure Susie never finds out about this. He said the polite thing, it wasn't my fault, and so on, and told me to go be with Tommy, they'd take it from here. I turned back and asked about Tommy's car. The constable shook his head and said he was lucky to be alive; the car was not.

He was asleep, and Susie was hanging over him like a rain cloud. I took a series of very deep, quiet breaths. I took a good long look at poor Susie, touching Tommy's still hand, looking as though she were floating away in grief.

I touched her arm. She turned to me, looking older than she was, thin-skinned, cornered. I said, "I'm sorry. I'm really, really sorry."

She spat, "I don't know what he sees in you, but you're going to get him killed. Go away, for God's sake."

I came back a half hour or so later. Tommy was awake, and Susie had left to get something to eat. He told me I couldn't call anybody, especially any Hannigans, because they hadn't arrested Frank yet. After they got him, I could talk to whomever I wanted. I ignored him only slightly to call Lizzie, mainly to give her an update on Tommy's health and to check up on the boys. I called my house, but there was no answer. I called her cell phone, but it was turned off. I wasn't worried at first, just curious, mildly annoyed. They should have been out of the movie by then; I assumed that Lizzie had turned the phone off in the theater and then had forgotten to turn it back on. I then tried Mo's house, thinking they might have wound up there, but only got the machine. Thoughts started moseying their way to the front of my mind, thoughts of Frank being all queasily avuncular and checking out my house, and worry started doing a sort of time-lapse blossoming. I told Tommy that I couldn't get hold of Lizzie and that she had the boys. His eyebrows lowered below the bandage on his forehead. All hope that I was being paranoid fled as he said, "Tell McCandless. Have him check it out. Now."

The constable's expression didn't change when I told him my concerns, but his actions were both reassuring and alarming. He quickly summoned Jed Paley, talking to him softly out of my hearing. Paley sprinted out of the hospital doors, and moments later I heard a police siren, presumably from his squad car. The constable guided me quickly back to Tommy's room. They exchanged manly, knowing looks that made me want to aim a flamethrower at both of them. I tried Lizzie's home phone just in case, remembering that her answering machine was broken. She didn't answer there, either.

I could feel small nibbles of panic at the edges of my internal organs. It hit me that there simply weren't that many deputies in Tenway, and at least one of them was out looking for Frank. How many could possibly be looking for my boys? No matter what they thought, no matter the urgency, if they didn't have the manpower, they couldn't be searching that thoroughly. I started to leave, saying I'd look for them myself, when the constable stopped me and told me that was a bad idea, although why was unclear to me. He suggested I was over-reacting, I needed to sit down, and so on. He followed me as I ran to the nurses' station and asked them to page Donna, and followed me as I paced back to Tommy's room. My fear was icy and very deep.

When my cell phone rang, I stared at it for a moment before I could bear to hear whatever was coming. The number on the display meant nothing to me. It took my shaking finger two tries before I could hit "talk."

"Gina, honey, I need you to do something for me." It was Frank.

"Do you have them? Do you have my boys?"

There was brief silence, then, "Well, not on me." A slurry chuckle. "Listen, you need to tell your boyfriend to get his buddies to lay off me. Think you can do that?"

The fact that my most outrageously paranoid fears were suddenly real, in the flesh, sent me somewhere I'd never been before, down some sort of weird emotional black hole. "Where the hell are they, Frank? You bastard, tell me where they are. If you've hurt them, I swear I'll rip your balls off with my bare hands and shove them down your throat." I had had no idea I could ever talk to someone like this. I wasn't in control of anything, my muscles, my words, my thoughts, anything. I was starting to come apart, to scream at him. "I'll kill you, you son of a bitch, I'll fucking kill you if you've touched them, you asshole bastard piece of shit." I was screaming so hard into the phone, my throat was burning. Someone with a big, strong hand was trying to take the phone out of my hand, and I wouldn't let go, turned to fight, and it was Tommy, pulling it from me. I was still screaming, I think, and I could see Donna coming in the door, her dark eyes wide and terrified. The constable had my shoulders, was holding me back, while I tried to attack Tommy, to rip the phone back. I heard the constable ask someone, maybe Donna, maybe another nurse, for a sedative. Even then I knew he meant for me.

Tommy was talking on the phone very reasonably, as if he and

Frank were frat brothers. I couldn't understand much of what they were saying, but it sounded to me as though Tommy was actually complimenting the son of a bitch on something, some cleverness, some wise course of action. There was a tiny, faint rational part of my mind left that knew that this was what you did with crazies, with violent hostage-holding psychopaths; you talked to them calmly, you gained their trust, you got them to believe that you were on their side. I knew this. But I couldn't act on it; I was unable to be anything but hysterical.

I felt a hot pinch; someone had injected me with something. I turned to beat on whoever had done it. It was a woman I vaguely remembered, Pam, Tommy's nurse. The constable and Donna kept me from hurting her by pinning my arms. I am pretty strong; it wasn't easy for them. In a surprisingly short time, I couldn't fight anymore. The drug had taken hold, and my manic anger drained, leaving a hollow, helpless sadness. I knew my boys were dead or mangled or being tortured and was powerless to help them.

I could hear Tommy more clearly now; he said, "Well, you're a family man yourself. I know you know a lot about kids, how to handle them." His voice sounded chipper and friendly. His face was dark with worry, his eyes on me. I started crying for real then.

Donna put her arm around my shoulder. For the first time I realized that Susie was still in the room. Her face was the color of a peeled potato; I thought, Go home to your kids. Tommy was actually chuckling at something Frank was saying on the other end of the conversation.

I don't know how long Tommy and Frank talked. Time distortion was only one weird effect of whatever sedative they gave me. The other was an immense slowing of my reactions. When Lizzie and my sons walked into the hospital room, at first I barely noticed.

If the circumstances had been different, the reaction of everyone, especially Tommy, still chatting amiably on the phone with my felonious uncle, would have been comical. The constable's eyes practically popped out, Donna started crying, and poor Tommy's head was whipping back and forth looking at everyone while he continued his insanely comradely phone call. Lizzie looked tense but nowhere near as scared or worried as she should have. As the horror slowly passed, a sad and relieved love, deep and painful, rolled into my heart, and I pushed to my feet, scooping both boys into my arms and falling at once back into the chair, holding them to my breasts. The boys were tired and whiny, and Lizzie was about to start talking; the constable shushed all of us and guided me, wobbly-legged, out to the hall. He waved Lizzie out there as well, and after getting me and the boys situated on some chairs in an empty room, he took Lizzie off to talk. I could hear his first question as they walked away: "Do you happen to know where your father is right now?" I could also hear her answer as she told him in which motel he was waiting for her to bring my sons.

It was late, and the boys were getting more and more upset, needing to go to bed. They hadn't been through any terrible ordeal; they'd just been roasting marshmallows on the patio in back of Lizzie's town house and were filled with sugar and exhaustion. I wanted to get them home but was still too wiggy from the drugs to drive; I remembered that I didn't have my car, anyway. I staggered back into Tommy's room, where he was mercifully off the phone.

I looked at him, seeing him for real for perhaps the first time in spite of the drugs in my system. Or because of them, who knows? A big, very strong, very smart man, handsome in his way, more handsome than I'd given him credit for when I first met him. Well muscled, soft-voiced, not as confident as he seemed. Sensitive and decent. So tired, in pain. I suddenly saw years of frustration ahead for him, years of not getting what he wanted. I could see no difference, suddenly, between me and Candace, except that I was more boring, more needy, and had two major distractions to keep me from attending to his happiness. I just as suddenly knew I couldn't do it. My love for him felt like dry ice inside me, so cold that it burned, damaged. The Universe had slapped me hard enough. I didn't want to be married again, didn't want to be hog-tied to anyone else, ever. I didn't want any more unasked-for love, any more people I couldn't take care of properly. No more. I had humiliated myself in front of him, too; I stank with shame, and I thought, I've got to get out of here. Home, home, home.

I saw Susie's streaked face, pasty and miserable, and said to her, into the murmuring room, "You win." I turned to the constable before I had a chance to see her expression, her response. I said, "Can someone take us home?" My words were mushy. "My car's not here. I couldn't drive, anyway." I pulled the twins out by their hands, and looked back quickly. "I'm sorry," I said to Tommy, hoping he'd be tired enough of me after this, maybe angry enough, that he'd get it and wash his hands of me. He was looking at the constable, talking about Frank, I assumed, but I couldn't make sense of any of it. "Goodbye," I muttered, slushy, thick-tongued, too quiet.

Jed Paley drove us home. His patrol car didn't have booster seats, but since he didn't seem to care, I guessed it was all right. After he left us, locked up and secure, I decided not to question the boys right away about what had happened; they were so strung out by that time, it was all I could do to get them into bed and asleep before midnight, the drugs slowly washing themselves out of my system. The next morning, however, I questioned them as casually as possible, as they can both get very squirrelly if they think the interest in their stories is too intense.

After Lizzie had brought them home from the movie, Uncle Frank had showed up. Stevie said that it was kind of creepy, that he was obviously drunk and kept calling her "my good girl" and "my golden girl." He frightened both of them, especially Toby, by trying to be clumsily and flamboyantly friendly. He wanted her to take them out for ice cream, then to some motel, the Little Apple Inn. I'd seen it, just north of town, outside the county line. Lizzie did the first part but then brought them to her home. They roasted marshmallows outside for a while before coming to the hospital. I made sure the twins had some fruit and whole-wheat toast for breakfast, a little concerned about the volume of sugar they'd had the night before. I knew I wasn't dealing with the main issues, but I wasn't sure how to do that at that moment.

Donna called, telling me that they'd arrested Uncle Frank not long after we left. She was home but was heading back for another shift in a few minutes. I wondered how any nurses anywhere could be sane and kind, given the hours they were commonly expected to carry. She said, "You need to talk to Lizzie."

"Why?"

"She's kind of falling apart, Gina. In a way, I think it's a good thing. But she's going to really need our help."

"Help with what?" Lack of sleep and the stress of recent events had made me stupid.

"Talk to her," Donna said again. "I told her to call you."

After we hung up, Josh showed up at the door with his new puppy on a leash; he wanted the boys to come out with him. I wouldn't let them go until I saw Patsy herself behind him. She assured me she wouldn't let any of the boys out of her sight, and after the puppy's short walk, they'd go right to their house to play. I knew she thought I was a completely psychotic, smothering mom; I didn't have the strength to explain myself. I was grateful for the moment of silence that followed their leaving. Unfortunately for me, Lizzie called moments after I'd closed the front door. I'd never heard her sound like she did, tremulous and exhausted, almost Jessie-like. She was calling, she said, because she still needed that boom box. In all the excitement the night before, she'd never picked it up. She said she was coming right over.

She pulled up less than twenty minutes later. I brought the boom box out to her car and put it in the backseat.

"I have another favor to ask, Gina," she said, still sitting in her car.

"What?" I squinted at her through her window.

"All my financial papers are at the Big House because my dad's accountant did my taxes for me. But I need them now, you know. My estimated taxes are late, and with all that's going on, I can't ask anyone else, Mo or Molly, to get them for me, and I just can't go there alone. I can't deal with Mom by myself right now. I mean, Dad's in jail, so that's all right, but not Mom, that's *not* all right." She was shaking and starting to cry, and I thought, Jesus, what is up with *this*? I got into the passenger seat, and for the first time in my life I hugged Lizzie while she cried and cried, moaning softly, palsied with despair.

She pulled away from me after a minute or so, wiping her face with her hands, as if her tears were acid, eating her skin. She wouldn't look at me. "You talked to Donna? Did she tell you about last night?"

"I talked to her, but all she said is that you could use some support just now. What can I do for you, Lizzie? Other than going with you to the Big House. What happened last night?"

"You don't know?"

"Not really. The boys told me that your father came to see you, but they didn't really understand what was going on, and so they couldn't explain it to me."

Lizzie's long sigh hitched in her chest. "Dad wanted me to help him kidnap Toby and Stevie."

Even though I should have guessed as much, my body chilled. I didn't need to ask his motive. But it was odd that he'd thought Lizzie was likely to go along with that. I said as much, finally, stammering, trying to make it come out as the compliment to her I meant it to be.

"My dad thinks of me more like a girlfriend or something than a daughter, Gina. And you may have noticed that he expects his girls to do whatever he asks, no questions."

I waited. I had a bad feeling about this.

"You know he sexually abused me, right?"

I was carefully trying not to act hysterical. "I was starting to suspect it. How old were you?"

"It started at about twelve. It stopped at around fifteen. I think it happened to Molly, too. I don't know for sure, but I'd bet money on it."

It shouldn't have surprised me so much. As I said, I myself had suspected it only a few days before. But I was still profoundly shocked and sickened. It was far more comfortable believing this than confronting it. Lizzie wouldn't look at me while she talked.

"I hadn't forgotten, exactly. I don't know if it's a repressed memory type of thing, really. It's just that I don't think about it. This is so weird, so horrible, it just kind of exploded into my mind, what kinds of things he used to do. I'm not a kid; I don't feel like I was ever a kid. It's like memories of being a kid are like watching a movie, and they're not real, so I don't think about them much. They don't usually have much to do with me. But of course they do. I'm not stupid; I know that this really screws you up. Oh Christ, I don't want to be so screwed up, but how can I not be when this happened? Oh Jesus, what am I going to do?"

I asked, trying to be gentle, about Aunt Rosa. Lizzie practically hissed. "What do you think? Of course she had to know. She's not as clueless as she acts."

I thought of Jeri and told Lizzie that I had a fabulous therapist I could talk to for her if she wanted. She wasn't crying anymore. It was as if she had hardened, solidified. She just nodded.

I told Lizzie to wait a second and went quickly back into the house. I called Patsy Hepplewhite; the boys were all safely ensconced in their playroom. I told her I had an errand to run. She agreed to keep the boys for an hour or so. I went back to Lizzie's car and said, "Okay, I'm yours."

Lizzie went into the house without knocking. The front foyer smelled of cabbage, vinegar, and onions. I wasn't looking forward to seeing Aunt Rosa; there was no telling what she'd been told about my involvement with Frank's arrest. Lizzie yelled, "Mom?" but there was no answer.

We went into the small office that was off the living room. Lizzie sorted through some papers on the enormous oak desk, and then we heard footsteps coming up from the basement. "Hello?" said Aunt Rosa, sounding frail.

Lizzie answered, and Rosa came into the study. She had a black eye.

Lizzie said, "Mom! What happened?" She knew, and so did I. But Rosa said, "I fell down the basement stairs last night. It was a stupid accident." She didn't look either of us in the eye as she said this, but then, she seldom did. Lizzie obviously wanted to go to her mother but stood in one spot, her arms stiff, at an angle, almost in hug position but not quite.

Rosa's brow darkened. "What are you going through my desk for? And why is she here?" Meaning me.

"My taxes. I have to get my estimated payments in the mail." She might have been a robot. No inflection whatsoever. It gave me the creeps.

Rosa didn't seem to notice. "I would have mailed them for you, Lizzie." She came to the desk to find them.

"They need my signature."

She found them and handed a thin stack of documents to Lizzie.

"You." She looked at me. "Frank told me what you did, you and your *lover*." An icky word made utterly slimy by her venom. "After all Frank's done for you, you treat him this way. He treated you like his own daughter, and look what you've done. Got him *arrested*. My God, what am I to do? They won't let him out on bail." She crumpled like a used tissue. Lizzie stood, obviously a mess of indecision. Without thinking it through, I went to Rosa and tried to put my arm around her shoulders. She jumped as though I'd bitten her. "Don't touch me! How dare you?" Her hair was up, as usual, but at least half of it was straying, floating around her head like milkweed spores. Her face was gray, thin, and flabby with exhaustion and grief.

I should have let it go, I know. But I couldn't help blurting, "I didn't get him arrested. The police have been gathering evidence for a long time now. I didn't have anything to do with it, really." Except to be connected to a cop, leading Frank to panic and try to kill him, thus making Frank's legal situation a whole lot worse.

"Frank got you your job, your house, your life, you disloyal girl. Everyone in the restaurant business cuts corners; you *have* to, to stay afloat. It doesn't hurt anyone."

I couldn't imagine that Tucker McCandless and Tommy were that bent out of shape because Frank was cooking the books a bit at Hannigan's, but I was smart enough to let this go, at least. But I couldn't leave the rest of it. "Wait. I'm sorry, Aunt Rosa, but Frank didn't get me my job *or* my house. Ivy helped me get the job at the college." That may have been the first time her name had been spoken in this house. "And I used some of my savings for the down payment. Again, Mo and Ivy told me about the house being for sale, but that's all."

Lizzie looked at me. "Daddy didn't give you the money?"

"Good heavens, no."

"Liar," Rosa hissed. She was starting to scare me. I wanted to get out of there. I said so, but Lizzie wouldn't move.

"So he lied about that, eh, Mom?"

"Your father isn't a liar. *She's* the filthy liar."

I thought, God, did they really think I was that beholden to Frank?

Lizzie looked at her mother, then said softly, "Did you know what he was doing to me? Did he tell you? Did he do it to Molly, too? You say he's not a liar. Did he lie to you about that?"

Rosa looked at her daughter with a sulfuric anger. "Of course not. He never did anything to you but be a good father. Stop it, stop it, stop it, stop it. Both of you, get out, get out, get out." She started hitting and hitting, first Lizzie, then me, thin arms harmlessly beating on us in turn, repeating get out, get out, over and over. It stung a little, but there was no bruising, no real force. In a movie it would have been good physical comedy. "Get out, get out, get out, get out" in little-old-woman tones, hissing and spitting. Her face was squeezed inward with a hostility bordering on madness. It sickened me in part because it was so familiar. I'd seen the same expression when I was a teenager, on my mother's face.

I grabbed Lizzie's hand, praying that she'd come with me. Together we fled the Big House, leaving Rosa staring at us both with hatred, mouth still working, arms twitching. I was shaking, and Lizzie was crying. She cried the whole way back to my house.

When we got there, I sat with her for a moment then said, "I'm sorry, Lizzie, I'm so sorry. Come inside. Stay here for a while." She shook her head and said, "No. Go inside. Later, I'll talk to you later."

I went to the Hepplewhites' house and collected the boys, including Josh, though without the puppy. Back at our house I made sure all the doors were locked. As I made the three of them a snack, I got one of the more disturbing phone calls of my life. It was Mo, sobbing and incoherent. At first I thought something had happened to Ivy, but then it became clear that she was upset about her dad. Not only about the attempted murder charges; Lizzie evidently had called Mo and told her she'd decided to press assault charges against him as well. Mo was beside herself and saw me, somehow, as to blame.

"You've always been jealous that we have a father, that our father took family seriously." There was a lot of talk about loyalty. I refrained from defending myself. There was no point. I thought I'd taken enough stands in the family to last a long, long time.

chapter thirty-two

Mechanically and logically it is easy to see that any system approaching perfect self-control is also approaching perfect self-frustration. Such a system is a vicious circle, and has the same logical structure as a statement which states something about itself, as for example, "I am lying," when it is implied that the statement is itself a lie. The statement circulates fatuously forever, since it is always true to the extent that it is false, and false to the extent that it is true. Expressed more concretely, I cannot throw a ball so long as I am holding on to it—so as to maintain perfect control of its movement.

ALAN WATTS, *The Way of Zen*

THAT AFTERNOON Susie brought Tommy to my house. Miraculously, he had no broken bones or serious injuries, just some bruises and a few cuts. He was pretty doped up, and Susie helped him stagger through the door.

I said, "Why is he here?"

"Don't you want him here?" she said, stumbling a bit under the weight of his arm across her shoulders. I wondered where Perfect Ben was.

"I told you, you won," I said. I could feel cold bubbles of hysteria trying to pop up past my breastbone. I breathed them back down. "Go away," I said.

"He wants to be *here*," she said, her voice quivering a bit. "He told me to bring him *here*. I'm doing what he *wants*. You can't tell me you don't want him."

I ignored her and looked into his big sad bloodshot eyes. "Do what you want," I said.

She somehow got him upstairs and put him in my bedroom. She came back down, obviously uncomfortable, which gave me a sickly satisfaction. She went out and came back in with an overnight bag.

"What's wrong with you?" she said as she left the bag by the stairs.

"I don't know," I said.

After I closed the door behind her, I heard the broomstick banging on the downspout again, so I went to see Jessie.

"My aunt Lottie says hello," I said as Jessie handed me a box of stale moon pies "for the boys." I had told her that Tommy was recovering from a car accident. I left out the juicier parts, thinking she might enjoy them later, when I could be more free with the details. I actually debated with myself for a tiny moment about talking to her freely about my life, trying to get some advice. I still don't know what prevented me: shame, embarrassment, or a simple unwillingness to impose. Whatever the barrier was, it was solid and it was oddly calming. It allowed me to tamp down my own unhappiness, even if just for a half hour or so.

I said, "Lottie was trying to remember what your mother's maiden name was. And your aunt's, of course."

"It was Tidwell."

"Oh, okay." Then, suddenly, I got it. All the concerns about my own family left me for a moment. I couldn't stop myself from blurting, "So you married your . . . aunt's husband after she died?"

I could have slapped myself, but the words hung there, suspended in the dust motes. Jessie didn't react much, just shrugged.

"He said his nephews wouldn't like him leaving me anything, but if we were married, I'd get everything when he died. He was taking care of me." I did the math silently. She would have been fifty-three. He would have been seventy-five. "After that we moved into this house. He thought people might be upset about things if we stayed where people knew us already." Her eyes narrowed. "Didn't Lottie know?"

"No, she didn't know you had married at all."

"I thought everybody knew. That's why we moved." Jessie seemed unconcerned. But then, it had been over thirty years ago. The obscene website now meant nothing to me, and just a few months earlier I had thought it would ruin my life. What parts of my past would I be worried about thirty years from now?

I threw away the moon pies as soon as I was back inside, feeling terribly guilty. I then pulled them back out of the trash, thinking I would give them to a food bank. Then I felt guilty about that, thinking should poor people get this crap? Then I thought, Who are you, girl, to decide other people's food choices, and on and on, till I drove myself crazy. I put them back in the trash and closed the lid; the phone ringing helped me stop obsessing. It was my mother. Evidently, Rosa had just called her.

"What have you done to Frank?" she yelled. "Rosa is beside herself. She says you got him arrested."

"He got himself arrested."

"By doing what?"

"Well, for starters, by trying to have Tommy shot."

"That's ridiculous. Frank didn't shoot anyone. Rosa is hysterical. Frank is fit to be tied. You have to be the center of attention, don't you, and bring everyone down with you. Rosa is furious with you. I've never heard her so angry."

"Frank hit her, you know."

Silence for a moment. "How do you know that? She certainly didn't tell you that."

"No, I saw her face. She has a black eye."

"Which she got from falling down the basement steps. You need to stop being so melodramatic, Gina, and stop causing so much trouble. You owe Frank an apology, and Rosa, too. You also owe her some money, I understand, for the rosebush Stevie helped destroy."

I sat there thinking. And thinking. Breathing and thinking.

"Gina?"

"Mom, did you talk to the Winterburns? Recently?"

There was a small silence. "No." Her voice was small, too.

"Okay. Did you contact them in some other way, maybe?" I waited.

Another pause. "Well, yes, I did write them a letter." I didn't say anything. She continued, "I assume they've contacted you by now. I told them that you should be more of a family and that you could use their help. Which is true. One of the brothers is still single, you know. It's something to think about."

"You didn't know about the boys' trust fund?"

"No! You've always been so closemouthed about that sort of thing. They have one? I thought, of course, that they might. I'm glad I was right."

"Well, sort of. They don't have it anymore."

"What did you do with it?"

"I gave it to the Winterburns."

"What?"

I told her the story, how her contacting them had technically violated the terms of our original agreement and how they had taken advantage of that. I told myself that I wouldn't be surprised if she said I should have given the boys to them and seduced the horrible Quentin, maybe let *him* get me pregnant, too, why not? But it was still an unhappy shock how furious she was.

"You gave it away? What were you *thinking*? You've always been so *stupid* with money."

"Go to hell, Mom." I hung up.

I felt like throwing up, wondering how many more people I could alienate in one day.

. . .

The constable came by that afternoon, checking on Tommy. He also had a picture, an actual mug shot, of Kenny Kelly. With my permission, he showed it to Toby, who said yeah, that was the man who needed help with the water fountain at the playground. Toby said that he hadn't looked sick then but that he looked sick in the picture. The constable said, "You're a perceptive boy. He's not doing so well right now, that's true. But don't you worry, son, we'll take good care of him." I told the constable that in all probability Frank had told Kenny to "keep an eye" on me. Frank's ideas about how to be a good uncle were, as usual, creepy.

I took care of Tommy while he was at my house, at least for the first few days. He understood something was wrong only later, when he stopped the pain meds and started being able to get up and around and was coherent for the first time since he'd been here. He was in my bed; I had been sleeping in the guest room.

"What's wrong?" he finally asked after I brought the boys back from swimming on Tuesday afternoon. The pain in his face made me want to cry so badly, the pressure actually hurt my eyes. But they stayed dry and burning.

"I don't know," I said honestly. "You can go home when you're well enough. You need to go back to the city."

"What's wrong?" he repeated.

I couldn't tell him. The pain of it was as unbearable as anything in my life had ever been. I thought I would do anything to stop this pain. I thought, go hug him, kiss him, fuck him, and you'll feel better, you'll both feel better, it will stop. But I couldn't.

My children seemed blissfully unaware of the pain and tension between the two adults in the house. But they amped up their voices, their play, their demands, their general volume, until it was all I could do not to leave the three of them in the house alone forever to fend for themselves.

Finally, on Wednesday, the boys were outside. Tommy cornered me and said, "You've got to tell me what's wrong. What the hell is going on?"

I'm crazy, that's what's going on, I thought. I blurted, realizing that this was true only as I said it, "I'm not visiting your grave, Tommy. I'm not taking my boys to visit your goddamn grave. Go home."

He was about to start yelling at me, was taking a mighty breath, nostrils flaring, face pale, when the doorbell rang. I thought, aha, finally Tim Solomon is here to kill us. Maybe that will even be a sort of relief. I still sensibly looked through the window in the door as Tommy stood in the living room, sad and miserable, his misery made larger by his physical size somehow. Through the little window I saw my mother standing on the porch, a taxi pulling away in the street behind her.

She had a small flowered suitcase at her feet and said hello pleasantly enough, picked up the bag, and walked in. Tommy looked exhausted from his efforts to try to understand what was going on. I thought anyone could see that we were having a horrible fight or discussion of some kind. My mother looked his way and said, "This must be Tommy." She smiled briefly. We just stared at her. I was too dumbstruck for even the rudiments of courtesy. She then said, "I'm going to go settle in and freshen up." Then she went upstairs.

Tommy left later that day, having used up as much sick leave as he was comfortable taking. He'd been fine since Monday, really, but had stayed anyway, taking care of the boys when I went shopping or ran other errands, straightening up, even making a few meals. Trying to get me to talk. I took him to the train station; he hadn't yet talked to his insurance company about replacing his car.

"Are we still getting married?" he finally asked, face pinched and gray.

"No," I said.

"Why not? Are you mad at me for getting shot at?"

"No."

Misery in his eyes. "Do you still love me?"

I looked at him, still incapable of lying to him. "I love you so much, it's killing me. Go home, Tommy, please."

"I love you. Don't do this."

"No" was all I could say. Maggie's right, I thought. I'm a mean, terrible heartbreaker. I deserve whatever I get. He hugged me and hugged me, and I terrified myself; I was like stone.

"So Gerald's going to have to have abdominal surgery next month. He's got a hiatal hernia. But he has insurance, so that's okay." My mother was sitting at the kitchen table while I cooked, talking very rapidly. She acted as though there was nothing strange about her coming up here and refused to talk about our last conversation or anything relevant. She was so obviously freaked out, I thought I'd let her get to the point at her own pace.

"What kind of pension will Tommy be entitled to? I mean, if he's going to quit, you should think about that. What are you going to live on? I can't believe you gave away the boys' trust fund. All that security gone, and the Winterburns couldn't possibly need it. I still don't know what you were thinking."

She paused. I said nothing, not disabusing her about anything. I thought about little warm heads in the crook of each of my arms and lullabies and promises.

"Maybe it would be best if you got out of Tenway. The Hannigans aren't going to like you being here, at least not for a while. These charges are just absurd. There's no way Frank was selling illegal weapons out of that restaurant. The whole idea is bizarre."

I sat down across from her. "Mom, why are you here?"

She looked at me as if I had started speaking in tongues. "Well, why can't I visit family when I want to?"

"You know what I mean. Do you want something? Do you want to see Rosa but don't want to stay there? What?"

"I just wanted to come up and see everyone. It looks like Rosa's going to have to sell the restaurant, which is a terrible shame, seeing that Frank's put so much into it."

I accepted that for the moment she wasn't going to tell me the truth. I'd had enough of Frank and Rosa. I decided to broach the adoption subject again. My last hope.

"I told you that Jessie Hays lives next door to me, right?"

"Oh, yes. Old Jessie."

"And she told me about Franny's baby. I don't see why she'd make something like that up. What I want to know is, what happened to the baby? Do you know? Or maybe they didn't tell you about it."

She got a frightened, pinched sort of look on her face and said, "Of course I knew about it." Her lips clamped together tighter. "All right. I guess you can know now. The baby was adopted."

"It was a girl?"

"Yes."

I waited.

"What?" she said, flustered and irritated.

"Well, by whom?" I knew my prissy grammar would irritate her further but I no longer cared.

"I don't know that you're entitled to know this, really, but I guess it can't hurt anything now. It was a very difficult time, and I'd rather forget it. But I'll tell you if you promise to then let it go and not bug me about it endlessly."

"Okay, I guess," I said, not sure if I was making a devil's bargain.

She took a deep breath. "She called me first. She had gotten pregnant and needed help, and that was about it. Your father helped arrange the adoption. One of his deputies—you remember Eddie Macomb?" I didn't, but she continued. "His brother was an attorney who knew about stuff like that."

"Who was the father? Did she ever tell you?"

"Why do you want to know this now?" The question was accompanied by a sharp look.

"Because I think that you guys kept the baby, Mom. I think it was me."

My mother stared at me for a few seconds, her eyes very slowly getting bigger and bigger. Madder and madder.

"What? You think you're *adopted*? Are you so ashamed to be our child? Is that it?"

"Oh, please, Mom," I said. "You've been angry with me for as long as I can remember. You were never that angry with Ellie." Although she sometimes was with Sylvia, I remembered uncomfortably. "You always seemed to hate me. Even now."

"Mothers don't hate their daughters!" This was said with such unmistakable venom that I started to get a little cold rock of fear in the pit of my stomach. She was getting really scary, reminding me of Rosa. But I couldn't shut up.

"You always seemed to. You don't even like my boys very much, and they're about the nicest kids in the world."

"I love my grandchildren. How dare you say I don't." She stopped and took a breath, her head pulling back as though she were preparing to breathe fire. "You've always been so goddamn *superior.*" Her eyes slitted, cracks in rock. "Your father thought you were so *special,* so much *in his image* or something. A mirror for his perfection. So much a *Paletta.*"

She was looking at me with a terrible inflating rage. I knew that look, but I had seldom seen it get this intense, this cold. Then she smiled, the tiniest whisper of a smile. Maybe not there at all.

"You might as well know, I guess. Your *sister* was Franny's baby."

Everything stopped, got a kind of weird clarity, like when you drive up a mountain too fast and your head compresses, your ears pop, and the world narrows down. There were sounds from the dining room, a computer game making *whoop, whoop* noises as Stevie shot aliens with a virtual laser cannon and Toby distantly and tunelessly sang the theme to a cartoon I recognized.

My mother almost seemed to be enjoying herself. "You were just too young to remember. You were only a toddler, after all. Any idiot can see how much you look like your father. What, did you think he had an affair with Franny or something?" Her eyes got bigger. "You did think that, didn't you? Your father would never have slept with Franny! She looked like a cow!" She even laughed, an eerie, terrifying sound. "You'll have to deal with the fact that I *am* your mother. I've had to deal with the reverse your whole life, after all. What are you complaining about, anyway? You were always your father's favorite, not to mention the old bat's."

This was true, I thought. I knew Grammy loved me. But it was no wonder I saw the icy and unforgiving Mary Glenn as a maternal figure. For me, she was more accepting than the real thing.

"You've never understood the depth of my pain, my loss," my

mother said. "And her death caused some financial hardship, too. You never understood that."

"How? Didn't insurance pay for her treatments? No one ever talked about bone marrow transplants or anything expensive like that."

My mother looked uncomfortable for a moment. "Not her illness." She seemed about to say something else, then stopped.

I couldn't imagine that the thought that popped into my head was true. "You don't mean that Franny sent you money?"

Her chin went up. "Well, she was her child, after all. It's not like she had many other expenses."

"She was a nun. How much money could she have had to send you?"

"Well, it wasn't just her. The father helped us out, too."

"Who was . . . ?"

"A priest. He was at Franny's funeral."

A thin black-robed figure sobbing in the back of the church. I remembered him. The father. It was almost black comedy, but of course, it wasn't funny at all.

"He came from a good family, lots of money. They were anxious not to have it made public."

"I'll bet they were." I turned it around in my head. "You mean you blackmailed them."

"What a terrible thing to say. Of course it wasn't anything awful like that. They were simply willing to pay us to keep her, to make sure she had a good life. There was nothing bad about it. You and your moralizing. You're just like your father."

"No, I'm not. I'm a lot nicer." I thought about Tommy. "At least I used to be. So how long after she died did they stop sending you money?"

She shifted in her seat, still expressionless. The answer was, obviously, a while. She wouldn't have told the poor man's family that his daughter was dead. It would have been easy to rationalize that the money was needed for the other girls, blah, blah, blah. Not that the other girls saw any of it.

"So did you get some money from Franny's estate? I mean, that Franny left to her? Is that what the visit to the lawyer was about?"

"Well, do you think *you* should have gotten it?"

"Of course not."

"Franny just never changed her will. I've had a difficult life. I'm entitled to some ease now. You and Sylvia are both well situated enough, and it's not like Ellie needs the money! It's not that much, but I can afford to take a cruise I've been looking at this summer."

I tried to imagine what I would do if one of the boys had a legacy from someone, some nonpsychotic Winterburn, maybe, that reverted to me because of his death. I couldn't imagine taking a cruise with it. But then, I don't like cruises.

I thought, I wonder if she ever rocked me to sleep? Then I thought, ask her. What is there to lose now?

She looked startled by the question. "Your father handled all that. I'm sorry, but the whole baby thing was too hard for me. You know how I can't miss any sleep; it's too hard to function the next day. Your father was happier with little kids than I was." She said this as though it was a character flaw. "But you girls were always so demanding."

I couldn't remember a single demand any of us had made on her other than the unstated ones for shelter, food, and clothing. We must have, though. We must have.

My mother continued, "Those were terrible times. My life was very hard when you were all young. And I lost a child. You can never know the pain of that unless you lose one, too. I've never been the same. I couldn't turn to you or Sylvia after Elena died. Especially you, in your own little world. Even if she was adopted, she was my best child."

"She was my sister, Mom. I miss Ellie, too."

"It's not the same, not the same at all."

At dinner, from somewhere a long way away, I fakely jollied the boys along as much as I could, then got them up to bed. Mom went into the living room to watch TV while I cleaned up. Tommy called. This time I picked up, not wanting to treat him like John Fagin. He asked why my mother was there. I said, "She wants money." He said, "Jesus," then "I love you." I said, "I love you, too. Good-bye."

. . .

Ellie was so mad at me about what I was doing to Tommy, she wouldn't speak to me at all.

Early the next morning, before the boys came down for breakfast, I got a cup of coffee and sat across from my mother, who was reading the sports section of the paper and drinking a cup of her own.

"Here's the deal," I said as she looked up. "You need to leave. I don't need your hostility and your obvious dislike right now."

Her brows rose, and her lips turned down. "I didn't know I was such a burden."

I paused. "If you had to—" I stopped myself. *If you had to choose between never getting any more money from me and never seeing Toby and Stevie again, which would you pick?* Stupid, pointless pain seeking. I knew the answer.

"I did some math," I said. "Altogether, I've sent you over five hundred thousand dollars from the time I was sixteen to now. I can't afford you anymore. Especially now that the boys have no trust fund to count on to pay for college. I'm sorry. I hope you saved some of the money. I always suggested you do that."

"You ungrateful little *bitch!*"

"You may be right; I don't know. Pack your things. I'm taking you to Rosa's. I love you, Mom, God help me. But you've got to get out of here right now or I'm afraid of what I'll wind up doing to you."

She came downstairs as the boys finished breakfast. She had left her suitcase at the top of the stairs for me to bring down. I took it outside and put it in the back of the car. She came out and silently got in the passenger seat. Then I drove across town.

When we got to Rosa's, I didn't go in. Before she got out of the car, I told the boys to say good-bye to their grandma. She didn't say good-bye to them. I waited to make sure someone was at the house to let her in; then the boys and I drove home.

chapter thirty-three

But the constant awareness of death shows the world to be as flowing and diaphanous as the filmy patterns of blue smoke in the air—that there really is nothing to clutch and no one to clutch it. This is depressing only so long as there remains a notion that there might be some way of fixing it, of putting it off just once more, or hoping that one has, or is, some kind of ego-soul that will survive bodily dissolution.

ALAN WATTS, *The Book*

In attachment there is pain, and in pain deliverance, so that at this point attachment itself offers no obstacle, and the liberated one is at last free to love with all his might and to suffer with all his heart. This is not because he has learned the trick of splitting himself into higher and lower selves so that he can watch himself with inward indifference, but rather because he has found the meeting-point of the limit of wisdom and the limit of foolishness. The Bodhisattva is the fool who has become wise by persisting in his folly.

ALAN WATTS, *Nature, Man and Woman*

I FINALLY TALKED to John Fagin again on the phone, consenting to an interview about Uncle Frank and Tommy's shooting. I knew I needed to prepare something but couldn't clear my head enough to do that. He showed up in a crumpled khaki suit that leached his complexion of the little color it had. I tried yet again to map his face with my eyes. But his face was just round enough, just soft enough, that you couldn't get to the bones underneath to see what its shape really was, independent of age or minor fluctuations in weight. His hair was no color, too, that cross between blond and brown in which each tone seems to negate the other rather than blend or enhance.

I wasn't able to lie or think on my feet or shape the truth into anything palatable that afternoon. He asked about Frank; I told him he was probably a criminal. He asked how the family was taking it; I answered that it seemed to be tearing the Hannigans apart. He asked about Tommy. I said he was recovering, which, as far as I knew, he was. Then he asked where Tommy was. I said I assumed he was in the city. He cocked his shapeless head and said, "Are you still seeing him?"

"No," I said. Oh, shit, I thought, here it comes. "No," I said again. No overly polite stalling this time. I declined preemptively.

He said, "Oh, think about it. You know I'm persistent!"

"Why me?" I said at last, though with only muted curiosity. "You don't know me at all, really. Why do you want to go out with me so much? I haven't even been all that civil a lot of the time."

He looked perplexed. "Well, I don't know. I guess I think you're the most attractive woman I've met in a long time. In fact, I think you're beautiful."

"Thank you," I said. "So what?"

His perplexity deepened. He plainly had no idea what to say. I decided on even more honesty. "Well, what's in it for me? What do you offer?"

His brow knitted even further. "Well, a relationship, I guess. I don't know."

"And that's good for me how?"

He stared at me as though I'd grown antennae and started levitating. He opened his mouth, closed it, opened it again. "Well, don't you want a . . . boyfriend or whatever?"

I cocked my head back at him. After a moment I said, "I honestly don't know." I thought some more. "I also really don't know what you think you'll get out of dating me. You can't just want to look at me all the time. You must have some other idea of what you want in your life."

He closed his notebook and said, "Every man deserves a woman like you. I truly believe that."

I considered this. Now we were somewhere, I thought. I said after a moment, "A woman like what?"

"Incredibly hot," he said, smiling now. It was the greatest compliment he knew, after all. The big guns. I thought about his wife, wondered if she was still "hot," or if she had done the unforgivable and aged. But all I said was "But then, what is a woman like me entitled to? Or a woman not like me, for that matter." I was genuinely curious about his answer.

He was getting more and more uncomfortable, his eyes no longer meeting mine. I wanted to say, I'm really not trying to be nasty. I really want to know. Explain this to me.

"A nice guy. To be treated well."

"So you're entitled to someone 'incredibly hot.' I'm entitled to someone nice. Are you entitled to niceness, too, or just hotness? And what about the reverse? For me, I mean. Or for a woman you don't think is hot. What is she entitled to?"

He actually got angry then. I had been wondering where the threshold was. I'd finally crossed it. He said something about "you women saying you want one thing but really wanting another." I had no memory of ever telling him anything about what I wanted, but it finally got him to go. He never called me again.

That night I had another dream, the last of the biggies, as I was to come to think of them later. It was the only one of them that was also part memory. I was in a gray-blue room, small, with two narrow beds six inches apart. The light was gray as well, weak sun through pale sheer curtains stained with swirls of old tobacco smoke. I was standing, holding a small, sweaty hand. The hand's owner was on one of the beds, but I was facing the window, not looking at her at all. I could hear her, though, and she said in a light voice, "G., I'm really scared. I don't want to die. What do you think happens, what do you think happens, what do you think happens?" I didn't answer, just stood there gazing at the glaring window with the ugly stained curtain. In real life my parents weren't religious. There was no comfort to be had in an expectation of mythical journeys to the light. I remember my father once, very drunk, telling my sister Sylvia and me that we were all just grease spots on a minute ball of dust. I'm pretty sure my dying sister heard him through the wall, two thin sheets of cheap drywall. In my dream I didn't answer Ellie as she asked me, "Do you think I'll just have to lie in the dark forever, G.?" In real life I had lied to my baby sister, "You won't die, you're not dying," as she stared up at me, eyes wide and dark, pupils dilated with fear.

The next evening Ivy showed up at my house. I'd never seen her in that emotional a state, stone cold sober. Mo, said Ivy, was moving out of the big Victorian on Circuit Lane. "She thinks her goddamn father pees perfume. She thinks everybody's lying, and if I don't *sieg heil* and say he's a goddamn *prince,* then I'm not being *loyal,* I don't love her, I'm siding with you, and that's a really terrible thing."

She was sitting at my kitchen table, crying. I'd sent the boys upstairs to watch a video in my bedroom. I asked her about Molly; Ivy said that she already had moved back to the Big House on Acton; Mo was following suit. Ivy, however, was getting custody of Frodo. That was not a difficult decision; Aunt Rosa hates dogs. They destroy rosebushes even more reliably than children do.

I tried to call Mo, but she wouldn't talk to me. I felt a tearing inside, a pain slowly growing larger and larger. Mo, I thought, Mo, what will I do without you? I would have done anything she asked me then, recanted anything, but it was too late; I had no power to affect anything about the Hannigans now. If I hadn't been talking to Lizzie regularly, I wouldn't even have known that Maggie had had her baby the night before, a healthy girl, seven pounds, six ounces.

. . .

The morning after Ivy's tearful visit I got a call from Yvonne Corbin. She wondered if she and her husband could take Toby and Stevie with them to Lavaland that day. Derek was beside himself that there were two boys his age in the neighborhood to play with, and his parents were eager to cement the bond among the three of them. I understood that desire, and so an hour later I was driving them the brief distance, yammering incessant instructions to mind Mr. and Mrs. Corbin, to use the money I was giving them to pay for their food and treats and rides. They bore it pretty well and left me without a whimper.

As soon as I knew I was to have a child-free day, I called Jeri to see if she could squeeze me in. That was in fact the reason I was driving; I needed to bolt over there immediately to be able to make it in time for the one slot she had open that day.

"I don't know what's wrong with me."

She was unusually silent, then said, "I have a theory. Want to hear it?"

"I guess."

"You think Tommy is a good guy? The problem isn't like Awful Bragging Man or even Scott, right? He's not a jerk or a liar or whatever?"

"No," I said, feeling sick. "He's a wonderful person. I love him."

"No doubt about it?"

"None."

"He's someone you can count on, right?"

I thought. "Yes," I said, feeling worse and worse, more and more twisted and lousy.

"Well, how are you supposed to know how to deal with someone like that?"

"What?"

"You've never had a man in your life you could count on, as far as I can tell. Nor many women, for that matter. They take some getting used to."

I sat with that for a moment. Then she said, "You've always been proud of the fact that you never gave in to anorexia and all that stuff from your former profession, although I think you're aware that that's partly just good luck, that you didn't need to. But you must realize that it's peculiar, someone like you not having even a serious crush on anyone for so long, after Riley, anyway, right? I think you've been experiencing something like anorexia all along. Instead of a disordered relationship with food, you've got a disordered relationship with love."

I swear, as unlikely as it sounds, I had not seen this till that moment. Jeri continued, "It's all about control. But you know, you don't have any, really. No one does."

I could feel the stone starting to melt, but it was so hot, I thought for sure the heat of it would kill me, burn me to ash. Jeri said, "Now we can finally get in there and do something."

As I left Jeri's office that afternoon, I saw Heather Mason sitting in the waiting room. She'd replaced her purple tights with jeans and looked ten years older than she had a few months earlier. I hadn't seen her in class since Tim Solomon had been arrested. I told her that she could come talk to me anytime she wanted. I knew something about fucking up your life. Her cotton T-shirt had a wide, fashionably torn collar; I noticed she had a mole on her left shoulder. Oh God, I thought. She's me.

I got out of the car on autopilot, went into the house, locked the door behind me: all the precautions I'd been taking since I left home, since I moved to New York, since I became a single mom, since I lived in places where people were looking to hurt you all the time, take your stuff, kill your cats. You locked things. I was used to that now. I just wanted to sit, either to think or to meditate, to try not to think. Either one. The house was quiet, and I thought, Please, God, let Jessie leave the downspout alone just for today, let me be, let me think.

So the knock on the door irritated me but didn't worry me much. I opened the door, intending to try to blow off whoever it was: John Fagin, Jessie, the mailman, Maggie, somebody, and I swear, the last person I expected was Tim Solomon.

. . .

Before I even registered anything but an awful gooey feeling in my stomach, he was in the house and had closed the door behind him, pressing in the thumb latch as he did so.

"Dr. P.," he said, then, "I mean, Gina. Can I call you Gina now? Really, I'd like to. I mean, you're not my professor anymore, so I can call you by your first name now, right?"

"Get the hell out of my house!" I was just mad now, just mad, just a seeing-red kind of mad. "Get out! I don't want you in my house. You have to get out now."

He looked genuinely hurt. "Look, Gina, come on, we need to talk. I just want to talk to you." He was an inch or two shorter than me but so thick, so muscley. Stubby and strutting and ridiculous, I thought.

"Get out," I said, feeling my jaws grind together.

"No," he said, pulling a small silver handgun out of his pocket.

Oh God, I thought. Guns. Again. "Where do you get all these guns?"

"This is America, the greatest fucking country on earth. It's freedom, you know. My dad practically *owns* the fucking NRA!" he said with great filial pride. It figures, I thought. He went on. "Look, Gina, you just have to listen to me. I don't want to hurt you. But you've got to listen, you've got to give me a chance. I know your kids aren't here, so we don't have to deal with them. I waited till they were gone. You don't understand. I love you so much. You need to think about this, because you don't understand how great it would be, how much I could do for you, how much we could do for each other. I mean"— he smiled an almost charming smile—"girls really like me, Gina. You've only really seen the student me. Wait till you see the charming me. I'm a great guy."

I remembered how I'd been talked to a lot recently, how you were supposed to calm crazies. So I thought, Be calm. To what end? I had no idea.

"So," I said, having no idea how to proceed. "What is it you have in mind?" We were standing in the hallway, his gun in his right hand, pointed loosely at my feet.

He brightened. "We have a house. It's really nice, in the mountains. I've got my own key, and I've got a Lexus full of gas outside. I've got some other stuff, too." He thought for a minute. "I got some clothes for you." Oh my God. "Nice stuff. Some of it's my mom's; some of it I bought."

Before the full horror of this could sink in, we both jumped when I heard a familiar banging sound. "What the hell's that?" Tim yelled.

"My elderly neighbor," I blurted. I kept thinking, don't get her involved, he's got a gun, you're putting her in danger. But I couldn't come up with a lie, I couldn't think, my head wasn't working at all. The banging started again. "What the hell is he doing?"

"It's a she." Shut up, shut up, I kept thinking uselessly. "She's banging on the downspout. She wants to talk to me. She'll keep banging until she sees me. She knows I'm home. My car's in the driveway."

Neither of us, I suspected, knew what to do. Tim grabbed my arm finally and said, "Well, let's go see her. But we better not tell her where we're gonna go. I think we should keep it a secret. For now."

He opened the door and pushed me in front of him, putting the gun theatrically in his pocket, keeping his hand in with it. I got the idea and walked out onto the porch. Jessie was standing on hers in her faded pansy housecoat. I looked at her but couldn't figure out what to say or how to act.

She saw Tim and said, "Who's that? Where's the big fella? I need to get my big chair moved. I wanted to know if he was around and could do it for me."

Tim said with a false hearty grin, "I'm the big fella now. Haha."

Jessie didn't crack a smile, just looked at him and said, "Wait a minute, you're that guy. That boy."

For the first time in this bizarre series of events I started to feel real fear. I thought, Yes, recognize who he is but shut the fuck up, Jessie. Just go call the cops. Before Jessie could blurt any more unfortunate observations to Tim, he said, sharp and hard, "Where the fuck did you get that?" It took me a second to realize that he was looking.

at the necklace. I hadn't thought about this, and now I thought, Oh, no, oh, shit.

"Watch your mouth, young fella," Jessie said, then reached up and grabbed the heart dangling at her throat with an anxious hand.

I interrupted. "Later, Jessie. We can't help you now." I looked bug-eyed at her, hoping she would get my psychic message: Call the cops, call the cops. Right now. Go inside and lock your doors. And call.

Tim was only inches behind me, and I could sense his whole body harden with anger and whatever other stress was operating in him. I half turned, not wanting to face him directly at that tiny distance, fearing our bodies would touch. I said, "Let's go inside. I'll make some food for the road."

He looked at me then and said, "How the fuck did she get that?" His eyes looked suddenly remarkably like his mother's.

I said, "We'd be better off talking about this inside, I think," having a terrible fear that he was going to start shooting at Jessie, and maybe at me as well, and from this close to both of us he was unlikely to miss even if he was a lousy shot. I had no idea how good a shot he was, but he had hit Tommy right in the back from a long way away at night. Good enough.

I yelled to Jessie, "I'll talk to you later. See you later. Go inside now, Jessie. Later, okay?" as she didn't seem to be moving at first. Then she turned and quickly disappeared through her door.

"She better not call anyone," Tim said.

"She doesn't have a phone," I lied.

Back inside, door locked, Tim said tightly, "How the fuck did she get it? I spent a goddamn fortune on that necklace. I got it for you. For you. But you would never wear the goddamn thing. I kept waiting to see it on you, and then I thought I'd tell you who got it for you, that I got it and how I felt about you. I mean, Christ, it was expensive. I got the nicest thing I could find, something that really said it all, you know what I mean? Then I see it on the scrawny chicken neck on that old bitch next door, and I'm thinking, how in the hell did she get it from you? Did she steal it? Is she some kind of thief? I'll go over there right now and get it back, and I swear I'll fucking kill her if she doesn't hand it over right now."

I thought, Calm him; you've got to calm him down. I interrupted, "Tim, Tim, no, she didn't steal anything. You've got to remember, I didn't know who it was from. I thought it was a mistake, and she really likes green. That's all. It was a misunderstanding. I'll go over there in a little while, and I'll ask her for it back. It'll be fine. It's okay. I understand now."

"I'm going over there right this minute and get it from the old bitch."

"Wait, wait, Tim," I said, my voice low and steady. "Let's wait. We can do that on the way out, right? I'll make some sandwiches. You know, for the trip."

He followed me as I walked slowly on shaky legs into the kitchen. I opened the refrigerator and started pulling out bread and lettuce and peanut butter, all the bizarre kid sandwich ingredients I had. Nothing normal, no jelly for the peanut butter, no meat to go with the lettuce, no mustard, nothing worthwhile. I couldn't see, was frustrated by the lack of light when the door opened. Who cares, I thought, just pretend. Make shit sandwiches, who cares, just do something, calm him down, stall for time, pray that Jessie is calling the constable right now. Please, please, please.

He stood in the middle of the room, looking loosely at me. He said, the gun out of his pocket now, hanging in his hand, "I'm the big fella now. Haha. I like that."

I couldn't fake any affect at that. I just kept ripping out chunks of lettuce, putting bits of pickles and hard-boiled egg on pieces of bread. I kept looking in the refrigerator for more things, more portable food, food that would take time to assemble. I found grapes. Good, everyone knows you have to wash grapes. I got them out, found a colander, saw the huge magnum of Tiger Lily champagne on the counter next to the fridge, and thought, Great, Tim and I can take it with us to celebrate. Fitting. He was saying that we were going to the Berkshires, that his family had a house there, but we wouldn't stay there because we wouldn't have a lot of privacy. Too many people knew about the house. But they had neighbors.

"There's a big family with this huge mansion next door, way bigger even than our cabin, which isn't bad. But this house, man, you wouldn't believe that tiled Jacuzzi and the indoor pool and shit. They have a bathroom that's the size of your whole ground floor."

I said, mostly to slow things down, "Somebody else lives there?"

"Well, no. Well, yes, but they're gone. Back to Iran. That's where they're from. Fucking Arabs. Towelheads had to go back to Iran, so afraid that they might get stuff thrown at them." He laughed. "Like bombs. Or dead rats. Or bullets."

Before I even knew I was talking, I said, "If they're Iranian, they're Persians, not Arabs." God, I hated myself sometimes. Don't make him mad, don't make him feel stupid. It doesn't matter if you think he is. Shut up, shut up.

"What the fuck difference does it make? I know how to get in; that's the important thing. I know the place well. It's a fucking mansion. They have tons of food, too. We'll never have to leave. They've got a kind of a closet sort of room with all kinds of food in it."

"A pantry." Shut up, shut up, shut up.

"Whatever. And a big freezer, a really big one you can walk into, that's full of stuff." He stopped for a minute, looking at the wall next to me, as though he'd thought of something. He opened his mouth, closed it, then smiled in a queasy sort of way. He thought something was funny, but not really. His gaze came back to me, and I quickly went back to making the shit sandwiches.

"Anyway, we'll have the run of the place. No stupid shithead Tommy Galloway or his stupid shithead fucking friends. I've taken care of him, in case you think he's coming back here; he's taken care of."

"What does that mean? How are you taking care of him?" I had remade the same peanut butter and olive sandwich twice now.

"Jason's dealing with it."

"How?" My sluggish brain, sluggish legs and mouth and hands were starting to wake up at this. "How?" I repeated.

"How do you think?" He laughed again. "Second time's a charm."

"Now? You mean today? In Manhattan? Jason's going to shoot him?" I was trying not to react at this, having some sense left that you didn't get them riled, the crazy people who liked hurting other people. I tried to keep my quivering voice even, low, steady. I sounded like I was fifty years older than I actually was. I sounded like Jessie.

"What do you think I mean? You got any beer?"

And suddenly, there it was, my brain kicking in and working for maybe the first time in a long, long while. I said, "Sure, it's on the bottom shelf of the refrigerator. You get it. I've got my hands full of lettuce."

And Tim, no great thinker himself, opened the refrigerator door and leaned down to find the nonexistent beer as I, with completely lettuce-free hands, grabbed the magnum of Tiger Lily champagne by its neck and, with a strength born of absolute terror for Tommy Galloway, heaved it up as high as I could backhand it and let it come down full speed at his shiny golden head.

It hit him at the base of the skull. It didn't make much of a sound, more of a *thunk* than anything else. Tim, however, grunted loudly, then said "Shit!" and flattened onto the floor, falling face-first. I managed to keep hold of the champagne bottle as it finished its arc; I kept it, pulling it away in case I needed to swing it again, even though I had certainly wrenched something loose in my shoulder. I thought with no emotion whatsoever, I bet it's my rotator cuff. Tim lay on the floor, still conscious but making a sort of "aaaaaaaagh" kind of noise and making slow and small movements. I stepped on his wrist, putting all my weight on it, which increased the volume of his yelling, and with my magnum-free hand grabbed the gun, pulled it away, and put it carefully on the counter as he tried to get up on all fours, tried to use his other hand to gain some purchase. I hopped back out of his immediate reach, thinking that I might have to kill him with either the gun or the champagne and that to do either would be too nightmarish; I imagined having to clean blood and brains and hair off my kitchen floor before the boys got back, and I'd have to live with having killed someone, even a piece of vomit like Tim Solomon, and all at once I thought, Oh Christ, what if I get another visit from his horrifying mother? He moaned a little bit more and tried to roll over, a flipped turtle in reverse, unable to push himself over to his back, going "Uuuuh, uuuuh, shit, uuuuh."

Still holding the horrendously heavy bottle by its neck, I said, feeling more powerful than I'd felt in a long time, "You boys killed my fucking cat. What, you think I'm going to want to love you forever? You know what I call you and Jason in my head? The few times I do think of you, I mean? Hitler Youth and Klan Boy. These are not compliments, idiot." He was still groaning, trying to get up. I chanced a quick step over to him and kicked him in the ribs, hard. He grunted again and went down. Then I turned around and threw up in the sink. I raised my head and saw Jed Paley looking through my kitchen window from the back deck, with the constable's thin tense face over his shoulder. I glanced at Tim, wiggling slowly on the floor like a gigantic blond slug, and heaved the leaden bottle up to the counter by the sink. Then I went to unlock the back door after tearing off a paper towel to wipe my mouth.

As soon as they were in the room and grabbing Tim, sacklike and leaking, I started hiccupping and couldn't stop for a long time. I tried to tell the constable about the threat to Tommy and eventually was coherent enough that he understood what I was saying. He called someone on his cell phone; I don't know who.

Hours later, who knows how long, the police were mostly gone. An ambulance had carted Tim away; the paramedics said he had a bad concussion, maybe a skull fracture, and possibly a broken wrist. They said he was lucky I hadn't broken his neck. He would live; he would walk again someday. I hadn't murdered him. It finally hit me that that was ultimately a good thing. Although, when I thought about it, Anita Solomon might not agree. I thought she meant what she had said.

A paramedic who looked seventeen checked me out as well; he diagnosed shock and a sprained muscle in my upper arm. Nothing that a blanket and an ice pack wouldn't fix.

The constable had questioned me and then had gone to talk to Jessie as well. As soon as he was done and said it was okay, I went over to see her. Her eyes were filmy with exhaustion. She looked yellow and terrible, holding the green heart with her right hand, warming the jade. I told her she'd saved my life, which might even have been true. She just looked at me, and I wondered suddenly if right then she knew who I was. All she would have was canned chicken noodle soup; I warmed some up in one of her dented saucepans and sat with her while she slowly slurped it through pale lips. Then I helped her upstairs to her dark, rickety bed. She lay down on it without changing, although I helped her get her shapeless loafers off. She closed her eyes, then said, "You're not like Maria, not at all like her." I patted her hard, chilly hands and left.

The constable made me call someone. I couldn't get hold of Donna or Bobbie and didn't want to tell Lottie all that was going on without her daughters around her, so on an impulse I called my boss, Kay Reynolds, who came immediately and brought Ida and Cindy with her. Vincent was out of town or, they said, he'd have been there as well. I started trying to cook for all of them, but Ida pushed me down onto the sofa and started making a salad out of all that lettuce. The Corbins then came back with the boys and wondered at the crowd. I explained what was going on, staying out of earshot of the three boys, and they offered their help. I thanked them and said I might take them up on it later, but for now I was in good hands. Kay sat with the twins while they showed her all their coolest toys and computer games, and it suddenly struck me that she missed her own children. I thought, I must remember this and share the boys with her as much as she'd like. The constable left, saying he'd call me whenever there was news about what was going on in Manhattan.

Eventually, Donna, Bobbie, Clark, and Lottie showed up as well, and my little house was swollen with help. I called Tommy's apartment and got his machine. I didn't leave a message, as I had no idea what to say. I called his cell phone, but it appeared to be switched off. I thought about calling the precinct but was afraid to expose both him and myself that way, so I didn't. I just waited with a rapidly beating heart for the constable to let me know if they'd caught Jason Dettwiler before he killed Tommy.

There was a lull during which Kay was drawing with the boys on the back deck, Lottie and Ida were chatting and heating up some soup in the kitchen, and Clark was watching some sort of sporting event on the television. My social worlds in collision. Clark then gave Lottie a ride home; after they left, I sat in the dining room with Donna and Bobbie and told them about Aunt Franny and Ellie's adoption. I was going to give them the big picture and spare them the grisly minutiae regarding my mother (and probably my father as well) and their blackmailing of the hapless priest. But being a blurter, eventually I told them everything. They were both gratifyingly stunned and thoroughly enthralled.

The evening wound down, and I still hadn't heard anything about Tommy. Kay and Ida and Cindy finally left when Clark came back; Donna assured the three women that she'd stay with me. Bobbie and Clark took the boys up to bed, saying that they needed the practice. Donna had just asked me to show her how to make a martini when there was a knock on the door. The teenage boy I'd seen on Jessie's porch those few times stood there, breathing hard through his mouth.

"Do you have a phone? The one in my grandma's house doesn't work. We think she might be dead."

The next morning Donna and I sat talking over breakfast. I said, "There have been so many ambulances and police cars here over the past few months. Every time, I always made sure I went next door to tell Jessie what was going on so that she wouldn't feel left out or scared. This time she was part of the excitement herself."

Donna let me cry for a while, then said, "It was really lucky the phone company didn't shut off her service until after she called the police. She must not have paid her bill for at least a couple of months." I thought she didn't bother to pay it because she knew she wasn't going to be around much longer.

Donna told me that Bobbie and Clark had gotten engaged the evening before. That didn't surprise me, although I felt bad that their big night had been colored by my weird life. Donna said that since the boys and I were okay, the whole evening was actually kind of exciting. She told me about Clark and Bobbie with a gentle envy that I understood; I thought then of Jed Paley. I was going to find out if he was single. He seemed healthy and kind, as far as I could tell, and was nice-looking. He and Donna both worked difficult, low-paying jobs with ridiculous hours. If nothing else, they had that in common.

Donna said, "So where was Tim going to take you, exactly? I mean, how dangerous was it? Would anyone have known where to look for the two of you?"

"I don't know," I said. I tried to remember, then said, "He was going to take me to some house in the Berkshires. His Persian neighbors." I thought about his face when he mentioned the walk-in freezer.

Donna made me go upstairs to shower and change into real clothes while she cleaned up the kitchen and prepared the boys to go outside to ride their bikes. I had just finished in the bathroom and was in my robe, ready to get dressed, when the phone rang. I let the machine get it in case it was John Fagin. It turned out to be McCandless, so I picked up.

"Where's Tommy? Is he okay?"

"He's fine. Although his partner isn't so good."

"What? Russell? Or Dan? Oh my God, Hazel."

Tommy and Dan had gotten the constable's message. It wasn't hard for plainclothesmen to spot Jason's car parked near the station house, with Jason waiting patiently inside. Tommy and Dan were part of the group that got him out of the car. They had on vests as a precaution, but Jason went berserk and managed to get one shot off before he was pounded to the pavement. It hit Dan Lowery in the leg. "He'll be all right. Getting shot is never a small thing. But it got him in the meaty part of the thigh, painful but not fatal. He'll heal up okay."

I found out which hospital Dan Lowery was in and then remembered what I wanted to tell the constable, something about Tim's face when he mentioned his neighbor's freezer.

There was still no answer either at Tommy's apartment or on his cell phone. Donna needed to go to work that day, so I called Ivy. She was so worried about losing contact with my boys, she offered to keep them overnight with Trevor while I tried to clean up my own mess in the city. I thought, This time I'm promising. No more running. If he takes me back. If, if, if.

It was midafternoon by the time I got to the hospital and asked for Dan's room number. The front desk staff looked askance at me; I told them to call his room first, get permission. They did, and I was allowed to know where to go, was allowed in past the guard at the door. I wasn't sure who they were worried about, then remembered that Tim's father was at least "part owner of the NRA." Jason's father might be equally crazy, mean, and gun-happy.

The first thing I noticed when I went in was that Tommy wasn't there. But I swear I could smell him, could tell by some lingering aura that he'd been there, maybe only moments before. Hazel Lowery was sitting next to the bed, holding Dan's hand, while Dan gazed at her, smiling, looking a little gray, perhaps, a little dry-lipped, but otherwise alive and conscious, even bright-eyed.

"Hey, can I come in for just a minute?" I asked softly, afraid that they might freeze up at the sight of me, afraid that they might be angry at me. Instead, both faces lit up gently. "Gina!" Hazel said, with what looked like actual pleasure. "It was so sweet of you to come." She stood up in greeting, then started crying, and I hugged her then, and I kept saying, "Oh, honey, I'm so sorry, but he's going to be all right, they told me so. Look, you'll get to have him home all to yourself for a while. You might be able to get something good out of all this mess." Dan looked at us both with vague, helpless confusion.

Hazel pulled away slightly then, sniffing. "It's hormones. I'm pregnant, Gina."

I said all the things you say, the hearty congratulations, what wonderful parents you'll both make, how beautiful your baby will be, and so on. I believed all of it, which helped. I let them talk about it for a while, understanding that the recent combination of events for them was incredibly potent and absolutely terrifying.

After they wound down, I asked if either of them needed anything, needed any errands run, and so on. They told me they were fine, then Hazel said, still sniffing a little, "You know, I should have said, you just missed Tommy. I think he was going back to the station."

At the precinct, again there was way too much interest in my presence. But the desk sergeant said that Tommy wasn't there, that he was pretty sure Detective Galloway had gone home.

I knew that by not calling first I was being stupid. But I wanted to see his honest reaction to me, not one he'd prepare to spare my feelings. If I found him out with or, worse, in with someone else, I'd certainly earned it. Standing on his front stoop, I thought, I have no right to do this. I'm entitled to nothing. He should be done with me.

No one answered the buzzer. I used the keys he'd given me, first on the front door and then to get into his apartment when there was no response to my trembling knock. The place was the same, a little messier: more dirty dishes in the sink, more books and papers strewn around, a few full ashtrays in strategic positions. A window air conditioner started up suddenly, obviously on some energy-saver setting; it caused me to practically jump through the ceiling. I didn't know what to do with myself, my stomach was so tight, my breath so thready. I decided to wash his dishes. That wasn't a great choice; my hands were shaking, and a glass slipped from my hot, soapy fingers. I juggled it gracelessly for a few seconds before it dropped to the gray and yellow tiles, shattering, of course, into countless shards. I yelled "Fuck!" as loud as I could, then remembered I was in an apartment; I might be heard. I had to search till I found a broom and dustpan, terrified all the while that Tommy would enter his apartment to find me riffling through his closets. Given how oddly I'd been acting, he might think I was out to rob him. "That'll teach him to give people like me a key," I said aloud, softly and a little creepily.

I got the glass cleaned up, put the broom and dustpan away, and finished the dishes. I walked around some more, wondering what else to do. I had both book and notebook in my bag but couldn't imagine sitting still long enough to accomplish anything with either of them. I checked the bathroom: no tampons or birth control pills. I wandered into the bedroom. His bed was unmade, and worn clothes were heaped in small untidy piles around the bed. I sniffed the sheets—glad I had no audience—both to see if they could use changing and to see if I could smell any womany scent. Nothing, just musky maleness. Relieved, I yanked up the covers and walked back and forth around the bed, straightening and pulling.

I didn't hear the front door open, but I heard something, I don't know what, a soft footfall, a breath, the rustle of clothing. My heart swelled and jerked as I took a quick hitching breath and turned toward the half-open bedroom door. He was suddenly in it, larger than I expected. He didn't look surprised; no doubt he'd seen my bag dumped on the sofa. "Gina," he said, in an expressionless voice, then took two quick long steps and crushed me to his chest. He said into my hair, somewhere between my ear and my neck, "Are you back? Are we back?" Yes, yes, I said, yes, and I'm so, so sorry.

Much later, as we sat enmeshed on his bed, Tommy told me he'd never expected our separation to be permanent. He knew I'd come around sooner or later. When I asked him why, he said, "I'd seen it in your face, even before we got together. You need me. But I knew you'd kill yourself before you asked me for anything." I made some sound, which he ignored. He put his face in my hair again, squeezed a little tighter. "I knew you'd come back, G. We went just a little too fast for you, I think. I was ready before we met. You just had to catch up."

We talked for a long time. He said he was taking a leave of absence, maybe permanent; he didn't yet know. But he'd found he liked the academic aspect of police work. He was thinking more about teaching.

"It took me a long time to come here; to say yes, this is what I want. Who I want. I'm not changing my mind. You're stuck with me, so you might as well face it. You have to decide for sure now. Do you want this?"

"Yes."

"You can run all you want; I'm not leaving. But I'd rather you didn't. I really hate it. Are you done running now?"

"Yes," I said.

"You know, you didn't promise me before. You squirreled out of it," he said.

"I know."

"Can you promise now?"

"I promise, Tommy. I promise."

This was followed by an interlude of tears and skin and heat and a painful sort of bonding that felt so deep, so visceral, that I knew that some fundamental chunk of me was somehow different than it had been only a few hours before. I had melted into someone who was, if not more normal, at least more complete. We didn't, couldn't, talk much for a while.

After an hour or so Tommy said, "Ask me for something. I want you to tell me at least one thing that you want from me."

I finally said, qualifying it all over the place with "you don't have to"s and "either way it's fine"s, "I want you to come live with us when you don't have to go into the city every day. You could use the guest room as a study if you want. I always use the dining-room table, anyway. We could share the cooking." I started to backpedal, to excuse him from this again, but he just said, "Sure. My insurance will pay for a rental car. We'll drive back tomorrow, okay? It's a holiday weekend, anyway, a long one. I'll bring some stuff." I'd forgotten it was nearing the Fourth of July. I was quiet. Something relaxed in my chest, and it was settled.

He later berated me for letting myself get way too close to a dangerous psychotic pervert yet again. I let him yell at me; I figured he was entitled. When he wound down, he paused and then said, "Jesus, G., a magnum of *champagne*?"

"Cheap champagne. Really, really cheap."

"Do we need to drink it for symbolism or something?"

"Karmically, we should. I mean, Jessie gave it to me. She saved my life with it, maybe, and by calling the cops. But I really, really don't want to."

"Let's put it in orange juice, drink it that way. Toast old Jessie."

"That's a good idea. You really are a smart guy, T."

. . .

It turned out that Bradley Franco's body was found wrapped in a tarp in the walk-in freezer of the Rashti house in the Berkshires, next door to the Solomons' well-appointed vacation cabin. The body had been stashed under about twenty frozen chickens. The police had been interested in the neighbors' house before but had had no legal justification for getting a search warrant, and the owners could not be reached to grant permission for a search. What I told the constable was enough to get a warrant, and voilà, there was poor Bradley. Tim wasn't talking, having a smart attorney for a father, but Jason had apparently gushed information.

Our first night back at my house, Tommy had a long chat with the constable on the phone while I put the boys to bed. Later he filled me in. "I hope you're not too upset, but Bradley apparently wasn't interested in you much at all."

"Well, thank goodness for small favors."

"But unfortunately, that's probably what got him killed." Tommy could see by my face that this was the wrong thing to say. "It wasn't your fault, G. There wasn't anything you could have done to keep him alive."

"But I don't understand. Why did they kill him?"

"He thought they were too weird. He just wanted money. From selling heroin on campus and from selling pictures. He took the grainy ones, the ones through windows."

"Who was he selling them to?"

"To your old friend Renouart. Or, rather, Renouart was paying him to take them."

"Oh my God."

"Yep. Amoral cretin that he was, Bradley still wasn't into the whole obsession thing and tried to disconnect from them. They were his frat brothers; they knew he was a blabbermouth."

"Oh my God," I repeated.

"But like the other two, he was no criminal mastermind. It didn't take much for Tim, and Jason, too, but mostly Tim, to lure him up to the Solomons' country house. They went up there a lot to get stoned. They liked breaking into the Rashtis' to use the Jacuzzi."

"Oh my God."

Tommy said he was pretty sure that even Claire Stanley couldn't mess up the case against Tim and Jason for attempted kidnapping, the murder of Bradley Franco, and the attempted murder of yet another New York police officer. I hoped he was right.

It was my third funeral that year. I hoped that the belief that things happen in synchronistic packages of three was true and that I was done for a good long while. I also wondered if on my karmic path the fact that Jessie was eighty-six when she died, just like Grammy, was significant in any way. One must, of course, be careful when assigning personal significance to the major life events of others. Or death events. Jessie wasn't in a position to care, probably, but most people understandably resent it when you decide that the point of *their* lives is to enhance *you* or to teach *you* some lesson.

The man I'd seen at her house was at the funeral home, eyes red and swollen. His name was Casey Willis. The sixteen-year-old boy was his son, Jordan.

The memorial service was sparsely attended. Few people came besides the two Willis men. Tommy had offered to come with me, but he had planned to go back to the city to get the paperwork for his leave started as well as to help Hazel get Dan home from the hospital; I told him to go ahead. I was going to bring the boys to the funeral, but Yvonne Corbin offered to have them come play with Derek at her house for a few hours that day, so I decided to leave them out of it. Jessie, after all, hadn't been that fond of children. Aunt Lottie surprised me by calling and saying that she wanted to go as well. I offered to drive her, as for once neither daughter was at her disposal. I was happy to step into the role of daughter for a day.

After the brief service I spoke to a small, tidy woman named Geraldine Ponder, a friend from the craft club at the senior center. She looked lost, sad, perplexed. I hoped she had more people in her life than her craft partner. I then managed to have a long chat with Casey Willis. Charles was his father. He had been a firefighter and had died on the job. Casey said he still owned the family farm, which was being rented to a writer who liked privacy, although it was nowhere near as isolated as it had been when Charles Willis had wanted to marry Jessie Hays.

"Dad married kind of late. After he died, my mother went into a bad depression, and she never really recovered. She died herself not too many years later. I was an only child, pretty lonely, and didn't have many other family connections. My father kept everything, and my mother didn't throw anything of his out after he died. So when I was going through all their things, I found a bunch of letters. After my partner and I adopted our son, I started pining for family, you know?" I said I did. "So I looked her up. I don't know why, exactly. An old white lady, what the hell was she gonna be to me? Or my son? But I did it, anyway, figured I'd give her back her letters, figured maybe she'd want them. It turned out she still had my dad's letters to her. She let me have them, which was pretty nice of her, if you think about it. So we got to talking, and she wanted to know about my life, and next thing you know, Jordan's calling her 'Grandma.' My mother wouldn't have been too happy about all this, but she wasn't that happy about much. And my daddy would have been pretty glad, I think."

He thanked me for keeping her company over the last few months. It had been a particularly miserable winter, and he'd been unable to get down to see her as much as he'd have liked. I told him I hadn't done much, had in fact mostly taken stuff from her. He seemed grateful, anyway; he introduced me to his partner, a slight, handsome, older man of indeterminate race named Brook. We shook hands with great cordiality. I was deeply ashamed at how begrudging I'd been with the little time I'd spent with Jessie. But at least her care hadn't been mainly in my hands. I invited him over later in the week, when we could drink mimosas and toast Jessie with the Tiger Lily.

By the end of the summer Tommy was more or less completely moved in, bringing frequent loads from the city in his new antique Mercedes, bought with hard-earned insurance money. The boys accepted this as though it were expected and natural. I told him all about my mother, of course, warning him what he could expect if John Fagin's prediction was true, that all women turn into our mothers. Tommy just said, "I don't think that's very likely. But if you do, I'll deal with it. Your mom's pretty hot for her age. Scary, but hot."

Under familial pressure, Lizzie dropped the charges against her father. But she didn't speak to anyone else in her family for a long time. Our relationship has shifted quite a bit. She's forgiven me for being the one to land Tommy, and she's started seeing Jeri. I actually am a bit weirded out by this, but Tenway is a small town, and there aren't that many good therapists. Lizzie's also been trying to get Molly to own up to her own past, but so far the rift between them has only deepened.

A month or so after Jessie's memorial service I got a letter in the mail from Casey's attorney. Jessie had left me all her clothing in her will, including the jade pendant. Not long after that, Casey, Brook, and Jordan moved in next door, as Jessie had left Casey her house. I brought them cookies. Unlike Jessie, they took them. It turned out that Yvonne Corbin was heavily involved with various animal rights causes. She let me know about a fund-raising auction for a cat rescue operation, and I donated the pendant. She later told me that it went for a lot. It goes to show, I thought, that having money doesn't necessarily mean having taste.

Tommy, the boys, and I all agreed that as part of the boys' adoption proceedings we'd change their last name from Winterburn to Galloway. I had not changed my name when I married Scott and didn't plan to change it now. I'd never really been comfortable being Gina Paulson; I needed to not do that again. Tommy wasn't particularly bothered by this. Neither of the boys seemed anything but excited that they would soon share the name of Tommy's considerable extended family. I, however, had a deep pang about asking them to abandon another link with their father. But Scott had abdicated much of his dadly responsibility when he got stoned and drunk and drove too fast on his motorcycle on an icy night. And maybe, just maybe—I have to consider this—maybe it wasn't accidental. Scott may have been a schmuck of a husband, but I was certainly no prize as a wife.

. . .

We got married in October, only a week or so after the end of Frank's trial and a month or so before Tim Solomon and Jason Dettwiler were scheduled for theirs. We weren't trying to be insensitive to the Hannigans; we had scheduled the wedding party to be held in one of the cafeterias at the university (Cindy has clout) and thought that Frank's trial would be well over by then. But Frank had a heart attack in prison, which delayed the proceedings. We then had a choice: cancel everything and put the wedding off till we could get another date or go ahead and hope that this event alone wouldn't keep Mo from ever speaking to me again. Not surprisingly, none of the Hannigans came to the wedding except Lizzie. Frank's health problems didn't prevent him from being tried and convicted; I wasn't surprised to learn that the FBI prosecutes people for selling illegal weapons, even if it's to people in Ireland and not the Middle East.

I invited my sister, Sylvia, but she didn't come. As usual, she used her job, making all that money, as an excuse. Maybe it wasn't just an excuse; there was no way to know for sure. We did have a long telephone conversation, though, which was more than we'd done in a while. She was cool but polite, wishing me well but making it quite clear that I was on my own as far as she was concerned. We rang off civilly, both knowing we might never speak again. I don't know if she found that as sad as I did.

That night I sat alone in my bedroom, looking at an old Polaroid of a nine-year-old Ellie, as old she ever got in real life. It had been easy to imagine her as a young adult, easy to know what kinds of things a grown-up Ellie would say. It wasn't so easy anymore. But I couldn't say good-bye forever. You never know when you'll need your baby sister. For now, she sleeps somewhere deep in my heart. For now.

One cliché that Grammy never would have let me get away with is the one where a marriage is a happy ending. After all, it's just more life, with crap and good stuff competing for first place each quivering moment. Somehow, though, a lot of bad shit is made a whole lot easier when there's a good person by your side. Most of us understand this; not all of us are lucky enough to get it, or to get it for long. But as the great philosopher Alan Watts would say (only more articulately), yesterday and tomorrow are just ghosts. Today is all you have to work with, all that's real. I'm doing my best to accept that, to stop hiding, or running, or pretending. And if the Universe is looking at me, She seems to be, for the moment, keeping Her hands to Herself.

It was my thirty-fourth birthday, the end of my year of reckoning, my year of waking up. I was cleaning up the mess from breakfast. I was also trying to keep our two new kittens, Lester and Chester, off the kitchen table. They liked licking up the milk puddles the boys inevitably left behind when they were finished with their morning cereal. Tommy came into the kitchen. "I plunged the toilet. It's okay now," he said, kissed me quickly on the cheek, and walked back into the living room, where the boys were watching Looney Tunes cartoons on the DVD player. All three of them periodically let loose great loud cackles of laughter.

I stood there, frozen in thought. I had plunged many a toilet. I had plunged them as a teenager in our run-down farmhouse, I had plunged them in apartments, and I had plunged the chipped and tilted toilet in this house countless times. But never, in my memory, had anyone plunged one for me. I went into the living room. Tommy was on the couch, between the boys, a big goofy grin on his face. Toby's head was resting on one wide shoulder; Stevie's whole slender body was perched on a broad knee. They were all laughing as the coyote on the TV fell from some great height, followed by a gigantic boulder, set to crush on impact. I watched quietly, not wanting in just yet. My heart swelled painfully till it felt big enough for all three of them to fit in it, growing bigger and bigger, round and full, pregnant with love and forgiveness, feeling hopeful that maybe the forgiving was moving both ways, in and out, and then I went to find a new pack of lightbulbs.

about the author

LILA SHAARA was born in Tallahassee, Florida, the daughter of an Italian-American writer and a German-American social worker. She attended a number of colleges before finishing her B.A. in religious studies at Duke University, then received a master's degree in archaeology and a Ph.D. in cultural anthropology at the University of Pittsburgh. Shaara has had many jobs, including (in no particular order) disc jockey (jazz, classical, and "beautiful music"), talk show producer, secretary, bartender, waitress, "crew member" at a fast-food chain, university professor, high school teacher, and in her lowest moment, a job handing out free cigarettes to homeless people on street corners. She has also sung and played guitar in various alternative rock bands, including the first all-female punk band in North Carolina. She currently resides in western Pennsylvania with her husband, two children, two cats, and six fish.

about the type

This book was set in Bembo, a typeface based on an old-style Roman face that was used for Cardinal Bembo's tract *De Aetna* in 1495. Bembo was cut by Francisco Griffo in the early sixteenth century. The Lanston Monotype Machine Company of Philadelphia brought the well-proportioned letter forms of Bembo to the United States in the 1930s.